# THE CAMARGUE BROTHERHOOD

Aristide Bertrand, an impressionist painter in the 1880s, vanished without trace from Provence leaving only three finished canvases. More than a hundred years later, Catherine Lacy is offered the chance to obtain six more Bertrands, but when the agent offering her the deal is fished out of the Thames, Catherine's husband Tim is less than thrilled. He decides to send his associate, Emma Kerr, to Provence but within days she is abducted and Lacy finds himself with a bagful of mysteries to solve...

# THE CAMARGUE BROTHERHOOD

# The Camargue Brotherhood

*by*

Derek Wilson

**Magna Large Print Books**
Long Preston, North Yorkshire,
England.

British Library Cataloguing in Publication Data.

Wilson, Derek
 The Camargue Brotherhood.

A catalogue record for this book is
available from the British Library

ISBN 0-7505-1231-8


First published in Great Britain by Headline Book Publishing,
1995

Copyright © 1995 by Derek Wilson

Cover illustration © Richard Jones by arrangement with
Headline Book Publishing Ltd.

Published in Large Print 1998 by arrangement with Headline
Book Publishing Ltd.

Magna Large Print is an imprint of
Library Magna Books Ltd.
Printed and bound in Great Britain by
T.J. International Ltd., Cornwall, PL28 8RW.

# Prologue

## SPOT THE FAKE

'Wow!' The word erupted involuntarily from Catherine Lacy's lips.

Genius screamed from the square metre of unframed canvas as the Frenchman whisked away the cloth covering, like a conjurer climaxing his best trick.

Slabs of colour vibrated from the painting's surface as though generating their own light. The nude's cascade of hair shone like polished mahogany against the gleaming white wall before which she was posed. The pigment seemed to have been laid on nonchalantly with hurried stabs of brush and palette knife. Yet every nuance of texture had been captured—flesh, plaster, grass and the burning Mediterranean sky, which created pools of deep shadow.

Catherine advanced across the sparsely furnished office, her short blonde hair glowing as she passed through a shaft of low winter sunlight. She lifted the picture from the typist's chair which was its makeshift easel. She looked at the monogram gouged into the paint of the bottom right corner with the handle of a brush. She examined the back. The stretcher, the canvas's discoloration and slight slackness certainly gave the right appearance of age.

'May we see the others, please, M. Jollibone?'

The young man nodded seriously and waved a hand round the room. 'Please.'

Emma Kerr, the younger of the two women, offered the solemn Frenchman the smile which usually relaxed tense situations. 'Great. We'll start at different ends and work our way into the middle.'

There were six paintings in all, including the one on the chair. The others had been propped on a desk and a battered filing cabinet—the office's only other items of furniture—and against one wall. Catherine and Emma took time to scrutinise and admire. All the pictures were of the same subject—a slender but firmly built girl of seventeen or eighteen. Yet each was very different. The artist had varied the settings for each study to display his versatility at depicting different textures. The model was arranged beside a river bank, before a barn door, in a clump of reeds, at an open window, seated on the edge of a boat.

Emma admired them. They were good; even she could see that. But Catherine was the expert and Emma left the job of appraisal to her. She was more interested in this bizarre situation and the intriguing Auguste Jollibone. She watched him surreptitiously as he wandered around the room trying to appear relaxed. Dark, athletic and definitely sexy. Perhaps twenty-three or four—certainly not much older than her. His double-breasted suit was very chic but somehow he gave the impression of being not altogether happy in formal clothes.

Catherine was still absorbed—and trying not to show her excitement. Emma let her gaze wander to the window which commanded a wide view of the Thames and a cluster of long-redundant warehouses on the south bank. The whole situation was too incongruous for words. Here they were in a drab, unused office in a half-empty dockside development block looking at a cluster of paintings whose value could be stratospheric.

Catherine stepped back and unconsciously smoothed imaginary creases from the linen skirt of her navy blue suit. Emma sighed inwardly, wondering whether another fifteen years would bestow on her a tenth particle of her friend's elegance and poise.

Catherine smiled at the Frenchman. 'Well, M. Jollibone, they're very impressive but, of course, I would have to have them examined by a specialist in Postimpressionism. And, then, I'd need to know about their provenance. On the phone you spoke of a large collection of Bertrands totally unknown to the art world. Can you elaborate on that?'

Jollibone frowned slightly. 'There are thirty-seven Bertrands in all. They have been in the owner's family ever since his ancestor acquired them from the artist. The owner has authorised me to explore the market, which is why I have brought these few here in order to hear your opinion.'

'And you haven't shown them to anyone else?'

The man shook his head.

'Well, I'm very flattered, M. Jollibone, but in all honesty I must point out that there are four or five top dealers right here in London, who are much more knowledgeable—'

Jollibone interrupted. 'My client wishes to avoid unnecessary publicity at this stage. A major cache of important paintings like these suddenly appearing in the London market would create enormous excitement, I think. But now, tell me, Mrs Lacy, what are your first impressions?'

Catherine knew she was expected to start talking figures. Tricky. Because she had no idea what valuation this art dealer had in mind and because it was quite impossible to tell what impact a collection of unknown Bertrands would make on the international market. 'I think they're absolutely fabulous and, providing we can establish their authenticity, I'd love to handle the sale. We'd have to exhibit the whole collection—no point trying to slip them onto the market in dribs and drabs. They'll attract massive publicity.'

Jollibone frowned again. 'That could be difficult. My client is anxious to remain anonymous.'

Catherine searched for reassuring words. 'Of course, that's very understandable with such enormous sums of money at stake. And there are ways we can keep him out of the limelight.'

Jollibone stepped softly across to the window.

Positively feline, Emma thought, watching him.

'And just what sort of "enormous sums" are we talking about, Mrs Lacy?' He asked the question casually.

Catherine tried to make her light laugh sound nonchalant but not dismissive. 'Oh, I don't think you'd find an expert anywhere in the world prepared to commit himself on that. This is a unique event. No one's ever put thirty-seven hitherto unknown works of a leading painter on the market before. What you're about to do, M. Jollibone is...' Catherine groped for the appropriate metaphor '...is write a whole new chapter in the history of Postimpressionism.'

There was a long silence. The Frenchman gazed down on the river's pewter surface, damascened with silver where a weak sun caught the ripples. Emma shook her long auburn hair and raised an enquiring eyebrow at her friend. Catherine shrugged.

At last she said, 'May I suggest that the next step is for me to take one of these and show it—very discreetly, of course—to a colleague of mine?'

The young man gave no indication of having heard. He seemed absorbed either in the view or his own thoughts.

'M. Jollibone?'

'Ah, je vous demande pardon.' He turned slowly. 'There is much that we must think about. I will discuss the matter fully with my client. You have been most helpful, Mrs Lacy...Miss Kerr.' He held out his hand to them in turn. 'For the moment I think there is nothing more to be done. I will, of course, contact you as soon as my client's wishes are clear.' He gestured them towards the door.

Catherine turned on the threshold. 'You

won't be doing a deal with someone else?'

Jollibone smiled. 'Rest assured, dear Mrs Lacy, that as soon as we have decided on the appropriate course of action you will be the first to know. Au revoir, ladies. We will be in touch.'

Five minutes later, as their taxi joined a convoy on Tower Hill, Emma said, 'Well, what do you make of our hunky friend?'

'I wish I knew.' Catherine leaned her blonde hair against the seat back and closed her eyes. 'I don't like having deals proposed in out-of-the-blue phone calls. They're usually very fishy. But I have to admit that Jollibone is a reputable dealer and that he is on to something very big.'

'Who was this Bertrand fellow? I've never heard of him.'

'Not many people have. There aren't more than half a dozen paintings of his known to exist and half of those are "iffy". He's one of the enigmatic might-have-beens of art history. In 1888 Van Gogh left Paris for Arles. He was excited by the light and the landscape of the South and did some of his best work over the next year. He wanted to set up an artistic colony there and wrote to several friends, urging them to join him. They didn't—except for Gauguin who came for a few weeks and proved to be really bad news.'

'They didn't get on?'

'They were at each other's throats most of the time. It helped to push Van Gogh over the edge.'

'You mean that business with the ear?'

'That and other things. Anyway, soon afterwards poor Vincent packed his palettes and brushes and left. But one younger painter had responded to his invitation.'

'Bertrand?'

'Yes, Aristide Bertrand. Legend has it that he belonged to a good Parisian family who disowned him when he decided on la vie de Bohême. He made his escape to Arles, stayed in the area after Van Gogh left, and produced a few paintings which suggested that he might be on a par with the mighty Vincent—perhaps in the fullness of time he might have been greater.'

'What happened?'

'Nobody knows. He disappeared without trace, leaving just a tantalising handful of pictures.'

'So what Jollibone's stumbled on is...'

'Just about the biggest find of the century.'

'Still, if he is genuine, we're in on the ground floor.'

Catherine bit her lip. 'I hope so. Dear

16

God, I hope so. This will put the gallery on the map in no uncertain terms. Think of the publicity...'

'Not to mention the astronomical commission.'

'Whenever I close my eyes I see noughts—rows and rows of noughts. Enough to put us in the black and keep us there; enough to pay for the boys' education; perhaps even enough to get Tim away for a long Pacific-island cruise. I sure hope this Jollibone guy's above board.'

'He looked OK to me.'

Catherine laughed. 'You were just lusting after his body.' Then she was serious again, reason wrestling with tingling excitement. 'He's much younger than I expected. And there was something odd about arranging a meeting in a semi-deserted office block. But if the whole thing was a con what was the point? He hasn't asked us for any money.'

'Why do you think he chose us? I mean, we're good but we're not exactly top drawer.'

The gallery and arts centre that Catherine Lacy had built up over the last six years was situated at Farrans Court, the Wiltshire house where she and Tim lived and from which Tim also operated his international security firm. Emma Kerr had recently joined them there as a general assistant with a view to becoming a partner—if it all 'worked out'.

'When he phoned last night, he said we'd been recommended to him but he didn't say who by.'

'Perhaps he'll just disappear—go away as mysteriously as he came—and we'll never hear from him again.'

'No way!' Catherine's green eyes flashed. 'I'm not letting M. Auguste Jollibone of 24 rue Gramont, Lyon, out of my clutches. You see, I've already done some homework and even memorised the address.'

The taxi deposited them outside the Victorian red-brick building off Great Smith Street where the Lacys maintained a small flat.

'Time for a leisurely cup of tea before we have to set off for the train, and boy, do I need it.' Catherine led the way up the stairs to the first floor.

'Is Tim meeting us here?'

'No, he's got meetings going on all day.'

She turned the key in the lock and opened the door. The first thing she saw was her husband leaping up from the sofa and stepping quickly across the room to greet them.

'Tim, this is a nice sur—'

He hugged her with an urgent vigour.

18

'Darling, are you all right?'

'Yes of course.' Catherine drew back and surveyed the anxiety in Tim's dark eyes. 'We've had the most extraordinary meeting. Haven't we, Emma?'

'Meeting?' Tim looked puzzled now. 'Who with?'

'Boy, you are getting forgetful in your old age.' Catherine lowered herself into an armchair and slipped her shoes off. 'With the Frenchman who phoned last night—Jollibone—I told you about him.'

'But you can't have!' Tim stared down at her. He picked up a copy of the *Evening Standard* from a coffee table. 'I saw this at lunchtime. That's why I cancelled my afternoon appointment. I tried to get hold of you but I didn't know where your meeting was. I've been pretty worried.'

Catherine looked at the short paragraph Tim indicated.

FRENCH VISITOR FOUND DEAD
The body of a man found early this morning in the river near New Caledonian Wharf was identified by the police as that of Auguste Jollibone, a French art dealer. The police have not ruled out foul play and are asking anyone who knew M. Jollibone or who had business dealings with him to come forward.

# I

## JOURS DE PEUR

Millet wept when he started painting...
Giotto and Angelico painted on their
knees...Delacroix was full of grief and
feeling... We are all soiled in the struggle
for life.

—Vincent Van Gogh

# CHAPTER 1

Inspector Edgerson prided himself on being decisive—'pro-active', he called it. He was one of the new breed of young DIs come into the Metropolitan Police straight from a degree course at one of the polytechnics recently raised to university status. As soon as he heard Catherine's story he phoned for a car. Within minutes the Lacys, together with Emma and the DI, were in a siren-wailing vehicle hacking an eastward path through rush-hour traffic. Half-turned in his front seat, Edgerson continued his questioning of the two women and punctuated it with imprecations directed at 'obstructive' road users and exhortations to the driver: 'Get a move on, Stevens!' 'This thing isn't a bloody hearse!' 'We'd get there quicker in a kid's pram!' Tim, whose army years had taught him a great deal about leadership, reflected that the young CID officer was demonstrably lacking in that quality.

Edgerson glowered at Catherine. 'And this fellow definitely called himself Auguste Jollibone?'

'Yes. Are you quite sure he wasn't?' The

man's tone made her feel absurdly guilty and she resented it. 'Perhaps it's *your* body that isn't Jollibone.'

Edgerson emitted a long-suffering sigh. 'The corpse our river police hoicked out of the Thames around breakfast time was carrying a passport—and the photograph matched. Judging by your description he bore little resemblance to the bloke you met. He was moustached, balding, below average height and just past his forty-first birthday.'

'That's certainly nothing like the man we saw,' Emma observed.

The DI treated her to a cursory nod. 'Thank you, Miss Kerr—or is it Ms Kerr?'

Emma shrugged and sank back into the corner of the seat.

Tim intervened. 'Surely, Inspector, passports can be forged? If someone wanted you to believe that the dead man was Jollibone...'

'The possibility had not escaped us, sir. Stevens! Why the hell are we going this way? Make a right at the next lights! My God! We'd be better off in a taxi! We've checked the details with French records. They all tally. The passport's gone to our lab as a matter of course, but right now I'm more interested in this other man you claim to have met.'

'Claim!'

Edgerson flapped a hand dismissively. 'Unfortunate choice of word, Mrs Lacy. It's just that I'm having a bit of difficulty understanding this mysterious imposter's behaviour. You reckon he made no attempt to flog you these pictures?'

'Quite the reverse.' Catherine shook her head. 'He wouldn't even let me keep one for verification purposes.'

'Worth quite a few bob, I dare say?'

Catherine paused slightly before replying. When she did so it was with calculated nonchalance. 'They were certainly interesting, but I couldn't possibly put a value on them on the basis of such a brief examination.'

'Hmm!' The policeman stared hard at the elegant American woman. 'But you must have some idea whether we're talking about thousands, or tens of thousands or, perhaps, even millions?'

Catherine returned his gaze. 'I really can't be drawn on that. It's more than my reputation's worth to give a snap valuation.'

'OK, let's try a different tack.' Edgerson rubbed his hand wearily over his eyes. 'If *your* Auguste Jollibone tried to sell any of these pictures through a dealer or an auction house, you'd get to hear about it, wouldn't you?'

'They would create a lot of interest in

the international art world.' Catherine was cautious.

'Which is a pretty small world with a well-developed grapevine?'

'Sure.'

'Hmm! So, if our murderer...'

Tim showed sudden interest. 'It *was* murder, then?'

Edgerson frowned at the interruption. 'It's pretty difficult, sir, to commit suicide by simultaneously jumping off a bridge and stabbing yourself in the back with a twenty-centimetre blade.' He turned back to Catherine. 'So, as I was saying, if our murderer wanted to offload these pictures he'd do it discreetly, through the underworld channels which you and I both know exist.'

'I guess so.'

'Odd, then, that he should deliberately draw attention to himself and the pictures by showing them to a highly respectable expert like your good self. Could it be that we're dealing with a nutter?'

Catherine was saved from venturing an opinion by their arrival at the office block. It took several minutes for the sole occupant of the security desk to locate a colleague to escort them to the tenth floor and admit them to the small suite of rooms the two women had come to earlier in the day. Catherine looked round the main office. It was exactly as they had left it, except that it contained no paintings and no 'Auguste Jollibone'.

Edgerson scowled his disappointment. 'You're sure this is the place?'

Catherine resented the policeman's sceptical tone. 'Yes, of course I'm sure. The paintings were arranged over there, along the wall and on those bits of furniture, weren't they, Emma?'

'Emphatically!' The younger woman nodded. Yet looking around the dismal, characterless box of an office, Emma found it hard to dispel the idea that the earlier episode had been only a bizarre dream. The room seemed to have shrunk, not only in size, but in significance. Early winter darkness had made the large window a sheet of shiny black, reflecting the four occupants and their dingy surroundings. Had there really been, only a couple of hours before, six radiant, vital canvases flooding this drab place with colour and light?

'OK. I'll get forensic in to give it the once-over tomorrow.' Edgerson turned to the security guard. 'I want this place sealed. No one's to be allowed in till we've finished with it. Meanwhile, we'd best not disturb anything. Not that there's much.' He gazed round mournfully. 'We'll also check with the agents, see what they know about whoever it is who rents the rooms, although I don't suppose...' He shepherded his little party towards the door.

On the way down in the lift he returned to an earlier question. 'Mrs Lacy, these pictures you say you were shown this afternoon—were they valuable enough to kill for?'

'As I said before, Inspector, I only had a few minutes to look at the paintings. They were certainly very well done but value is determined by the market. These things get pored over by dealers and experts and auctioneers and critics. So, whether they would ever fetch big money in the rooms is anyone's guess.' Catherine glanced quickly at Tim and, not for the first time, recognised quizzical disapproval in his expression. She hurried on. 'I can't help feeling that the whole thing's a dreadful muddle. As you say, the man's behaviour is quite inexplicable. He didn't look to me like a thief, and certainly not like a murderer.'

Edgerson smirked. 'And just what do thieves and murderers look like, Mrs Lacy?'

Catherine was still fuming half an hour later when she, Tim and Emma took their seats in the rapidly filling dining car of the Penzance train moments before it eased its way smoothly out of Paddington.

'Why does anyone ever bother to help the police? We do the good citizens' bit. We trot along to Scotland Yard. We give up hours of our time. For what? So that some kid fresh out of college can make snide remarks and grill us like prime suspects.'

Tim grinned. 'Don't let yourself be phased out by little men in big jobs. Anyway, it's all over now. Have a drink and relax. Evening Jim.' The last words were spoken to the chief steward who appeared with an assortment of cans and miniature bottles.

'Evening, Mr Lacy, Mrs Lacy. Good to see you again. I reckoned you'd need some fortifying after a long day in the smoke.' He set down the drinks on the white tablecloth. For some minutes the travellers busied themselves pouring out the measured doses and scanning the menu cards.

Emma took several gulps of her Coke. 'What an odd business it is. I can see that life with Lacy Enterprises is never going to be dull.'

Tim laughed. 'It's mostly routine but we do have our moments.'

Emma studied the round face with its dark eyes and topping of hair just beginning to be flecked with grey. She tried to imagine away the half-generation which separated them. It was easy to picture a sleeker Tim Lacy in his mid-twenties in the battledress and beret of an SAS major. He still looked more like a soldier in mufti than a highly successful international businessman, in demand by museums and collectors the world over, wanting the latest high-tech security systems. If only they could have met in those earlier days—before Catherine had come on the scene. Not that Emma resented the Lacys' excellent personal and business partnership. She owed both of them too much ever to want to endanger the friendship and trust she enjoyed with them. But still...

Catherine watched Emma watching Tim and hoped that they had not done the wrong thing by expanding their team to incorporate this bright, effervescent young woman who was all the more attractive because she was ignorant of her own good looks.

Tim's thoughts were in a very different sphere. He sipped his brandy and ginger, twirling the ice cubes in the glass. He asked his wife. 'Why were you so cagey with our ill-mannered friend?'

'Cagey?' Catherine's eyebrows rose in innocent surprise.

'You know very well what I mean.' He hitched his voice a few tones higher and mimicked. 'Oh, I couldn't possibly put a value on the paintings, Inspector. They might be important but then, on the other hand, they might not.'

'Well, that's perfectly true.'

'So how come that when you got back from your interview with pseudo-Jollibone this afternoon, your eyes were glazed and your feet were scarcely touching the ground? You were jabbering about changing the pattern of art history and earning millions in commission.'

The appearance of the steward serving slices of parma ham and melon gave Catherine time to think out her answer. When he had moved on to the next table she sipped her gin and tonic, set the glass down, and elaborately separated it from other pieces of tableware against which it was rattling. She took up her knife and fork and applied them with surgical precision to the contents of her plate. Without taking her eyes from this delicate operation, she said, 'It wasn't relevant.'

Tim rubbed a finger along the bridge of his nose. 'Surely that's for the police to decide.'

'Hell, no!' Catherine dropped her knife and fork with a clatter. 'What does it matter to a Philistine like Edgerson that someone may have discovered a cache of important Postimpressionist paintings?

31

That's not going to help him find a murderer.'

'But can't you get it into your head that keeping this information to yourself is technically withholding evidence—and that's a criminal offence.'

'So, turn me in!' Catherine violently speared a cube of melon.

Tim sighed and turned to Emma. 'Surely *you* can see that I'm right?'

The young woman raised her hands defensively. 'Don't make me a referee in this domestic bout.'

'Well, you saw the paintings and the fake dealer. What do you think?'

'Three months with Lacy Enterprises and I'm supposed to be an expert on French Postimpressionism?' Emma sipped her Coke thoughtfully. 'Well, I thought they were pretty fantastic paintings. I can quite see that they could be the real McCoy. And, in that case—'

'In that case,' Catherine interrupted excitedly, 'this discovery is so big it'll blow your mind. And, oh, Tim, we're actually in on the ground floor. We're the only ones in the art world who know about it.'

Tim nodded. 'And that's the real reason you were keeping mum with Edgerson, isn't it?'

'If we tell the police what we suspect

about these paintings it'll be splashed all over the media in hours.'

'And Catherine Lacy will have lost her exclusive coup.'

Catherine flushed with anger. 'Don't take a high moral tone with me, Tim. You'd have done exactly the same. This is the kind of opportunity that doesn't get repeated—and besides, do you really think we can afford to chuck it away? We can't put off re-roofing Farrans Court much longer and next year we have to start finding school fees for the boys. Once news about a batch of unknown Aristide Bertrands leaks out every dealer and auctioneer from Tokyo to New York will have his bloodhounds on the scent. We shan't get a look-in.'

Tim swallowed his last mouthful of ham and pushed his plate away. 'But we don't have a look-in now. Pseudo-Jollibone has disappeared, taking his canvases with him. Now that the police are after him he's going to keep a very low profile. He's hardly going to write and invite you over to appraise the entire collection.'

The train slowed into Reading. Catherine gazed out at the sparsely populated platform. 'I've thought of that. If Mohammad won't come to the mountain... Well, I'll have to track down these paintings myself.'

'What? No way!' Tim snapped the words angrily.

Catherine responded in kind. 'Tim, don't be silly! Of course I must follow this lead. I'll go over to Lyon and see what I can find out at Jollibone's gallery. There must be someone else there who knows the owner of the Bertrand paintings.'

'Catherine, absolutely no!' Tim glowered at his wife. 'One man's already been killed—probably on account of these paintings—and his murderer is still on the loose. I don't care how valuable these pictures are, I'm not having you—'

'Don't you come the heavy Victorian husband with me, Tim Lacy!' The atmosphere was eased by the chief steward who reappeared carrying a bottle.

'Your usual Burgundy, Mr Lacy?'

'Yes please, Jim, we could all do with it tonight.'

'Do you know, the same thought had crossed my mind, sir. What you need to do is relax and enjoy your meal.' He smiled as he set down the opened bottle.

The dining-room staff reappeared with their loaded platters.

When the main course had been served, Tim tried a tone of calm reason. 'Look, this afternoon you came face to face with a killer.'

'We don't know that!'

'Well, my money's certainly on pseudo-Jollibone until a better suspect turns up. Now this chap knows that you can identify him. That's worrying enough in itself. But the thought of you wandering France actually looking for this character... Well, it's just not on.'

'Oh, for heaven's sake!' Catherine's dark emerald eyes glinted almost black under lowered lids. 'Don't be so melodramatic! Do you expect me just to shrug my shoulders and say, "Oh well, it's the chance of a lifetime—several lifetimes—but I'm going to pass on it"?'

'I expect you to behave like the intelligent woman you are. Don't get carried away by your excitement. Stand back. Give it a few days, a few weeks. See what happens. If these paintings have been hidden away for a hundred years they'll wait a little longer.'

'But, Tim, you could just as easily argue the opposite: the owner of these Bertrands has decided that, after a century of obscurity, they should go on the market. He hired Jollibone to act for him. Jollibone gets himself killed and perhaps allows some of the paintings to be stolen. Chances are the owner will find another agent, p.d.q. That would leave us right out in the cold.'

'But still alive.' Tim carved up his steak with enthusiasm.

Catherine stared, appetiteless, at her grilled plaice. 'If we miss this one I'll never forgive myself—or you.'

Tim matched his wife's stubbornness. 'And if you go chasing after it and something happens to you, I'll...'

'Children, children, please!' Emma pushed back her tumble of shoulder-length dark hair and frowned at them. 'There's a perfectly simple answer to this problem: I'll go.'

Tim and Catherine protested in unison. 'You can't possibly!'

'Why not?' Emma spoke nonchalantly between mouthfuls of steak. 'I've met Jollibone, or whoever he is. I've seen the sample paintings. I speak pretty good French. All I have to do is locate the owner and the rest of the collection and report back to you.'

Tim shook his head. 'All the reasons I gave Catherine apply just as much to you. It's too risky.'

'I didn't join Lacy Enterprises for a dull, safe life. Catherine's absolutely right: this could be vitally important for us. And Tim's right: you can't possibly go, Catherine; you've got a husband and two sons to look after. So, that leaves me.'

'No. I'm sorry, Emma.' Tim was adamant. 'It's great of you to suggest it but I can't let you.'

'Tim, you can't stop me.' She gave him the wide-eyed smile that seemed to wither most men's ability to resist her wishes. 'Technically you're not my employer. I'm just learning the ropes at Farrans with a view to possibly coming in as a partner. If you upset me I might consider investing the Kerr family fortune elsewhere.'

Catherine intervened. 'Look, Emma, this business is our life. That means it's quite in order for us to run risks...'

'And if I come in with you, it'll be on the same basis. No one's going to keep me under a glass dome for protection.'

The argument continued all the way to Pewsey, where the three combatants alighted, and throughout most of the fifteen-minute drive in Catherine's car from the station to Farrans Court. The headlights panned across medieval stone and struck reflections from the tall windows of the hall as Catherine swung the small Ford to the right and entered the old stable block, now converted to offices and garage space. Tim and Emma scrambled out in the courtyard, unspeaking, and waited while Catherine ran the car into its customary cubicle.

At last Tim said, 'OK, I give in—on two conditions.'

'Namely?' The harsh security light emphasised Emma's suspicious frown.

'You spend no more than a week in France and George goes with you.'

'George! Tim, I don't need—'

'That's it, Emma. Take it or leave it.' He helped Catherine close the garage door.

Somewhere in the nearby woods a tawny owl hooted as they crossed the yard and let themselves into the house by a side entrance.

## CHAPTER 2

'Ladies and gentlemen, your attention for a moment, please, if I may.' Brigadier-General Eustache d'Erigny-Duchamp rose to his feet at the head of the long table, an impressive white-haired and moustached figure resplendent in the dress uniform of a cavalry officer of the Third Republic.

Three dozen pairs of eyes turned towards one of the army's most respected leaders, a hero of campaigns in Algeria and Indo-China and one of the few field commanders to acquit himself well in the disastrous 1870 conflict with Germany. It was a military occasion. Almost all the men present were vividly splendid in jackets and facings of blue, gold, white and scarlet. Their panache was enhanced by the pale silks and laces and the glistening purity of diamonds and sapphires worn by their consorts. The room itself added to the glitter of the occasion with its gilt mirrors, elaborate chandeliers and the family silver and crystal which graced the table's glassy surface.

The general benignly surveyed the faces of his guests, most of whom were colleagues and subordinates and their wives. 'The longest speech I ever made was to my corps the night before we took Tiensin back in 1860. As I recall, it consisted of about a dozen words—though, judging by events, they were rather effective.' He paused for the polite laughter. 'Well, that was twenty-eight years ago, and ever since then I've tried to live by the maxim that brevity is a virtue. I've no intention of keeping you much longer from the ballroom which is where I know the younger ones among you would rather be. I simply want to ask you to drink the health of my lovely daughter and Captain de Bracieux.' He smiled at the young couple sitting on his right. 'It isn't merely a pleasure for me to bestow Eloise upon the elder son of my old friend, Colonel de Bracieux; I venture to believe that, in these troubled times, France needs the stability provided by the union of old military families such as ours. We're the guardians of tradition, of national pride, of discipline. It is in that spirit that I ask you to drink to the happiness of Eloise and Albert.' Obediently, the company rose to do the old campaigner's bidding.

Minutes later, the newly engaged couple led the way to the ballroom where a hundred less intimate friends had already gathered to help them celebrate. The two were of much the same height, although Eloise looked taller because her long black hair was drawn up into a lustrous pyramid. As she and her fiancé made their way around the room, Eloise received the greetings of her father's guests with intelligent, smiling eyes and handsome features which never for an instant lost their composure. She wore the restraining corset of formal correctness with serene self-assurance. Albert did not. His movements were brisk and erratic. His blue eyes fixed people with a stare that was intense, yet at the same time distracted, as though he was seeking a meaning beyond the proffered congratulations and friendly smiles.

The orchestra struck up a waltz and the couple took the floor alone to begin the dancing; Albert set a style of impatient vigour his partner had difficulty adjusting to. When the music ended, they separated and embarked on their round of duty dances with relatives and friends. It was an hour or so later that Albert took temporary refuge in the library where, for a few minutes, he sat alone smoking a cigar and reading *Le Figaro*.

It was there that his younger brother found him. The two men were superficially similar. Edouard wore the same regimental uniform and was of a comparable stature to Albert though, at eighteen, he still had time to grow taller. He had the same thick fair hair and blue eyes, inherited from their mother. There the resemblance ended. In temperament Edouard was all that Albert was not—extrovert, self-assured, aggressive.

'Bertie, there you are!' The younger man came and stood squarely in front of his brother, looking down with a disapproving frown. 'I've been commissioned to find you and restore you to your neglected friends.'

Albert looked up with a distracted smile. 'In a moment, Ed. Our friends will survive without me a little longer.' He returned to his reading.

Edouard perched on the edge of a solid library table. 'I must say, you don't look much like a man on whom the gods are positively beaming. If I were in your position I wouldn't be hiding away and looking glum. Here you are, getting married to the darling of the regiment,

41

marked out for rapid promotion and soon to be sent to Madagascar as ADC to the governor. Not bad for someone just past his twenty-first birthday!'

Albert stared at his brother over the top of the newspaper. 'Yes, it is nice, isn't it?'

'Nice! Nice! Is that all you can say? Don't you appreciate the strings Father has pulled for you? My God, I wish he'd do the same for me. But then...'

'Yes?'

'Forget it.' Edouard turned away.

'You were going to say that I've always been Father's favourite. Don't you think we've worn that old argument to death, Ed?'

'I suppose so.' The younger man returned to the door and looked back with one hand on the knob. 'What irks me is the way you take it all for granted.'

'Ed, your chances will come. Father will do all he can for you too. And you're bound to fare better than me in the long term. You're more fitted to this soldiering life than I am.'

The door opened. Edouard fell back and made a military bow as Eloise entered. Albert stood up and extinguished his cigar in an ashtray on the table.

Eloise let fall the elegantly held fold of her cream satin, long-skirted dress and surveyed the brothers with her grey eyes. 'Have you two been arguing again?'

Edouard moved to the doorway. 'Just fraternal discussion. Elli, you persuade him to return to his duty. I've failed.' He went out, closing the door behind him.

'What was all that about?' Eloise sank onto a leather sofa and motioned to Albert to sit beside her.

'Oh, the usual—jealousy. He thinks I've been handed everything on a plate.'

'Including me?'

'Especially you. You know he's in love with you?'

'Yes.' The unemotional monosyllable expressed simple fact. 'But it's you I'm going to marry.' She laid a gloved hand lightly on his.

Albert stared moodily at the newspaper, now lying folded across his knees. 'I don't deserve you. I don't deserve any of this.'

'Few of us get what we deserve in life. Perhaps it's as well.' After a pause she added, 'Do you want to tell me why you're unhappy? I have to begin on my wifely duties some time.'

Albert nodded but for reply only gripped his fiancée's hand firmly. It was some moments before he asked, 'Do you think husbands and wives should have any secrets from each other?'

'Oh, certainly. Few marriages would

survive the unclothed truth.'

'That sounds like a smart line from the latest operetta.'

'It's a fact, nevertheless. Have you some terrible confession you think you ought to make to me?'

He looked into the candid grey eyes. 'I wish I knew when you were mocking me and when you were serious.'

Eloise laughed. 'Oh, Bertie, after all these years, can you still not read me as fluently as I read you? Well, then, I'm now being serious—philosophical even.' She tilted her head to one side. 'I think there are secrets and secrets. Some are quite harmless. Others damage their owners. They eat away at the soul; they erode happiness and contentment. If I felt that you had such a secret then I should want to share it.'

'Even if it meant sharing the unhappiness?'

'Yes.'

Albert sighed deeply. 'Would you mind terribly if I resigned my commission?'

She considered the question carefully. 'I think Papa would be very angry. He thinks the army is the only honourable life for a gentleman. He looks to you and me to raise another generation of soldiers.'

'But what do you think?'

Eloise detected a new urgency in the question. 'I think there are several other respectable professions. I shouldn't mind being married to a banker or a landowner or even a manufacturer.'

Albert smiled briefly. 'I can't imagine myself as any of those.'

'Nor as a soldier?'

He shook his head wearily. 'I don't know. If I could feel that it meant something... It all seems to be so...out of date...like this fellow Boulanger.' He opened *Le Figaro* and pointed to a report on the front page. 'He's been in Paris again, making speeches in secret to his supporters.'

General Georges Boulanger was the name on everyone's lips in the winter of 1887–8. Some regarded him as a dangerous rabble-rouser; others as the saviour of France, who would restore the glorious days of the Second Empire that had vanished with the humiliating defeat of 1870. Since the Franco-Prussian War the nation had gone republican and become the playing field for rival politicians. Twenty-three governments had risen and fallen and the administration of the doddering Pierre Tirard had no look of permanence about it. Boulanger, with his nationalistic tirades and his distinguished military record, had suddenly appeared in the political arena two years before. An increasing body of royalists, imperialists and disenchanted republicans looked to him to cut through the tangle of government corruption and incompetence. A worried prime minister had banished him to the relative obscurity of Clermont-Ferrand, four hundred kilometres away from Paris. Now he was back.

Eloise glanced at the lines of print. 'Papa says he's France's only hope.'

'My father believes in him, too. So do most of the officers in the regiment.' Bertie tossed the paper aside in disgust. 'Can't they see the man's a posturing idiot—prancing around on that black horse of his like a latterday Don Quixote, talking about a war of revenge against Germany? Well, they can follow Boulanger into mass suicide if they like, but I shan't!'

Eloise looked at him sharply, her eyes narrowed. 'You mean you would resign your commission to avoid going to war? You know what that would mean. You would be branded as a coward. Ostracised. None of our friends would ever speak to you again. As for me...' She pulled away from him. 'Bertie, is this your guilty secret, that you have lost your patriotism, your sense of duty, your honour?'

'No, that's not it.' He shook his head wearily. 'I'll fight—die—in any just cause. But I don't think Boulanger will ever amount to anything. He's nothing but a windbag. It's just that I can't see that this political posturing, this militant bombast, these colonial adventures have any meaning.' He jumped up and began pacing the carpet with short jerky strides. 'We talk about freedom while we exploit women and children in our factories and conquer savages in Africa and Asia. We talk about democracy while over two-thirds of the adult population have no voting rights.'

Eloise frowned. 'Bertie, do sit down. You're ranting like a radical demagogue.'

'Huh! They're just as bad. They get into power by making promises to the mob. The next anyone sees of them, they are living on le Faubourg, driving their smart carriages in le Bois and sitting in their own box at l'Opéra.'

Eloise stood abruptly. 'I'm sure I don't know what you're so concerned about, Bertie, but I do know you're spoiling my party. Are you going to come and be sociable or do you intend to sulk in here all evening?'

Albert took her hands in his own. 'I'm sorry, Elli.' He looked awkward and miserable. 'I don't know what I want half the time. It's all so confusing.'

'It would be nice if, tonight, you wanted to show our friends how happy you are at our engagement.'

'Yes, of course.' He smiled and squeezed her hands. 'But...'

'Yes?'

'Look, Elli, could I show you something tomorrow?'

'Your secret?'

'Yes.'

'I'd like that.' She bent forward and kissed him lightly, quickly. 'Now, come and dance—before everyone assumes we've eloped.'

She slipped her arm through his and they made their way back to the ballroom.

Vieux Lyon keeps itself very much to itself on the right bank of the Saône, content to glare across at the modern vulgarity of the commercial city centre which sprawls over the terrain bordering the convergence of Rhône and Saône. Its jumble of old narrow streets networks the steep ascent from Quai Romain and the cathedral to the heights of Fourvière, where nineteenth-century piety raised the monumental Eglise de Notre Dame and twentieth-century curiosity uncovered extensive Roman remains. Rue Gramont skirts the foot of the escarpment and begins close to the funiculaire station. It is home to several exclusive galleries, antique shops and restaurants whose prices are in inverse proportion to their seating capacity.

48

It was in one of these centres of gastronomic worship that the two representatives of Lacy Enterprises consumed a superb lunch and surveyed the modest exterior of *numéro* 24 opposite.

'Not up to much, is it?' George Martin had been Tim's right-hand man ever since the early days of Lacy Security. He was stocky, with a head of grey-black bristles. Though nudging fifty, he was fit, tough and sharp-witted.

Emma found George's old-fashioned, paternalistic attitude towards women irritating but, although she would never admit it, there was something reassuring about this gruff ex-sergeant major.

She gazed at the unimposing premises of the late Auguste Jollibone. The frontage was small and in need of repainting. She wondered whether the neglect was deliberate, designed so as not to distract attention from the items on display to the passing public. At the moment this amounted to one brightly coloured abstract, centrally placed on a velvet-draped plinth.

Emma smiled at her companion. 'It certainly looks shabby but I'll bet the price tag on that picture in the window would blow your mind.'

'Wouldn't give it house room, myself.' George prodded unenthusiastically at his plate of lightly cooked pigeon breast, *mangetout* and *asperges en feuilleté*.

Emma giggled. 'For once, George, I agree with you. But we must suppress our philistinism when we go in. We want them to take us seriously.'

'What's the game plan, then?'

Good question, Emma thought as she banished a wisp of hair which had escaped from the swept-back arrangement she had spent several impatient minutes fixing in an attempt to appear efficient and sophisticated. In her determination to be in charge of this important mission she had given little thought to what she would actually do when she got to Lyon. Catherine had plied her with advice about how to extract information without arousing suspicion but, as the moment of confrontation drew nearer, Emma knew that she would have to rely on instinct and hope for luck. 'Well, I'll ask the questions and you watch carefully for reactions. If you get a chance to snoop around any desk or back premises, grab it.'

'I can try the old "May I use your bathroom" routine, I suppose, but what exactly am I looking for?'

Emma shrugged. 'Postimpressionist paintings. Lots of vivid colours. All the ones we saw were nudes but I imagine Bertrand tackled other subjects as well. If you strike lucky you'll see a monograph signature—"AB". Have a look on the back. There might just be a label.'

'You'd better go easy on the questions, miss. Those people are sure to have been well grilled by the gendarmerie. They'll be wary of English visitors prying into this Bertrand business. We don't want to find ourselves in the local nick "helping the police with their enquiries".'

Emma was stung into an annoyed response. 'Have you got any better ideas?'

George was unruffled. 'I'm not paid to have ideas, miss. I leave that to people with a university education.'

'Oh, for heaven's sake, George. I know you resent having me around at Farrans, but can't you try to get used to the idea?'

He laid down his knife and fork and considered the question. 'I dare say I shall in time—get used to it, I mean. We certainly need some more top brass. The Major's been under too much pressure for a couple of years now. That's the price of success, I suppose.'

'But you don't think I'm the right person to help the Major—Tim?'

'Not up to me to say, miss.'

'Oh do stop, "Missing" me! My name's Emma. And of course it's up to you to say. I want to make a success of this job. I'm very fond of Tim and Catherine. I owe them a lot. It's not going to help anyone if you and I are at odds. Apart from anything else I need you to help me find my feet. Look, George, I'm not some snooty Oxbridge brat who thinks she knows all the answers—honest!'

'OK...Emma, if you want me to be frank, I'd like to start by asking you what you think we're doing here.'

'Surely you know?'

'What I know is that the Major, as I said, is up to his ears in work. What he doesn't need right now is having to worry about your safety. The fact that I'm here keeping an eye on you means that half a dozen jobs I was working on are back on his desk.'

'But, George, if I hadn't come here, Catherine would have insisted on coming. Tim would have been a hell of a lot more worried about that.'

He gazed back at her unblinking. 'You're sure that's the real reason? You're not just trying to prove you can track down a lot of old paintings? Because however valuable they may be, they're not worth putting more strain on the team at Farrans.'

Emma stared mournfully at her cooling *quenelles de brochet* and avoided the question. 'It was Tim's idea for you to accompany me, not mine. I don't need a minder. If you want to go back that's fine by me.'

George shook his head. 'Oh, no. When I'm given a job I see it through. We all do. That's why Lacy Security is successful. If there's pictures to be found we'll find 'em—or, at least, have a damned good try. As to you not needing a minder—well, Emma, you've got a lot to learn about this business. Art is like rotten meat, it attracts some very nasty flies—thugs, fraudsters, drug dealers, killers, thieves, kidnappers, rapists, every kind of scum you could imagine and several you couldn't. The Major and I, we've seen 'em all. We know what you're getting into. Frankly, you don't.'

Emma sat back and pushed her plate away. 'So you'd be quite happy to see me sitting around at Farrans writing letters, answering the phone and fluttering my eyelashes at prospective clients as long as I don't get involved in the sharp end of the business? Well, if that's your attitude you've got a lot to learn about the modern woman. God! I pity your daughter!'

After several minutes of silence, during which George, ostentatiously calm, cleared his plate, Emma rose abruptly and strode to the ladies' room. When she returned she had beaten the flames of anger down to glowing embers. 'Any sign of life over the road?' she asked casually.

George laid aside the dessert menu.

'Can't make head or tail of this. You'll have to translate again. Number 24? Yes, a smartly dressed woman came up a couple of minutes ago and let herself in with a key. Looks as though they'll be open for business soon. Strange, that.'

'What do you mean?'

'Well, what with the boss dying—and murdered at that—you'd have thought the shop might have been shut for a few days as a mark of respect.'

Emma shrugged. 'Perhaps it was his own partners who bumped him off.'

George took the intended joke seriously. 'Could be. Nothing would surprise me in the art game.'

They finished their meal in leisurely fashion. By the time they were ready to tackle number 24, rue Gramont had emerged from its lunchtime interlude. Shoppers meandered along its cobbles and window displays were illuminated.

'M'sieu, 'dame, puis-je vous aider?' The elegant, fortyish lady who advanced to meet them was dressed in a beige linen suit of classic design with dark brown trimmings. She exuded charm, caution and cool efficiency.

Emma explained in French that she and her 'father' had met M. Jollibone 'several months ago' and that he had invited them to call on him in Lyon in the hope that he

54

could help them to add to their collection of minor Postimpressionists.

'Oh, but how very unfortunate!' The lady slipped into faultless English. 'Auguste is away at the moment! He will be devastated to have missed you.'

Emma looked suitably disappointed. 'I'm sorry. He said that this would be a good time to find him at home.'

'Normally, yes, but he had to go to New York suddenly. There was a chance to obtain some items from a very distinguished collection which sadly is being dispersed. Perhaps I can help. Josephine Tarantin, Auguste's partner.' She held out a heavily ringed hand to Emma and George in turn. 'And you are?'

George, who had met several wealthy connoisseurs during his years with Lacy Security, assumed the cultured air of a man who could both appreciate and afford to collect turn-of-the-century originals. 'George Martin, madame. It's a pleasure to meet you. Auguste, of course, mentioned you warmly. This is my daughter, Emma. She shares my passion for Postimpressionists.'

'Ah yes, Mr Martin; now I remember Auguste describing your meeting.' Mme Tarantin ushered them through the main gallery into an office-cum-sitting-room beyond. Will you permit me to check our files? Auguste was very fastidious about keeping a card index of our clients' requirements.'

' "Was"?' Emma pounced on the word. 'I beg your pardon?'

'You said Auguste *was* very fastidious about keeping a card index.'

If the Frenchwoman was thrown she covered her confusion very expertly. 'Well, of course, now we keep all our client details on computer. Poor Auguste hates this modern technology: he calls it "impersonal". But I tell him we have to move with the times.' She motioned George and Emma to chairs of ebonised wood and scarlet fabric which were more artistic statements than pieces of furniture. 'Actually, since you are here it will be simpler if you explain your requirements. But first, permit me to offer you a drink.'

George accepted a brandy and Emma a peach liqueur which turned out to be sickly sweet.

Mme Tarantin perched on one of the forbidding chairs. 'Now, tell me about your collection and I will see if we can help you fill any gaps.'

Emma had carefully rehearsed this part of her act. 'We can't afford works by the leading artists so we're trying to accumulate examples of their followers.

56

We're particularly interested in exploring how the Postimpressionist vision developed in different countries. We have a small Munch and some representative paintings by Harold Gilman and others of the London Group. We've managed to acquire items by Ensor and Heckel and—recently— a magnificent Kirchner. But, of course, no collection can be even respectable without some of the French disciples of Van Gogh, Gauguin and Renoir.'

Josephine Tarantin switched on a smile. 'What an exciting little horde. I should love you to show it to me one day. Now, let me see, what can I offer you? How about a very unusual Marquet, or a Maurice Denis?'

George nodded enthusiastically. 'That sounds very interesting, madame.'

Their hostess stood. 'Excellent. They are not on current display. I shall have to fetch them from my strongroom. Will you excuse me for a moment?'

George rose also. 'I wonder whether I might visit your bathroom while you're doing that.'

'Of course. Come with me.' She led the way to a rear door giving on to a flagged courtyard with an inoperative fountain at its centre. She indicated a door opposite. 'Through there and on the right.'

George crossed the enclosed space

quickly. At the doorway he paused and glanced over his shoulder. He saw Mme Tarantin unlock an imposing portal of studded oak. He entered a dark passageway, half-closed the door behind him and kept watch from behind it. Moments later Josephine Tarantin emerged carrying a canvas in each hand. As soon as she had disappeared George moved swiftly to the storeroom. The door opened to his touch, and he was confronted by a row of wooden racks holding dozens of paintings.

In the office Emma was trying to sustain an intelligent conversation about the items selected for her inspection, to give George as long as possible for snooping. About Albert Marquet and Maurice Denis she knew absolutely nothing. So she bluffed. Holding her head slightly to one side she stared intently at the canvas Mme Tarantin had placed on an easel in the corner of the room. It was a riverside scene with sketchy figures and buildings. 'An early work.' The inflection could be taken as either statement or question.

'About 1902 or 1903, I would say. The Fauvist influence is very obvious. Marquet was already exhibiting with the group, as I'm sure you know.'

Emma nodded sagely. 'May I see the Denis again? I'm sure it will appeal to my father.'

Mme Tarantin removed the Marquet with its geometrical shapes and deceptive simplicity to reveal a complex composition of sumptuous, swirling shapes and mysteriously dark colours. Men and women were depicted playing cards, discoursing or striking attitudes in a wooded landscape whose trees and foliage resembled wallpaper design or an atmospheric stage set.

Emma approached the canvas with a pensive frown. She peered at the combined monogram and date—M.A.U.D. 1897—and tried to think of something perceptive to say.

It was the Frenchwoman who spoke. 'Your father seems to be taking rather a long time. Is he all right? Should I go and check?'

Emma thought quickly. 'I'm afraid the poor dear does have a problem with his waterworks.' She watched Madame Tarantin anxiously.

The other woman frowned and moved towards the outer door. But at that moment George reappeared. Their hostess seemed to relax and the talk turned once more to the two paintings which were on display. George perspired with the effort of sustaining the rôle of knowledgeable collector and steered the conversation as naturally as he could to a rapid conclusion. At last he and Emma were on their feet and being escorted back through the gallery.

'You'll let me know then, about the Denis?' Mme Tarantin struck an attitude of professional nonchalance over the potential sale.

George shook the proffered hand. 'Certainly, madame. In a day or two. We're staying nearby at the Hotel Cour des Loges until the end of the week.'

The outer door opened as they reached it. Two men entered. As the English couple stood aside to make way for the new arrivals Emma dropped the gallery catalogue she was holding. She retrieved it and ducked through the doorway, leaving George to say the final goodbyes. She had taken several quick paces along the street before her companion caught her up.

She stopped and drew him into a doorway, trembling with excitement. 'George, we've cracked it! That was him! The man I met in London.'

# CHAPTER 3

'You're sure?' George put the question insistently. 'Quite sure?'

'Absolutely.'

'There's no chance that your memory's

playing tricks—that you thought you saw the imposter because...well...because you wanted to see him?'

Emma burst out impatiently, 'Oh George, for heaven's sake, I'm not an idiot! One of those men back there is pseudo-Jollibone.' She was struck by a sudden thought. 'Do you think he might have recognised me too?'

'Well, the dropped papers ploy wasn't exactly subtle but I don't think that either of the men noticed you. They were looking at the gallery owner and I'll tell you this much: she was *not* pleased to see them.'

'So, what happens now?' Emma was glowing with self-satisfaction.

'You go back to the hotel and keep out of the way, just in case. I'll wait for these two and tail them.'

Emma scowled. 'George, that's not—'

He ignored the protest. 'If we can find out where they're based we can decide what to do next.'

Emma pulled a face but knew that George's plan made sense. 'OK. See you later.' She sauntered along the street.

George did not have to wait long. Within a few minutes the two men left the gallery, turned to the right, walking rapidly and, to judge from their gesticulations, locked in fierce argument. George followed them across the Pont Bonaparte towards the city centre. They went down the metro steps at Place Bellecour and rode the train a couple of stops northwards. The pursuit ended in a shabby sidestreet, inappropriately named rue d'Etoile, behind the Musée des Beaux Arts. George hesitated at the end of the street. Apart from his two quarries it was deserted and he could not follow without becoming conspicuous. He watched from behind a parked van close to the corner. He saw them stop before an apartment block halfway along. The taller and younger of the two men opened the door with a key.

As soon as they had entered the building, George walked rapidly along the narrow pavement. The door bore the number 15. There were six names listed on the intercom. He backed away and stared up at the building. There were lights in the top two storeys. George returned to the doorway and scrutinised the top two names—'Fournelet' and 'Lebec'. He retreated to the corner, turning his overcoat collar up against the drizzle that had now set in. An hour later he was very cold and very wet. No one had entered or left the building. Deciding that no useful purpose would be served by his catching pneumonia, George turned his back on rue d'Etoile, made for the bright lights of the nearest main thoroughfare, found a cab and, within fifteen minutes, was thankfully soaking his weary limbs in a hot bath.

The fiacre climbed the hill slowly and the wheezing horse finally came to a halt in the open space before Sacré Coeur. Particles of stone dust hung in the still sunlit air. Sounds of hammering and sawing and the shouts of workmen fell from the scaffolding encasing the great basilica which had already been fifteen years in the building. Albert descended, then held up a hand to help his fiancée from the cab.

She stepped down warily, watching where she put her feet. 'We would have been much more comfortable in the carriage,' Eloise complained.

'We would have attracted too much attention.' Albert held her arm firmly as they crossed the uneven surface towards the row of tall, ramshackle houses facing the church. 'These Montmartre people still think of themselves as villagers. They're suspicious of "smart" people from the big city.'

'I suppose that's why you're wearing that unbecoming garment.' Eloise glared disapprovingly at the brown topcoat Albert had thrown over his suit.

They began to negotiate a narrow street that descended the Butte in a cataract of slopes and steps. A man lolling in the doorway of a bar waved a bottle and called out, 'Hello, Aris.' A few paces further on a young woman wearing a shawl over a ragged dress crossed the street to stand in their path. 'What's this then, Aris?' Her grin revealed a row of yellowing teeth. 'Bringing your own? Ain't I good enough for you, then?' She looked Eloise up and down appraisingly. 'Fine feathers—but we all look much the same plucked.'

Albert laughed. 'Marie, don't be a pest. I'll see you soon.' He steered his fiancée round the obstacle and towards an open doorway on the right.

Eloise clung tightly to his arm. 'Do you really know these dreadful people? Why do they call you Aris?'

Albert smiled fleetingly but made no reply. He led the way across an internal courtyard where two barefoot girls were playing with a spinning top. He inserted a key into the door on the far side and ushered Eloise into a dingy passageway.

She peered into the gloom. 'Bertie, what an awful place. Why have you brought me here?'

'Just be patient a little longer, Elli.' He struck a match and lit a gas lamp which threw some light on a narrow staircase. He took his fiancée's hand and drew her up to the first floor. 'Here we are.'

He threw open the door at the top of the stairs and waved her into a spacious room. He crossed to a large window, drew back heavy curtains and allowed the bright winter light to burst in.

Eloise observed a chamber the like of which she had never seen before. It resembled a half-dressed stage set or a room partially cleared for redecorating. To the left, comfortable and expensive furniture was tastefully arranged—a perfectly respectable drawing room. On the right, carpet gave way to bare boards. Two kitchen chairs, one draped with grubby, stained sheeting, stood beside a deal table strewn with rubbish. By the window there was a huge easel supporting a framed canvas of which only the back was visible. Unframed pictures were stacked against the bare side wall.

The elegant young woman moved instinctively to her left and stood beside a rosewood table whose gleaming surface was obscured by a layer of dust. 'Bertie, what on earth is this place?'

Albert moved to the centre of the room and spread his arms in proprietorial pride. 'This is my studio.'

'You mean...' Eloise struggled with the concept.

'This is where I come to paint.'

'But why?' She laughed a nervous laugh.

'You could follow your hobby just as well at home.'

'You think so?'

'Of course. Everyone admires your drawings. I treasure the sketch you did of me in the rose garden last summer.'

'Oh, that!' He waved a hand dismissively. 'I could have done that just as well with a camera. That's not art.' He walked across to the easel and gazed at the uncompleted painting. 'I couldn't do this sort of thing at home—not that it's much good,' he added gloomily.

'Why ever not?'

'A couple of years ago I made the mistake of asking Father for a room to use as a studio. He refused. "No son of mine is going to be a namby-pamby artist," he said.'

'You shouldn't worry about him. He's terribly old-fashioned. When we have our own house you can have as big a "studio" as you want. The whole attic if you like.'

Albert frowned and momentarily looked away from his unfinished work. 'That's not the real reason why I have to come here. Painting isn't just about putting pigment on canvas. It's about *ideas*. It's about the search for *truth*. It's about how to get what I feel here, inside, out onto a flat, white surface. In this place, in Montmartre, there are men who *can* do it; men I can learn from. Oh, Elli, there are artists here—geniuses—who can do *anything.*' He advanced into the centre of the room waving his arms enthusiastically. Vuillard, Bonnard, Charente, Denis, Van Gogh, Deribault—they're all doing fantastic things. Even old Degas comes here sometimes to meet and encourage us.'

'Degas? Wasn't he one of the ones exhibiting at Durand-Ruel's gallery last year? You got cross with me because I said I couldn't understand his pictures.'

'They call themselves Impressionists. They're amazing—some of them, anyway. But they're out of date now. Art is moving on. It's the younger men who are really doing astonishing things. They'll be famous one day, long after your father and my father and all our blessed politicians are forgotten.'

Eloise laughed. 'Now you're letting your enthusiasm carry you away.'

'No, it's true. These are the men who are exploring the meaning of things, looking behind mere appearances. That's what I want to do. To understand! To communicate! To do something important and lasting.'

'But you don't have to be here to meet these people. If you want lessons they can come to our house in the Faubourg—just as my piano teacher does,

67

and the dressmaker.'

'Oh, for heaven's sake, Elli!' The covering slipped from Albert's frustration. 'These aren't tradesmen or musical hacks! They don't sell their services to fashionable dilettantes who think it would be quite nice to pass the occasional afternoon painting flowers in the garden!'

Eloise came back vigorously. 'Presumably they have stomachs that need filling, like ordinary mortals. I don't imagine they'd be too proud to earn a few extra sous. It would be much more seemly for them to come to you than for you to lead this degrading double life.'

'You don't suppose I enjoy it, do you? If society weren't so topsy-turvy I'd be able to study art quite openly and my family and friends would be quite happy about it. As it is, people—our class of people—think it's splendid to be a soldier, learning how to kill, but frightfully infra dig to be an artist pledged to creating something beautiful, something life-enhancing. Don't imagine that I'm the only one caught in this trap. There are several of us. There's a young fellow called Henri Matisse. He rents a room just along the street. His father thinks he's in Paris studying law. You call it degrading, this secret of mine, but it's not me who's degraded; it's society. Can't you understand that?'

It was Eloise who broke the frozen silence which followed. 'I can certainly try. I want to understand, but you'll have to help me. Will you show me some of your paintings?'

'I'd like to.' He looked sheepish, like a small boy taking the lid off his little box of treasures. 'But you must promise not to laugh.'

Albert moved an armchair close to the window, established his fiancée in it, and for the next half hour he displayed canvas after canvas, eagerly explaining the effects he was trying to achieve in each. It was obvious even to Eloise that the artist was experimenting with various techniques. Some subjects were depicted naturalistically. In other pictures she found the colours jarringly harsh and the shapes distorted.

At last she stood up and began herself selecting paintings she wanted to look at more closely. 'So what is important to you is not so much depicting what things look like as what you feel about them?'

'That's my main objective—yes.'

'Hmm! I think I begin—' She stopped abruptly. She had turned round one of the larger canvases which had been facing the wall and stood back to appraise it. When she spoke again after several moments her tone had changed. 'And just what do you feel about that?'

Albert came to stand beside her and look down at the picture. It was a virtually complete nude study that he had done several months before and almost forgotten about. He turned from it to Eloise, whose cheeks glowed red and whose lips were tightly clenched. 'I was struck by how relaxed she was, how...'

'Perhaps "provocative" is the word you're looking for. Other adjectives come more readily to my mind. That is your little friend Marie, isn't it? I suppose this is what she meant by having her feathers plucked.'

'Yes, nice girl. She models for several of us.'

'And is that all she does for you?'

'It's all she does for me. Elli, you don't really think... By God, you do!'

'Well, what am I supposed to think? You obviously enjoyed looking at her like...that. Oh, for goodness' sake, turn it round. It's disgusting!'

'It's nothing of the sort!' Albert reacted angrily. He looked again at the seated figure, face turned to the spectator with an expression of slight humour. 'It's a picture of someone who feels no shame about her body.'

'Manifestly! There's a name for women like that.'

'Marie is a respectable girl. She wouldn't be accepted in your mama's salon but she's none the less a lady for that. And she needs all the money she can get. She has two small children to support.'

'Huh! That's hardly a surprise!'

'Eloise!'

'No, Albert, don't say any more! Just take me out of here and find me a cab. I've decided I don't like your secret and I want no part of it.'

When George had dried and changed he made two internal phone calls. The first was to room service. The second was to Emma. Twenty minutes later he was pouring tea for his young colleague and contemplating a plateful of cholesterol-packed cakes. He described his pursuit of the two Frenchmen.

'So you reckon that's where they're staying?' Emma forked fragile pastry and *crème pâtisserie* into her mouth.

'Maybe, maybe not. The way I see it, it doesn't much matter.'

'But if they're not there, whoever is in the apartment won't tell us where to find them.'

'He'll soon sing if we threaten him with the police. He won't want to find himself an accessory to murder.'

'Hmm.' Emma looked doubtful. 'What

about your snooping at the gallery? Did you find anything useful?'

'Not a thing. There were lots of pictures in Mme Tarantin's storeroom, but nothing much like the ones you're looking for.'

'She's a pretty cool customer. What did you make of her?'

George drained his cup, dropped another teabag in it and added hot water and milk. 'She's such a fluent liar it's hard to know whether to believe anything she says.'

Emma nodded. 'Why do you suppose she spun that yarn about Jollibone being in America?'

'Perhaps she thought the truth was bad for business. Having a partner stabbed and dumped in the Thames can't be very good for customer confidence.'

'Possibly. Or it might be a case of bad conscience. She obviously knows the fake Jollibone.'

'That's right. Whatever's going on, it's a pound to a penny they're in it together.'

Emma sat back with a frown of concentration. 'Let's think this through... The fair Josephine and these other characters plan to bump off poor Auguste. They wait till he's out of the country so that they can cover their tracks.'

'That would certainly explain why Mme Tarantin didn't want her confederates hanging round the gallery. But what's the motive?'

Emma's eyes widened with sudden inspiration. 'Got it! Someone turns up at the gallery with a bunch of long-lost Bertrands. The dealers realise they've been presented with a goldmine. But Josephine gets greedy and decides not to share with her partner. So she plans to have Auguste killed when he takes some of the paintings to London *and* to fake a theft. When the heat's off Josephine will dispose of the Bertrands on the underground market. Not only that, but eventually the insurance company will have to pay up.'

'So milady and her toyboys cop the lot, which will run to millions.'

'That's right. And I'll bet she gets Jollibone's share of the gallery into the bargain.'

'Do you want that?' As Emma shook her head, George helped himself to the last cake. 'That still doesn't explain why our young villain displayed himself and the pictures to you and Catherine.'

Emma had also seen the flaw in the argument. She shrugged it off. 'Everyone makes mistakes.'

'Oh well, ours not to reason why. We've done what we came over for. It's up to the police now.'

Emma shook her head vigorously. 'No,

George! We came to find the pictures.'

'We've found the crooks. When the police have bagged them they're sure to get the pictures, too.'

'But then we'll never get to handle them. Anyway, everything we've worked out is only a theory.'

'You sounded very convinced about it just now.'

'Yes but, as you said, our scenario doesn't cover everything. We could be wrong. People are presumed innocent till proved guilty, even in France.'

George stood up, walked over to the bedside table and picked up the telephone. 'Well, there's nothing more we can do here.' He pressed in a number. 'I'm sure the Major will agree that we've followed the trail as far as we can.'

'No, wait!' Emma was on her feet now. 'There's the apartment in rue d'Etoile.'

'So what do we do—march in and say "Please hand over the stolen pictures"? I don't know about you, but I want to live a bit longer. Sally?' he spoke into the phone. 'George here. Is the Major around?'

Emma went up to him. 'Look, let's just think a bit more before we report back.' She heard Tim's voice on the other end of the line and knew that it was too late. She listened while George gave a résumé of the afternoon's events.

'So there you are, Major—all tied up, and within twenty-four hours. Not a bad bit of work, if I do say so myself. Thanks, Major. What do you reckon, now? Make a report to the local plod and get back to Farrans a.s.a.p.?... Yes, I see. I hadn't thought of that... Yes, she's right here. I'll put her on.' George handed over the receiver.

Emma spoke brightly but wondered how she could convincingly convey her misgivings. 'Tim, hi! Look, I'm not sure—'

'Emma, congratulations. It sounds as though you've done a great job.'

'Thanks Tim, but—'

'I was just saying to George that if you get tied up with the local police they could keep you there for days. What I suggest is that you write a cryptic, anonymous note for the gendarmerie and give them the address in the rue d'Etoile. Then there'll be no reason for them to connect us with the business at all.'

'Well yes, Tim, we could do that. The thing is I'm not sure we've got this thing right. If Catherine wants us to track down the paintings, then I think we ought to take things just a stage further.'

'Sorry, Emma, but there are two things wrong with that. The first is that you are almost certainly dealing with a ruthless and

75

vicious gang. The second is that if you don't tell the police what you know, you are technically breaking the law. It's called withholding evidence. If it ever came out we'd all be in hot water.'

'But, Tim...'

'No, Emma. I realise how wonderful it would be to be able to trumpet to the world that Lacy Enterprises has made a historical discovery—and perhaps we're still in there with a chance of handling the Bertrands—but right now the police of two countries have a murder investigation on their hands and I don't want you mixed up in it.'

'Tim, just give us another twenty-four hours...'

'You can have twenty-four hours—for shopping or sightseeing. I know you're disappointed but there's nothing more you can do. Look, have a good dinner with George this evening, and a bottle of champagne on me. You deserve it, both of you. I'll see you at the end of the week. Bye for now.' He rang off.

Emma dropped the receiver onto its rest disconsolately. 'That's that, then.'

George offered an encouraging smile. 'Cheer up. He is right you know.'

'I guess so.' Emma moved to the door. 'I think I'll banish the gloom with a bit of shopping.'

'You do that. I've got some paperwork to catch up on. See you downstairs for dinner?'

'Sure, George. I'll be in the bar about eight.'

But she was not.

# CHAPTER 4

Albert knocked on the mahogany double doors.

'Come!' The terse command struck unmuffled through the solid timber.

Albert entered the study, closed the door softly behind him and walked with firm tread across the wide carpet. He stopped, standing stiffly before the desk. Silent. He had learned in childhood only to speak when spoken to.

After some seconds his father looked up from the letters he had been opening. He removed his pince-nez and scrutinised his elder son with pale eyes beneath thick, arched brows. 'What's all this nonsense I hear?'

'Sir?'

'Don't play the innocent with me. You know I'm referring to your broken engagement with General d'Erigny-Duchamp's girl. What's it all about?'

'That question would be more appropriately addressed to Eloise, sir. It was she who returned the ring.'

'Yes, and mightily upset the general is, too. So am I. You know how important your marriage is to us and to the regiment.'

'With respect, sir, if Eloise no longer wishes—'

'Don't talk nonsense. If women's whims were allowed to influence such matters no one would ever get married.'

Albert opened his mouth to protest. 'With respect—'

'Don't "with respect" me!' The old man cut him short. 'Respect means obeying parents, being guided by those who are older and wiser, doing your duty.'

Albert had always been intimidated by his father. So had the entire household. But whereas his brother accepted the dominance of the head of the family just as their late mother had done, Albert increasingly resented it. With the resentment went self-loathing. He despised himself for not standing up to the balding old tyrant. He looked down at the pinched face and rheumy eyes and wondered yet again where the strength lay which forged and maintained the iron shackles by which his father bound others to his will. He clenched his fists and pressed them firmly against his thighs. 'Sir, we are approaching the end of the nineteenth century. Attitudes are changing...'

'Yes, and not for the better. You'd have to be blind not to see the mess this country's in. And why? Because there's no leadership. And why is there no leadership? Because those in power don't command respect and obedience. Politicians pander to the people instead of enforcing policy.'

'France is a democracy, sir.'

'Aye, more's the pity. Have you ever heard a more damned-fool idea than democracy? All men equal? Pah! Take that to its logical conclusion and what have you got? Grocers who think they're as good as government ministers. Corporals who think they know as much as officers. Workers who band together to dictate terms to their employers. Women who demand to be educated alongside men and even believe they've as much right to vote. Heaven help us! Democracy is the rot in—'

'I don't agree, sir. I—'

'Don't interrupt!' The old man scarcely raised his voice but Albert fell silent. 'As I was saying, democracy is the rot in our society and it's the duty of every one of us to stamp it out. We must make sure that wherever we have any authority—in our homes, in our families, in the regiment—we exercise it firmly. That brings me back to you and what's-her-name...Eloise. I have spoken to the general and we're agreed that you're to patch up your quarrel. Write to her this morning. Be firm. She's going to be your wife, so you mustn't stand any nonsense from her.'

'I don't think Eloise...'

'The general will talk to her and she will obey his wishes. Now, off you go and write that letter.' Colonel de Bracieux replaced his pince-nez and returned his attention to his correspondence. The interview was over.

But as Albert reached the door his father spoke again. 'Oh, by the way. The wedding will be on sixth June. That's a week before the military review. Everyone of any consequence will be in Paris. It will be a splendid affair. You and what's-her-name will have an excellent start to your married life.'

Albert ran down the wide staircase. He crossed the hall, whose walls were hung with spears and lined with glass cabinets filled with carved masks, ivory figurines and other colonial trophies. He made a direct line for the front door only to find his way blocked by Edouard, emerging suddenly from the drawing room.

'I want a word with you.' The young

man stood hands on hips, glaring.

'Ed, get out of the way. I don't have time for your silliness.' Albert struggled to keep his bubbling anger under control.

He made to sidestep but Edouard put the flat of his hand against his chest. 'I said I wanted a word and, by God, you will listen!'

Albert brushed the arm aside. 'Not now, Ed.'

'Yes NOW! You've been avoiding me for days.'

'Don't be stupid!'

'Don't call me stupid!' Edouard screamed the words through clenched teeth. 'I've taken all I'm going to take from you! I'm tired of sticking up for you in the mess. I'm tired of watching you make the family name a laughing stock. Now you've broken the heart of a woman who's far too good for you.'

Albert looked at the quivering adolescent and took a deep breath. He forced himself to say slowly and calmly, 'Ed, what nonsense have you got into your head now?'

'It's only nonsense to you because you choose not to see what's under your nose. You're a weakling. Your own men call you names behind your back. If it weren't for father's reputation you wouldn't stand a chance of promotion. You're a sham soldier!' The boy's blue eyes glistened with tears of rage. He gulped for breath.

'Right, you've had your say. Now let me pass.' Albert pushed Edouard roughly aside.

But Edouard clutched his arm. 'Not so fast, *brother!* It's not enough for you to dishonour this family, is it? You have to cause pain and distress to Eloise—and that I cannot forgive.'

'You don't know what you're talking about. What passes between Eloise and me is our business.'

'No it isn't! You don't care anything about her. But I do and I can't bear to see her unhappy or listen to jokes being made about her in the mess.'

Edouard stood breathing heavily and glowering with a hatred that consumed him utterly. For several moments the two brothers stood immobile like cardboard figures in a child's toy theatre. Then, impelled by Albert's lack of reaction, Edouard let out a roar of rage. He drew back his right arm and swung a wild blow at Albert's chin.

Albert turned his head just in time to take the force of the punch on the side of his face. A torrent of released emotions surged through his body. They were transmuted into strength. He grabbed Edouard by the lapels, swung him off his feet and hurled him across the hall. He stepped to the door. As he wrenched it open he heard the crash of breaking glass. Without looking back he rushed into the street, hailed a cab and was driven to Montmartre.

Instead of going to the studio he wandered the streets for several hours, hands thrust deep in pockets against the biting wind. His mind was in a turmoil. Questions spun around as agitatedly as the scraps of paper and leaves caught in the wind eddies of the cobbled alleys. Eloise? The army? Art? Family? All imponderables eventually coalesced into one: what did he want from life?

As light drained from the sky it came on to hail and Albert blundered into a bar. He sat alone at a corner table with his cognac. Edouard was right; that was the damning truth. He *was* a weakling. He would marry a woman he did not love and continue in a career he did not like because he lacked the courage to do anything else. Because doing what his father called his 'duty' would ensure him comfort, wealth, social status, respect. And one day he, too, would be a shrivelled old man sitting behind a desk, confronted by a son he did not understand because he did not want to understand.

He was staring morosely into his third

brandy when he became aware of the voice.

'I said, "Hello, Aris, what's bothering you?" '

Albert looked up into a ruddy face fringed with black beard. He managed a faint smile. 'Hello, Joseph.'

'Can I join you or is this a private wake?' Without waiting for a reply the tall man tweaked a chair from the table and lowered his bulk onto it. He raised a glass of absinthe to his lips and drained it at a gulp. He set a second down carefully on the marble surface. 'My God, how's a man expected to work in this weather? My hand nearly froze to the chisel.'

'What are you working on?'

'It's a commission, that's the devil of it! I shall actually be paid—if I ever get it finished.' He scowled as the door opened, admitting a surge of icy wind. 'Hey, Henri, close that damned thing! Do you want us all to freeze?'

'Just for that, Joseph, I won't buy you a drink.' The newcomer was enveloped in an expensive-looking coat with a fur collar. The shabby cap pulled down over his ears made an incongruous contrast. He collected three glasses from the bar, came across, placed them on the table and sat down. 'There you are. Just as well for you I'm in a good mood. I sold a couple of articles to the *Revue des Arts* this morning. That'll keep Madame Forget off my back for a while. She's been threatening for weeks to throw me out of the apartment and let it to someone "respectable".' He spoke the last word in a fruity falsetto.

The sculptor laughed. 'And where would she find anyone respectable round here?' He nodded at Albert. 'Although our young friend is looking very smart today. Aris, in that suit you might almost pass for a gentleman.'

Henri, a thin-faced man with a wispy moustache, winked. 'Ah, but then Aristide Bertrand isn't his real name, you know. Joseph, you are the product of a chambermaid and a syphilitic carter and I wouldn't recognise my father if I passed him on the boulevard, but our little painter here has breeding.'

Albert stared at the speaker in genuine alarm. 'What do you mean?'

Joseph scowled. 'Have you been snooping, Henri? You know the rules here.'

The writer giggled girlishly. 'Oh, don't I just: everyone to be accepted at face value and no questions asked. But that's what makes Montmartre so fascinating. It's a place of secrets. And I *love* secrets. Now, drink up friends and I'll tell you all the latest gossip—that is, if you're interested, Joseph.'

Albert only half listened as the two locals discussed the doings and misdoings of mutual acquaintances. His own problems continued to tumble around his brain although the repeated brandies softened their edges. He heard Joseph repeat his grumble about the cold weather. He heard Henri's reply: 'Perhaps you should go and join Van Gogh—you know, Van Gogh, the mad Dutchman, studied in Cormon's studio, went off to the South a month or so back. Well, he's been writing glowing letters—Provence is wonderful; Arles is wonderful; the countryside is wonderful; the light is wonderful; the people are wonderful; he's painting again and his paintings are wonderful; Vincent says he's "found himself" and has discovered that he is wonderful! He wants all his friends to go and join him and discover just how wonderful it all is.'

Aristide heard, like an echo in a distant room, the two men laughing. Someone pushed another glass across the table towards him. He emptied it at a gulp.

That one brandy changed his life.

George gave Emma twenty minutes, then put a call through to her room. There was no reply. He ordered another drink and waited another quarter of an hour before allowing himself to become concerned. The most likely explanation, he told himself, was that she had been trying on dresses and had lost track of time. Even so, the shops shut at seven. He went to the reception desk and quizzed the professionally smiling duty clerk.

Yes, Mlle Kerr was out; her key-card was in its pigeonhole. No, there did not appear to be a message, but had monsieur checked his room? Personal delivery was part of the Cour des Loges's high quality service.

George strode rapidly to the lift. He saw the envelope as soon as he pushed open his door. It was propped on the dressing table. He tore it open and, with difficulty, deciphered Emma's enthusiastic scrawl.

In haste 7.50

George, we've got it wrong. The man we saw in London and at the gallery is Charles Dubec. He didn't steal the Bertrands and he didn't kill Jollibone. He's going to show me the paintings and explain everything. I'll be a bit late for dinner. Please start without me. See you soon.

Emma.

George sank on the bed, head in hands.

'Stupid woman! Bloody, bloody, bloody stupid woman!'

He looked again at the piece of crisp hotel notepaper. Seven fifty: that meant that Emma and Charles Dubec (if that was his real name) had an hour's start. They could be anywhere in the city by now—or on one of the roads out of Lyon. Well, there were two places he could try.

He ran most of the way to the gallery. It was shut up. He found his way round to the back but there was no sign of life. He checked at the hotel before getting the concierge to summon a taxi.

At 15 rue d'Etoile George gained entry by slipping in behind another visitor. He climbed to the top floor and pressed the button beside the nametag. 'Fournelet'. An elderly man in slippers opened the door on a security chain. He peered suspiciously at the stranger, and when George tried to question him, made it clear that he spoke no English. Nor did his wife, who hovered anxiously in the hallway behind. George made a stumbling enquiry about M. Lebec. The man pointed to the stairs, muttered something about 'jeune homme' and 'quatrième étage' and slammed the door. When George descended to the next landing and rang the bell of the apartment below there was no reply.

Hoping against hope that his suspicions

were wrong, George hurried back to the hotel. Emma had not returned and frantic questioning of the desk staff brought forth no more information. Wearily George returned to his room and put through a call to Farrans Court.

He was surprised to hear his own daughter's voice at the other end of the line. 'Tina? What are you doing there?'

'Hello, Dad. Are you having a good time in France? I'm babysitting for Mr and Mrs Lacy. They're having dinner with friends in Marlborough, and it's the nanny's night off.'

'Damn! Just my luck.'

'What's up, Dad? You sound dead worried.'

'Nothing serious, luv, but I must talk to the Major urgent. Have they left a phone number with you?'

'Yes of course, they always do. Hang on, I'll get it.'

She was back after a few seconds and gave him the information he needed. 'You sure you're OK, Dad?'

'Yes, fine, luv. You'd best get back to your homework, or whatever it is you're doing. Give my love to your mum. See you in a couple of days. Bye.'

Two minutes later he was listening to Tim Lacy's clear, authoritative voice. 'Hello, George, what's up?'

'Sorry to disturb—'

'Cut the apologies! You wouldn't be calling if it wasn't important.'

George gave a succinct summary of the events of the last couple of hours.

'How did this Dubec character get on to you?'

'He must have recognised Emma at the gallery and found out from Mme Tarantin where we're staying.'

'So he waited for Emma at the hotel and spun her some yarn to get her to go with him.'

'That's how I see it, Major. She should have had more sense.'

'It's my fault. I ought to have realised she was too stubborn to give up just because I said so.'

George gave voice to his worst fear for the first time. 'Do you reckon they'll have done away with her, because she recognised one of them?'

'They'd be pretty stupid to do that. It's only going to hot up the hunt. More likely they're using her as a hostage to warn us off—I hope. The best thing you can do, George, is stay put in case they phone you. I'll get the first plane out in the morning.'

'Shall I inform the police?'

'Better not—not immediately, anyway. At the moment Dubec and his cronies have got the initiative. Let's wait a few hours and see what they do with it. Call me immediately if you hear from them. Otherwise I'll see you tomorrow.' Abruptly, the line went dead.

George ordered a bottle of scotch and a plate of sandwiches from room service. An hour later he undressed, rolled into bed and tried to sleep. Unsuccessfully.

She was back in her prep school, running along an interminable corridor, terrified, pursued by screaming bullies waving hockey sticks, and the air was heavy with the familiar smell of boiling cabbage. Then she was in a cavernous, dripping sewer teetering on a slippery ledge above a seething black pool from which a foetid miasma assailed her nostrils. With a scream she fell—and in falling, she woke.

The nightmare visions dispersed to be replaced by a small room whose low ceiling was crossed with thick beams. As she lifted her aching head from the pillow, Emma saw that light was being filtered through a piece of sacking or other loose-woven material nailed over a solitary window. The panic was still there. So was the smell; not as strong as in her dream but no less unpleasant.

She lay back, heart racing, perspiration standing out on her forehead. Questions tumbled around her bewildered mind: Where was she? How had she got here? What was going to happen to her? Could she get out?

She drew the back of a hand across her brow. 'Emma Kerr, pull yourself together!' she commanded. 'You're an intelligent, self-reliant woman. You can handle this—whatever it is.' She took several deep breaths. 'OK. Step one—analyse the situation.'

She eased her legs out from under a duvet and got herself into a sitting position. No use. The pounding in her head grew worse; she felt sick; and the dimly perceived shapes in the room performed slow gyrations. She lay down again and closed her eyes. OK, plan B—get to work on the memory. Various images presented themselves in jumbled form but, with painful concentration, Emma threaded them into a comprehensible sequence.

The hotel foyer. She had come in from the street. The man was there—the man who was not Auguste Jollibone—sitting in a chair flipping through a magazine, obviously waiting. He had stood up and come across to her, holding out his hand, smiling disarmingly.

'Miss Kerr, it is a pleasure to see you again so soon.'

Emma remembered the mixed emotions

she had felt at being accosted by the imposter. There had been alarm but also mingled excitement and triumph. She had come to Lyon on a fairly hopeless mission to track down this man and a bundle of important paintings. Against all the odds she had accomplished half her task. Would her luck hold and lead her to the Bertrands?

She had returned the man's casual smile. 'Good evening, M. Jollibone—only, of course, that's not your name, is it?'

The dark-haired young man had placed a hand over his heart and dropped his head in mock contrition. 'Ah, you have discovered my little masquerade. I was foolish to think that I could deceive two such intelligent ladies. But I assure you, it was necessary. Please, give me a chance to explain.' He had motioned towards a cluster of chairs.

Glancing around the comfortingly busy foyer and across at the two lift doors from one of which George would be emerging within about half an hour, Emma had allowed herself to be led to one of the bergère-style fauteuils. She had stared fixedly at the man taking his seat opposite. He was compellingly attractive. Dressed now in an expensive-looking leather jacket over a red roll-neck jumper he seemed much more relaxed than he had at their previous meeting. 'So, what do I call you?'

'My name is Dubec—Charles Dubec. I'm studying art here in Lyon.'

'Well, M. Charles Dubec, I assume you know that the British and French police are both looking for you. A little matter of murder and theft, I believe.'

Dubec had nodded gravely, his brown eyes fixed unblinkingly on Emma's. 'I reported to the local gendarmerie yesterday, as soon as I heard of Jollibone's death.'

'You went to the police yourself!'

'Of course. Why should I not? I have nothing to hide. I didn't like Jollibone. The man was a crook. But I was horrified when his partner told me that he had been killed.'

'Did you explain to them that you had been imitating the dead man in London?'

'Naturally.'

'Would you care to explain to me?'

Dubec had taken out a packet of Gauloises and offered her one. She had refused. Emma remembered thinking how steady his hands were as he extracted the cigarette, lit it with a lighter, and returned the pack to his pocket. He had not seemed the slightest bit nervous.

Only after exhaling a stream of blue smoke had Dubec begun his narrative. 'It's really not as mysterious and sinister as it must appear. The Bertrands belong to me and my brother. They have been in our family for many years. A few months ago, we decided to look into the possibility of selling some of them. I had met Jollibone at a lecture and—unfortunately, as it turns out—I confided in him. He was, naturally, very excited when I showed him a couple of the paintings. Conrad, my brother, was not very happy about trusting a dealer. We come from southern, peasant stock—naturally suspicious of all strangers. I'm afraid it was I who persuaded him to allow Jollibone to take a sample batch to London. Well, Conrad was right and I was wrong. He made some enquiries about Jollibone and discovered that he was involved with some pretty unsavoury characters.'

'Was it Conrad I saw you with earlier?'

'No. That was my father. He was on Conrad's side. He insisted that we went to London to get our property back before anything happened to it. We confronted Jollibone in his hotel. There was a fierce argument. Jollibone tried everything—threats, entreaties, promises of immense wealth. I've never seen a man so angry and so frightened.'

'Frightened?'

'Oh yes. He was afraid of someone. My guess is he had a deal going with a very powerful customer. Then we'd come along and *bouleversé*—messed up—everything.'

'So you weren't surprised to hear that someone had put a knife into him?'

'Not altogether. If you mix with the *canaille* you have to watch your back.'

'So you made Jollibone give up your pictures?'

'Yes. He tried to tell us that he hadn't got them; that a client had taken them on approval, but...well, let's just say we persuaded him to change his story.'

'If all this is true—and I'm not saying that I'm convinced—why the charade of posing as Jollibone and showing the paintings to us?'

'My idea again. Jollibone told us about the meeting he had set up with Mrs Lacy. We still wanted to know about the value of the pictures. So I thought I'd keep the appointment and see what I could discover.'

'So what are you going to do about the Bertrands now?' Emma had tried to sound casual.

'Oh, we're still planning to sell them—or some of them. And we're still looking for expert advice. But it's going to have to be someone we trust—totally.'

'You can trust Lacys.'

Dubec had nodded sagely and smiled at her with his brown, guileless eyes. 'Only if you trust me and believe that I'm not a cold-blooded assassin.'

'Well...I'm not...'

'Suppose I were to show you a couple more Bertrands? I have them in my apartment here.'

' "Come up to my room and look at my paintings"? It sounds like the corniest line in the book!'

'Oh, no!' He had looked genuinely shocked. 'I would not presume... Look, there's a bar on the ground floor of the apartment block. We'll order a drink. I'll leave you there and fetch the paintings down. You'll be perfectly safe, I promise you.'

'I'm supposed to be meeting my colleague here for dinner.'

'It will only take a few minutes—twenty, thirty at most. You can leave a note for your friend.'

Emma had hesitated. Dubec had seemed to understand. He had stood up. 'I'm sorry. That wasn't a good idea. You're quite right to be cautious. It's just that, having these valuable paintings, we're anxious to do the right thing; make sure that someone really reliable handles them for us.'

'Clever bastard!' Emma gazed up at the ceiling's flaking whitewash. Dubec had known that the paintings were a bait she could not ignore. As the pounding in her head slowly subsided, she once again heard herself making her fateful response the previous night. 'OK, I'll come. Hang on while I scribble a note for George.'

The small drinking establishment Dubec had taken her to was a five-minute cab ride from the hotel. Three middle-aged men sitting on stools at the bar had ignored the two newcomers. Dubec had seated Emma at a corner table close to the door, brought her a glass of Sauvignon and left. Then...nothing. Emma probed the amnesiac darkness of her mind. Hazily she recalled wondering what was taking Dubec so long. She remembered looking at her digital watch and being unable to understand what the numbers meant. Beyond that—blackness, grotesque nightmares and the stench of rotting vegetation. Lies. All lies. But why? What did Dubec...

Emma drifted back into sleep. This time no dreams were thrown up by the vortex of her unconscious.

# CHAPTER 5

Albert woke with a pain in his head that seemed to course through his veins down to his fingers and toes. With an effort he prised his lids apart and forced them to stay open.

The room was very dim. Francine had not drawn the curtains. She was getting very slack. He would have to talk to Jacques, the butler, about her. It was only as his eyes grew accustomed to the gloom, and shapes began to assume greater definition, that he realised he was not in his bedroom. He fumbled for the sheets but they were not there either. He forced himself into a sitting position. He was on a sofa and he was still fully clothed. He turned his head cautiously from side to side and realised that he was in his studio. He also realised that he was very cold.

He blew on his hands, stumbled across the room and drew back the heavy curtains. He winced in the sudden light of a cloudless February morning. He pulled the gold watch from his waistcoat pocket and, with difficulty, focused his eyes on its enamelled dial: 9.23.

In the corner by the door there was a washstand. He had to break the thin coating of ice on the water in the jug before pouring some of the liquid into the bowl. He sank his face into it. The shock went through him like an electric charge. He dabbed the moisture away with a towel and peered into the mirror. He saw blotchy features, a bristly chin and hair which looked like a storm-ravaged haystack. It was while he was trying to smooth his fair locks that someone turned a key in the door and came into the room. Albert looked round to see Henri, still clad in his heavy topcoat and floppy cap.

'Good morning, Albert.' The thin man closed the door and leaned against it. 'Back from the realms of Morpheus, I see.'

'Good morning, Henri. Was it you who brought me back here?'

Henri laughed. 'Single-handed? Hardly. It took three of us.' He crossed the room. 'Breakfast,' he observed, placing a jug and some bread down on a table. From one of his large pockets he produced a cup and saucer.

Albert smelled the pungent odour of strong coffee as the writer poured steaming liquid from the jug. 'That's very kind, Henri.'

'From the bar across the street.' Henri watched keenly as Albert sat by the table and thankfully lifted the cup to his lips.

It was good. Albert tore off a hunk of bread and realised that he was hungry. 'I'm sorry to have put you to all this trouble.'

Henri shrugged. 'We all help each other here—even those we've adopted.'

Albert chewed the coarse bread and poured himself more coffee. The mist inside his head dissipated rapidly. Suddenly he looked up with a frown. 'You called me Albert just now. Does that mean...'

The other man stared back unembarrassed. 'I went through your pockets, Captain de Bracieux. I am insatiably curious. As well for you, perhaps, that I am.' Henri waited for a response to the innuendo. When it was not forthcoming, he continued, 'Would you like to tell me what happened yesterday?'

'What do you mean?'

'Joseph tells me he found you in Gaston's place sunk in melancholy—or was it guilt?'

Albert met the other man's gaze levelly. 'I still don't see what you're getting at.'

Henri shrugged. 'Very well. If you insist on remaining aloof I'll not plague you with my presence.' He pulled a newspaper from his pocket. 'But in the light of this, I'd say you need all the friends you can find.'

Albert took the copy of *Le Petit Journal*

and read the frontpage paragraph indicated by the other man.

Catastrophe visited the residence of Colonel Louis de Bracieux yesterday afternoon. Edouard de Bracieux, the colonel's younger son, suffered severe injuries as a result, we are informed, of an altercation with his brother, Albert. Servants, hearing a commotion, rushed to the young man's assistance and discovered him lying among the ruins of a glass display case. He was bleeding profusely from several lacerations, including, apparently, one severed artery. Before medical aid could be summoned Lieutenant de Bracieux, recently commissioned in the Hussars, succumbed to his appalling injuries. He expired in his father's arms. Examining magistrate Duroc has authorised an exhaustive search for Captain Albert de Bracieux who has not been seen since the incident.

Tim Lacy arrived at the Cour des Loges just before noon and found a worried colleague waiting for him in the foyer.

He dropped into a chair beside him. 'Any news, George?'

'Not a whisper, Major. I've told reception to tell me if any calls come in and not to try my room. But, so far nothing. I'm sorry I let you down. You sent me to keep an eye on Emma and—'

'Enough, George!' Tim snapped the words. 'You can't nursemaid a twenty-three-year-old woman day and night—especially one as headstrong as Emma.'

'That's right enough. Still it's very worrying for you and Catherine.'

'I haven't told Catherine. She'd go berserk and blame herself for not insisting on coming here in person.'

'What do you reckon their game is, Major?'

Tim shook his head. 'I've been asking myself that question over and over again ever since you phoned. As I see it, it depends whether we're up against professionals or amateurs. I hope to God they're professionals.'

'How do you mean, Major?'

'If they're amateurs they're likely to panic. They could do anything. All they know is that Emma has recognised one of them. They might think no further than making sure she's silenced. Professional art thieves will be more careful. The first thing they'll want to do is find out how much Emma knows, and who else knows what she knows. Then they'll use her to make sure that we don't go to the police.'

George gazed mournfully into space.

'I hate a hostage situation. It's like a game of Russian roulette with no winners. Whichever way you look at it, Emma's in dead trouble.'

Tim jumped up. 'Well, I don't intend to sit around waiting for this character...what did you say his name was?'

'Charles Dubec, according to Emma's note—if that's his real name. It certainly wasn't the name of the bloke whose apartment I followed him to.'

'Well, whatever. If he's in no hurry to call us let's see if we can jolt him into action. You'll have to carry on waiting for a phone call. I'll follow up the only leads we've got, starting with Jollibone's gallery.'

'Worth a try, I suppose.' George shrugged. 'But if the Tarantin woman's in league with the others the chances are she's done a bunk.'

George was wrong about that. When Tim entered the gallery at 24 rue Gramont the proprietress was expatiating to two customers on the qualities of a canvas of superimposed blocks of pale colour which might have begun in the structured chaos of Orphic Cubism but which had decidedly lost its way thereafter. Tim wandered around the long room, seemingly engrossed in the exhibits, and waited until the couple had departed. The elegant brunette turned her attention to her new prospect.

Before she could speak, Tim extended his hand. 'Mme Tarantin, how do you do?'

She swiftly covered her surprise and was obviously searching her memory.

Again Tim forestalled her. 'No, madame, we haven't met. My name is Tim Lacy.' He watched closely but the name drew no response. 'You're acquainted, however, with two colleagues of mine, George Martin and Emma Kerr.'

She smiled, but not before anxiety had flickered momentarily in her eyes. 'Ah yes. Monsieur Martin and his charming daughter. Although, I thought...I had not realised that the young lady was married.'

'Emma is not married, nor is she George's daughter.' As he spoke, Tim sauntered casually across to the street door, flicked the lock and turned the card in the window to 'Fermé'. 'But I'm sure you know this already.'

Josephine Tarantin stepped briskly forward. 'Mr Lacy, what do you mean by this outrageous behaviour?'

She had her hand on the catch of the door when Tim said sharply, 'I strongly suggest an early lunch break—that is unless you would prefer me to say what I have to say to the police.'

She remained motionless for several

seconds, then turned. 'Monsieur, it is I who will be summoning the police, if you do not leave instantly.' But she made no attempt to unfasten the door.

'Madame, I have no time for a game of bluff and counter-bluff.' Tim spoke brusquely. 'I need information urgently and I have no intention of leaving without it.'

Madame Tarantin returned his belligerent stare but said nothing.

Tim went on. 'Last night my assistant, Emma Kerr, was abducted. I require the names of the men responsible.'

The Frenchwoman's mouth opened in what appeared to be genuine shocked surprise. 'Abducted! You mean—'

'She was lured from the hotel shortly before eight o'clock and has not been seen since.'

'How terrible! M. Lacy, you have my sympathy. But why should you suppose—'

'I said I had no time for bluff. Emma was kidnapped because someone thought she could identify the murderer of Auguste Jollibone.'

Mme Tarantin gasped.

'Yes, madame, and you know the name of that someone.'

'Oh, this is really absurd. I was appalled, grief-stricken by poor Auguste's death. I still can't grasp it.' She walked through

106

into the office and dropped into the chair behind the desk.

Tim followed into the smaller room but remained standing. 'I know nothing about your late partner but no one deserves to be knifed and dumped in the Thames. While I'm sorry for him and for you, I'm more concerned about Emma. I don't intend the same thing to happen to her. I want a name and frankly, madame, I don't much care what I have to do to get it.'

He glared down at the chic, expensively dressed woman. Her head was now cupped in her hands. She said nothing and suddenly Tim realised that she was sobbing. Her shoulders quivered. She pulled open a desk drawer, grabbed a tissue from a box and feverishly dabbed her eyes.

While Tim was wondering whether or not this was all an act, Josephine Tarantin shuddered a deep sigh, struggled to compose herself and said in a quavering voice, 'Oh, when will it end! Auguste's death was terrible but at least I thought...' She took a couple of deep breaths.

Tim sank onto one of the red and black chairs. 'Tell me about it—from the beginning, if that's easier.'

She nodded. 'Auguste brought me into the business a few years ago because things were bad and he needed extra capital.

Unfortunately my money was not enough to save the gallery. Auguste borrowed heavily from...someone who wasn't quite...'

'From a crook?'

'Yes. I wasn't supposed to know anything about it, but, well when things started happening..

'What sort of things?'

'At first it was just a question of giving him some of our best pieces. We could refuse him nothing that he took a fancy to. Balancing the books was a nightmare. But then he started bringing paintings to us. Stolen, of course. We were expected to dispose of them quietly to unsuspecting clients.'

'He was using you as a fence.'

'Yes, but that wasn't the worst.'

'Let me guess. He started putting large bundles of cash through your accounts.'

Josephine Tarantin looked up with wide, moist eyes. 'That's right. How did you...?'

'It's one of the favourite methods drug syndicates have of laundering money.'

'Yes, I suspected that's what it was. I was sick with worry. Everything was getting so complicated I just knew it would all collapse some time. Auguste would never tell me what was going on. I suppose it was his way of trying to protect me. Then, a couple of months ago, he came in one day, terribly excited. He said he had an enormous deal to put through and that this crook had promised it would be the last. If it all went smoothly the gallery's finances would be set on an even keel and we'd escape from this man's evil clutches. Only, of course, it didn't go smoothly. Something went very wrong in London.'

'Did this deal involve some paintings reputed to be by Aristide Bertrand?'

Once more she looked at him in surprise. 'My God, Mr Lacy, you seem to know more about this business than I do.'

'My colleagues and I have pieced together quite a lot of the story. That's why Emma is in such danger. So, madame, the name, please.'

Josephine Tarantin stared up in genuine anguish. 'But surely you can see that I dare not give you his name. He is very powerful and quite ruthless. Look what happened to Auguste.'

'I'm afraid you have no choice. Unless you give me a name I'll tell the police all you've told me.'

'I shall deny everything.'

'And who do you think they'll believe; the partner of a shady art dealer who's recently been murdered or an international businessman with friends in several police forces?'

The Frenchwoman sat up straight, suddenly regaining her composure. 'I think you are bluffing, Mr Lacy.'

'I told you I had no time for bluff and counter-bluff. I am desperate to find my friend and colleague before anything happens to her. I understand your dilemma, madame, but a few minutes ago you asked when it will end. It will only end when justice catches up with your partner's murderer. You won't be free of him as long as he's at liberty. He'll turn the screw on you just as he did on Auguste. If you give me his name I promise to do everything in my power to put him out of action.'

Long seconds of silence followed, during which the two stared across the desk, each willing the other to yield. At last, Josephine Tarantin drew a pad and pencil across the polished leather, scribbled something, tore off the top leaf and held it up, finger tightly clenched. 'Please, whatever use you make of this, keep my name out of it. If the police or anyone else question me I shall deny that this meeting ever took place.'

Tim took the small slip of paper. 'I agree to those conditions and thank you.'

'I'm doing it for the girl, you understand. I hope you manage to get her back safely. For yourself, I would say, take great care. This man is younger than you and, as well as being powerful, he is very clever, very plausible, absolutely without a trace of moral scruple.'

Tim read what Mme Tarantin had written. There was a telephone number and below it a name—Charles Labardie. 'Thanks,' he said. 'I'll watch my back.'

Albert read the newspaper report over and over again, understanding yet not understanding the simple words. His mind and body were numbed with shock.

At last, Henri eased *Le Petit Journal* from his fingers and pressed the coffee cup to his lips. 'Tell me about it,' he suggested.

Albert stared vacantly before him. 'Edouard? Dead?'

'That's right.' The little journalist spoke softly. 'There was a fight. What was it about? What happened?'

'Yes...a fight. Edouard said... But I didn't... Oh my God!' He pressed his hands to his face; a barrier against reality.

Henri's tone sharpened. 'Aris—Albert, you must talk. You are among friends here, but we can only help you if we know the truth.'

Slowly, falteringly, Albert told his story to this virtual stranger. As he came to the end he stood up. 'And now I must go to my father.'

'You won't get near him. As soon as

anyone recognises you you'll be denounced to the police.'

Albert shrugged. 'What does that matter? I must go to the police anyway. Explain.' He moved towards the door.

'The only thing waiting for you out there is the guillotine.' Henri's tone was matter-of-fact, yet urgent.

Albert half turned. 'No, no! It was an accident. They will see that.'

'You really think so?' Henri leaned forward in his chair. 'You may be right. Personally, I would find death preferable to a lifetime on Devil's Island.' He added conversationally, 'I suppose if you were lucky they might send you to the New Caledonia penal colony. And then, of course, there's the trial. It will be one of the most sensational of the year. I wonder how your father will cope with it—you manacled in the dock; the hectoring prosecution; the jeering crowds; the newspaper reports day after day; details of family life made common property; old friends rejecting him; society turning its back.' He stood, buttoning his topcoat. 'However, if you're determined, I will come with you. I want the exclusive rights to your story. It will be worth a fortune.'

'But, what...' Albert faced him, irresolute.

Henri wandered over to the canvases

112

stacked against the wall. 'You won't have any need of these, will you?' He held one at arm's length, appraisingly. 'Not bad; not bad at all. May I have these? They will sell like Leonardos during the trial. Or perhaps I'll hang on to them, in case they do send you for an assignation with Madame. They'll be worth much more after you're dead.'

'Stop it!' Albert screamed. He snatched the picture from Henri's hands. 'What are you trying to do to me?'

'Bring you to your senses. Come, sit down.' He led Albert back to the sofa. He strode to the centre of the room like an actor dominating the stage. 'You have accidentally killed your brother. That is tragic. It will haunt you the rest of your days. Remorse will never leave you. For a moment's impetuous rage you will pay an appallingly high price. In my opinion, that is punishment enough. But society will also want its revenge. Well.' He shrugged. 'If they cut off the head of Captain Albert de Bracieux or lock him away, what is that to me, or the world? Nothing. France has strutting, arrogant cavalry officers in plenty and to spare. But terminating the career of Aristide Bertrand? That is another matter altogether. That can only impoverish the world. You have a rare talent. I knew it the first time I came in here and saw

113

you painting little Marie. The work was barely half-finished but she was there—on your canvas. Not some anonymous female. Not a meaningless life-class model. Marie as the girl—woman we all love and find so infuriating. You must carry on. Aristide Bertrand must live and develop and perfect the genius which, as yet, few people know he possesses.'

Slumped on the sofa, Albert shook his head. 'Ridiculous. Impossible. Even if I believed what you were saying was right, honourable, I could not escape detection. Sooner or later the police would find me. The fact that I'd tried to evade arrest...'

Henri waved aside the objection. 'Certainly, if you hang around here waiting for the knock on the door you'll be taken within days. No, you must go to the country.'

'The country? What? Where?'

'To this "wonderful" Provence Van Gogh keeps eulogising.'

Albert jumped to his feet. 'You are suggesting I become a fugitive, an outlaw, skulking in caves and mountain hideouts!'

Henri nodded. 'Why not? It's a wild country. People have found refuge there from justice and injustice since the time of the Cathars and before. Van Gogh says that it's the sort of place an artist's soul can be free—away from the pseudo-sophistication of the city, the idiocy of critics and academicians, the pomposity of philistine patrons, the cramping conventions of society. Think of it, Aris—that's what I shall continue to call you—a beautiful world; a secret world; where the peasants know nothing of what happens beyond their own horizon and care less; a world where an artist can be truly free.'

'Free to starve?'

'No. Leave some of these canvases with me. I will sell them and get the money to you. It won't be much—at first. But it will buy you paints and simple food. Then, as your work improves...'

Albert shook his head violently. 'You mean well, Henri, but this is madness—criminal madness.'

The other replied quietly. 'It is what you have secretly wanted for a long time. To be free to create. To escape from all other distractions and obligations. To be truly yourself. Now fate has opened the way for you. Don't turn your back on it. Fate can be very cruel to those who despise her.'

'Nothing?' Tim asked the question as George opened the door of his room. But one glance at his old friend's gloomy features revealed the answer.

'How'd you get on with the Tarantin

woman?' George asked.

'I got a different name out of her, and judging by her reluctance to give it to me I'd say it was the right one. I'll tell you about it over lunch. Come on. We'll get the switchboard to transfer any calls to the dining room.'

They chose a corner table and Tim related his conversation at 24 rue Gramont.

'So, are you going to call this Labardie character?'

'Not before I've checked him out. And for that, of course, we're in precisely the right place.'

'Interpol?'

'Yes. Right here on our very doorstep. Bob Stonor's still on secondment from the Met, isn't he?'

'Must be. He's doing a three-year stint and he came just after we'd helped him out with that business at the Henty Museum. I suppose you're right to spend time talking to Bob.' George's tone of voice indicated that he supposed no such thing.

'You think we shouldn't wait before getting in touch?'

'I'm worried that Labardie hasn't contacted us yet. In a normal kidnap situation the crooks make their demands pretty quickly.'

'I guess we both know this isn't a normal kidnap. Labardie grabbed Emma because she recognised him. He wants to find out what she knows.'

'Or simply silence her so that she can't tell the police what she knows.'

'Don't imagine I haven't thought of that. I've spent hours looking at the situation from every possible angle. On balance, I don't think he'd do anything drastic. Not yet, anyway.'

'What makes you so sure?'

'I'm not sure. I'm just trying to put myself into his shoes and assuming that he's not a complete idiot. He knows that Emma's not alone in trying to track him down. He's confident about keeping out of the clutches of the police but he doesn't know who we are or what we're up to. He's got to find all that out from Emma.'

'And when he's squeezed her as hard as he can, he'll get rid of her.'

'I don't think so. Emma will make it pretty clear that if anything happens to her we're not the sort of people to shrug our shoulders and walk away.'

'That's for sure. Miss Kerr's a pain in the backside as far as I'm concerned but she's one of us and if—'

'I know that, George, and my guess is that by now Labardie knows it, too. He's going to have to negotiate.'

'So why don't we make contact?'

'Because at the moment he holds the ace

of trumps. I'd like to see if I can't deal us a better hand before play commences. That's where Bob Stonor comes in. He owes us. He's going to help us tap the world's biggest databank of criminal activity.'

## CHAPTER 6

Next time she woke Emma found herself looking up into the face of the man who called himself Charles Dubec. 'How are you feeling?' His expression seemed to convey genuine concern.

Emma sat up, head clear now and memory intact. 'Just what the hell—'

He held up both hands and backed away a couple of paces. 'OK, OK. You've every right to be angry—angry and frightened. But let me assure you that you're perfectly safe. We mean you no harm. We've brought you some breakfast.'

Emma looked past him at the ramshackle table in the centre of the room. It had been spread with a cloth and she could see a plate piled with croissants and an opened steaming vacuum flask. She could also see another, older man standing in front of the door, like a heavy immovable piece of furniture.

He was broad-shouldered, barrel-chested and muscular with dark hair falling to the collar of his open-necked shirt. She transferred her attention to Charles Dubec. 'The last time I accepted a drink from you I ended up drugged to the eyeballs.'

'I regret that—honestly—and I assure you that this food is perfectly safe. Look, I'll share it with you.' He crossed to the table, poured black coffee into two mugs and sipped one of them. He pointed to a short bench. 'You must be hungry. Come and eat while I explain.'

Emma got to her feet slowly. 'Explain! I don't want to hear any more explanations from you. I wouldn't believe anything you told me. All I want you to do is take me back to the hotel.' The smell of coffee was enticing. She perched on the bench and picked up a mug suspiciously.

'Go ahead, drink it.' The young Frenchman sat opposite her. He took a croissant from the dish, dunked it in his coffee and ate appreciatively. 'These are very good—fresh baked in Edgar's kitchen this morning. He keeps a guest house not far from here.'

'Edgar? Huh! I'll bet that's not his real name, any more than Charles Dubec is yours.'

'Well, the Charles bit is right. It's best

119

that you don't know any more than that, for the moment.'

'So much for explanations!' Emma took a gulp of coffee and enjoyed the feeling of it in a mouth that seemed to be lined with desiccated leather. 'Well, what about telling me where I am—or is that classified too?'

'Certainly,' Charles nodded. 'You're in the middle of the Camargue.'

'The Camargue, but that's...'

'The Rhône delta, about three hundred kilometres south of Lyon. We made quite a journey last night.'

'I don't believe you.'

He shrugged. 'See for yourself.' He waved towards the door.

Emma crossed the room. Edgar stood aside and lifted the iron latch. Outside the hut three saddled white horses were tethered to a post and grazed a small plot of grass. To the right channels of black water pocked with yellow-green weed snaked between islets of tall reed. To the left the fringe of vegetation gave way to a steely expanse which, at the point where a horizon might have been, merged imperceptibly with a grimy sky. A drear waterscape smelling of death, for now Emma knew that the malodour which had pervaded her dreams was the stench of perpetually rotting vegetation. She had never been to this part of France but she knew the Camargue's reputation as one of Europe's few remaining wildernesses—thousands of acres of lagoon and treacherous marshland hospitable only to waterfowl and birds of prey. This desolation, she realised, was as effective a prison as anything involving high walls and barbed wire.

She shivered, turned her back on the stark view, went into the hut and attacked the simple food hungrily, as much to keep her spirits up as to satisfy her appetite.

She was aware of the eyes of the two men watching her closely as she ate. She tried to go through the motions as casually as possible. Tried not to think of her vulnerability. Tried not to speculate how far she was from a road or human habitation. Tried not to wonder what the murderous thugs wanted of her. 'Have you called my colleague in Lyon?' she asked casually.

Charles shook his head. 'Not yet.'

'Shouldn't you make your ransom demand before George goes to the police?'

'What makes you think that we're demanding a ransom?' A quizzical, mocking smile rose briefly to the surface of his face.

Emma snapped. She crashed her mug down on the table. 'For God's sake, stop playing games! What is all this about?

What do you want?'

Charles stared back at her impassively but the man called Edgar stepped across the room, scowling. He whispered angrily sibilants in his colleague's ear.

Charles nodded and waved the bulky man away. To Emma he said, 'You appear to have made a conquest. My friend chides me for forgetting my manners. I will answer your questions—but not just yet. I have a promise to keep. I must ask you to accompany us on a short journey. You'll need something rather more suitable than that charming dress.' He gazed at her body in a way Emma did not find flattering. 'I've done my best to find some things which will fit you reasonably well. Edgar, les vêtements!'

The other man went out and returned seconds later with a bundle which he placed on the table.

Charles pushed them across to her. 'We'll wait outside while you change.'

When the door had closed Emma unrolled the parcel and discovered a man's thick checked shirt and jeans, some woollen socks and a pair of calf-length boots. She took the garments into the building's only other room, which turned out to be a primitive bathroom. She took her time about changing. Although the boots were a couple of sizes too big the whole ensemble was surprisingly comfortable and certainly more appropriate for the horse ride which Emma guessed lay before her. In one corner stood an ancient pump. She pressed the handle experimentally and, the second time, water gushed into a stone trough. There was a bar of soap on its rim and a cracked mirror on the wall beside the pump. Emma washed, pushed a comb through her hair, took some deep breaths and tried to persuade herself that she felt more like herself.

When she went outside Charles was already mounted. 'That looks much better.' Again the appraising scrutiny. 'I'm afraid there's one more little formality I must insist upon.' He nodded to Edgar who produced a silk scarf, which he tied around Emma's head as a blindfold. 'You would be quite unable to find your way through the maze of causeways across the marsh but I prefer to be over-cautious.'

Emma felt for the saddle and stirrup. Edgar gave her a leg up and she swung astride the small, muscular animal. She felt the reins being put into her hands. Seconds later her mount started abruptly into motion. Emma was comfortable on horseback; she had ridden and enjoyed riding since childhood. But nothing had ever prepared her for this eyeless, disorienting expedition.

Soon the horses were splashing through water and she felt the spattering of drops on her hands and face. A sudden terrifying possibility struck her. Was she being taken to some still-more-deserted spot to be hustled into the lagoon and held under its surface by muscular hands? Or would she, like Jollibone, be knifed in the back before being consigned to the water? Emma shivered. Perhaps she could snatch off her blindfold, heel her horse into a gallop and try to make a break for it.

Charles, riding beside her, broke in on her terrifying thoughts. 'I hope this isn't too uncomfortable for you. It won't take us long to get where we're going. And I promise you, you'll find it worth the trouble. You're in for the experience of a lifetime.'

Albert de Bracieux left Paris. Eight days later Aristide Bertrand, a young man with an immature fringe of beard to his fresh features, arrived in Arles. The circuitous journey had been planned with makeshift ingenuity. It had begun in a suffocating wine cask, rolling back and forth on a lumbering cart, and subsequent stages had involved an infuriatingly slow but inconspicuous farm horse, a river barge, an overcrowded country train and more than a few kilometres on foot. At first the merest glimpse of a village gendarme had been enough to impel Aristide into the nearest alleyway but as the days passed and no one took any interest in the dusty traveller he relaxed and even felt exhilarated by his new freedom. His leisurely progress enabled him to delight in the changing landscape and its inhabitants. He was fascinated by walls of ochre stone and terracotta roofs glowing in the southern sun, by the Provençal women in their black dresses and lace caps, by the encampments of polychromed gypsy caravans, where men in wide-brimmed hats smoked their long pipes or pranced around on their spirited stallions. The sight of orchards in blossom and hedgerows bristling with spring flowers set him reaching for the pastels and sketchpad he kept at the top of his shoulderpack. He itched to turn all his new experiences into paint.

Journey's end was an initial disappointment. Aristide discovered Arles to be a medieval town overwhelmed by modern vulgarity. It had bulged out from the inadequate restraint of its ancient walls to spread in undisciplined and unpicturesque suburbs and slums on either side of the Grand Rhône. An ugly steel bridge linked the two bits of the city and its skyline was dominated by the tall chimneys of locomotive sheds and factories which eternally spewed their slatey smoke into the sparkling purity of the atmosphere. Was this the artistic haven with which Van Gogh was so enraptured?

Aristide found lodgings over a *charcuterie* in the Place Voltaire in the old town. He called at the address he had been given for Van Gogh, only to be confronted by an irate landlord who flew into an immediate rage. At one moment he was on the point of flinging Aristide into the street, but an appraisal of the young man's robust body dissuaded him from physical violence. Instead, he berated his ex-lodger in vigorous tones that sometimes slipped into unintelligible patois. The essence of the diatribe was that Van Gogh was a madman who had departed owing him money. He neither knew nor cared where the Dutchman was, he thundered, prior to slamming the door in Aristide's face. Other locals of whom Aristide enquired took a less extreme but not dissimilar attitude. Van Gogh was a foreigner, he was poor, and he was 'odd'. Those facts were sufficient for his Arlesien acquaintances to turn their backs on him and to regard this new stranger with suspicion.

It was when he went to buy paint and canvases at a bookshop not far from his lodgings that he learned of the other artist's whereabouts. Van Gogh had recently bought a large consignment of materials and had them sent to the Café de la Gare in the Place Lamartine, just outside the ramparts. But now that he had an address Aristide hesitated about making contact. He had met Van Gogh only twice. Both occasions had been impromptu parties at which several other Montmartre denizens had been present. He had listened on the edge of the crowd, enthralled by the emaciated painter enthusiastically, argumentatively airing his opinions on colour and form. He had seen a couple of Van Gogh's canvases and found their uncompromising primary hues disturbing and compelling. For months he had deliberately copied the older man's style, before realising that he had to go in a different direction. What would Van Gogh make of Aristide's ideas, which had now developed away from his own? The fugitive decided that he could not confront the daring innovator until he had some work of his own to show.

Aristide spent the next six weeks in a frenzy of painting. It was as though years of pent-up creativity were released in an uncontrollable flood. Everywhere he went he saw things he wanted to capture on canvas or sketch in his book. On fine days he was out all the daylight hours. Mostly he took his folding easel into the country to paint as many facets as possible of this exciting new landscape. He went at frantic speed, throwing pigment or chalk at the virgin surface as though a moment's delay would allow to escape for ever the effect of light or shade or texture that had captivated him. Often he scraped the paint from his canvas or tore the sheet from his pad in angry frustration at his failure to capture the passing moment and his emotional response to it. When rain or cloud draped the fields in drab or the mistral did its best to tear the world apart, Aristide spent time indoors touching in remembered or sketched detail. It was the river and the canals that fascinated him most. He painted boats and boatmen, and overarching trees speckled with the first leaves of spring, and surfaces rippled by fish, and the hunched anglers on the bank who stalked the fish, and the water's skin which soaked up colour and at the same time reflected it, muted and glowing.

If this vigorous activity was a response to his changed environment, it was also an attempt to overlay past horrors with vibrant impasto. But however hard and long Aristide worked, suppressed memory took its revenge when his exhausted body and mind succumbed to sleep. Few nights passed unhaunted by visions of blood, of Edouard's accusing, death-frozen features, of his father weeping behind his pince-nez, of the guillotine's plunging blade—visions from which the dreamer woke sweating and cold amidst a chaos of strewn bedclothes.

By the middle of April his money was running out. Irregular modest subsidies arrived from Paris in the letters Henri sent, full of news and gossip expressed in self-congratulatory prose, but it rapidly became evident that this income would not keep pace with Aristide's expenditure on essentials and painting materials. He parcelled up a few small canvases, sent them off to his benefactor and waited impatiently for some reaction. Apart from acknowledging receipt of the new work, Henri made no reference to it. He was too absorbed with events in the capital. The 'political jack-in-the-boxes' were still jumping; currently Tirard was 'down' and Floquet 'up'. Boulanger, 'the posturing patriot', was back in parliament and planning a coup—'l'Empereur Georges Premier—what a prospect!' Meanwhile, in the real world, the conflict was still between Seurat and the 'technicians' on the one side and the Impressionists on the other. Art, like politics, was plagued by 'the anarchy of rival theories'. Oh, and as for the monster dubbed by the press 'de Bracieux the Butcher', he had slipped from the front pages. The affair was, as Henri had always prophesied, a nine-days' wonder. The police had put a price on Albert de Bracieux's head but no one had come forward to claim the money. However, there could be no question of Aristide emerging from hiding for a very long time. 'Keep up the painting, my dear friend; that is all that matters.'

Aristide stuffed the letter into his pocket. 'Keep up the painting'! All very well for Henri to say that but there was a limit to what an artist could do in isolation. He needed people to see his canvases—especially other painters. He needed informed criticism. He needed to discuss his work with others who understood what he was trying to do. Perhaps the time had come to talk to Van Gogh. Yes, he would seek out the 'mad Dutchman'.

It was past midnight when Aristide sidled into the Café de la Gare with a bundle under his arm. The room was brightly lit and noisy. A dozen or more men—railway workers, soldiers, down-and-outs and husbands delaying their return to their wives—were talking, laughing and drinking at the small round tables. A couple were slumped forward, head on arms, sleeping. No one took any notice of them or sought to disturb them. Aristide anxiously scanned the customers, and at

130

last spotted Vincent Van Gogh, seated alone in the far corner. His red hair was close-cropped but his beard, by contrast, straggled unevenly around his thin cheeks and jaw. His blue jacket was open over a shirt unfastened at the neckband. Before him on the table a battered straw hat lay beside a clutter of empty glasses. The painter sat straight in his chair, hands in his lap, eyes staring from expressionless features. He might have been in a trance or even dead for all the interest he took in his surroundings.

'M. Van Gogh?' Aristide approached diffidently.

There was no response.

'Monsieur, may I buy you a drink?'

The drawn face arranged itself into a frown, but the eyes remained unfocused. 'Certainly.'

'What would you like?' Aristide seated himself in the other chair.

'Cognac, if you're paying.'

Aristide signalled to the waiter and ordered. As the other glasses were cleared he noticed that Van Gogh had been drinking both brandy and absinthe.

Neither man spoke until generous measures of amber fluid and a jug of water had been set before them. Then Aristide held up his glass. 'Your health, monsieur.'

The other nodded and condescended to gaze at his patron.

'I'm a fellow artist. We have actually met. I was—'

Vincent groaned. 'Not another damnable amateur! I'm sick of talentless dabblers wanting me to give them lessons or look at their hideous daubs!' He returned to his pose of Buddha-like withdrawal.

Aristide was determined not to be overawed. 'No, not an amateur, a serious artist. I was in Paris—Montmartre—till recently. I saw you a couple of times with mutual friends. The first occasion as I recall was at "Père" Tanguy's in rue Cluzel. You were there with your brother and Paul Gauguin and several—'

'You know Gauguin?' Van Gogh showed sudden interest.

'Not well. I—'

'He is the master of us all. He is the only one who knows where he is going. You've seen his work?'

'Some.'

'He's the only one among us who is doing something really new. New and yet...ancient. He's trapped the primeval in man. He's travelled so much. You should hear him talk about the simple life of primitive people, moving with the simple rhythms of nature. That's what he gets into his paintings. God, how I envy him. He's coming here, you know.'

'Gauguin, here? That's wonderful. I heard that you wanted to set up an artistic commune in the South. That's why I came. But I had no idea that Gauguin—'

'Yes, yes!' Vincent was suddenly animated. 'And when he comes others will follow. This time next year there will be a studio of artists dedicated to the new movement. And it will be here, far away from Paris and the stick-in-the-mud academicians and the big-heads who spend all their time arguing about their pet theories. It will be here! In the South!'

Aristide was still trying to adjust to his companion's complete change of mood when Vincent suddenly jumped up. 'And you must help me prepare! Marie, have you got a lamp?'

The question was shouted at Marie Ginoux, the proprietor's wife, who stood behind the bar. Quite unphased by her tenant's impulsive demand, she went into a back room and emerged with a small hand lantern which she proceeded to light. Without a word, Vincent took it, clapped his hat onto his head and led the way from the café. Aristide gulped down his cognac, gathered up his bundle and followed.

'It's only a few paces along here. I bought it just last week. I wondered whether I'd taken on too much. But now

133

you're here...er...what's your name?'

'Aristide. Friends call me Aris.'

'Now you're here, Aris, things will be just perfect.' He marched rapidly to the edge of the square opposite the city's Porte de la Cavalerie. 'There!'

He waved the lantern towards a double-fronted house with closed shutters. There was a full moon and Aristide did not need the light of the lamp to see the building's shabby, peeling frontage.

'Come on!' Van Gogh fumbled in his pocket for a key, inserted it in the lock of the front door, pushed it open on stiff hinges and advanced into a wide hall.

The scene which met Aristide's eyes as they grew accustomed to the gloom was one of dereliction. Paper hung from the walls and debris littered the floor. Boards creaked ominously as Vincent moved with heavy tread from room to room.

'It's not all that large but it will do for a start. Half a dozen of us can live here quite comfortably. And we shan't be plagued with grasping landlords. Why, you and I can move in as soon as we've tidied the place up a bit.'

After a complete tour Vincent locked up with proprietorial care. Back on the street he smiled at Aristide. 'We'll start tomorrow. See you in the morning. Bring

134

some of your work—I'd like to see it. Goodnight.'

Aristide strolled under the Cavalry Gate and through the quiet streets of the old town. He discovered that he was doing something he had not done for many weeks. He was laughing. Laughing at the impetuosity of Vincent Van Gogh and at fortune who was once more looking on him with favour. He would have a rent-free home and the company of fellow artists. He could, he really could, build a new life. That night his sleep was undisturbed by dreams.

But his sense of well-being did not long survive the dawn.

## CHAPTER 7

Tim stepped out of the taxi by the gates to the Parc de la Tête d'Or. He stood on the pavement waiting for the pedestrian crossing light to halt briefly the avalanche of one-way traffic heading out of town along the Quai Achille Lignon and gazed at Interpol's modernistic HQ. Whoever designed it, he reflected, must have been given the brief to create a twentieth-century version of a Norman keep. It

135

was a seventy-foot-high mass of concrete and glass surrounded by concentric circles of fences and surveillance equipment. Even the ornamental pool encircling its gleaming façade gave the impression of a moat. Crossing the road, he appraised the assortment of antennae bristling on the roof.

He approached the gate in the outer ring of Interpol's defences. An intercom panel demanded his name and business and released the lock on receiving his satisfactory reply. The next hurdle was the security booth. A door beneath a guard's bullet-proof grill opened to receive Tim's passport. Another accepted his briefcase. While he waited for Bob Stonor to be informed of his arrival, he appraised the security arrangements professionally. He could suggest one or two refinements, but basically this building which, minute by minute, received and disseminated information about criminal activities world-wide, was well protected. Not that any modern villain would bother trying to get into the building. The real target would be Interpol's computer network. Tim wondered how well that was safeguarded and what back-up existed in the eventuality of some technocrook hacking into the system. Having received the necessary information, the guard invited Tim to enter the screening chamber, a glass tube with a sliding door which now opened to admit him. Seconds later the inner portal moved noiselessly allowing Tim through the second ring of the defences. He collected his case and walked over a 'drawbridge' towards the main building.

Bob Stonor—mid-thirties with the build of a rugger full-back—came out to meet him. They shook hands. Bob showed his ID card to a scanner and the glass double doors glided apart. The impression of a castle was reinforced for Tim as he followed his host into the atrium, a hexagonal courtyard into which light streamed through a glass dome five storeys above. Bob led the way to one of the lifts set in the inner wall and they ascended to the third floor. The door did not open until Stonor again presented his ID card for examination.

'Do you have to use that wherever you go in the building?' Tim asked.

'No way. I'm strictly a floor-three man. If I want to visit another department this gizmo is no use to me. I have to be collected by someone authorised to be on that level.'

'So, if I had you in an arm-lock and said ' "Take me to the Secretary-General..." '

'No could do.'

'I'm impressed.'

'That's flattering coming from you.'

They reached Stonor's office and Bob fetched coffee from a vending machine in the corridor. Tim asked how he was enjoying his spell in Lyon.

'It's a real eye-opener. Back in the Met we were understaffed and under-informed but at least we had a fine art squad. You'd be amazed at the number of countries where the police simply have no specialist departments.'

'No I wouldn't.'

Bob smiled, ruefully. 'Sorry, Tim. I was forgetting. You get around quite a bit. Well, you know the size of the problem.'

'I guess the problem is that art theft isn't high profile.'

'Right. A bunch of Arabs hijack a plane or someone's caught bringing in a few kilos of heroin and it's front-page news. But a gang turns over some tycoon's pad and makes off with a couple of priceless paintings and the level of public outrage is zero. People just don't understand the size of the problem. Take Russia. Everyone knows about the narcotics problems, the murders, the violence, the breakdown of law and order. But theft accounts for 90.56% of all crime there and the greater part of it is related to looting art and antiques. The stuff's flooding into Western Europe by the truckload.'

'And most of the traffic's controlled by syndicated crime.'

Bob nodded vigorously, eyes glowing with evangelical conviction. 'Exactly. You can't draw tidy lines between dope-dealing, terrorism, money-laundering, white-collar crime, extortion, prostitution and art theft. They're all bundled up together. The bastard you're interested in is a case in point.'

'Thanks for letting me pick your brains. So what have you got on Charles Labardie?'

'That depends which Charles Labardie you want.'

'How many are there on offer?'

'Two. Father and son. Dad's a major crime boss operating out of Marseille. He's grooming Charles Junior to take over his organisation. Charles is the younger son—the brighter of the two or possibly just his father's favourite. He's cut from the same cloth as the old man. They're both vicious and totally unscrupulous, though the son likes to consider himself cultured. He was educated at the Sorbonne and picked up a master's degree in some tenth-rate American university.'

'What did he study?'

'Art history.'

Tim raised an eyebrow. 'Sounds like my man.'

'I thought it might. I've done a print-out

139

of our blue notice on him.' He picked up a sheet of paper from beside his computer terminal.

'Blue notice?'

'We circulate information under four categories: red, blue, green and black. Red means "If you come across this bloke, grab him." We put out red notices when a police force somewhere has issued an arrest warrant. I'd love to have red flags out on the Labardies. All we've got is a blue notice, an enquiry notice. The signal that sends is "We know damned well this chap's a crook but we can't prove it. Please, dish any dirt on him that you come across." Here's Charles Junior's CV.'

Tim read the sheet that Bob handed him.

LABARDIE—Charles Antoine
Born: 27.6.1968 in Nice, France
Son of Charles and Giselle, née Renouille
OCCUPATION: Business executive
NATIONALITY: French
ALIAS: None known
DESCRIPTION: Height 5′ 11″, dark brown hair

There followed a set of fingerprints, two photographs (full face and profile) of a cleanshaven young man with a smile of arrogant amusement on his lips.

140

PREVIOUS CONVICTIONS:
FRANCE: Paris 30.4.92: two months suspended sentence for illegal possession of a firearm.
MISCELLANEOUS INFORMATION:
FRANCE: Questioned in Paris 17.4.92 in connection with handling items of jewellery, antiques and paintings stolen from private addresses in the Paris area. ITALY: Held in Turin 5.1.93-7.1.93 on suspicion of cocaine dealing in collusion with members of the Fabrizi organisation. Released due to insufficient evidence. GERMANY: 13.6.93 a warehouse owned by Labardie under surveillance by Munich police in connection with a series of art thefts was destroyed by fire. A known associate of Labardie was imprisoned for arson. USA: Interviewed in Paris 14.9.93-15.9.93 by NYPD officers in connection with the murder of his mistress, Tania Gregorian, in New York, 7.8.93. Labardie is the sole owner of Caltech Electronics (Paris) and Calroutiers (Paris) a transcontinental haulage firm. Labardie's father (See Enquiry Notice B 4832/7G—LABARDIE, Charles Louis) has been twice convicted for narcotics offences. The subject of this notice is known to work closely with his father and with other criminal associates.

ADDRESS: Subject has known residences in Paris, Zurich, New York and St Petersburg but is based at Château d'Orgnac, Tarascon, 13150, Bouches du Rhône.

REASONS FOR THIS CIRCULATION: Issued by the General Secretariat of ICPO—Interpol for information purposes. Please supply any information concerning this person, his movements, business contacts and known criminal associates, particularly any investigations of Calroutiers in connection with the suspected movement of illicit substances or stolen objects.

Tim rubbed a finger along the bridge of his nose. 'Slippery customer.'

Bob nodded. 'Positively greasy. He's come within an ace of being nabbed two or three times, as you can see, but he's always walked away with a smirk on his face.'

'What was this murder in New York all about?'

'Labardie uses his haulage firm to carry stolen artefacts, drugs, arms and God knows what to and from Russia. We're certain he's hand-in-glove with one of the big Moscow syndicates. Somewhere along the line he picked up this Russian girlfriend, Tania Gregorian. While they were in America she contacted the FBI. She offered information on Labardie in exchange for a US passport and enough cash to live comfortably in the States. The next thing anyone knew she wasn't able to say anything—ever again.'

'What happened?'

'She was found, neatly knifed, in Central Park.'

'And Labardie?'

'Very conveniently, 35,000 feet over the Atlantic on Concorde at the time the killing occurred, heading back to Europe.'

Tim thought of Emma and clenched his fists tightly. 'And this place, Tarascon—where's that?'

'It's on the Rhône not far from Arles. Very usefully situated near some of the wildest country in Provence yet close to the autoroute network and very handy for Marseille. By private helicopter or small plane he can be there inside an hour. He has to be, because he runs the transport system for the whole organisation.'

'And he has a penchant for fine art.'

'Oh yes. Get inside Château d'Orgnac and I bet you'd find yourself in a treasure house stuffed with items that have gone missing from major collections over the last few years.'

Tim took a scrap of paper from his pocket. 'Would that telephone number correspond with Labardie's palatial hide-away?'

Stonor tapped several keys on his computer terminal. Seconds later the machine delivered its verdict.

'Yes, that's one of the lines at Château d'Orgnac. Now, supposing you tell me all you know about this unpleasant specimen?'

Tim shook his head. 'Sorry, Bob, I can't. Not yet.'

'Oh come on! Have you any idea what strings I had to pull to get you in here?'

'Bob, I'm enormously grateful, and I'm going to do everything I can to help nail this Labardie bastard. I've got very personal reasons for wanting to put an end to his activities. But right now, you've got to trust me to go it alone—just for a couple of days. As soon as I can I'll give you a full brief.'

Stonor scowled. 'Not good enough, Tim.'

Tim folded the blue notice carefully and tucked it into an inside pocket. Thinking hard. 'OK. Here's a couple of snippets that may be of some use. Labardie has been using the alias Charles Dubec. And he has an apartment in Lyon—15 rue d'Etoile—rented under another name. I don't know much else—honestly.'

'You haven't told me why you are suddenly interested in Labardie.'

'Sorry, Bob.' Feeling very mean, Tim stood up. 'Is this place as hard to get out of as to get into?'

'You can take the blindfold off now.' Charles spoke as the horses slowed to a halt.

Emma pulled the scarf down from her eyes and let it hang loose round her neck. She squinted in the sudden sunlight and looked about her. The scene seemed little different from the one she had left at the beginning of her short journey. Waterlogged marsh accounted for most of it but here there were trees intersected by beaten paths of solid earth.

Charles slipped from the saddle and held up a hand to help Emma. She ignored it and sprang expertly to the ground. She stood, back to her captor, stroking the horse's soft muzzle. Edgar tethered the animals, then smiled at her and, in a strangely incongruous gesture, offered her his arm to escort her along the track. Emma thought quickly. If there was a possible difference between these thugs about her treatment she would exploit it. She returned Edgar's smile and linked her arm through his.

The path turned sharply to the right after a few metres, then came up against a barrier of trees and tangled undergrowth.

Charles took a dozen paces to the left along this wall and ducked into a small opening. Edgar held back a springy sapling for Emma to follow. She peered into the gloomy copse and shrank back. This was where they were to do it!

'No! Please!' She looked at Edgar, desperately appealing. For the first time she saw with horror the long, sheathed knife attached to his belt.

The Frenchman grasped her arm firmly but not roughly. 'Soyez calme, mam'selle! Soyez calme! Ne vous vous troublez pas. C'est OK.' He propelled her into the thicket.

Charles waited with evident impatience, then moved forward through what transpired to be a narrow belt of trees. When they emerged Emma saw a long, low, semi-derelict building. At first sight it looked totally abandoned, in the process of being swallowed up by the flourishing vegetation. Then she saw that the thatched roof was in a good state of repair and that a narrow strip of earth round the building had been kept clear of encroaching creepers.

Edgar went ahead and unlocked wide double doors. Then he busied himself removing shutters from two glassless windows.

'What is this place?' Emma tried to keep the tremor out of her voice.

'It was built as a sheep barn. Years ago there were thousands of sheep and goats in the Camargue. The shepherds moved their flocks over long distances, from pasture to pasture, over much of the year. But they wintered and lambed in places like this. There aren't many left now. The sheep people were never exactly popular with my ancestors. The real Camargue dwellers looked on them as tramps who invaded their precious grasslands. They often pulled the sheep barns down while the shepherds were away. Nowadays there aren't many sheep around here anyway. This building would have collapsed long ago if we hadn't looked after it. Let's go inside.'

Emma stood her ground. 'If you think I'm going in there with a pair of murderers...'

Charles pursed his lips in annoyance. 'Look, how often do I have to tell you that we didn't murder Jollibone?'

'I believed you when you told me in the hotel, but that was before you drugged me and dragged me to this Godforsaken place!'

Charles shouted, 'If we were going to kill you, don't you think we'd have done it by now? You're in absolutely no danger. I brought you to the barn to show you something.'

'Well show me here...out in the open, where I can keep my eyes on you!'

'You stupid woman!' Charles glared at her. 'That's imposs—Oh, very well. If that's the way you want it.'

He exchanged a few words with his colleague, who nodded and disappeared inside the barn. When he emerged he was carrying a bundle, wrapped in heavy oilcloth. He rested it against a sawn treetrunk and began untying the cord which fastened it.

Charles said, 'There you are. Help yourself.'

When Edgar had removed the outer covering and then an inner layer of hessian, Emma found herself gazing down at a painting that was all blues, greens and yellows. Even to her untrained eye it was obvious that here was another picture by the same hand as the ones she had seen in London. The subject matter was quite different. She guessed that it had been executed not far from the spot where they were standing. Three young boys were sprawling on a wooden jetty engrossed in a game which seemed to involve small pieces of wood or bone. Beyond them the broad expanse of the lagoon vibrated with reflected light. The painting spoke of childhood days and innocence and the radiant simplicity of unexploited nature.

'Bertrand?' Emma asked the unnecessary question.

Charles nodded. 'Of course. I told you we had several. Now, do you want to come and see some more?'

They went inside the barn. Along the far side a low, slatted platform had been built, supporting a row of racks. There were the paintings, each in its protective layers of waterproof cloth or sacking, stacked on end and kept clear of the earthen floor. Someone had obviously taken a great deal of trouble to look after them. But why here? Why in this remote, marshy wilderness where no one could ever appreciate them?

As Edgar lifted out pictures at random and began unwrapping them, Emma turned to Charles. 'What is it with these paintings? Why all this cloak and dagger stuff? Why are people getting killed and kidnapped because of these beautiful objects?'

'I'll come to that in a little while. I've kept my word. I've shown you our Bertrands. Now it's your turn to answer some questions. Why did you follow me? What have you told the English police? What are they doing?'

Emma stared at the row of canvases, hoping that her apparent absorption in Bertrand's superb work would cover the fact that she was thinking carefully how to reply. It was only a half-deception.

The paintings really did compel attention. Those on view had all been painted in the Camargue. Most of them were landscapes with figures. Emma recognised the girl who had modelled for Bertrand's nudes, though in these pictures she was clothed and seemed younger. The boys on the jetty also reappeared in several of the paintings. 'This is the reason I followed you.' Emma waved a hand at the collection. 'You introduced us to these amazing pictures and then disappeared. We wanted to do business with you. We still do—if you have legal title to the paintings.'

Charles looked at her shrewdly, head on one side. 'I suppose I believe you. All dealers are vultures. Jollibone certainly was. He was itching to get his hands on our Bertrands. There are so many crooks in the business. That's what makes it so difficult to know what to do with these.'

'We're not all tarred with the same brush. Lacys would be immensely excited to handle such an amazing collection. Obviously we'd make a lot of money in the process. But we always put our clients first and try to do the very best for them.'

He shrugged. 'You all say the same. Now, what—exactly—did you tell the police?'

Emma hesitated. If she gave the impression that Edgerson was hot on the trail of his prime suspect, Charles might be panicked into desperate measures. Equally, if she let him think that Scotland Yard were floundering he might conclude that he could safely get rid of her. 'Well, obviously we had to tell them about our meeting and give them a description of you. But there wasn't much more we could say.'

'You described the paintings?'

'Well, only in very general terms. We couldn't say anything authoritative. We'd only seen them for a few minutes.'

'That man with you at the gallery—your "father"—was he police?'

'Oh no! He was...a colleague.' Emma saw a piece of flotsam on the dark pool of her fear. She grabbed it. 'Actually, you've got much more to worry about from the Lacys than the police. I can't imagine Scotland Yard tracking you down here, even with the help of their French counterparts. But my friends will certainly find me. They know what you look like. Tim Lacy, Catherine's husband, has lots of important contacts. He won't give up till he's found you. You wouldn't be the first criminals he's helped to put behind bars.'

Charles opened his mouth to reply angrily but the arrival of a third man checked him. The newcomer strode into the barn with jerky steps. He was the other man Emma had seen in rue Gaumont. He was short, wiry, with a high colour and a drooping moustache. Late fifties, Emma guessed, and not very happy.

'Que fais-tu, imbécile?' He marched up to Charles and stared him straight in the eye.

The two men launched into a rapid exchange of French, mostly in local dialect. Emma could not follow it closely but had little doubt that she was the object of the violent disagreement. Both men glanced at her from time to time. At one point Edgar joined in the argument but was immediately cowed by a torrent of abuse from the older man and shuffled away into a corner of the barn. The others were now shouting at each other. Emma distinguished the word 'confrérie' which was repeated several times. Then Charles turned his back and walked away. But his combatant had not finished. He grabbed the younger man by the shoulder and spun him round. Again he pointed to Emma, then drew a finger across his throat. For several seconds the two men glared at each other in silence. Then, the newcomer turned and walked out as briskly as he had arrived.

Emma gasped, 'Was that your father?'

'Yes.'

'I gather he doesn't think much of me.'

152

'He doesn't think I should have brought you here.' Charles glared in the direction of the open door. He was still quivering with rage. 'But I don't care what he thinks—the old fool.'

'He was ordering you to...dispose of me, wasn't he? Is that why you killed Jollibone—because Daddy said so?'

Charles grabbed her by the shoulders. 'Look, whether or not you choose to believe it, we didn't kill Jollibone! What I said last night was true...substantially.'

'Run it by me again—with the insubstantial bits left out.'

'It was as I said: we discovered that Jollibone was trying to swindle us. We went to see him and had a row. We collected the paintings and left...but we went back again. A few hours later, the devious bastard phoned us at my brother Conrad's place—he lives in London—and begged us to give him one more chance. He told us he'd set up a meeting with you and suggested that we came along, too. We returned to the hotel and found Jollibone dead.'

'He was killed at the hotel?'

'Yes.'

'Then how...?'

'How did he get into the river? We dumped him there.'

'What on earth for?'

153

'It may not have been a very clever thing to do but all we could think was that we'd been seen with Jollibone. People might have heard us arguing. Anyway, our fingerprints would be all over the room. We sat down and tried to work out what to do. Conrad's apartment overlooks the river. He knew how we could get the body into the water if we could smuggle it out of the hotel. With any luck it wouldn't be discovered for a long time. In fact, getting it to Conrad's car at the back of the hotel proved quite easy. We waited till there was no one about, put Jollibone into one of those chambermaid's trolleys, went down in a service lift and *voilà.*'

'So you didn't report to the police, as you said?'

'Would you have done?'

Edgar called out something about being left to do all the work and Charles went over to help him replace the paintings. Emma watched him, wondering how much to believe of this new version of events. If it was true her chances of survival were even more slender, as Charles's father had vividly indicated. She was a real threat to the Dubecs, or whatever their name was. Yet there were, she told herself, a couple of glimmers of hope: George and Tim were sure to be doing their utmost to trace her; and these unsavoury characters

154

were at odds with each other.

As they walked from the barn she asked, 'What was it your father kept saying about a *confrérie,* a brotherhood?'

Charles glanced at her, frowning. 'Your ears are too sharp. I've got things to do. We must get you back.'

'Well, at least tell me about the paintings and why you're hiding them in a derelict sheepshed. You promised me that.'

'It's a very long story.'

'You could make a start.'

'Oh, very well.' He stopped at the edge of the trees and looked down at her. 'You're a remarkably self-possessed young woman. I was afraid we'd have tears and tantrums.'

When they had remounted their horses and Emma was once more blindfolded, Charles began his story. 'Once upon a time there was a handsome young cavalry officer.'

# CHAPTER 8

'Move on. Don't let anyone know your whereabouts—not even me. Don't make contact for at least a year. Good luck. Henri.'

That was the message which accompanied 500 francs in grubby notes and a cutting from *Le Figaro*. When Aristide, sitting at a pavement café table in the sunlit Place Voltaire, read the latter he understood the brevity and urgency of his friend's letter.

For several weeks we have been demanding the answers to some simple questions. How can a well-known citizen of Paris disappear without trace? Why have the police not made more strenuous efforts to locate Captain Albert de Bracieux, who is suspected of fratricide? Is there a conspiracy in high places to suppress any information which might embarrass close friends of General Boulanger among the officer corps? We have not been given answers to these questions. The police and their political paymasters appear more preoccupied with deliberate obfuscation than with justice and the apprehension of a killer who may yet claim further victims, if he is suffered to remain at large.

Recently, vital new information reached this journal from an impeccable source. We conveyed it to the examining magistrate who enjoined us to secrecy while he carried out fresh investigations. We have waited impatiently for evidence of renewed police activity. We have waited in vain. We can remain silent no longer. The public deserves the truth.

The revelations of our informant are alarming in the extreme. They expose Albert de Bracieux as a violent man in competition with his brother (Edouard de Bracieux, the victim) for the affections of a lady. Still more alarming is the allegation that the fugitive is a known companion of the worst elements in the Paris underworld who may well be harbouring him at this very moment. Albert de Bracieux has long been, it appears, a man with a double life. His public persona is that of an undistinguished cavalry officer, a member of an old military family. However, when he is not on the parade ground he may be discovered, shabbily-dressed, walking the streets and alleys of Montmartre and posing as an artist. The companions of his *alter ego* are *demi-mondaines*, petty criminals, unruly bohemians and other social outcasts.

Since no man in full possession of his mental faculties would forsake his respectable family and friends in order to associate with such riff-raff, we must doubt de Bracieux's sanity. We must renew our warnings to the citizens of Paris to be alert to the dangers they face until this man is apprehended. We redouble our demand for effective action by the police. Let them explore every tenement and garret in Montmartre. Let them subject its inhabitants to rigorous interrogation. Let them concentrate all their resources on discovering de Bracieux's alias. Let them not be deterred by the efforts of those who wish to draw a veil over this modern Cain and Abel affair. Let them persevere until the elusive Albert de Bracieux is brought into a court of law to be accused of the most ancient and most bestial of crimes.

Aristide read the report three times in mounting panic. Who was the newspaper's 'impeccable source'? Some confidante of Eloise? Eloise herself? She was certainly the sort of earnest young woman who would have had a tussle with her conscience and who might have felt obliged to reveal—anonymously—information which could only bring further distress to his father, not to mention dishonour to General d'Erigny-Duchamp and the regiment. Well, it did not matter who had revealed his secret. What was important was that, hounded by the press, the police would be forced to seek evidence of Albert de Bracieux in Montmartre. They would be showing his photograph in the bars and brothels. They would be offering money to starving painters, writers and sculptors. Sooner or later someone would put a new name to the face in the posed, studio portrait. 'Why, that's Aristide,' he would say, 'Aristide Bertrand, the painter.' Then the alias would be revealed in every newspaper in the country.

Perhaps it already had been. He looked anxiously around. Two customers at nearby tables were reading local journals. A man crossing the square had a copy of *Le Figaro* under his arm. Aristide felt numb, immobile. How stupid he had been. How absurd to think he could remain undetected, start a new life. He must have been mad to let Henri talk him into running away. All it had done was confirm his guilt. Now, if he were dragged back to Paris in chains—a dangerous, captured fugitive—no court would believe his version of Edouard's death. The mark of Cain was upon him—indelible, fatal. Better to accept the inevitable. Salvage what fragments of honour still remained. Give himself up.

Having made the decision he felt suddenly very calm. He stared unseeing across the Place Voltaire. Groups of men were pulling carts to block the exits from the square and tying ropes between the young plane trees which

159

bordered it. Behind this barrier small groups of citizens began to congregate for the twice-weekly *encierro*. Aristide was too busy with his own ordered thoughts to notice. He had earlier loaded most of his few belongings on a handcart, ready for transporting to Van Gogh's house. He would go back to his apartment, collect the remaining items, then trundle them down to the Place Lamartine. He would explain that he was unable to join in Vincent's new enterprise and make him a gift of his canvases, paints and personal possessions. Then he would head for the gendarmerie. It was all very simple. He paid for his drink and enjoyed the proprietor's surprise as he offered a tip. Then he walked with slow, purposeful strides across the square.

It took only a few minutes to complete his arrangements but when he re-entered the Place Voltaire the *encierro* was in full swing. It was a local custom he had observed with some curiosity. The Arlesiens were passionate about their bull games. Talk in the bars and cafés was of little else but the highlights of the previous years *courses* in the great Roman arena and the prospects for the coming season. The *encierro* was a traditional way of providing the citizenry with some excitement during the cooler months of the year. Young bulls would be driven into town and herded into enclosed spaces like the Place Voltaire so that young gallants could play at being *torreros*. Egged on by the taunts of rivals, and the squeals of their female admirers, the lads of the town competed to see who could get closest to the dangerous black beasts, provoke them to charge, avoid being gored or, most daring of all, run up to touch the lyre-shaped horns.

Aristide had often watched these diversions; had even tried, in rapid sketches, to capture some of the excitement of the *encierro*. Today the event held no interest for him. He circled the enclosure, pushing the swaying cart over the uneven cobbles. As he turned the corner by the open fishmongers' stands, the vehicle tilted too far. A bundle loosely wrapped in cloth slipped to the ground and spread brushes among the feet of the people clustered along the rope. Aristide went down on all fours to gather them.

That was the moment when he became aware of a different noise from the crowd—a gasp of some emotion that was not excitement. He was on his knees by the rope. Suddenly the feet around him leaped backwards. Looking into the makeshift arena he quickly grasped the drama taking place only a few metres away. A group of young boys, no more than twelve or thirteen years of age, had joined in the dangerous sport. They had baited one of the two bulls, provoked it into chasing them and then scattered. Three of them ran and swerved nimbly to reach the safety of the barrier. But the fourth, a stocky, black-haired lad, tripped. He lay sprawling in the dust. He looked up, straight into Aristide's face, pain and fear glowing in his dark eyes. A few paces away the enraged bull saw the boy, turned and charged, head lowered.

Aristide's move was instinctive. He sprang from his crouching position. He grabbed the lad's arm. He part-lifted, part-dragged, part-threw the youngster out of the path of the angry animal. His own impulsion carried him forward. He stumbled. Regained his feet. Then the bull's lowered head struck his upper leg. The impact sent Aristide rolling over and over. His head hit the base of a tree and all sensation ceased.

'M. Labardie is not here at the moment. May I take a message?' The secretary who answered when Tim phoned sounded efficient and spoke passable English.

'Please tell him that I'd like to speak with him as soon as possible about Auguste Jollibone. My name is Tim Lacy. He can reach me on this number.' Tim read off the figures on the receiver and replaced it.

George stood by the window, staring moodily down into the rue du Boeuf where shop lights were beginning to glow in the late winter afternoon. His anxiety and sense of helplessness had become almost unbearable. 'Think that'll do any good? Shouldn't we be paying this Labardie character a surprise visit?'

Tim sat down on the bed. 'I thought about that in the taxi on the way back from Interpol, but now that we know who we're dealing with I don't see it as an option. His sort are always well protected. This Château d'Orgnac is probably as well fortified as the name suggests. Anyway, it's pretty unlikely that he's got Emma there.'

'He holds all the cards. Why should he return our call?'

'If he knows we're bluffing about Jollibone, he probably won't. I'm just hoping against hope that he won't be quite so sure. If he thinks we might know something about the murder he'll want to find out what it is.'

'And if he calls our bluff?'

'Then we'll look at your option. Don't worry, George. We'll get Emma back somehow.'

'If she's still alive.' The older man drew the curtains. He picked up the bottle on the dressing table and poured himself another scotch. With a heavy sigh he dropped into an armchair.

The two men waited in gloomy silence.

Twenty-three minutes later the telephone rang.

'Charles Labardie here. I assume I'm speaking to Mr Timothy Lacy.'

'You know damned well who I am. How is Emma?' Tim tried to keep the angry tension out of his voice. Tried to match the other man's languid calm.

'She is in excellent health—for the moment.'

'Just what is it you want, Labardie? Why haven't you called earlier?'

'I thought it would do you good to sweat for a bit. I also wanted to find out how anxious you were about your colleague's safety. I congratulate you on discovering me so quickly. Presumably you extracted the information from Josephine Tarantin.'

'You haven't answered my question. What do you want in exchange for Miss Kerr?'

'I'm not convinced that you have anything to offer that would interest me.'

'I know who killed Jollibone and why. Unless Miss Kerr is returned unharmed within twenty-four hours that information goes to the police.'

'You're bluffing, Mr Lacy.'

'There's one way to find out.'

164

There was silence at the other end of the line. Then, 'The ancient theatre in Arles. Ten o'clock tomorrow morning.' The line went dead.

Emma had plenty of time to explore her prison after her captors left. Despite her fear, she had found herself listening enthralled to the story, or part story, of Aristide Bertrand that Charles had told her on their way back from the barn. If ever the incredible hidden paintings went on sale their remarkable history and the dramatic events leading to their creation would produce massive media interest. Catherine was closer to the truth than she realised when she spoke of the commercial possibilities of the rediscovered Bertrands.

If Charles was telling the truth. How could you believe a man who changed his story every time he told it? A man who protested that he intended her no harm while keeping her locked up in the middle of a swamp. A man who refused to tell her what he was planning to do with her. And even if Charles was to be believed, what about his gruesome accomplices—the shambling, well-intentioned Edgar who carried a vicious knife and obviously knew how to use it; Charles's sinister father who regarded her as an embarrassment to be disposed of as quickly as possible. She

165

shivered at the thought of the old man. Only one thing was clear to her amidst all the terrifying confusion. Somehow she had to escape. Purposefully, Emma surveyed every nook and cranny of the little building.

Charles had explained that it was a *cabane,* a simple shelter once used by the *gardians* who eked out a living on the Camargue—herding the black bulls or white horses, fishing on the *étang,* wildfowling. They were originally built from marsh mud and roofed with marsh reed. Emma's hut was still thatched but the inside of the roof was boarded, and investigation with a nail file proved that the walls were made of sterner stuff than wattle and daub. The only window had been fitted with horizontal bars and the door, she knew, was heavily padlocked. When she peered up the chimney she saw that it was blocked. Just as well, perhaps, since there was no fire; at least draughts were kept to a minimum.

The tour of inspection left Emma depressed—and cold. She sat on the bed, drew her legs up beneath her and wrapped herself in a couple of blankets. The simple act flashed a childhood memory into her mind. This was exactly what she had done on those, seemingly frequent, occasions when she had been ordered to her room for some misdemeanour. She remembered her father's fierce scowl and his instruction that she was not to return until she felt 'utterly ashamed'. She remembered stamping up the stairs, slamming her door and leaping heavily on the bed in self-righteous rage. But those infantile tantrums had existed within a world of comfortable security. That was the difference.

Emma banished nostalgia and self-pity. 'Think clearly,' she told herself. 'There's no problem that doesn't have a solution.' If the walls were impenetrable the only possibility of escape was when the door was opened by her captors. Slowly she pieced together a desperate plan.

The *cabane*, which was gloomy even in the middle of the day, had surrendered to almost total darkness when she heard the sound of hooves outside. Moments later the hasp on the outside of the door rattled as the padlock was unfastened. Emma saw Edgar outlined in the doorway. He was carrying a large storm torch in one hand and what looked like a bucket in the other. She watched her jailer carefully, noting every movement. He came into the room, set down his load, turned, shot the bolt and then moved to the table. He hung the torch from a hook on one of the beams and set about unpacking his 'bucket', which turned out to be a hot food container. She noticed how the man bent over the table setting out dishes, absorbed in his task. Appetising aromas soon filled the small room.

'Thank you, Edgar. That smells delicious. What is it?' Emma tried to engage the man in simple French, hoping that she would be able to understand his heavily accented responses.

She learned that he had brought fish soup and a salmi of wild duck prepared by his wife who was acclaimed as one of the best cooks in the district. There was fresh-baked bread, some apples and pears and, in the plastic container, wine from the vineyard of his cousin in the Ardèche. There were also two half-litres of mineral water in case mam'selle felt thirsty during the night. He hoped she would enjoy the food. From a deep pocket in his waterproof coat Edgar produced some dog-eared guidebooks and magazines. Perhaps mam'selle would like to read to pass the time. He would leave the torch for her.

Emma was effusive in her thanks. She deliberately detained her keeper with small talk. Was it true he kept a hotel? Yes—a small one, she must understand, but of a high quality. Several of his customers, some of them English, came back year after year. Summer was very busy, what with the hotel and the fishing and taking guests out on riding parties. Emma pushed her luck a little further. She hoped that Edgar had not had to come very far with her food. He smiled and put a finger to his lips. The ruse had failed. When Emma asked how long she was to be kept here, he shrugged and moved back to the door. He wished her a good night, asked her to let him know if there was anything she lacked and went out.

Emma tackled her supper with the array of spoons provided—she noted that there were no knives or forks, which might easily be used as weapons. It was good. Madame Edgar's reputation was, clearly, well deserved. As she ate she pondered. This was the best time of day to carry out her plan; when growing darkness would hamper any pursuit. Though, if it worked there would be no immediate pursuit. She set aside most of the fruit and one of the water bottles. If she were to spend hours wandering around the marsh she would need it. Tomorrow evening. That would have to be the time. She dared not leave her bid any longer. Until then she would be a model prisoner.

Her meal over, Emma examined one of the benches with the aid of her torch. Yes, it would be fairly easy to detach one of the truncheon-shaped legs.

Tim collected a hire car that evening and left for Arles early the following morning. George accompanied him down to the foyer.

'Three hours—that should be plenty of time.' Tim checked his watch with the one above the reception desk. 'With any luck I should be back this evening.'

'And if you're not?'

'If I'm not, and if you haven't heard from me, call in the local plod. Give them Labardie's name and address. That should interest them. Not that it'll come to that. As soon as I meet up with our murdering, kidnapping friend I'll make it very clear that my back is covered.'

'I still think I should come with you, Major.'

'George, we've been over all that. I know thumb-twiddling isn't your forte but there has to be someone here, someone who knows what's going on and is free to take whatever action is necessary. Right, I must go. I'll be back either with Emma or with definite news about her.'

'Good luck, Major.'

The two men shook hands and Tim went out, through the swing doors. George wandered towards the newsagent's stand in the vain hope of finding a London paper.

'M. Lacy. Telephone call. Are you M. Lacy?' A bored clerk called to him from the desk and indicated the booth beside the lifts.

George went across and picked up the receiver.

'Mr Lacy?' A French voice but speaking in English. 'Listen carefully, please. You are, I'm sure, anxious about your colleague, Miss Kerr. She is quite safe and I wish to discuss her fate with you.'

'Who are you?'

'Please don't waste time with unnecessary questions. Just do as I say. I will come to your hotel at midday. Meet me in the foyer—alone. If there is any sign of the police I will not come and you will not see Miss Kerr again.' The line went dead.

George rushed out into the street but there was no sign of Tim's car. Distractedly, he went back into the hotel. He returned to his room and when, minutes later, breakfast arrived, he worked his way through it mechanically. Over and again he posed the question, what the hell is going on? Over and over again he failed to discern an answer. It was like trying to solve a crossword with the wrong set of clues. The Major had gone off to Arles to negotiate for Emma's release. Someone else was coming to Lyon apparently for the same purpose. Was there a double-cross going on? One of Labardie's cronies trying to cash in on the situation

171

by doing a private deal behind his boss's back? Or perhaps the Marseille syndicate was splitting into factions. Father and son not seeing eye-to-eye perhaps? Whatever the truth, Emma had got herself into water that was turbulent as well as hot.

In the whole confused situation only one thing was clear: George would have to go along with this latest development. He could not contact the major. Calling the police was out of the question. The ball was in his court. He wrote a note for Tim and took it to reception. Then he made his escape from the anxiety-ridden claustrophobia of the hotel. He spent most of the next few hours walking the streets of Lyon in the crisp morning air.

He returned at 11.45. One of the Cour des Loges's pink message slips was on the dressing table. George grabbed it. There had been a telephone call. Would he please return it? With relief he recognised Catherine Lacy's direct line number. He picked up the receiver and pressed the requisite buttons.

'George? Thank God! I tried to get hold of Tim but he's out. I've had the police—Edgerson—on the phone asking some odd questions. What on earth's happening over there?'

George took a deep breath and tried to keep his voice relaxed and even. 'Catherine, everything's fine here. There's a lot to do...various leads to follow up. That's why the major's out at the moment. I'll get him to call you as soon as he gets back.'

'Don't bullshit me, George! You're a lousy liar! What's wrong? Is it Emma? Tim left here very suddenly, without telling me a word. That always means trouble. Is Emma with you? Let me talk to her.'

'I'm afraid she's out, too, at the moment.'

'Where?'

'Oh...making enquiries...I'm sure—'

'George, I'm getting on the first plane to Lyon!'

'That's really not a very good idea.' He looked anxiously at his watch.

'If anything happened to Emma I'd never forgive myself. Tell me honestly that she's OK, George.'

'Emma's absolutely fine. Never better. Look, Catherine, I'm afraid I have to rush. Someone's coming to see me in a few minutes. Could be an important lead. Please don't do anything till the major's had a chance to talk to you later. Goodbye for now, Catherine.'

'George!' Her voice was shrill. 'Don't hang up! I've got to tell you about the police.'

'Later, Catherine, later. I really have to go now.' Catherine was still talking as he put down the receiver.

George left the room at a run. He just missed the lift and waited what seemed an age for its return.

As he emerged in the foyer he immediately saw the young man from the gallery, the man who called himself Charles Dubec. The man approached him.

'Mr Lacy? Follow me!' He turned and walked abruptly out of the hotel.

## CHAPTER 9

Aristide became aware of a jolting movement, a throbbing head and a beautiful face, in that order. He seemed to be lying in a confined space that was constantly moving. He tried to sit up but pain stabbed at his eyes and flashed like lightning across his temple.

'Don't move, please. You're quite badly hurt.'

Aristide gazed up at a girl of about seventeen with brown eyes and shoulder-length hair which had hints of copper and gold. She laid a cool hand on his forehead. 'You have to stay very quiet,' she announced solemnly. 'Aunt Lou has looked at your head and she says you will

174

be all right if you keep still and let it heal itself.'

'Who are you?' Aristide was shocked at how faint and hesitant his voice sounded. 'And who is Aunt Lou?'

A slight blush brought a trace of carmine to the girl's glowing, outdoor complexion. 'I'm Yvette Bardol. It was my brother, Jean-Marc, whose life you saved. Stupid show-off! He might have killed himself and you. Do you remember about that?'

Aristide closed his eyes. Remember? What did he remember? What was there to remember? Who was he? Images flitted across the pained darkness of his mind. Frightening images. Angry faces. Shattering glass. A black bull with lowered horns. A nude, leering woman called Eloise. And water everywhere. Water of an unbelievable blue...streaked with blood. And a face in the water. An angry, accusing face... He threw his lids open with an effort.

'What's the matter? What is it?' The girl's eyes were wide with anxiety. 'You must stay calm. Aunt Lou says it will be very serious if you develop a fever.'

Gazing back into eyes that were miraculously dark yet glowing with intense emotion, Aristide felt a vibrant tranquillity exerting itself to overcome the panic and the pain. 'Perhaps, if you could tell me why I'm here and where "here" is...'

175

'Well, let me see.' The girl frowned slightly and listed recent events, like a child painstakingly reciting learned lessons and concerned not to forget anything. 'It was at the *encierro* in Arles this morning. We had come in for the market and to see Uncle Pierre's bull. He lives near the town and often runs his bulls there in the winter. We keep ours for the real games. Jean-Marc was there with his friends and I was supposed to be looking after them. Well, you know what young boys are like—twelve years old and they think they know everything. Jean-Marc has only just begun as a *gardianon,* helping to herd the horses and the bulls. Already he thinks he's a *razetteur* in the big arena at Arles or Aigues-Mortes. He and the others slipped under the rope before I could grab them. They started running one of the bulls—skipping round and round him to get him angry. When they had made him charge, the next part of the game was to see who could stand his ground the longest. Well, Jean-Marc left it too late. In his hurry to get back to safety he fell. The bull saw him and started to charge. It was terrible. I couldn't look—only I did, of course. And then you appeared—from nowhere. *Marie Mère,* but you were brave! You ran right in front of the horns. It was wonderful! You threw Jean-Marc to

176

safety. Then you hit your head. And you were lying there in the dust. And there was blood coming from your head. And I thought you were dead. Oh, if you had been dead I should never have forgiven myself. Do you not remember all this?'

'I don't think so. I don't know. You tell it so well that I can see it all but whether it's imagination or memory... What happened next? And how is Jean-Marc?'

'Jean-Marc is fine—more's the pity. If he'd been gored it might have taught him a lesson. Anyway, he got a good strapping from M. Simier. Now he and his friends are walking home. It will take them hours but I don't suppose they'll learn their lesson. As for you, they dragged you under the rope and a crowd gathered. And people were asking who you were. Fortunately someone sent for Aunt Lou and she took charge. No one argues when Aunt Lou gives orders. She sent for water and cloths and bound your head and made you swallow one of her potions. Then we tried to find out who you were and someone said you were a stranger here and all alone. So, of course, you became our responsibility. A life for a life.'

Aristide closed his eyes, head throbbing with the effort of thought. It might have been seconds or hours later that he said, 'You are very beautiful.'

The girl blushed again. 'And you are delirious. I must take over the driving from Aunt Lou and leave you to sleep.'

'No, don't go.' Aristide weakly lifted a hand and the girl took hold of it.

'Very well, but only if you promise to sleep. We won't be home for another hour yet.'

'And where is home?'

The girl's reply seemed to come from the far end of a long tunnel. It reverberated in Aristide's brain as he slipped into unconsciousness. 'Mas Maraques in the Camargue...'

Tim reached Arles in a panic. A jack-knifed lorry near the Avignon junction had turned southbound traffic into a sluggish stream of revving vehicles and frustrated drivers. The hold-up had threatened to make him late. A church clock was chiming the hour as he drove through the town centre and threw the hired car into the first parking spot he saw. He jumped out and moved along the street at a half-run, desperately trying to assemble enough French to ask his way. Then he saw a sign, *Théâtre Antique,* pointing up a side street. He walked briskly along the narrow thoroughfare, past the gendarmerie, and came suddenly upon an opening in the high wall on his right. Two ladies were deeply absorbed in conversation but as Tim entered one of them sighed deeply, put down the poodle she was cradling and shuffled into a small ticket office. Having rapidly disposed of the tiresome business of the rare visitor's admittance, she returned to her interrupted tête-à-tête.

Tim hurried into the amphitheatre. To his left a semi-circle of stepped tiers rose skywards. They faced a stage backed by a line of broken columns. Elsewhere in the enclosure clumps of Roman stonework were engaged in an inconclusive contest with creeping vegetation. Tim walked to the centre of the ancient stage and looked around. Apart from the two women by the gate there was no one in sight.

He climbed the stone tiers of the auditorium to get a better view. Behind the stage area blocks of part-wall stood out from the clinging undergrowth like disorganised tombstones. Tim scanned the unkempt area of overgrown paving and columns. He had an excellent view of the whole enclosure. There was definitely no one lurking among the ruins. Had he missed Labardie? He had only been two or three minutes late. Perhaps the man was a punctuality freak. The cracked bell of a neighbouring church clanked the quarter. Some children were released noisily into a nearby playground. A squadron of black pigeons wheeled over the wall and settled hopefully on the seats around him.

They squawked away protestingly as he stood suddenly. Something was very amiss. Either Labardie was playing games with him or this was the wrong place. Surely there was only one *théâtre antique* in Arles? He descended the steps towards the stage. He passed one of the entrances that led to the area behind the seating. Perhaps. He stepped through into the gloomy, curving passage.

He had gone only a few paces when he heard his name called.

'M. Lacy?'

Two young men stood in an embrasure beneath the banked seating.

'Yes...*oui.*'

One of the men beckoned to Tim to come over and stand facing the wall. The other expertly frisked him. Satisfied that the Englishman was not armed, he said, 'Allons!' and waved an arm.

Tim stood his ground. 'M. Labardie—où est-il?'

The man shook his head. 'Allons, à votre auto.'

Tim walked warily back into the arena, then to the exit. The two men followed casually, some fifty metres behind. Tim led the way briskly to where he had parked the hired Renault. The taller of the two men climbed into the passenger seat and motioned Tim to start the car.

They drove northwards for about twenty minutes, Tim's guide giving directions by means of gestures and grunted mono-syllables. When they had passed the nameboard for Tarascon he indicated a road to the right climbing away from the town. After a kilometre he pointed out tall gates on the left. These opened in response to a remote control operated by Tim's passenger. The Renault passed through into wooded grounds followed by a Mercedes driven by Labardie's other henchman. After a few twists and turns the drive ended in a gravelled terrace overlooking the Rhône.

The Château d'Orgnac was a Renais-sance-style sumptuosity, well embellished with round towers and pinnacles. Gazing upwards, Tim noticed an elaborate flag fluttering from the highest point of the multi-gabled roof. He reflected that its heraldic device was probably spurious and wondered if its motto read 'Crime Does Pay'.

As he was taken through a wide, marbled hall and a succession of anterooms Tim was forced to acknowledge that Charles Labardie Junior had taste, as well as the illicit income to indulge it. He paused to admire Brussels tapestries, cabinets displaying fine Sèvres and Limoges and French furniture created by eighteenth-century *ébénistes* who understood precisely at what point exuberance fell over into vulgarity and avoided the trap. This cultural pilgrimage ended in a library-cum-study whose tall windows provided a wide prospect of the Rhône valley. The room glowed with soft reflected light. The lime green background of the Savonnerie carpet was taken up in the colour of the walls and fitted bookcases whose mouldings were picked out in gold leaf. Impressionist paintings had been hung to embellish this bowl of light. A beach scene in the centre of one wall had to be a Monet and Tim reckoned that the more stylised group study facing it was probably a Lebasque.

The proud owner of this display was seated behind a miraculously elegant black lacquer *bureau plat* gleaming with crisp ormolu. Charles Labardie was either studying or affecting to study a file of papers. He rose as Tim approached and held out his hand across the desk. 'A pleasure to meet you, Mr Lacy. Your reputation goes before you.' He waved his guest to a deep, gilded *bergère fauteuil*.

Tim saw a slim young man with dark hair and slightly pinched features wearing a pink silk shirt over tailored jeans. He said. 'Nice place you have here. You must let me do you a security quote for it. It would be a tragedy if anyone dishonest were to get in here.'

Labardie ignored the sarcasm. 'What do you like to drink at this hour, Mr Lacy?'

'Coffee would be fine.'

Labardie pressed a concealed button and gave instructions to the young woman who appeared at the door almost instantly. 'Would you like a tour of my little treasure house?'

'Some other time, perhaps. Right now we have some pressing business to attend to. Where is Miss Kerr?'

Labardie leaned forward, elbows on the desk's polished leather, hands cupping his chin. He looked straight at Tim for several seconds and then said, 'I haven't the faintest idea.'

The answer was so unexpected that for several seconds Tim could only stare back. At last he said, 'Don't play games with me, Labardie.'

At that moment the coffee arrived. After it had been poured and the girl had withdrawn, the criminal opened a desk drawer and took out a packet of photographs. 'Any "game" that is being played involves us both, Mr Lacy. And this is the prize.' He pushed the envelope across the shining leather.

There were twenty or so photographs—

amateurish and some a little blurred. Twenty snapshots of obvious masterpieces. The very range of the artist's talent was breathtaking. There were landscapes, nudes, still lifes, figure studies, but they all glowed with light and life.

'Magnificent, aren't they?' Labardie sat back in his chair. 'I want them. You're going to find them for me.'

'You know what you can do!'

'You have a reputation for intelligence, Mr Lacy. Please don't disappoint me.'

'My interest begins and ends with Miss Kerr's safety. You haven't convinced me yet that your thugs aren't holding her somewhere.'

'Do I really have to spell it out? I want the Bertrands. You want the girl. If I had your precious Miss Kerr that would put me in a very strong position to encourage your assistance. I wouldn't hesitate to use her as a bargaining counter. I got you to believe that I had her for the very purpose of initiating this conversation. You wouldn't have come here otherwise.'

'What do you mean *you* got me to come here?'

Labardie smiled an infuriating, superior smile. 'You thought you had extracted the information about my involvement from a reluctant Josephine Tarantin. She is a very accomplished actress. As I was saying, I could have used your friend as a means of ensuring your co-operation. But you would certainly have demanded proof that I have her in my clutches. So I have decided to lay all my cards on the table and be honest with you.'

'That must come hard.'

'Not to a pragmatist.' Labardie stood up and walked round the *bureau plat*. 'You can moralise as much as you like but while you're striking attitudes do you know what I shall be doing?'

'Getting rich at the expense of others. Selling drugs and misery to kids so that you can live in style.'

Labardie ignored the taunt. 'Establishing a dynasty, a benevolent dynasty. Come with me and I'll show you what I mean.' He led the way from the room. 'All the great families of history—Medicis, Habsburgs, Bourbons, your own Tudors and Stuarts—how did they start out? Brigands, swindlers, murderers, unscrupulous accumulators of capital and power. And what did they become in the fullness of time? Intelligent rulers, munificent patrons, arbiters of taste and fashion, encouragers of genius. Take this chess set...' He indicated an inlaid, silver-mounted board on which exquisite porcelain figures confronted each other. 'Commissioned by Frederick the Great for a visiting diplomat.'

Labardie strolled through a succession of rooms showing off his treasures. 'That secrétaire is a signed piece by Jacques Dubois. What would have become of his talent without the support of Louis XV? This monumental silver Tiffany ewer was created for an American millionaire whose father made a fortune running guns to the Indians. The family became leading philanthropists and founders of charities. The little Titian over the fireplace was painted for a corrupt cardinal and was later in the collection of a royal saint and martyr—your own Charles I.'

The tour lasted almost an hour. Despite himself Tim was fascinated by the younger man's magpie collection. Over and again he had to remind himself that these precious objects had been brought together at the cost of thousands of ruined lives. At last his guide opened the door to a small circular sitting room or cabinet in one of the building's corner turrets.

Labardie motioned his guest to a chair and busied himself pouring drinks. 'An apéritif before lunch, Mr Lacy?'

'I didn't come here to socialise.'

'Of course not. You came to discuss business. I know quite a lot about you—from colleagues and friends in our own little world of art and antiques—and I have made it my business to find out more over the last twenty-four hours. It was only fair that you should also discover something about me. I wouldn't want our negotiations to be wholly one-sided.'

'If you're not holding Emma Kerr we have nothing to negotiate.'

Labardie handed Tim a glass of sickly-sweet-smelling liqueur and seated himself opposite. 'It's a reasonable guess, wouldn't you say, that whoever has your friend also has some or all of the Bertrands?'

Tim nodded.

'So we're both looking for the same person. Therefore it makes sense for us to work together. Or rather for you to work for me. I will pay you generously if you find the paintings. If in the process you manage to free Miss Kerr, safe and sound, that will be a bonus.'

'I don't need your help.'

'Oh, but I think you do. I have information that will help you, not to mention resources—money and muscle—which will be at your disposal.'

'I don't accept commissions from crime syndicates. As well as a personal distaste I have for everything you stand for, our association wouldn't do my reputation much good.'

Labardie shrugged. 'If you wish to continue your investigation with one hand tied behind your back, that's your affair.

It makes little difference to me. I shall have you followed, whatever you decide. If you are successful you will lead me to the paintings—eventually. Of course, by then it may be too late for Miss Kerr. You obviously haven't heard from the kidnappers yet. That's serious. In these situations every hour that passes is crucial. If I were in your position I'd be very worried and I'd want to gather every scrap of information, irrespective of its source. I certainly wouldn't be sitting there like a virgin guarding her honour.'

Tim stared back impassively. 'Tell me what you know.'

'We have a deal?'

'I'm not taking money from you. I'm only interested in finding Emma. If I locate the pictures that, as you say, will be a bonus. So, what can you tell me?'

Labardie stretched his legs before him. 'OK. It all began about six weeks ago. Josephine Tarantin brought me the photographs I showed you.'

'*She* did? She told me the whole deal was Jollibone's.'

Labardie laughed. 'Jollibone? Poor little Auguste was a mere cypher. The Lyon gallery belongs to me and Josephine runs it for me. She's been an associate of mine for years. She helps me to build my collections. She tells me all the artworld gossip. She's valuable to me in many ways. A while back I decided I needed a legitimate front. Jollibone was a respected dealer with money troubles. I took care of his financial problems, put Josephine in as his "assistant" and kept Jollibone on for his reputation.'

'So who approached Josephine about the Bertrands?'

'She doesn't know. The photographs were sent anonymously. Someone followed up with a phone call and offered to show her some sample paintings in London.'

'Why London?'

'The collection is in England. That's where the photos and the telephone call came from.'

'I see. And then?'

'We despatched Auguste to make the initial contact. We wanted to make sure the paintings were genuine and he was a considerable expert in Impressionist and Postimpressionist art. He vetted them and showed them to Josephine. She told him how to handle the negotiations.'

'Mme Tarantin went to London?'

'Yes. When she had seen the pictures, she called me and I authorised her to go ahead. Next thing either of us knew Jollibone was dead and the paintings had vanished.'

Tim sat thoughtfully, rubbing a finger

along the bridge of his nose. 'There's something here that doesn't hang together. The whole idea, I presume, was for you to get the Bertrands at a knock-down price.'

'I certainly intended to buy privately. It's terribly important to keep such a unique collection together. After a century it would be a tragedy to have galleries and collectors squabbling over it, scattering it round the world.'

'Spare me the public-spiritedness. What I can't understand is why Jollibone arranged to show the paintings to my wife.'

'That took us by surprise, too. He certainly mentioned nothing to Josephine about bringing anyone else into the deal. You can imagine that I would have had something to say about that. My guess is that the owner of the paintings demanded a second opinion. Auguste couldn't go to a leading dealer of comparable standing. The art world would have been trembling excitedly within hours. So on the spur of the moment he contacted an out-of-town gallery, just to keep the customer happy. The first thing we knew about your involvement was when you turned up in Lyon asking questions. As soon as I realised the celebrated Mr Tim Lacy was involved I was convinced we needed you on our side.'

'But...'

'Yes?'

'Oh, it doesn't matter. So, we come to the sixty-four-thousand-dollar question: who killed Auguste Jollibone and made off with a carload of priceless paintings?'

'Presumably he fell out with the owners of the pictures.'

'Why on earth should they want to knife him and dump him in the river? All they had to do was say, "No thanks," pick up their belongings and disappear back into obscurity. Anyway, the man who impersonated Jollibone to my wife was French—definitely not English. Isn't it more likely that wily old Auguste was not as much under your thumb as you thought? Suppose he was doing a deal with some other shady characters—a deal that came fatally unstuck.'

Labardie looked thoughtful. 'I could certainly make some enquiries.' He hesitated. 'There is another possibility.'

'Yes?'

'The organisation I'm a part of is very big. There are...factions...disagreements over policy...'

'In other words, Daddy doesn't approve of all this money you spend on fine art?'

Labardie eyed him shrewdly. 'You've done your homework. I'm glad I was right about your intelligence. Yes, my father and I don't see altogether eye-to-eye. He

191

had to know about the Bertrand deal. There was, potentially, a very large sum of money involved. It might have meant diverting funds from other operations. He opposed that, very firmly. But I don't think he'd have gone over my head. However... Look, before you go, I'll give you a name to contact.'

'If this person is in the know, why don't *you* talk to him?'

'It would be better if the enquiries came from someone outside the organisation.'

'So, if Daddy doesn't like my snooping I end up in the river with a rear incision while you act the innocent?'

Labardie smiled. 'There's an element of risk. Whether or not you're prepared to take it will depend on your degree of commitment to your friend.' He looked at his watch and stood up. 'Let's have lunch.'

Two hours later Tim was heading north along the autoroute du Sud. All the way to Lyon he went over and over his conversation with Labardie. He analysed things said and unsaid. Struggled to unravel truth from lies. There was much to think about. Somewhere along the motorway he passed a totally nondescript Citroen roaring south at around 140 kph. If he had noticed it at all he would only have observed that its driver was yet another Frenchman in too much of a hurry.

The soft thud of hooves approaching the *cabane* took Emma by surprise. Edgar was very early. She looked at her watch: 4.13. She had expected her jailer to come with supper around six o'clock. She jumped up from the bed, heart racing. 'It doesn't matter,' she told herself. 'Everything's ready. Now, just keep your head.'

She had spent most of the day making preparations for her uncomplicated escape bid. When Edgar had appeared with breakfast and lunch she had watched, carefully, his routine: come in, bolt door, lay out food on table, collect used dishes, unbolt door, go out. She had made relaxed, though sparse conversation with the big man and knew from the way he looked at her that he liked what he saw. He would not be expecting her sudden move.

From the table she quickly grabbed up the cloth bundle containing scraps of food and the makeshift, bench-leg cosh. She climbed onto the intact bench she had already placed behind the door.

With her ear to the crack, she could hear the clink of harness and the sound of her captor dismounting. She weighed her weapon and did a trial swing. 'Mustn't hit him too hard!' Frightened and angry though Emma was, she could not bring herself to channel all her emotion into a single savage blow. She had spent much of the afternoon practising, trying to remember everything her school tennis coach had told her about controlled aggression, about putting the right amount of effort into a shot, no more and no less. She didn't want to inflict serious injury on Edgar, just to stun him for a few vital seconds—long enough to slip through the open doorway, and fasten the padlock on the outside. Then the brute could yell all he liked. As her abductor had callously pointed out, no one was within earshot. After that it was simply a question of mounting Edgar's horse and trusting the animal's instinct to find its way through the marsh to a road, people, civilisation.

There was a metallic scrape of key in lock.

Emma lifted the cosh above her head.

The door opened. A man's head and shoulders came into view. Emma's arm swung in a free arc.

Only in the last split second—too late to divert or soften the blow—did she realise something was wrong.

The force of the contact jolted her arm. Her victim grunted, staggered forward, fell to his knees and rolled sideways onto the floor.

Emma dropped the truncheon. 'George!' she screamed.

The wounded man sat on the floor, shaking his head slowly from side to side, rubbing a hand tenderly over the point of impact.

Emma was on her knees beside him. 'Oh, George, are you all right? I'm so sorry. I didn't—'

'George? Who is this?'

Emma looked up at the three men in the doorway—Charles, his father and Edgar.

Charles was glaring down, angry, suspicious. 'Why do you call him George? This is Tim Lacy. What's going on here?'

Emma looked from her captor to her dazed colleague and back again—bewildered. 'Oh, shut up!' she blurted. 'Help me get him to the bed!'

'It's OK, Emma. I'm all right.' George struggled to his feet.

Charles stepped forward to face him. 'Who are you? Police? Why have you been masquerading as Tim Lacy?'

George glared back. 'Case of mistaken identity, chum. You got it wrong. I just didn't bother to put you right. And if there's any explaining to be done, you're going to do it!'

The oldest of the three Frenchmen shouted something. Charles spun round and answered him angrily in dialect. Within seconds a violent argument was underway, both men screaming and waving their arms. Eventually they went outside, followed meekly by Edgar. Through the closed door the prisoners could hear the row continuing.

'Come and sit down. Let me look at your head.' Emma guided her colleague to the bed and sat beside him.

'I'm OK. Had far worse than that in my time. The important thing is, how are you?' He put an arm round her shoulder. 'Have they...mistreated you?'

Emma managed a wry smile. 'Well, this isn't exactly the Ritz, but...how did you find me? Oh, George, I'm so glad to see you.' She threw her arms around him and burrowed her head into his shoulder. 'I've been so frightened.' Her long-pent-up tears gushed forth and her body shook as George hugged her.

He muttered consoling words while reflecting that his bungling had only made matters worse. Now the criminals had two hostages instead of one.

After about ten minutes the Frenchmen came back in. Edgar took up his accustomed position by the door. The others sat on the undamaged bench which they dragged into a position to face their captives. The atmosphere between them was still almost tangible but the older man did not interrupt as Charles, with an obvious effort, spoke calmly.

He glared at the English couple. 'So who exactly are you, "George"? Where is Mr Lacy? Have you got the police looking for Miss Kerr?'

George explained who he was. 'As for Mr Lacy, you should know where he is, Mr Labardie. You sent him on a wild goose chase to Arles.'

'What are you talking about? And why do you call me Labardie? My name is... No matter. What is going on?'

George's head still throbbed but he began to prise apart some crossed wires. 'Yesterday, Mr Lacy spoke on the phone to someone called Charles Labardie who claimed to be holding Miss Kerr prisoner. He told Mr Lacy to meet him in Arles. If that wasn't you, then whoever it was was lying.'

'It was not me. What do you know about this man called Labardie? Who is he? What does he want? Why is he involved in this?'

'I've done enough explaining for the moment. Now it's your turn.'

The older man now interjected. 'Qu'est-ce qu'il dit? Qu'est-ce qu'il dit?' He gestured agitatedly.

Charles translated his exchange with

George. His father shook his head, muttering a string of words among which Emma could only make out the oft-repeated 'Fini! Fini!'

The younger man responded slowly, with strained patience. The gist of his words was much clearer. 'We must find out what they know—what is happening. If Lacy is looking for us, and the police, and this Labardie, whoever he is, someone will find us. We must trust somebody. I say we tell them everything.'

The old man was clearly not convinced. Edgar was brought into the conversation which lasted several more minutes. At last Charles reverted to English. 'You are right. It will be helpful if we, as you say, clear the air. My name is Charles Lebec; not Dubec, Lebec—a small deception. This is my father, Denis Lebec and our friend Edgar Robert. Apart from Conrad in London, we are all that is left of what we call the Brotherhood.'

# II

## ANNÉES SECRÈTES

A picture dies after a few years like the man who painted it. Afterwards, it's called the history of art.

—Marcel Duchamp

# CHAPTER 10

Aristide's restoration to full health was a slow business. Even when the exploding fireworks behind his closed lids had subsided and he had successfully sewn together most of the shreds of memory, there were still days when his head felt as though it was clamped in a vice and nights when he spent sweating hours in a vain quest for the few missing patches of his past life, one in particular that he longed and yet dreaded to discover.

Not that he had anything to complain of about his new existence. At Mas Maraques he was treated as a hero. The sprawling farmstead deep in the Carmague occupied a position where arable land, marsh and lake were often indistinguishable. The fields of summer grazing where horses and bulls were corralled and the womenfolk grew vegetables lay under water every time the Rhône and the Petit Rhône burst from their ill-defined channels. These visitations left fresh, welcome layers of silt over the meadows but made it impossible for all but a few score families to live a settled life. Theirs was a tough, introverted subsistence, their isolation reinforced by their own, very localised patois, their unremitting feud with *les intrus*—a term embracing all outsiders from sheep farmers to town dwellers who invaded their watery kingdom to shoot and fish—and an especial loathing of all government officials, who seemed to labour under the delusion that the Camargue was a part of France.

A few seconds of spontaneous bravery had lifted Aristide out of the ranks of the strangers, whose lot it was to be permanently treated with suspicion. In the uncomplicated Camarguais code 'a life for a life' had a positive as well as negative connotation. Aristide's intervention had preserved Jean-Marc Bardol from being killed or—equally disastrous for his community—crippled. It followed that Aristide's life must be preserved and enhanced to the best of his hosts' capacity. Jean-Marc's survival was particularly important since he was, potentially, the head of the family. He and his sister, Yvette, had been orphaned three years before. A sudden mistral had overturned their father's fishing boat on the *étang* and on receiving the news of the tragic accident their heavily-pregnant mother had gone into premature labour which neither she nor the baby had survived. It was then that Aunt Lou, their father's unmarried sister, had accepted responsibility for her nephew and niece.

Aristide soon discovered that she was as formidable as she was kind as she was wise. There was nothing matriarchal about Camarguais society—it was very much a man's world—but no one at Mas Maraques would have dreamed of contradicting Aunt Lou or going against her wishes. She was the only literate member of the little community. Having been as a girl untroubled by suitors, she had devoted herself to study. The breadth of her self-taught knowledge was amazing—or at least it amazed everyone in her small, intimate circle. In addition to book learning she was the repository of the community's folklore and possessed a considerable knowledge of simples and herbal remedies. During Aristide's bed-ridden days at the *mas* she put in frequent appearances, watching over her patient with keen eyes deep-set in a weathered face. It was Aunt Lou who posed the searching questions designed to help the patient re-establish contact with his identity—or, perhaps, to add to the store of information upon which her own authority rested. Yet, as Aristide's faculties returned, the old woman delegated most of the nursing to Yvette, wisely reasoning that the presence of a beautiful creature just breaking out from the shell of uncertain adolescence would have a valued restorative affect all of its own.

Yvette became Aristide's tutor in all things Carmaguais. With her help he gradually learned the dialect of the region, came to know the other members of the community and to understand the workings of their common life. Three other families shared the *mas* with the Bardols—the Roberts, the Simiers and the Lebecs. The total population was twenty-one—soon to become twenty-two if all went well with the fecund Elisabeth Simier. Madeleine Robert, forty-five and embittered, envied her neighbour the unruly brood of children. Only one of her offspring, the gangling François, had survived infancy. It was to this scion of the Robert dynasty that Yvette was pledged. Aristide thought it strange, given their 'understanding', that the two young people spent little time together. He taxed her about this as they sat one steamy June afternoon on the rickety jetty which reached out into the lagoon, dangling their feet in the water.

'Is it different, then, between men and women where you come from?' Yvette tugged off her lace cap and let it fall on the rough boards. 'What do they do?'

Aristide described the promenade in the Bois—men and women, arms linked, exchanging glances beneath fringed parasols

—the visits to the theatre and the opera, the balls, the stolen moments on balconies. Yet again, he wondered why such half-memories brought pain.

'We have dances. Are yours like ours?' Her wide eyes glowed with enthusiasm.

Aristide laughed. 'I doubt that very much.'

'You don't know. You haven't seen. There'll be dancing soon at cock-killing. You'll enjoy that.'

'Cock-killing?'

'When the last mare has foaled we kill a cock and have a party. It's a thanksgiving and celebration in one.'

'Who do you sacrifice this poor bird to?'

Yvette tossed her head impatiently. 'I don't know. You'll have to ask Aunt Lou. Oh, I feel so drowsy.' She stretched her arms above her head. The black dress, a touch too small, stretched tight across her upper body.

Aristide jumped to his feet and moved away a few paces. 'Can you stay like that for a moment?' He pulled his sketchpad and a stick of charcoal from his satchel.

She smiled at him languidly and kept her arms raised. 'Why do you keep on drawing me, Aristide?'

'Because you're beautiful.'

'And the boys? Do you draw them

because they're beautiful, too?'

He grinned. 'Well...yes. In a different way, of course.'

Jean-Marc and his friends had attached themselves firmly to the novelty in their midst. They had become Aristide's virtual disciples, gathering around him at every opportunity when they weren't watching over the animals, carrying feed, leading the horses to water, immersing hides in brine, stretching them on the curing frames or performing menial tasks about the *mas*. This god who had come into their humdrum lives from some exciting, far-distant Olympus was possessed of all kinds of magic. They were astonished at his skill with pencil and brush. They clamoured to have Aristide draw and paint their likeness. They sat for hours while he relayed to them stories about military exploits in distant lands culled from the mythology of his regiment. But what above all earned their admiration was his prowess as a horseman. As soon as he was active, Aristide had offered to help with breaking the colts, rounding up the bulls for branding, and herding the untamed animals. Even the most experienced *gardians,* as the Camargue herdsmen were called, acknowledged Aristide as their equal.

The newcomer's varied skills did not

endear him to all the inhabitants of Mas Maraques. Madeleine Robert, whose mind was well trained to distinguish the worst in everyone, cast Aristide in the rôle of a rival to her son for Yvette's affections. Since she was the dominant member of her household, her husband dared not show any favour to the mysterious stranger. A few of the other men were wary of someone they had neither the wit nor the will to try to understand. But one fact outweighed all jealousies and misgivings: Aunt Lou had thrown her protective mantle around Aristide Bertrand. That being the case, no man's hand or voice would be openly raised against him.

The boys, of course, sensed these undercurrents of disapproval and mis-understanding—and were, as a result, even more possessive of their hero. There were five members of the gang. Jean-Marc, though the youngest, was the liveliest and most innovative. He was the one the others looked to to dream up pranks and exploits. These children of the Camargue knew no childhood in the conventional sense of the word. From their earliest years they were involved in the day-to-day work of the *mas*. Their 'games' were extensions of their labours—racing the horses, running the bull calves, walking the ridge of the big barn for a dare. Paul Lebec, at thirteen already tall and serious as befitted the elder of five siblings, was the acknowledged leader of the group, his quick temper and hard knuckles effective deterrents against mutiny. He feared no challenge from the Simier twins, Gaston and Philippe. The sandy-haired, genial pair were Paul's elders by some six months but were too good-natured and easy-going to assert any authority based on age.

The fifth member of the gang was Yvette. Mortality had removed from the *mas* community any other girls of a similar age and she had gravitated naturally towards her brother and his companions. She had helped to nurse them when they were babies and she little more. She had watched over them when they were vulnerable toddlers whose parents were often occupied elsewhere. She had become their confidante and playmate, running and tumbling with them throughout the pre-pubescent years, and when her body had begun sending out ever stronger hints about the need for a changed relationship her mind was reluctant to respond. She no longer swam naked with the boys from the jetty or relished the thrill of their dangerous games with the animals, but the ties which bound her to them were still strong.

In fact, though neither her nor the young people realised it, Aristide's appearance at the *mas* had given the little group a new cohesion at the very moment when, in the normal course of events, it was breaking up. Unconsciously, Yvette and the boys clung to the newcomer because he reinforced a communal identity they were afraid of losing. Aristide responded to their admiration and loyalty. His painting took on a new confidence. Not only were his devotees eager models, they were also unsophisticated critics. Having no preconceived ideas about what art 'ought' to be, they listened without prejudice to his ideas, asked questions which were no less intelligent for being naïve and offered frank opinions which not infrequently helped him to find his way through problems.

One afternoon, Aristide set up his easel in a corner of the *mas* yard. He laid out a limited palette—cadmium, white, carmine and sienna—and concentrated with sweating intensity to convey onto canvas the blindingly vivid intensity of light on plastered walls, throbbing earth and an assemblage of tools, jars and buckets he had arranged on a bench.

Yvette came barefoot from the kitchen and sat beside him. After a few moments watching him work and receiving mono-syllabic replies to her attempts at con-versation, she rummaged in Aristide's knapsack. There were three books among the painter's few possessions, at least one of which he often had with him when he was working. Yvette slipped out a well-worn volume entitled *Italian Masters* and began idly looking through the coloured plates. She stopped at one picture, stared hard for a few seconds, then held it up to Aristide, giggling. 'Was this painted to hang on someone's wall—for everyone to see?'

Aristide glanced briefly at a reproduction of Titian's *Danaë*. 'Yes, I suppose so. Why?'

Yvette appraised the dolorous, reclining nude watched by a nonchalant cupid. 'Do all the ladies in Paris have their pictures painted like that?'

'No, not all.' Aristide, struggling to combine his pigments to match an elusive shadow tone that deepened by the minute, was too engrossed to explain that Titian's model was an Italian woman who lived three hundred years ago.

Yvette continued to stare at the picture. 'Do you know her?'

'No, of course not.'

'Do you think she's beautiful?'

'The man who painted her did. And he's enabled us to see her through his eyes.'

'Is she as beautiful as me?'

He looked at her briefly. 'Yvette, please. I'm trying to concentrate.'

She scowled at him, shut the book with

a snap and thrust it untidily back into his bag. A few moments later she walked back across the yard, singing a song, deliberately emphasising the high notes.

As the summer and the autumn of 1888 passed, Aristide discovered a freedom and an excitement in his art that he had never known. There were days when he worked frenziedly. The life of the *étang* and its borders fascinated him. Reeds, marsh flowers, waterfowl, bulls, horses, the men and women who strove to survive in this Spartan environment—there was so much to set down, to record, to respond to in terms of paint, pencil or chalk. Absorbed in his new life, sustained by his new friends, Aristide gradually abandoned the quest for the tragedy and unhappiness he believed to lie beneath the black waters of his unconscious. But they had not ceased to exist.

And in the world outside the Camargue there were those who had by no means abandoned the search for Albert de Bracieux, the murderer.

Three surprises, varying in their degrees of unpleasantness, awaited Tim when he returned to the hotel.

He had a faint premonition of things to come when he collected his key. The clerk handed it over wordlessly then turned abruptly to enter the manager's office. While Tim waited for the lift he looked back and saw both men staring at him with frowning disapproval.

Two messages awaited him in his room. The first was from Catherine—short, to-the-point and infuriating, even when rendered into English by someone with an incomplete grasp of idiom.

'I will come to you about midnight. I could not speak with you or Emma by telephone. George was evasive. Something smells of fish. Love. Catherine.'

If that was alarming, the note from George was even more so.

8.07 a.m. Major, just after you had gone I had a call from someone who says he has got Emma. I don't know whether he has got anything to do with the lot you have gone off to see. Presumably not. He is coming here to meet me at midday. I don't know what is going on but suppose I will have to go along with this bloke and find out what he knows. If I am not around when you get back I will be in touch a.s.a.p. Hope one of us gets to the bottom of this. Regards. George Martin.

Tim strode along the corridor and knocked on his colleague's door. There was no answer. Back in his own room Tim peeled off his clothes and took a shower. As the hot water eased his body he forced his mind to take in yet another twist in the turn of events. George's news, he realised, was both good and bad. The real kidnapper had, it seemed, been in touch. That was a relief after the wild goose chase that had taken Tim to Tarascon. If 'Charles Dubec' was talking to George it was presumably to discuss terms for Emma's release. At least Tim would know the score. Would know whether he was dealing with a French mafia faction or a bunch of amateurs. The flip side was that now George was in the criminals' hands, too. Tim stepped out of the shower and reached for a towel. That was the moment of the third surprise.

There was a knock at the door—firm, authoritative. Tim swathed his lower body in pink towelling and went to answer. Two grey-suited young men moved forward as soon as the door opened. Tim groaned. Policemen were the same in any language.

The taller of the two held up an identification card. 'Inspector Picart, Lyon Sûreté. Please, you will accompany us to headquarters.'

Argument would be futile. Tim dressed, unhurriedly, and went with the Frenchmen to their car. Minutes later, he was shown into an office in the gendarmerie close to the Gare de Perrache. The room had one occupant.

He swivelled his chair to face the door. 'Well, well, Mr Lacy, fancy meeting you here.'

'Good evening, Inspector Edgerson. If you observe that it's a small world I shall inflict serious injury upon your person.'

'Nothing was further from my thoughts, I assure you. I've no doubt about what brings you to Lyon. My only question is, Why? Merci, Jacques.' He smiled at the French officer. 'Puis-je prêter votre bureau pendant quelque temps?' When the others had withdrawn he waved Tim to a chair. 'Obliging chap. Perhaps there's something to this EU thing, after all.'

'Could we get to the point?'

'I very much hope so, sir, but that rather depends on you.' His tone sharpened abruptly. 'Right, for starters perhaps you'd tell me what you were doing on the night of the seventeenth.'

Tim stared at the policeman incredulously. 'The night of Jollibone's murder? You're not seriously suggesting...?' Meeting Edgerson's stolid gaze, he abandoned the protest. He took out his diary. 'The seventeenth? Ah yes, here we are. I was in Manchester most of the day, got back home soon after six and had to change hurriedly to drive to Salisbury. We were attending a charity dinner in aid of the Wessex Fine Arts Fund.'

'We?'

'My wife and I and some friends. We made up a party of eight. It was one of those dos where you're expected to fill a table.'

'And you could give us the names and addresses of your friends?' If Edgerson was disappointed he did not show it.

'If it's really necessary, yes.'

'And it was while you were getting ready to go out that this Jollibone character phoned Mrs Lacy?'

'Yes, Inspector, as she mentioned in her statement. He called just before seven. He only just caught us.'

The policeman nodded gravely. 'That tallies with the hotel switchboard's records.'

'Oh, you've found out where he was staying, then?'

Edgerson ignored the question. 'They logged a call to your number at 6.51. That tells us *when* he phoned but, of course, it doesn't tell us *what* the conversation was about. We only have Mrs Lacy's word for that. But let that ride. What time did this function of yours end?'

'Officially around eleven but people tended to hang about quite a while afterwards. You know what these events are like.'

'And you and your wife were there all evening?'

Tim's exasperation got the better of him. 'Oh, no, Inspector. We slipped out after the dessert, popped up to London, murdered a foreign visitor, dumped his body in the Thames and drove back to Salisbury just in time for the cheese board.'

Edgerson restrained himself with difficulty. 'I haven't travelled all the way here, Mr Lacy, to listen to your feeble attempts at sarcasm. If you wouldn't mind confining yourself to answering questions. Now, I need to know Miss Kerr's movements for the critical time. I gather she's with you in Lyon but she's not at the hotel. Do you know where I can find her?'

Tim tried to divert attention from that question. 'If it's a matter of an alibi I can help you. Miss Kerr was with us in Salisbury that evening.'

The policeman swivelled his chair around —a movement he seemed to enjoy. 'OK, we'll leave that for the moment. Would you mind telling me what the two of you are doing in Lyon?'

'You just said you knew, Inspector.'

'Confirm my suspicions.'

Tim looked Edgerson in the eyes. 'I came to Lyon for a chat with my friend and your colleague, Bob Stonor.'

'At Interpol!' The reply shook the inspector. 'How do you know him?'

'I know quite a few people in the Met. Try asking your Fine Art Squad. Dick Pratchet or Jock Armstrong will give you all the lowdown you need.'

'Tossing names around doesn't impress me, Mr Lacy—not when I'm on a murder inquiry. Your wife told us a very odd story about someone impersonating the late M. Jollibone, art dealer of Lyon.'

'A story which she volunteered, as a good citizen, entirely on her own initiative.'

'A story she was unable to corroborate and for which we have been able to discover no evidence.'

Tim scowled. 'I don't like the drift of this conversation. Are you still suggesting that my wife was somehow implicated in Jollibone's death?'

Edgerson continued levelly. 'Yesterday I called your place in Wiltshire, to ask you and your associates some more questions. No one was available but your secretary let slip that you and Miss Kerr were in France. That seemed a bit of a coincidence to me. So I had mes amis here in Lyon to do a bit of checking around the hotels. And what did they discover? That the two of you were tucked up in the Cour des Loges, just along the street from the late lamented's gallery. Now, I wouldn't be much good at my job if I didn't follow up something pretty suspicious like that, would I? So I want to find out—from both of you—exactly what you're doing here. Where is Miss Kerr, by the way?'

Tim's mental cogs were whirring at speed. What could he say? How much could he get away with not saying? With Emma—and now possibly George—in the hands of unscrupulous men, the last thing he wanted was the police blundering about. Then there was Labardie. If the mobster was having him watched, which Tim had no reason to doubt, he could not but be alarmed at the news that, within hours of their meeting, Tim was at Sûreté HQ.

He affected a nonchalant smile. 'I see now why you're so concerned, Inspector. Miss Kerr is here to see some of our French clients. She's visiting various collectors and dealers over quite a wide area.'

'She hasn't booked out of the hotel.'

'She's doubtless planning to return here in a day or two.'

'You don't sound very sure.'

'Emma plans her own itinerary.'

'Seems to me she's being pretty profligate with the firm's money. Can Lacy Enterprises afford to foot the bill for unoccupied hotel rooms?'

'We encourage staff initiative.'

'Do you take me for an idiot?' Edgerson's

voice rose in pitch and volume. 'I haven't come all the way here to be fobbed off with answers that wouldn't fool the greenest rookie out of Hendon. A man's been killed and some valuable paintings have gone missing. Either you and your sidekick know where those paintings are or you've come searching for them. If it's the first, then, at the very least, you're looking at a conspiracy charge. If it's the second I'll have you for withholding evidence.'

Tim decided to try another tack. 'You're right, of course. I should have known better than to pit my wits against a university man.'

'Watch it, Lacy!'

'Yes, we are on the track of a valuable cache of paintings. It seems to us that the pictures my wife and Miss Kerr were shown are almost certainly in the hands of criminals. Jollibone's murder confirms as much. Now, I have certain contacts in the world of fine art crime—on both sides of the law. I thought I might be able to get some useful leads to pass on to you. That's why I wanted to see Bob Stonor, among others.'

Edgerson watched him closely. 'You expect me to believe that you've got nothing better to do than interfere with police business?'

'Some of your colleagues have been

quite glad of my interference in the past. But don't take my word for it. Ask Jock Armstrong to tell you how the silver stolen from the Henty Museum was located. I understand he got his last promotion largely on the strength of that case. Of course, I know that officers have their own ways of working. If you want to warn me off I shall quite understand. As you suggest, I have got plenty of other things to do.'

Edgerson stared back in silence for some moments. 'You still haven't explained where Miss Kerr fits into all this.'

'She really is away in the country somewhere meeting with clients. I'm afraid I don't know her exact whereabouts, but as soon as she makes contact I'll certainly tell her to call you.'

Edgerson was not so stupid that he could not see the corner he was being edged towards. 'Very clever, Mr Lacy. But you don't seriously expect me to believe that you and Miss Kerr just happen to be in Lyon on quite different business.'

Tim looked rueful. 'No, Inspector. You've shattered that rather pathetic subterfuge. Let me be quite frank with you. Emma is very new to the firm. She's still on probation—not ready to handle business single-handedly. I wanted an opportunity to introduce her to some of our French clients. Then, when this Jollibone business cropped up I thought I'd do a bit of ferreting around... Very wrong of me I know, but, as I say, I have been able to help with these sorts of enquiries in the past. So I decided to kill two birds with one stone. Emma went to talk to Mme Tarantin. A waste of time, I'm afraid. Then I sent her off on a little tour of business contacts while I went to see Bob. I thought Interpol might have got wind of these mysterious paintings. Some of them are bound to surface somewhere—offered to collectors or dealers. Unfortunately, Bob had no useful information on this particular cache. There you have it. I'm sorry we've caused you so much bother. How's your enquiry going?'

Edgerson swung the chair round again. 'I'm following up several leads over here.'

Tim thought, In other words, you're floundering. He said, 'Well, best of luck. With the help of your French colleagues I'm sure you'll crack it.'

'How much longer are you planning to spend in Lyon, Mr Lacy?'

'Oh, we'll be on our way home in a couple of days.'

'Well, I still want to talk to Miss Kerr.'

'I'll have her phone you as soon as I see her.'

'No need, Mr Lacy. We'll know when she gets back to the hotel.' He waved a hand and turned his chair to face the opposite wall. The interview was obviously over.

At about the time that Tim was being grilled by DI Edgerson, an extraordinary discussion was in progress in an isolated thatched hut some three hundred kilometres to the south. George and Emma had listened enthralled to Charles Lebec as he told the story of Aristide Bertrand, his paintings and the Brotherhood. The narrative concluded with an account of the Lebecs' movements on the night of Jollibone's death, which tallied with what Charles had already told Emma. The light from the suspended storm torch illumined the circle of intense faces as the prisoners and their captors debated the implications. It was a slow business. Charles had to act as interpreter for his father and Edgar, and then translate the elder Lebec's excited dialect responses for the English couple.

George was sceptical about the proffered account of the Lyon dealer's death and the Lebecs' innocence. His only concern was to get Emma out of their clutches. Emma found her own attitude changing. Her growing familiarity with her kidnappers, the comforting presence of her burly

222

colleague and the story she had just heard—surely too detailed and fantastic to have been made up—aroused in her a growing sympathy with the Frenchman's predicament. 'I think they're telling the truth,' she muttered.

George's only response was a non-committal shrug. He assumed the certainty and authority which came naturally from his military training and spoke firmly to Charles Lebec. 'Snatching Miss Kerr and keeping her here against her will is not the sort of behaviour that will convince the police you didn't murder Jollibone.'

Charles nodded gloomily. 'It was a mistake, an impulse. When you both turned up at Jollibone's gallery I panicked. I had to find out what you were doing there and whether you recognised me.'

'Seems to me you've panicked all the way along the line. That was a crazy stunt, dumping old Jollibone in the river.'

'We did not know he would be found so soon. We thought, perhaps, he might never be found.'

'Well, your only hope now is to release Miss Kerr, go to the police and make a clean breast of it. Tell you what, so that it will be easier for you, we'll say nothing about Miss Kerr's abduction.'

Lebec père interposed. 'You think your English police will believe my sons? I tell you what they will say: "Jollibone was French! The Lebecs are French! So they must have done it!" '

Charles relayed the complaint. 'There is a lot of truth in what my father says.'

'But how is holding Miss Kerr against her will going to help?' George kept his voice low, level and, he hoped, soothing.

Edgar put in a surprise contribution, translated by Charles. 'She is our insurance policy. The police cannot arrest us while we have her. If they do, we will not tell them where she is. It would take them weeks to find her unaided, and by that time...'

Emma tried to move the conversation forward. 'Look, what you're proposing is a stalemate—'

Charles shrugged. 'A stalemate is better than a lost game—especially if the penalty is life imprisonment. We are playing for our continued freedom.'

Emma persisted. 'What I was going to say was that it's a stalemate but one that can't go on for ever. If you face the police now and tell them your story—'

'They will lock us up and congratulate themselves on a case solved. I know how the police work; what matters is getting a conviction, not finding the truth.'

'Oh, do stop interrupting, Charles!' Emma shouted. 'I'm trying to help. I believe your story. I'll support you. So will George.'

Denis Lebec would have nothing of that suggestion, as Charles explained. 'My father says you are only saying that in order to escape.'

Emma glared at the old man, matching his stubborn anger with her own. 'Oh, you... This isn't getting us anywhere!'

George reintroduced a note of calm. 'Look, gentlemen, let's face facts. In a few days Emma's family and friends are going to start getting worried about her. She'll be reported missing and the search will start in Lyon.'

Edgar blurted out, 'But no one will be able to trace her to us. You're the only other person who knows about us—and you're here.'

George produced his ace slowly and deliberately. 'That's where you're wrong. Mr Lacy arrived in Lyon yesterday and I gave him a full report, including our bumping into you in Jollibone's gallery. So you see, the police will very quickly get on to Mme Tarantin. They'll grill her and you can bet your life she's not going to protect your identity—not when she's facing a charge of conspiracy to abduction and murder.'

That made the sparks fly. As soon as Charles relayed the message, the shouting and gesticulating began again. George let the argument run for a couple of minutes, then called out, 'Stop!' The three Frenchmen turned to face him, angry, bewildered, but mainly, as George could see, frightened.

When he had their attention he said, 'There's only one sure way out of this—for all of us.' He paused while the younger Lebec translated. 'Charles, if neither you nor your brother knifed Jollibone, someone else did. If we can find out who, then you're off the hook.'

The old man growled his scepticism. 'How can we do that? Are we police?'

'We could be the next best thing. Whoever killed Jollibone must have been after the Bertrand paintings. Now, the Major—Mr Lacy—has something of a reputation for tracking down villains in the art world. I believe that, in return for Miss Kerr's freedom, he would agree to help you find the murderer. Believe me, he can get to places where the cops can't and talk to people who'd run a mile from a blue uniform.'

Charles scoffed. 'Oh yes, Mr Martin? We release you and Miss Kerr and you run straight to the nearest gendarmerie.'

'No! George is right!' Emma jumped up and stood in the centre of the room. 'If anyone can get to the bottom of this, it's

Tim Lacy. I know he will help you.'

The captors stared at her dubiously, then went into a huddle.

Charles conveyed their decision. 'If what you say about Mr Lacy is true we will co-operate with him. If someone ruthless enough to kill is after our property we cannot be safe, or do anything about selling the paintings, until he is behind bars. I will go to Lyon and talk to Mr Lacy. But Miss Kerr stays here.'

George shook his head emphatically. 'No deal. Either Emma and I leave tonight or you take your chances with the police.'

'Non! Impossible!' Denis and Edgar shouted their rejection.

As all the men glowered at each other it was Emma who broke the silence. 'OK, I'll stay—of my own free will. But not as a prisoner in this hovel. Somewhere more comfortable, as your guest.'

George shook his head. 'That's not a good idea. I can't walk away and leave you here. Anyway, it could take weeks—months—to get to the bottom of this business.'

'Somewhere along the line, someone has to start trusting, George.' Emma returned to her seat on the bed. 'It was my idea to get involved in the first place. I guess it's up to me, to see it through.'

After another half hour, most of which

he spent in fruitless argument, George allowed himself to be blindfolded again and led away on horseback through the marsh.

He did not relish having to make his report to the Major.

# CHAPTER 11

In 1889 the men of Mas Maraques won their long war with the shepherds. The spring of that year was mercilessly dry. The Rhône stayed within bounds, its channels defended with an ever-extending system of earthworks built to government order in the name of progress. By early May the pastures bordering the marshlands were parched and fissured. The foraging horses and wild cattle spread over an ever-widening area, and where they went the *gardians* followed. During the foaling season several mares died, lacking the strength to give birth. More perished in the ensuing weeks, literally sucked dry by their offspring. When the sheep folk arrived, driving their flocks onto the overburdened meadowland, the usual skirmishes broke out, but this time the situation was more desperate. This time all the combatants knew that they were engaged in a fight to the death.

One evening a meeting was called. The Mas Maraques *gardians* rode over to a neighbouring farmstead and joined more than a hundred men from all over the region. The audience stood or sat in semi-circular ranks facing a waggon from which their leaders tried to keep order. It was a chaotic, ill-disciplined assembly. Much as the conveners tried to follow an agenda, proceedings were constantly interrupted by outraged herdsmen relating the provocation they had endured from *les intrus,* and others angrily demanding 'action' they were unable to specify. 'We must work together,' someone urged to a shout of approval. 'Yes, but what are we going to do?' a voice from the back called out. Another added 'We need a plan—a campaign.'

It was then that one of the Simier men stood up—the twins' uncle, a rangy figure in a much-patched shirt. 'We've got someone here who can draw up a plan. He's a military man. He knows all about campaigns and great victories.' He turned to the row behind and hauled Aristide to his feet. 'You tell them,' Simier urged, 'like you tell the boys.'

There was a murmur of laughter. A fat man spat tobacco juice between blackened

229

teeth. 'Why, it's that artist fellow. What does he want us to do—hack the sheepmen to pieces with paintbrushes?'

Aristide looked around bewildered. He would have sat down again, speechless and embarrassed, if the self-appointed chairman, clutching at straws, had not called out, 'Shut up, Leo! If you've got nothing useful to say let's listen to the artist.' He smiled down at Aristide from the cart. 'M. Bertrand, isn't it? Well, can you help us?'

'Well...I...' Aristide floundered for words. He gazed over the heads of the rough herdsmen. Sitting on the ridge of a small shed were four smaller figures, watching him intently. Watching their hero. Willing him to seize his moment of glory. Jean-Marc waved. Aristide returned his attention to the immediate audience. 'Well, we won't get rid of the sheepmen if we just go on fighting them whenever they appear. Defensive action doesn't win wars. We ought to take the battle to them. The first thing we need to know is the enemy's weak points. That means reconnaissance...'

The words and ideas tumbled out in an enthusiastic yet coherent stream. Aristide was surprised. Part of his mind seemed to be detached. He heard himself speaking with confident authority, repeating principles of strategy and tactics learned at St

Cyr and retelling stories of past campaigns. He watched his audience fall under the spell of this unaccustomed oratory. The restlessness, the private conversations, the shouted ribaldry were gone within less than a minute. Aristide surveyed, as through a stranger's eyes, rows of absorbed and increasingly eager faces. When he concluded his address by stressing the importance of a sound command structure, men responded immediately, putting forward names of those best suited to fill certain positions. Someone proposed that he should assume overall command and several voices were raised in support.

The idea appalled him. Giving something back to these people who had welcomed him into their midst, contributing his experience, advising them in their desperate struggle for survival—that was one thing. Riding into battle at their head—that was another. Aristide was not a man of action. And there was something deep inside him that repelled even the thought of violence. That was—he supposed, for he could not remember—why he had left the army to take up the life of a struggling artist. He was an observer, a recorder, a lover of the world; not one of its prime movers.

He held up a hand. 'No, my friends. You have your own natural leaders: men

231

you look up to; men who know you; men familiar with every hectare of the terrain you must fight over. These are vital qualities in the cool of the strategy meeting and in the heat of the battle. You must choose not an *intru,* like myself, but someone you trust implicitly and will follow without question. You may, of course, count on me for any support I can give.' He sat down to a hail of cheers and applause and noticed as he did so that his limbs were trembling and the sweat was pouring from his brow.

Over the next couple of weeks the herdsmen became an organised cavalry corps. They met most days for an hour's training in formation drill. Being superb horsemen accustomed to riding in groups to move the bulls from place to place, they assimilated the manoeuvres very quickly. At the same time they carefully monitored the movements of their adversaries. Aristide drew a map and helped the 'officers' to read it and use it in working out their strategy. They looked to him to work out every tactical detail but he refused to be responsible for drawing up the battle plan, preferring to nudge them towards their own decisions.

For Aristide these were only interludes, interruptions in the serious business of painting. He spent most of his days not only sketching and producing finished pictures, but also making up canvases. His belongings, including a dozen or so prepared surfaces and some rolls of material, had come with him from Arles, but they were inadequate for his surge of creativity. When waggons were going to St Gilles, Arles or Les Saintes Maries de la Mer for market he took the opportunity to replenish stocks, but his limited resources did not keep pace with his output. He was obliged to make up frames from scrap wood and beg old shirts and even discarded sacking to cover them. Even so, he not infrequently over-painted earlier subjects.

That spring the womenfolk of the *mas* journeyed more frequently than usual to the nearer towns. Mortality among the animals and the need to augment basic income had led to an increase in the production of leather goods. Mas Maraques had to take every opportunity to sell its bridles, saddles, harnesses, boots, belts and other goods.

An hour before dawn on a Thursday morning at the end of May found Aristide loading one of the two waggons setting out for Les Saintes Maries. He carefully stacked a few finished paintings. Wealthy people came with their yachts to the coast town and often stopped for provisions and sightseeing. There was always the possibility of a sale. Les Saintes Maries would, in fact, be even more crowded than usual. This was pilgrimage time, when the bedecked images of three female saints, whose boat had been miraculously wafted from Jerusalem to the French coast, were paraded through the town. Normally it was a holiday for everyone at Mas Maraques, but today the men would be riding eastwards along the fringe of the *étang* for their confrontation with the shepherds. Even as the women prepared for their journey to market their husbands and brothers were saddling horses and checking their assortment of weapons.

Pierre Lebec, young Paul's burly, bearded father, crossed the yard to speak to Aristide. 'You're determined, then, not to ride with us?'

The artist fastened the waggon's rear flap. 'You don't need any more men, Pierre. You outnumber the enemy and you have the advantage of surprise. It will be over very quickly, probably with no fighting at all.'

The older man tilted his wide-brimmed hat. 'Some of us would feel happier if you were there. Supposing something goes wrong and we need to make quick decisions?'

'You have the trumpet calls I taught old Esmé—advance, retire, regroup. As long as every man keeps his head and you act together on the signals there's no reason why anything should go wrong.'

'Why won't you come? Some of the men from the other farms say you're an armchair general, afraid to get hurt.'

Aristide shrugged. 'Perhaps they are right. All I can tell you is what you already know: I was once a soldier but now I am a painter. I can't remember why I changed. I only know that I did—and that I've no desire to return to a military life.' He walked along the side of the cart and climbed to the driver's seat. 'Good luck, my friend. Tonight you can tell me all about your success.'

The open area around the great battlemented fortress church was already bustling with people when Aristide and the women set up their pitch in the shadow of the *campanile*. The square and the narrow streets leading from it steadily filled with people. Pilgrims and visitors drifted past the Mas Maraques stall. Several stopped to admire the craftsmanship of the leatherwork. Some peered with curiosity at Aristide's pictures. A few bought trinkets. By mid-morning, Aristide was bored and restless; he picked up his paintbox and a blank canvas and shambled away from the crowds.

He wandered onto the beach. In the

curve of a rugged groin the grey sand had banked up. Some children were playing with a dog at the water's edge. Aristide pulled out his sketchpad and charcoal. He filled several pages with his own pictorial shorthand. Rapidly he felt excitement welling up inside—the excitement that only came when he knew he could capture something and release it into pigment. He unfolded his easel, clamped the canvas onto it, assembled his palette and rushed his brushes through the splashes of colour.

He was unaware of time, except as a force which constantly moved, intensified or softened areas of light and shadow. He knew that people on the promenade behind him occasionally stopped to gaze at his work. He half-heard the flippant comments some exchanged before resuming their progress. He never turned to look at them. Neither they nor their opinions were of any interest. So there was no obvious reason why a stifled gasp should have distracted him; why he should have lowered his brush and spun around. But he did.

The woman who stared back at him was beautiful. She was dressed in palest yellow which emphasised her dark hair and she carried a matching parasol: a wealthy society lady. For what seemed minutes she stared at Aristide, eyes and

236

mouth wide with horrified disbelief. Then she sagged and fell back in a faint. The tall, moustached man who accompanied the woman half-caught her and laid her gently on the ground. He began patting first her cheek, then the backs of her hands. He called in an effort to rouse her, 'Eloise! Eloise, dearest! What is it? What's the matter?'

Aristide watched the little drama motionless, his feet seeming to have taken root in the sand.

The woman began to moan and move her head.

Aristide leaped backward, knocking over the easel. He turned and ran wildly along the beach leaving the unfinished painting behind him.

George walked straight in on a marital row. When Charles Lebec dropped him back at the hotel at half-past midnight he made straight for Tim's room. As he raised a hand to knock on the door he was aware of angry voices. He hammered loudly in order to make himself heard.

Tim yanked open the door, still shouting over his shoulder. 'Don't be stupid! Of course I know you're worried, too! But that's no excuse—George!'

George walked quickly into the room. He saw his boss in shirtsleeves, neck open, tie loose, hair tousled. Catherine Lacy, by contrast, sat rigid and crisply immaculate, as though sculpted in ice.

Seeing George, however, she threw composure aside and jumped from her armchair. 'Have you seen Emma? How is she? Where is she?'

Tim was also firing off questions. 'Who is this Dubec character? What does he want? What the hell's going on?'

George held up his hands. He sat down on the end of the bed. 'I've seen Emma. She's OK. Exactly what she's mixed up in is going to take a long time to explain. First, I could do with something to eat. Oh, and the people who've got her are called Lebec, not Dubec.'

Tim phoned room service and ordered coffee and sandwiches. He sat down in the other armchair and Catherine also resumed her seat. The Lacys knew their friend well enough to realise that, if he was allowed to report in his own way, he would do so clearly and without omitting any important detail.

He embarked on his story, paused to fortify himself when the food arrived, and concluded his narrative shortly before two a.m. Finally he pulled an envelope from his pocket. It was bulky and not properly fastened down. The address had been crossed out and 'Tim and Catherine'

238

scrawled along the top. 'Emma made some notes. She thought they might be helpful.'

Catherine removed the contents of the envelope—a scrap of glossy paper obviously torn from a magazine and an old diary in which several pages had been covered with cramped writing. She read the separate note aloud: 'Dear Tim and Catherine, What can I say? I know you'll be worried sick and I'm so sorry I screwed up. Try not to worry too much about me. These characters are probably as scared as I am. Perhaps more. They are looking after me as well as they can. I've seen the Bertrands and they are fabulous. I've written some notes on the story Charles Lebec told me about them. Pretty amazing! Seems this "Brotherhood" really has looked after them for a hundred years. Charles showed me a genealogical plan of all the members and I've done a copy. This will all make a great story when we come to do the exhibition catalogue, Catherine. Gulp!—almost out of paper. These guys are...'

The writing got smaller and turned to run along the side of the paper. Catherine squinted to read the last words: 'a bit weird but *innocent*. Try to prove it PLEASE! Don't say anything to my Ma. Love Emma.'

Catherine looked up. 'How much more

can she take, George?'

'She's coping. It took enormous guts to volunteer to stay and it was a smart move. She assessed the situation quicker than I did. She knew we had no real choice, but instead of going all weepy and pleading with them to let her go she took the initiative. That impressed the kidnappers.'

Tim looked anxiously at his colleague. 'OK, George, let's have it straight. What are her chances? What sort of men are we dealing with?'

'Well, Major, they're amateurs and they're divided among themselves. That makes it pretty difficult to know how they'll react. The old boy exerts a lot of authority. He's a real peasant type. Spent all his life among those Godforsaken swamps. Knows little about the real world and cares less. I wouldn't put anything past him. The other one—I call him The Hulk—is probably much the same. Emma reckons he's a bit simple. He certainly goes along with what old Lebec says. Young Emma, of course, reckons she can handle them, but I shan't be happy till she's well away from there.'

'And she's not going to get away unless we can prove they didn't murder Jollibone—great!' Tim rubbed tired eyes. 'Well, I suppose the first question is, Did they? Any ideas on that one, George?'

'The case against them is about as watertight as it can possibly be. They thought the dealer was trying to rip them off. That gives them a motive. They were at the scene of the crime. They tried to dispose of the body. And, hours later, they were openly showing Catherine and Emma the pictures taken from Jollibone's room.'

'But the Bertrands belong to them!' Catherine leaned forward to make the point. 'We know that now. So they have been telling the truth about that.'

George poured the last half-cup of cool coffee from the pot. 'Emma was certainly impressed with the way the pictures have been looked after.'

Catherine continued eagerly. 'And they do admit all that business about moving the body. Surely that suggests their innocence. If they had killed Jollibone, they'd have tried to concoct an alibi.'

Tim shook his head. 'That's not going to cut much ice with Edgerson. Hell! I wish I knew just what evidence he's got! That's something I'll have to work at.'

To break a long silence Catherine said, 'Perhaps it would help if we thought a bit more about the paintings. They're obviously at the centre of this business. Why have they been hidden all this time? Why haven't the Brotherhood tired to sell them before? Any ideas, George?'

241

'I asked young Charles the same question on the way back this evening. The answers were a bit garbled but I reckon they make sense. The original members of the Brotherhood felt a sense of loyalty to Bertrand. The pictures became a sort of sacred trust. Keeping them from the prying eyes of strangers was a point of honour. The Camargue was cut off, a private world. The feeling's strong—even now. You have to meet these characters to realise how mentally isolated they are.'

Catherine followed the explanation closely. 'And I suppose none of them had any idea of the value of the paintings?'

'Not a clue, I'd say; not till recently, at any rate. It's obviously the new generation—Charles and Conrad—who want to cash up their assets. Like I said, they argued about it with their father. He was violently opposed to selling—said it would bring them all bad luck. And the Hulk went along with whatever the old man said.'

Tim gave a wry smile. 'I bet Lebec senior is saying "I told you so" now.'

'Loud and clear, Major.'

Catherine pursued her own line of thought. 'Can we just go back to that bit of the story. Charles claims that it was this difference of opinion that made him go to Jollibone and Tarantin, instead of one of the big auction houses or dealers?'

'According to Charles, that was his brother's idea. He thought if they could get a discreet valuation they could persuade Dad to sell. That's why he had to remove a few sample pictures secretly and take them to Conrad's place in London. Then, as I said, they sent the snaps to the gallery. Jollibone and Tarantin were interested—to put it mildly. The next step was to arrange the private view in London. And that was where their scheme began to fall apart at the seams.'

'And Jollibone—acting on orders from Josephine—tried to steal them?'

'That's right, Catherine. At their second meeting he said they might have difficulty proving right of ownership. Since the artist had never made a will, under French law the state could claim his property. He advised the brother to let him sell the pictures very privately.'

'Oh yes,' Tim grunted. 'And we all know the customer he had in mind.'

'Well, anyway,' George continued, 'the dealers had reckoned without the Lebecs' peasant cunning. Charles and Conrad smelled a rat, picked up the pictures and said they'd take their business elsewhere.'

Tim asked, 'Have you any idea why the brothers were so keen to sell?'

George nodded. 'They've both got good reasons. Conrad is some sort of financial whizz kid. He's looking for capital to buy into a top broking firm. As for Charles Lebec, he fancies himself as an artist but realises there's precious little money in that game. He talks a lot about getting the Bertrands put on public display, giving the man his proper place in the history of art and all that. I reckon he's really got his eyes on the independence that his share of several million francs will give him.'

Tim closed his eyes in concentration. 'If we assume the Lebec brothers are innocent and are not stringing us along, that leaves three other suspects; Charles Labardie, his father and Josephine Tarantin. Bumping off poor old Auguste would be quite in character for any of them.'

George stifled a yawn. 'What's Labardie's game? Why was he making out he'd snatched Emma?'

'Because he wants the Bertrands and he reckons we're going to lead him to them.'

George nodded. 'Just like the Lebecs. They think we'll track down the killer.'

Catherine sighed. 'And Edgerson seems convinced that we either murdered Jollibone ourselves or that we know who did.'

'Talk about pig in the middle,' George concluded mournfully. After the depressed silence that followed he added, 'What do we know about the other three?'

'The only good thing is that they're at each others' throats. Labardie Junior suspects his old man of trying to louse up his attempt to get the Bertrands. As for the fair Josephine, she's certainly trying to double-cross young Charlie.' Tim went over the main points of his meeting at Château d'Orgnac.

When he had finished, Catherine observed, 'I guess the Tarantin woman's the key to all this.'

Tim shrugged. 'Could be. I can't make up my mind whether she's very clever, very stupid or just a compulsive liar.'

George agreed. 'She certainly pitched a yarn to me and Emma.'

'Yes, and she played me for a sucker. She actually had me believing that she was a helpless female caught up in the machinations of evil men. Then, as soon as I'd gone out the door she was on the phone to Labardie.'

Catherine said, 'And she's been lying to him, too.'

'That's right. I spotted at least two deceptions. She told Labardie she didn't know the owner of the Bertrands but George and Emma had seen her talking to the Lebecs. And she claimed to know nothing about our involvement despite the fact that Charles had recognised Emma in the gallery.'

'And now we know that Josephine Tarantin was in London.' Catherine made the point as though it proved the Frenchwoman's guilt beyond any doubt. 'When she discovered that Jollibone had screwed up...'

'She took out the long knife she always carries in her handbag and stabbed him?'

Catherine scowled at her husband. 'And why not?'

'I see her as cold, calculating, fastidious —hardly the type to kill in hot blood.'

'Huh! Don't you believe it, Buster. She's pulled the wool over your eyes once.'

'Well, you haven't even met her!'

'I can't wait for the pleasure!' Catherine glowered.

George cleared his throat loudly. 'So, Major, where to now?'

Tim thumped his temples with both fists, as though to jolt his mental machine into more rapid motion. 'The key question is, how much time have we got?'

'Emma's due to go home for her mother's birthday at the weekend. If she doesn't show up, Mrs Kerr will be on the phone within minutes. You know how close they are. If we tell her the truth she'll go bananas and alert every police force in the country. If we don't...well, I guess we could stall her for a couple of days but then all hell would break loose—and friend Edgerson would have us in for the third-degree treatment.'

Tim agreed. 'There's no way we could go on holding out on him. That means swarms of police all over the Camargue. And God knows what would happen to Emma if her captors panicked.' He jumped up and went across to the phone. 'I'm going to get some more coffee. I need to think. God, I wish I hadn't been talked into letting Emma come here!'

Catherine flashed her response. 'Don't start that all over again! We're all to blame and somehow we've all got to figure a way out of this mess—and in the next four days.'

Tim shouted his order into the phone and slammed down the receiver. 'I know what I'd like to do—throttle the truth out of La Tarantin.'

Catherine laughed. 'Get in line. That's my privilege. First thing in the morning...'

'No, it won't do,' Tim interrupted. 'Not unless we get really desperate. With Labardie's men watching us we can't be seen to be taking too much interest in his trusted accomplice. If he suspected anything, he'd find out what she knows, make the Camargue connection and have his own heavies down there within hours. All we can do about Mme Tarantin is keep an eye on her for the time being.

Labardie doesn't know you, George, so that'll be your job—that and staying in touch with the Lebecs. Speak to them as often as you can. Be encouraging. Tell them we're following up important leads. Tell them anything you like but keep them as relaxed as possible.'

'What shall I do?' Catherine asked.

'We get the first plane back to London. I've got to pull every string I can find at Scotland Yard to discover what I can about Jollibone's murder. Until we know how, when and where he was killed we're stumbling about in the dark. Then there's the lead Labardie gave me to follow up. He's got a Paris address.'

'So what do *I* do?' Catherine's voice rose a few decibels.

'Hold the fort at Farrans. We do have a business to run, not to mention a couple of kids to bring up.'

'Nuts! If you want to be mad at me for coming over here, that's your problem. But I'm not letting your pique cut me out of the action. Of course, things at home are important, but they'll have to be put on hold for the moment. Emma needs the best shot we can give. That means all of us.'

The arrival of the waiter cut off Tim's angry response. By the time the old tray had been cleared, the new one set down and fresh coffee poured he had his derailed reason back on track.

He took a gulp of the thick, black liquid. 'Sorry, darling, I guess this has put us all on edge. Of course, there is another lead that needs following up—brother Conrad. What we need from him is a minute-by-minute account of the events of the fateful night. Get as much detail out of him as you can: exact times; who said what to whom; where they found the body; what they did in Jollibone's room; whether they saw anyone or anyone saw them; what—'

'OK, OK, I get the picture.'

George looked at his watch. 'Well, if that's all for now, Major, I'm off. You two can either carry on your domestic row or kiss and make up. I'm going to try and sleep away what little is left of the night.'

# CHAPTER 12

Aristide had no idea where or for how long he walked. Sometimes he was alone on the seashore. Sometimes he was deep in jostling crowds following the draped statues of the local saints as they were borne, shoulder-high, through the streets. All he was aware of was struggling with memories. Memories or phantasies? The terrifying images which now vividly flooded his mind fell into a logical sequence. They neatly filled the gaps in his hitherto obscure past. But could they be true? Was Edouard really dead? Had he and his brother quarrelled in that way? Had he...done that terrible thing and then rushed from the house leaving Edouard's blood to ebb away? Aristide had learned to live with lost memories. Could he continue to do so now with found ones?

The town quietened towards dusk. The marketeers had packed away their stalls. The statues had been returned to their shrines for another year. Most revellers had left the streets and squares. The cafés and bars were thronged. Lamps began to appear in windows.

Inside the church it was dark already, save where pools of light from votive candles illumined the painted faces and gaudy trappings of the images. The crypt sanctuary was better lit. On one wall a group of paintings had been arranged: primitive daubings donated by grateful devotees to mark the miracles wrought by the Saintes Maries in answer to prayer. Two fishermen scrambled ashore while their boat was splintered upon the rocks. A widow's son sat up in bed while his mother clasped her hands in thanksgiving. The saints stood among the flames of a burning house while two young children were lowered to safety from an upper window. Aristide stood before these testimonies to the power of holy intercessors and prayed with all the fervour he could muster that his memories were false. That Edouard lived. That their father experienced no grief or shame for his sons.

'Aristide.'

He did not hear the soft voice behind him.

'Aristide.'

He opened his eyes and turned slowly. 'Yvette.'

'Aristide, where have you been? We've been so worried. We looked everywhere. Most of the others have gone home with one of the waggons. Aunt Lou and I stayed for a last search. I came here to pray for you.' She laid a hand gently on his arm.

He made no answer but let the girl lead him slowly from the church.

Twenty minutes later they sat side by side on the box of the cart as it lurched and waddled northwards. Yvette handled the reins skilfully but made no attempt to hurry the shambling horse until Aunt Lou, perched on a bale behind them, said, 'Best get a move on, child; there'll be little moon tonight.'

When the animal had settled into a quicker pace, Yvette gathered the leather straps in one hand and felt for Aristide's with the other. 'What is it? What's wrong?'

He grasped her fingers firmly. 'I'm sorry I went off and put you to all this trouble. I saw someone I used to know. Then I remembered...'

Yvette looked at him sharply. 'Does that mean you have to go back to your real life?'

'No, I can't do that.'

She brightened. 'Good! Then you can stay with us for ever and ever.'

He shook his head. 'I can't do that either. It could be dangerous for you.'

'Dangerous? I don't understand. How can it possibly be dangerous for you to stay at Mas Maraques?'

'I can't explain. Not now. Perhaps one day.'

'Well, you can't go!' Yvette flicked the reins and the surprised horse broke into a trot. 'We're all very fond of you, aren't we, Aunt Lou? You're our hero.'

Aristide groaned and shook his head. 'Heroes have feet of clay, Yvette.'

'Don't be silly. And don't try to make me believe anything bad about you. You won't succeed.' After a pause she added, 'Have you remembered everything now?'

'Yes, yes I think so.'

'Are you...married?'

The question brought a sudden laugh to Aristide's lips. 'No, I'm not married—thank God!'

'Why do you say thank God? Is it not good to be married?'

'I'm sure for many people—most people—it's excellent. But there are those of us...'

Aunt Lou intervened at this point. 'We must talk soon of your wedding, child.'

Yvette pouted. 'Why? There's no hurry.'

'François is getting impatient.'

'You mean his mother is getting impatient.'

'It will be good for Mas Maraques for you to be settled.'

'Why? You aren't married. Aristide isn't married. Why have I got to be?'

'Perhaps it is because Aristide is not married that you should be.'

The farmstead was quiet when they arrived back. There were few lighted windows. Jean-Marc came out with a lantern when he heard the waggon. Aristide helped him unharness the horse and turn him out in the meadow behind the big barn.

As they closed the gate the boy said, 'You haven't asked about the battle?'

'I'm sorry, Jean-Marc. I've had other things on my mind. Was everything OK?'

'I suppose so...well, almost.'

'Tell me about it.'

'We caught the sheepmen all together. They were moving their flock across the dried marsh near Méjanes. We surrounded them and advanced all together. They couldn't break out. We forced them back towards the *étang,* just as you said.'

'So they had to surrender.'

'No, not straight away. Some of them had guns. They tried to shoot their way out.'

'So you charged before they could reload?'

'No. Some of us panicked and pulled back. It was chaos. They split us into two groups.'

'But you regrouped quickly?'

'Old Esmé was hit. He couldn't blow the signal. We scattered. Then the men of Mas Rollan got together and charged into the breach. That stopped the sheepmen long enough for us to regroup. We pushed them right back to the water. They didn't stop till they'd lost several sheep. If I'd been in charge I'd have driven them all into the *étang* and drowned every last one of them.'

'You forced them to leave. That's what matters.'

'Yes, we saw them on the road. They know what to expect if they dare come back.'

'I'm glad it all worked out.'

'But it didn't!' The boy turned and almost shouted. 'Mas Rollan are claiming all the credit. They say your plan didn't work. That any success was all due to their courage.'

'It doesn't matter what they say, Jean-Marc. The important thing is that you won.'

'You don't understand us, do you? Of course it matters!' Aristide could hear the sob in the youngster's voice. 'It's our honour that's at stake. You were our hero. Now everyone's saying that you're a coward because you didn't come on the raid and that your battle tactics didn't work.' After a pause he added, 'And there's worse. We lost three men. One was Jean Robert, François's father.'

Later Aristide lay sleepless in his narrow bed and knew that the time had come to move on.

Neither Conrad Lebec nor his habitat were what Catherine expected. The door of the apartment was opened by a slender, mid-twenties brunette clad in designer jeans and cashmere. 'Hi! I'm Alison,' the welcoming committee said, in that tone somewhere between friendliness and condescension that Catherine immediately recognised as English public school. Alison led the way

255

into a wide sitting room whose windows provided an extensive view of south-bank lights reflected in the river. The decor was sparsely modern and very expensive. Conrad was pouring the contents of several bottles into a large glass bowl, but came across to greet her, hand outstretched. Catherine saw a thirtyish figure already developing an unhealthy paunch. The Frenchman was balding prematurely and had grown a flamboyant moustache by way of compensation.

Alison retreated. 'Do excuse me. Things to do in the kitchen. Party. Don't forget the vodka, Connie.'

Catherine sank into an armchair that was more comfortable than it looked. 'Have I arrived at an inconvenient time?'

'Not at all. Just a few friends coming round.' Conrad's English was impeccable.

Catherine gazed round the room. 'This is all very pleasant.'

He laughed. 'Yes, isn't sexual equality great? Ali insists on paying her way and since her father is MD of Grenville-Baring her way is gratifyingly sumptuous.'

'So you're virtually a kept man?'

Lebec's eyes flickered but the bon-hominous smile did not leave his face. 'I suppose so. What a delicious thought.'

Catherine decided on an abrupt end to the pleasantries. 'Look, you know why

I'm here. Can we get right down to business?'

'I checked with Charles, of course, straight after you rang this morning. I'll do what I can, but frankly I'm getting very tired of sorting out little brother's problems.'

Catherine raised an eyebrow. 'Little brother's problems? I should have thought you were both in the mire up to your necks. It's only a matter of time before the police get on to you and if anything happens to Emma Kerr I'll give them all the help I can to put you away for a very long time.'

Conrad winced and glanced anxiously towards the kitchen. He said, very loudly, 'Would you mind if we took a little stroll? I've been commissioned to lay in some extra booze. There's a shop just along the street.'

It was not to a liquor store that the Frenchman led the way. He guided Catherine to a wine bar round the corner from the apartment block. He seated her at a corner table and fetched two glasses of Sancerre. 'We can talk more comfortably and privately here,' he said as he sat opposite her. 'I suppose I ought to begin by apologising for Charles. Abducting your friend was bloody stupid. I'm afraid he's not renowned for clearheadedness.'

'Well I am, Mr Lebec, and I don't give a damn for your fraternal squabbles. My only concern is to get Emma Kerr back in circulation. Unfortunately, it seems that can't be done without somehow extricating you and your brother from a little matter of murder.'

Lebec stared straight back, anxiety now breaking through the shell of his poised self-assurance. 'We did not murder the dealer.'

'So, convince me. Let's go through it —slowly, in as much detail as you can remember.'

'Well, if you're going to understand, we'll have to go back to the beginning.'

'I've got all night and I guess the party will start OK without you.'

'Have you ever been to the Camargue?'

'No.'

'Well, don't bother. It's a backward, stinking, soul-sapping dump. I can't remember the time when I didn't want to get away. Charles felt much the same. Most of our school friends had no greater ambition than to be *gardians* and work on the salt pans at Salins-de-Giraud or run hotels or riding centres for the tourists. Our parents wanted us to settle there among all our inbred relatives, marry local girls and provide them with a healthy crop of grandchildren. I suppose our father hoped that introducing us to the "great secret" would strengthen our commitment to the community.'

'The "great secret" being the Brotherhood?'

'Yes. I was twenty and Charles sixteen when the Day of Initiation came. I was home from the Sorbonne for the summer vacation and I'd already made it clear that I planned to go in for international banking. Well, one sunny morning we were driven over to Uncle Achille's place—Father, Charles, me and Father's faithful shadow, Edgar; he's—'

'Emma's met him. She drew up this sort of family tree.' Catherine took the old diary out of her handbag and found the appropriate page.

Lebec looked at the diagram quickly. 'Yes, that's right. The names underlined are the members of the Brotherhood. We both had to memorise it. It was part of the initiation ceremony. We were supposed to realise our enormous responsibility—maintaining honour and tradition and all that sort of thing. You've no idea what we went through—worse than any Masonic ritual. It took most of the day. First, we were sworn to secrecy. Then we were told the story. Then we were taken through the marsh on horseback to this deserted barn to see the pictures. It all seemed very silly but the others were deadly serious about it and I suppose some

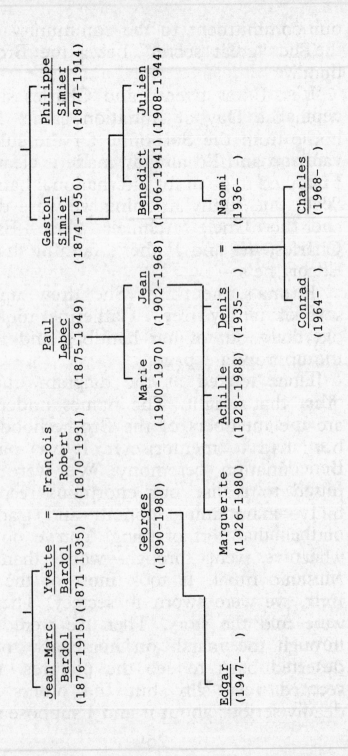

THE BROTHERHOOD

of their earnestness rubbed off. We kept the secret. It would be more honest to say that we almost forgot about it.'

'It's a bit surprising that the secret was kept all those years, isn't it?'

Conrad shrugged. 'Not if you know the Camargue. It's a country full of secrets. Then, of course, the Brotherhood was never very large. It was exclusively male and there were never many men around to be admitted. We had to learn about all of them. Let me have another look at that chart and we'll see how good my memory is. Right, of the original five, two—Jean-Marc and Philippe—died trying to stop the Germans in World War I. There was a story about Yvette having other children but they were carried off by an epidemic—diphtheria, I think. Hitler's war accounted for the Simier brothers. Benedict was in the Resistance and Julien fought with the Free French.'

'I see that you and Charles are the last of the line.'

'Unless poor Edgar surprises us. I suppose that's possible. His father was well smitten in years before he sired a son. Anyway, the Brotherhood's finished now. If Charles or I have kids we shan't put them through the mumbo jumbo we went through.'

'When did you realise the commercial

possibilities of the paintings?'

'Well, that was Charles, of course. He started studying art four or five years ago. It was only a matter of time before he came across the otherwise obscure name of Aristide Bertrand. About three years ago he told me he reckoned there was a fortune in Postimpressionist paintings sitting in our semi-derelict barn in the middle of the marsh. As you can imagine, we both read up everything we could find about Bertrand, which wasn't very much. I managed to get an introduction to Everett Sondheim in Philadelphia. He has two of the only three fully authenticated Bertrands. To my untrained eye they seemed to be very similar to our collection. So we eventually plucked up courage to broach with Father the possibility of selling at least some of the pictures. My God, you could have heard the explosion here in London. We were accused of being madmen, criminals and traitors. We had no love of family; no respect for tradition; no loyalty.'

'So you dropped the idea?'

'For the moment. But, Mrs Lacy, how would you have felt in our position? An important and valuable collection of paintings was rotting away in the middle of a swamp where no one could enjoy them. Wouldn't you have wanted to do something about that?'

'I suppose I might have consoled myself with the thought that one day the Bertrands would be the exclusive property of myself and my brother.'

'What, in forty years or so? Even if our beloved père doesn't survive long beyond his three-score years and ten, there's Edgar to consider. His father was still going strong at ninety and he only croaked then because he choked on a chicken bone.'

Catherine stared at him, her penetrating green eyes watching for every nuance of his reaction. 'Then, of course, there was the money—a great deal of money.'

The Frenchman met her gaze but moisture glistened on his brow. 'Sure, neither of us was thinking in terms of a comfortable old age. We wanted, needed, the cash *now*. My job's in the currency markets. It's a profitable business but it takes its toll. I've seen younger men than me burned out and tossed aside. Some of my colleagues are living—or dying—on stimulants. I don't kid myself that I can keep going much longer. I have to make a career move soon and that means capital. Well, there's more than enough tied up in those bloody pictures. And it's not as if I—we—were planning to steal them. They're our birthright. Why shouldn't we benefit from them?'

'So you removed some of the paintings and brought them over here in order to get a valuation? What made you choose Jollibone?'

'Charles knew him slightly. He'd given some lectures at the Musée des Beaux Arts in Lyon. Charles thought he'd be discreet and trustworthy. God! How wrong can you be?'

'What happened—exactly?'

'We took the sample along to Jollibone's hotel, the Wellington Tower at the bottom of Park Lane. Mrs Lacy, you should have seen his face. He tried hard not to react but he couldn't help himself. That was the moment I really knew we were on to something big—I mean seriously big. He wanted a couple of days to examine the paintings. That seemed reasonable, so we asked for a receipt and left them with him. Now, all we wanted at that stage was a figure so that we could go back to our father with a written valuation. We reckoned that once he realised that the Brotherhood's treasure was worth not hundreds, not even thousands, but millions, even his objections to selling would break down.'

'And when you went back to see him?'

'The man had changed completely—or reverted to his true colours. The respectable art expert had disappeared. In his place there was a cheap hustler. He said he'd found a buyer who would take *all* the Bertrands. This would have several advantages, he said: the collection would be kept together; we would be spared lots of unwelcome publicity; the money could be paid in such a way as to avoid tedious taxation problems.'

'How much was his mysterious client offering?'

'Ten million francs.'

Catherine laughed aloud. 'Less than a million pounds for a unique collection of over thirty genuine Postimpressionist paintings? He must have thought you very gullible.'

Lebec bridled at the suggestion. 'Well, he was wrong. I saw through him immediately. He had scraped together every penny he had or could borrow in the hope of buying at a knock-down price. His plan, then, was to split the collection and sell at a huge profit. When we told him we weren't interested in selling all the pictures, and certainly not at that price, he tried to lean on us. He suggested that if we attempted to sell the paintings through the rooms or top dealers we would have to prove title and that would be difficult. He said the French government would refuse to let the collection out of the country. He conjured up the spectre of expensive litigation running on for years. When he saw that that tactic didn't work he started wheedling and pleading. He actually ended up looking very pathetic. We, of course, decided to have nothing more to do with him. He was almost in tears when we picked up the paintings and left.'

'What time was that?'

'Late afternoon—five, perhaps five fifteen.'

'But you went back again?'

'Yes, much against my better judgement.'

'OK, now we're getting to the crucial bit.' Catherine took a small tape recorder and put it on the table. 'I want every detail about the rest of that evening.'

Conrad glanced nervously at the machine but spoke firmly. 'Jollibone phoned soon after eight. He apologised and said he had obviously misunderstood our wishes. He suggested that, to set our minds at rest, we get a second opinion. He told us he'd spoken to an English dealer who was prepared to meet us at short notice in a discreet location and give us an independent assessment. I told him straight that I didn't believe him—that he was obviously planning to wheel out some crony to back up his story. That was when he gave us your name and address, Mrs Lacy, and suggested that we check your credentials with people in the London art world.'

Catherine nodded. 'That certainly ties in with what I know. He called me just before seven and asked if I could spare some time to look at some important pictures which were only going to be available "very briefly". Naturally I was as suspicious as hell, but I knew of Jollibone by name and reputation so I decided to risk a wasted journey. But let's get back to your movements.'

'Charles and I argued about Jollibone's proposal but we eventually said we would, at least, go back for another chat at about eleven.'

'Why so late?'

'We were in the middle of dinner. We had some friends from the embassy here. We certainly weren't going to spoil our evening for Jollibone.'

'OK, so you drove back to the West End?'

'That's right. We went straight up to his room.'

'What was the number?'

'518.'

'Did anyone see you? Think carefully.'

Lebec nodded gloomily. 'That was the problem. The foyer was very quiet and I suppose the girl on the reception desk was bored. Anyway, she decided to be chatty. She said something like, "Good evening, gentlemen. Back again? I've just seen your friend go up. Between you and me he was looking a bit under the weather." '

'Was there anyone else in the lift?'

'No, we went up alone. There was someone waiting for it on the fifth floor...a man in a DJ. He was looking a bit the worse for drink, so he probably wouldn't remember us.'

'And there was no one in the corridor?'

'No. We definitely didn't pass anybody. We got to Jollibone's room and he was lying face down on the floor.'

Catherine glanced sharply across the table. 'Hold it right there! If the corpse was lying inside the room and you were outside, how come you got in?'

'Sorry, I forgot. The key-card was on the floor.'

'What?'

'The card. It was on the floor.'

'That didn't strike you as odd?'

'A little, perhaps. But he was expecting us. We knocked, got no answer, and let ourselves in.' The explanation came quickly, easily.

'Describe what you saw—minutely.'

Lebec supported his head in his hands. 'Oh, God, I've tried hard to forget.'

'If you want to spend the next twenty years as a free man you'd better remember.'

Conrad nodded. He took a deep breath. 'Jollibone was lying just inside the door...

face down...arms spreadeagled. There was only a bedside light on. I assumed he'd fainted or had a heart attack or something. It took us a few moments to notice the gash in the back of his jacket...and the stain around it...blood.'

'What was the first thing you did?'

'It seems strange, looking back, but we were both remarkably cool. I felt for his pulse. Of course there wasn't one.'

'Was he still warm?'

'Yes. He can't have been dead long. There was nothing we could do for him. No point in calling for an ambulance. Our first thought was to get away quickly. I opened the door to check that the coast was clear... It wasn't. There was obviously a conference in the hotel; several men and women in evening dress—executive types—were coming along the corridor. So we had to stay there...with the...body. That was when it dawned on us what a spot we were in.'

'We'll come to that in a moment. Tell me first what impressions you had of the room. What was it like? Had it been disturbed? Was there any evidence of anyone else being there? Was there a murder weapon?'

'The answer to all those questions is no. The place looked just the same as when we had left it several hours before. Even the glasses we'd had drinks from were still on the table.'

'You're sure they were your glasses?'

'Oh yes. It was that that made us start to panic and eventually do something...frankly ...stupid!'

'I'll say it was stupid!'

'OK, OK. It's easy to be wise after the event. But put yourself in our position. First of all, we were in a state of shock. How'd you like to find yourself in a room with someone who's just been stabbed to death? Before we knew quite what we were doing we were washing the glasses and wiping down any surfaces that might have fingerprints on. Then we went through his pockets and his briefcase to remove any letters, diaries and so on that referred to us. Then, of course, it dawned us that this was all a waste of time. We'd been seen coming to Jollibone's room. So we stopped and tried to collect our thoughts.'

'It didn't occur to you to phone the police?'

'Of course it did!' Lebec snapped his anger and exasperation. 'But then we asked ourselves what their reaction would be to the truth. A Frenchman goes into a hotel room. Minutes later two other Frenchmen go to the room. They "discover" the other man dead. In the investigation it

270

comes out that these three men had had a business row.'

'So?'

'So I came up with a plan. Other people knew that we were in that room but nobody knew that there was a body there—except the murderer, and he wasn't going to come forward. Therefore, if there was no body there would be no problem.'

'That's a pretty big mental jump.'

'Call it lateral thinking. My job is all about making big, snap decisions, then having the balls to see them through.'

'Even so...'

'You don't get it, do you? Even supposing that, by some miracle, Charles and I avoided a criminal prosecution for murder, that would only be after weeks or months of media exposure. Do you realise what that would do to my career? My bosses are paranoid about the bank's good name. Two of my friends were sacked last year—one over a case of sexual harassment which was never proved; the other because he got involved, very marginally, in an insider-dealing scandal. If my name appeared in the papers as "helping the police with their inquiries" in a serious criminal investigation I'd be out with a leaden kick rather than a golden handshake.'

'And Charles went along with this crazy idea?'

'He took a lot of convincing, but we had plenty of time to discuss it. Actually, I have always been able to talk him into things, ever since we were kids. In fact, there wasn't much he had to do. Anyway the plan wasn't all that difficult once I'd started to think it out.'

Catherine watched the Frenchman actually relax into self-congratulation as he got engrossed in his story.

'There were three phases to the operation. The first was to leave the hotel and be seen leaving. The second was to smuggle the body out. The third was to dispose of it. Stage one was easy. We discovered the staff entrance. Then we left the hotel by the main door, being careful to say goodnight to the receptionist. Of course, we immediately went round the back and returned to Jollibone's room. Then I scouted around and found a chambermaid's trolley. I took some dirty sheets from it and we wrapped up the body. I moved the car close to the hotel's back entrance and collected the trolley and brought it to the room. We put Jollibone in it. We picked up his case and all his belongings and dumped them in with him. Then we waited till about two thirty. Charles went down the back stairs.

We arranged that I'd bring the body down in the luggage lift if he wasn't back in five minutes. That was the only nerve-racking part. But, as they say, fortune favours the brave. We got the trolley out the back, moved the body to the boot of the car and I even wheeled the trolley back into the hotel. No sign of life anywhere. Stage three was simple. There's a ground-floor terrace at the back of my apartment block. It's right over the river.'

Catherine sighed deeply. 'Well, when you've stopped congratulating yourself perhaps you'd like to give some more thought to the question of how we're going to prove your innocence. Wasn't there anything in room 518? Some clue that you might have cleared away in your obsessive tidiness?'

Lebec shook his head mournfully. 'It didn't look as though anyone else had been there since we left.'

Catherine switched off the tape recorder. 'If Jollibone was killed shortly before you arrived you've got no alibi at all. Let's hope that the police never get to question you.'

'Oh, but they already have.'

'What?'

'A couple of days ago a plain-clothes chap called. It was a bit of a shock but I think I carried it off.'

'How did they—'

'They were checking all Jollibone's phone calls.'

'Of course! I should have realised. What did you say?'

'I said that dear old Auguste was an acquaintance and that, being in London, he'd phoned up for a chat. That seemed to satisfy him.'

Catherine said, 'Good,' and thought, I wonder.

## CHAPTER 13

While Catherine was looking for a diamond of hope in Conrad's Lebec's slagheap of memories Tim was standing in a pub on Victoria Street trying to keep pace with the alcohol consumption of a rotund, bespectacled humorist. Jock Armstrong did not look like a policeman nor a heavy drinker, perhaps because he was fastidious in all his habits. His suit had been cut by a tailor skilled in imparting linear stylishness to globular, over-indulged human frames. He consumed—at least when someone else was paying—only the finest malt available. His conversation was larded with literary and classical allusions.

He raised his fourth whisky and

winked at his companion. 'Remember Tam O'Shanter's mare!'

Tim laughed, careful not to sip his own drink. 'What's that supposed to mean, Jock?'

'Tut, tut, mon!' Jock affected an accent far broader than his usual soft Highland brogue. 'D'ye no ken yer Burns? "Whene'er to drink ye are inclined Or cutty sarks run in your mind, Think, ye may buy the joys o'er dear. Remember Tam O'Shanter's mare".'

'And what happened to Tam O'Shanter's mare?'

'She had her tail snatched off by a witch. Is there no poetry in you at all, Tim?'

Lacy shook his head. 'Strictly a visual arts person. And that brings me—'

'Pity, pity—a man without poetry in his heart is a man without wisdom in his head.'

'Dr Johnson?'

'No, Jock Armstrong.' The fat man roared his laughter. 'You should start reading poetry, Tim. It's never too late. It's a perfect accompaniment to grape and grain.' He emptied his glass and broke into recitation again.

' "Sweet in my bold endeavour now, To chant unuttered strains divine, And seek the god, who on his brow Wears the green blossom of the vine." Horace,

275

"Ode to Bacchus". Now, whose shout is it? I quite forget.'

'I'm OK for the moment, Jock.'

'Nonsense!' He attracted the barmaid's attention with an imperious gesture and two more tots of tawny liquid appeared on the counter between them.

Tim tried again. 'Jock, I was wondering—'

'Why this stuff doesn't dissolve the grey cells? Well, all I can tell you is that it doesn't. It lubricates my genius. That's what you need in the Fine Art Squad—sheer, intuitive genius.'

'It's not just a question, then, of computerised lists and stolen art notices and patient plodding, these days?'

'Replace the PC with the PC, eh? Out with the police constable and in with the personal computer? Get it all on some encyclopaedic databank and your problems are solved? What a positively surreal conceit. You know what they say, Tim: "To err is human but for a real cock-up you need a computer." ' He tapped his temple. 'Here's the only machine that counts. When they invent the computer that can tell the difference between a masterpiece and a fake, or even between a Uccello and a Utrillo, then I'll become the lean and slippered pantaloon. Until then I'll continue to get results with what the ancients called "inwit", that *understanding* of beautiful things and unscrupulous people that no amount of megabites can encompass.'

Tim saw a way in. 'Talking about unscrupulous people, I was lunching the other day with someone you'd love to meet—Charles Labardie.'

The glass paused on its way to Armstrong's lips. 'Labardie? Now there's a name to conjure with in hell. I trust you were using a long spoon.'

'He has a magnificent château and some fine things in it.'

'Did you see the official collection or the unofficial one?'

'Oh, I'm sure everything I was shown was come by quite legally. He's very proud of his patronage of artists and dealers. I was treated to quite a lecture on the crime baron as modern Maecenas.'

'And what was the purpose of this tête-à-tête? Is he employing you to keep his treasures safe from dishonest rogues?'

'No thief with an interest in self-preservation would risk crossing the Labardie syndicate. I was investigating his connection with a certain French art dealer—Auguste Jollibone.'

'You mean the late Auguste Jollibone.'

'You know of his unconventional exit from this vale of tears?'

'Of course.'

'Did you also know that he was a front man for Labardie?'

Armstrong's eyes opened wide. ' "What news? What news? Your tidings tell. Tell me you must and shall".'

'Would you like to be the officer who put young Labardie behind bars?'

The policeman took a mouthful of spirit and ran it round his palette before replying. 'Beware of Greeks bearing gifts. You've wheeled your Trojan horse out before, Master Lacy.'

'Have you ever been on the losing end of a deal with me?'

'I've found myself in some pretty hot water.'

'And emerged smelling of roses. Think of it, Jock; arranging a long, paid holiday for Labardie. It wouldn't shut down the Marseille mafia but it would give it a very nasty jolt. Charles Junior runs their European transport system. It would be good to disrupt that, even for a few months. And just imagine getting into his private horde. Labardie's been behind the biggest campaign of art looting since the heyday of the Jackdaw of Linz. If you found his Aladdin's cave I'll bet you could close dozens of files.'

'As ever, you're suspiciously well informed, Tim. Your horse is painted in garish colours, but I want to know what's inside before I even contemplate opening the gates.'

'Jollibone's gallery in Lyon was being used for laundering criminal proceeds and shifting stolen works of art. The mastermind behind this particular part of Labardie's operation was Jollibone's partner, Josephine Tarantin. She's up to her pencilled eyebrows in all sorts of shady art transactions. Jollibone stepped out of line, so they disposed of him.'

'You have proof of all this?'

'You're the detective.'

'But I'm not on the Jollibone case.'

'You could get put on to it.'

'What makes you think that?'

'I happen to know that the investigation is getting nowhere at the moment. If you told the powers that be that the case has Fine Art Squad implications and that you have some vital information, I'm sure they'd let you in on the act.'

'I sense the water temperature rising again. That would make me extremely unpopular with the investigating officer. I suppose you can tell me who that is?'

'DI Edgerson.'

'Huh! Edgerson by name and edgy by nature. He certainly would get tetchy about someone else muscling in. Why don't you go to him with your evidence?'

'He doesn't take very kindly to help from me. I've tried. Anyway, he isn't a big enough man for the job. Labardie would run rings round him. This is the kind of case that needs your breadth of vision.'

'Now you're overdoing it—smothering your wooden horse in the glossy varnish of flattery. If I were to agree to your suggestion I'd need some hard facts to lay before the super.'

Tim wondered just how much more elaborate his masquerade would have to become to convince Armstrong. 'The best way of obtaining them is to go over what Edgerson's got on the killing. As soon as you find the smallest link to Tarantin you can persuade the Sûreté to lean on her. She'll certainly crack.'

'That'll depend on how frightened she is of Labardie.'

'She won't be frightened enough to face a murder charge for him.'

Armstrong took a gold half-hunter from the pocket of his floral waistcoat and peered at it closely. 'Someone once said—damned if I can remember who—"Counsel is cheap; we can all afford to give it away." This has been a fascinating chat, young Timothy. I'll give some thought to what you say.' He drained his glass. 'Must dash now. I'm supposed to be speaking at some crime writer's shindig. I hope their booze is better than their prose.'

Tim watched with alarm as the other man buttoned his jacket and began moving towards the door. 'Hang on, Jock! This is important. We can't afford to lose any time.'

'Where's the urgency?' The fat man threw the question casually over his shoulder.

Tim followed in the swathe Armstrong's bulk cut through the crowd. 'Edgerson's sure to bungle things. As soon as Labardie gets a whiff of police interest in his connection with Jollibone he'll be off to South America by private jet.'

Armstrong paused in the doorway. 'And as soon as I get a whiff of why Tim Lacy has an urgent and compelling interest in this particular investigation I shall decide whether or not to take a hand in it.' He marched out into the drizzling evening, brandishing his umbrella and roaring for a taxi.

Minutes later Tim and Catherine were sharing a depressed silence and a supper of sandwiches and coffee in the Westminster flat. Tim gulped down several cupfuls of black liquid in an effort to clear his head. Then he spread himself out on the sofa.

He groaned. 'Without knowing what

Edgerson has discovered about the crime we're hamstrung.'

Catherine curled her legs beneath her in a deep armchair. 'Isn't there any other way of getting it?'

'Short of breaking into Scotland Yard at dead of night, no. Armstrong was my only hope.'

'Well, I fared no better with Conrad Lebec. He's implicated himself so convincingly that he might as well walk into Edgerson's office with his hands up.'

'He won't have to. Even our short-fused DI is bright enough to put two and two together as soon as he starts going through his paperwork. Conrad is French; Conrad spoke on the phone with Jollibone; Conrad has a flat overlooking the river. He's bound to pull the frog financier in for questioning.'

'And when his brother and father get to hear about that...'

'You've no need to spell it out.' Tim jumped up and wandered aimlessly round the room. 'God, I feel so useless! The hours are slipping by and we're achieving nothing.'

'If only we could prove that one of our other suspects was at the hotel just before eleven on the night Jollibone was murdered.' Catherine set down her empty plate on the coffee table beside her. 'Gee,

I'm still hungry. Do you want to send out for a pizza?'

Tim turned slowly. 'No, I've got a better idea. How about a nice steak in the Wellington Tower grill room?'

Edgar's wife was diminutive and plain but her culinary reputation was indeed well deserved. Emma forked the last morsels of seafood and miraculously light *feuilleté* pastry into her mouth, crossed her eating implements on the plate and sat back grateful for this symbol of civilisation. She had only exchanged prison for house arrest but, she reflected, the conditions of her confinement could be a lot worse.

She had been brought to l'Auberge du Cheval Blanc, Edgar and Jeanne's little hotel on the bank of the Petit Rhône, immediately after George's visit the previous evening. It was a modest hostelry at the end of a long track leading from the main Arles-Stes Maries road. Edgar assured her that in the season they did a roaring trade but now, in late November, with no cars in the wide yard, unused children's swings moving squeakily on rusty chains, and plastic chairs and tables stacked in a corner of the terrace, it looked shabby, forlorn, unwelcoming. Inside, however, the hotel was cosy—especially the kitchen, with its ancient range radiating heat, its aromas of garlic, fish and fresh-baked bread and its wide, cluttered deal table.

It was around this well-scrubbed board that Emma sat with her host and hostess enjoying an evening meal and reflecting that summer guests to the White Horse Inn must be remarkably well fed. The conversation was desultory, as it had been most of the day, consisting of measured sentences in standard, non-colloquial French which often had to be repeated. Emma noted that Jeanne understood her more readily, but that often, instead of responding for herself, she translated for her husband's benefit and left him to answer or ask questions.

Emma politely declined both cheese and coffee. She realised that she was yawning uncontrollably every two or three minutes. She told herself that it was the heat of the stove that was making her feel tired, but she did not believe the explanation. She recognised her own nervous exhaustion—the body demanding its price for days of emotional strain.

She felt like a ship being tugged from its moorings by storm winds that could not be resisted. One by one the hausers were snapping. It had been wonderful to see George, to re-establish contact with the comfortably familiar. But George had gone and she was alone again. It was encouraging to know that Tim was doing all he could to secure her freedom. But what chance did he have of solving a crime that was still defying the resources of the police? She made herself think positive thoughts. Her hosts/captors were attentive to her needs. But they also watched her incessantly and last night had locked her in her room. Edgar had been at pains to show her the two alsatians which had the run of the grounds after dark. Charles—and probably Edgar, too—wished her no harm. But Charles had gone back to Lyon, and his father—a man well beyond the reach of reason—was now in control.

Emma decided to give in to the oblivion of sleep. She smiled at her hostess. 'Merci, Jeanne. Maintenant je suis fatiguée et—'

The telephone rang. Edgar went to the corner of the room to answer it. After a brief exchange he held out the receiver to Emma. She went over and took it eagerly.

'Hello.'

'Hello, Emma. How are they treating you?'

'George, how lovely to hear you. I'm OK.'

'You're sure?'

'Well, Charles's father is around here most of the time. He gives me the creeps but I don't think he'd do anything nasty, not yet, anyway. The others are OK. Edgar's wife is quite sweet.'

'Look, if there's any problem—any problem at all—give me a ring without hesitation. You've got the number.'

'Yeah, of course. How are things with you? Any...developments?' She turned her back on the room.

'Nothing from the Major and Catherine yet, but that's probably a good sign. They must be busy following up leads.'

'And what are you doing, George? Keeping an eye on Mme Tarantin?'

'That's right. She's a cool one. Seems to be carrying on as though nothing had happened. It's business as normal at the gallery. She's certainly got a big shock coming to her.'

'I wish I could be there to see it administered.'

'Perhaps you will. We'll have you out of there in next to no time. Meanwhile, keep your chin up. I'll talk to you again tomorrow.'

'Thanks for calling, George. It's a real help. I'm sorry about the trouble I'm causing everyone.'

'Don't you worry about that.' The voice was suddenly stern. 'You just look after yourself, OK?'

'OK, George. Goodnight.'

Minutes later Emma was standing by

her bedroom window looking down into the yard. By the light of the security lamp she saw Edgar let the dogs out of their shed. They leaped around him excitedly, barking with joy at their sudden freedom. Without undressing Emma lay down on the bed. She cried herself to sleep.

Aristide did not leave Mas Maraques. He intended to. His resolve strengthened as he sensed the changed attitude of the older members of the community. No one spoke words of reproach, but glances, whispers and turned backs were eloquent testimony to his altered status. He had been a talisman. Now he was a Jonah. Yet Aristide did not leave. The past, now rediscovered, appalled him. He feared for the future. Eloise had recognised him. In all probability she would tell her friends, her father. They would alert the police and the murder hunt would shift to Les Saintes Maries. Sooner or later someone would say, yes, they knew the painter. He came to market with the people from one of the *gardian* farmsteads. The gendarmes would venture into the closed world of the Camargue. And someone, somewhere would direct them to Mas Maraques. Yet Aristide did not leave. In the days following the recovery of his memory he found work impossible. He wandered the marshland, sometimes on foot, sometimes on horseback. He sat for hours looking out across the *étang*. He always took a sketchpad or canvas with him but invariably returned without drawing or painting a line. Inspiration had deserted him. Yet Aristide did not leave.

He told himself he was awaiting the right moment. He would slip away when neither Yvette nor the boys were around. His going would distress them. The disapproval of their elders had made the Bendol siblings and their friends even more fiercely loyal. They had started calling themselves the 'Brotherhood', a secret society pledged to his welfare. Aristide was touched and wanted to make sure that his departure caused his supporters the minimum of sadness. Certainly he would have to wait until after Yvette's wedding to François—now fixed for mid-July. She would be very miserable if he missed that. He gave himself another reason for procrastination: he needed to plan his future. It would be senseless just to wander off. He would have to go *somewhere*. Perhaps he should walk to Marseille. There he could work his passage on a boat—to Italy? Greece? Algeria? Perhaps even farther afield—the French Pacific colonies?

A few days after the journey to Les Saintes Maries, Aristide was down by the lagoon turning these ideas over yet again. The afternoon sun bleached the marsh vegetation into straw-coloured fronds. It burned on the rippleless surface of the water. Aristide was in one of his favourite places. A tongue of land protruded into the *étang* and was completely enclosed by tall reeds. If he lay down they afforded a modicum of shade and enabled him to watch the comings and goings of moorhens, herons and egrets without being detected.

He must have drowsed for he was suddenly aware that he was not alone. Someone had come to the water's edge a few metres away. Aristide parted the stands of rushes and peered out. It was Yvette. She was standing in one of the small boats used for fishing and was engaged in pulling off her dress. She laid it and her few other items of clothing in the stern and crouched for a few moments looking at her reflection. Then she lowered herself into the water. Aristide watched entranced as this beautiful, unselfconscious creature swam in lazy circles with leisurely strokes. He sat up to see her more clearly but took care to remain concealed. He fumbled for his sketchpad and pastels. He dashed in suggestions of colour—water, sky, boat, vegetation—and waited for Yvette to emerge into full view again.

She did so at last and sat on the

sternboard, her legs in the water, squeezing the wetness from her long bronze hair. Aristide was awestruck. He applied his chalks deftly, dashing in the highlights and shadows of the girl-woman's body. The glowing paleness of her skin contrasted with the coarse texture of the boat's planking. Her reflection had a numinous quality. This was Venus rising from the waves, but not as Botticelli saw her: ethereal, untouchable, an eternal symbol of idealised woman. Yvette was of the earth, not of mythical Arcadia. Her body existed not to be adored from afar. It awaited a husband's touch in worship of a different kind.

After a while the girl swung her legs over the side and lay down in the boat to be dried by the sun. Now she was largely out of sight. Aristide carefully repacked his knapsack and stole quietly from his hide.

Fifteen minutes later Yvette, now fully dressed, made her way along the bank to the place where her silent watcher had sat. She looked down at the flattened grass and bent reeds. And she smiled.

In the corner of a barn he was permitted to use as a studio Aristide brushed the dust from a clean canvas, set it on his easel and began to translate his sketch into paint. The sluice gates of his talent were suddenly open. The ideas gushed forth in almost uncontrollable exuberance. Aristide had the feeling that he was throwing pigment at the prepared surface without any calculated plan and yet somehow every brushstroke was falling on precisely the right place. He worked on and on, pausing only once to light a lamp.

'I've brought you some soup.'

Aristide had not heard Yvette come in. He looked round to see her standing just outside the circle of light holding a steaming fish-kettle. She was staring intently at the painting, head on one side.

'Am I beautiful?' She seemed quite unabashed.

'Very.'

'As beautiful as the woman in your book? As beautiful as all the women in Paris?'

Aristide laughed. 'You've no need to compare yourself with anyone else.'

Yvette advanced several paces and peered closely at the canvas. 'I think it is good.'

Aristide nodded. 'I think it's perhaps the best thing I've done...and yet...' He sighed.

The girl frowned. 'What's the matter? You don't like it after all?'

'No, no... It's just that... It doesn't say everything I want to say. Perhaps one study can't.' He stared at the painting's glistening surface, looking for faults of

291

technique, failures of interpretation.

Yvette laughed. 'Then we will make several more—until you are happy with them.'

Aristide stared at her. 'You don't mind?'

She tossed her head. 'No. Why should I?'

'Some of the others might not understand.'

'Then we won't tell them. No one will ever know. They don't look at your pictures. Anyway,' she spoke with a sudden fresh excitement, 'we've got a surprise for you. Something that will make everything much easier. Now, eat your soup quickly and I'll show you.' She slipped out of the barn.

When Aristide emerged a few minutes later there was still a lot of light left in the evening sky. Yvette was waiting by the boundary fence with two horses. He mounted and they rode for about a quarter of an hour, northwards, away from the *étang*. When they reached the point where marsh vegetation gave way to vestiges of old woodland Yvette led the way through a grove of poplar, ash and elder. She reined in beside a small sheepfold where other horses were already tethered.

'Aristide!'

He looked up to see the Simier twins

perched precariously on the ridge where they were carrying out repairs to the thatch. Sounds of banging and sawing came from inside.

Yvette jumped nimbly from the horse's bare back. 'Come and see!' She led the way into the building.

By the light of a couple of lamps Paul Lebec and Jean-Marc were constructing what looked like a wooden cage. Paul, now almost as tall as Aristide, put down his hammer and came to meet the new arrivals. He wasted no time on preliminaries. 'You need a proper studio. All artists have studios.' He waved a hand around the shadowy interior. 'No one will disturb you here. We're just making somewhere for you to stack your canvases—off the floor, away from the damp and the rats. That's right, isn't it?' His anxious frown begged for acceptance.

'Paul, this is marvellous. I don't know what to say. You must all have put in a lot of hard work...'

'It was mostly a question of cleaning out,' Yvette explained. 'The shepherds left the place in a terrible mess.'

Jean-Marc sauntered across grinning. 'Well, they won't want it any more. That's for sure!'

Paul, as leader, felt the need to explain more fully. 'The Brotherhood wanted to make up to you for the way some of the others are treating you. After all you've done for Mas Maraques they should be grateful, not grumble about you and tell lies. We don't want you to leave. We thought that if you had everything you need here you wouldn't feel you had to go away.'

Jean-Marc interposed. 'You can be our own hermit—like the ones Aunt Lou used to read to us about from her old books.'

Paul scowled at the interruption. 'Come and look round. Tell us if there's anything else you want us to do. We don't know what a studio is supposed to look like.' He led a tour of inspection.

Yvette grasped Aristide's hand. 'So you see, now you can paint me whenever you like.'

## CHAPTER 14

'Would you ask the head waiter to step across when he has a moment?' Tim asked the question as a Greek or Cypriot carefully served two helpings of what the menu called *maigret de canard Wellington*.

'There is something wrong?' The young man paused anxiously.

Catherine smiled at him, 'Not at all. The food looks excellent. We'd just like a word with him about something else.'

Moments later the head waiter glided confidentially to their table, his mask of professional solicitude securely in place. 'Sir, madam, are you enjoying your meal?'

'Very much, thank you. This duck is cooked to perfection. I'm with the *Daily Express*. I must get our food and wine chap to pay you a visit.' Tim decided that if he was going to lie he might as well go the whole hog.

'Thank you very much, sir. I'll pass your remarks to the head chef.'

'There was something else I wanted to ask you about.'

'Sir?'

'That bit of unpleasantness you had here last week.'

'You mean the poor gentleman who was murdered?'

'That's right. Did you—'

'I'm sorry, sir. We're under strict orders not to talk with the press.'

'Bad for the hotel's image?'

'Just so, sir.'

'I quite understand. I don't want to probe—though, of course, we do pay well for information we use *and* we protect our sources. I'm not going to press you for staff gossip. I just wondered whether the

295

victim—what was his name?'

'Jollibone,' Catherine prompted, with a disarming smile addressed to the waiter.

'Yes, Jollibone. I just wondered whether he dined here on the evening of the tragedy. That's not privileged information, I imagine. Would it be possible for you to check?'

The man's austere pose did not alter as he enquired, 'And what might that piece of information be worth, sir?'

'Twenty for starters. Of course, if you have more and we print it...'

'Fifty—on the strict understanding that this conversation never happened.'

Tim nodded.

'No need for me to check, sir. I ended up having to look after the unfortunate gentleman myself.'

Tim thought, Bingo! He said, 'Why was that?'

'M. Jollibone was one of our last diners. It was getting on for nine thirty (that's last orders) when he came in and he certainly didn't hurry over his meal.'

'He was alone?'

'Yes. As I say he lingered over every course. We all like to be away by eleven and Grégoire, who was looking after the gentleman's table, was particularly anxious to get home. His girlfriend's pregnant and having rather a tough time of it, I believe.

Eventually I told Grégoire he could go; I'd finish off for him.'

'So what time did Jollibone leave the grill room?'

'Between five and ten to eleven.'

Tim glanced quickly at Catherine. He said, 'You're quite sure about that time?'

'Oh yes, sir. At the end of a long shift one notices these things. I thought he was going to go a few minutes earlier but then he ordered another bottle.'

'I don't quite follow.'

'He'd drunk a bottle of the Aloxe-Corton '88—a particularly fine wine; may I recommend it to go with the *canard*, sir?'

'Thanks very much but I'm trying to keep a clear head. You were saying?'

'Well, M. Jollibone was just about to leave. He'd signed the bill. Then he asked for another bottle of the Burgundy. He said he had some friends coming round. By the time I'd organised that and changed the bill it was gone ten to eleven. Next morning they fished him out of the Thames. Seems to me whoever his drinking partners were, they certainly weren't friends.'

'Thank you very much. That fits in with the story we're putting together.'

'Thank *you*, sir.' The man pocketed the notes Tim passed below the level of the tabletop. 'If I can be of any further help just ask for Alfred.' He slid away as though on silent castors.

Catherine groaned. 'Everything we do, everything we find out, only seems to make things worse for the Lebecs—and Emma.'

Tim nodded. 'Jollibone can't have got to his room much before eleven. If Charles and Conrad were on time then how on earth would someone else...? It looks as though we're going to have to face up to the fact that they've been lying to us.'

Catherine shook her head. 'I won't believe that—not until I have to. My money's still on the Tarantin woman. Hey, I've got an idea! Don't go away!' She hurried from the room.

In the foyer she went up to the reception desk.

'Can I help you, madam?' A bright-looking girl in the hotel's dark-green livery smiled up at her.

Catherine put on her lost-American-tourist act. 'Well, I surely hope so. I have to meet a friend here, from Lyon, France. Would you mind calling her room to let her know I've arrived. Her name is Josephine Tarantin.'

'Could you spell that surname please, madam?'

Catherine did so and the clerk's fingers rattled swiftly over the computer keyboard.

'I'm sorry, madam, we don't have anyone of that name staying in the hotel.'

'Oh, but that's not possible!' Catherine's face registered mingled annoyance and amused indulgence. 'Why we arranged this meeting months ago. Check again, dear.'

'There is no need, I assure you, madam. The computer displays guest details immediately if they're registered.'

Catherine looked flustered. 'Oh dear, this is terrible. I have it right here in my diary.' She fumbled in her handbag and produced a slim black book. 'There, look. Thursday 18 February.'

'Today's the 25th, madam.'

'Oh, my goodness gracious. Don't tell me... Do you mean to say Josephine was here a week ago and I never... Did she leave a contact address? I must write a note and get you to send it on. She'll be so upset.'

'I'm afraid that won't be on our current instant retrieval programme. I'd have to get a print-out if your friend's name is on an earlier guest list.'

Catherine smiled sweetly. 'Would you mind? I'm so sorry to be a nuisance but if Josephine and I have missed each other after all these years...'

The girl resigned herself. With a patient smile she stood up. 'It may take a few minutes.' She walked into an inner office.

By the time she returned carrying a snake of computer print-out a small queue had formed behind Catherine. She sat down and began looking through the list of names. 'We had the ICN international convention here most of last week. They pretty near filled the hotel, so there weren't many other guests. Now let's see Philipson...Jonquil...Roberts...Andries ...Labardie...James... Ah yes, here we are, Tarantin J. There is a forwarding address. If you'd like to write a note I'll be happy to send it on.'

Catherine stared down at the paper—speechless.

'I said, would you like to write a note? You'll find paper and envelopes at the end of the counter.'

Catherine came to. 'I'm sorry. Yes, I'll do that. Thank you, dear.'

She felt elated, triumphant. Two birds with one stone! Then she made herself think calmly. Proof. The police would need proof.

She collected a sheet of headed notepaper from the box on the reception desk. She carried it to a small table in a corner of the foyer, took out a pen and pretended to write a letter. Carefully she watched the desk clerk. The girl spent several minutes dealing with a couple checking in. Then she had a short telephone conversation. Then she just sat. Catherine's spirits drooped. Would the woman never leave her post? A few seconds, that was all Catherine needed. After five minutes that seemed like fifty a tall man put his head round the door of the inner office and called to the girl. She disappeared behind the scenes, leaving the door slightly ajar. Catherine almost ran across the expanse of carpet. She leaned over the counter. The print-out was still lying there. Cautiously Catherine reached a hand over, rolled it up and slipped it into her handbag.

As she sat down opposite Tim again Catherine whispered excitedly, 'Boy, have I hit pay-dirt!'

'Josephine Tarantin?'

'She was here the night Jollibone was killed. I've got the hotel computer's guest list.'

Tim pushed his empty plate to one side. 'You mean you stole it.' He grinned. 'You realise that's against the law.'

'Yeah? Well so's murder. Tim, this is just what we need to give Armstrong's arm that extra twist. But there's more. Do you know who else was here?' She took the roll of paper cautiously from her bag, scanned the list of names, then folded it to reveal the information she wanted. 'There: suite 2A!'

Tim's eyes opened wide. 'Labardie C. and two others—presumably bodyguards. Wait till Jock sees this!'

Catherine attacked her cooling dinner. 'At last we're beginning to get somewhere. Which Labardie do you think was here?'

Tim shrugged. 'There's a Marseille box number shown, so I suppose it could be either of them. I'd better chase up that contact Labardie Junior gave me.' His eyes moved on down the list. 'Ah yes, here's Tarantin J. Room 409.' He rolled the print-out up again and handed it back. 'You'd better take this to Jock first thing in the morning. Tell him—nicely of course—that he must follow up the Labardie connection.'

'What will you be doing?'

'Taking my first ride through the Channel Tunnel on the earliest available Paris train.'

Over the weeks of high summer Aristide felt a gnawing sense of foreboding. The ruthless sun scorched grassland and marsh. It burned the colour from the land. It sucked moisture from the *étangs* whose retreating shorelines lay white with salt. It killed animals—or did not permit them to live. Among the Camargue's people it ignited desiccated fears and inflammable rivalries. Men came to blows over trifles.

*Mas* vied with *mas* over the shrinking pastures.

Aristide had less and less to do with the life of the farmstead. The menfolk shunned him and he was too absorbed in his work to make efforts of friendship. 'Work' meant Yvette. He was in the grip of a vision so intense that it was, like the unremitting sun, both clear and dazzling. Everything about this harsh, beautiful, simple, exuberant, primal land and people had its concentrated distillation in this child of the Camargue. With Yvette as his model he worked with a fervour and fluency he had never known. He still slept at the Bardols' house and took some meals there but otherwise he spent every available minute in or close to his new studio.

It was there that Yvette came to pose for him—although 'pose' was the wrong word. A white stallion pawing the air did not pose. A buzzard resting on the wind did not pose. A clump of asphodel pointing its blanched spikes at the sky did not pose. No more did Yvette. Whether stretched against the sheepshed wall, sitting half-concealed among the reeds, or leaning from an open window, she was a natural part of the vista. The scene was made for her and she for it just as an actress and a stage set were designed to complement one another. Aristide had to complete this series of pictures, this composite revelation of time, place and mood while it was on offer from the gods. He knew that it would be his finest work; that if he never began another canvas he would have fulfilled himself, completed whatever he had been sent to this world to achieve. This conviction drove him forward with mounting excitement. It also frightened him. The intensity of the present had overwhelmed the future so completely that the future had ceased to exist. He felt as though he was part of a wild cavalry charge—magnificent but fatal.

Most of the time he let these feelings possess him. When they became too strong he rationalised them. His haste, he told himself, was simply to make the most of an opportunity. Once Yvette and François were married it would vanish. The situation would change. There would be no more long afternoons of sunshine and laughter, of Yvette's solemn questioning and his own half-mocking response. The last vestiges of the child would have become absorbed in the woman. Yvette would be a wife and soon a mother. The possession of her husband. A part of the birthing and rearing cycle of her community. Then, Aristide told himself, then the time really would have come for him to move on.

But now was now, intense, glorious and

never to be repeated.

'Have you killed many men?' It was just another matter-of-fact question in the unending catechism with which Yvette occupied the hours when she was being painted. On this particular day they had discovered one of the few rivulets crossing the *marais* which had not been swallowed up by the thirsty earth. Pools of water were linked, like beads on a necklace, by the stream which trickled in its narrowed course. Here rushes still grew, green and lustrous. It was their colour Aristide wanted as back drapes for the girl's body. He needed to show the tints of the verdure reflected in her flesh and hair: to contrast the erect, swaying stalks with Yvette's suppleness. He located her in the little grove of reaching shoots, set his easel up on the other side of the stream and began work.

'Killed? No, not many.'

'What does it feel like?'

'In battle there's no time to consult your feelings. Your main concern is to stay alive. You kill in order not to be killed.'

She tossed her head to look at him. 'No, but afterwards, when you are wiping the blood from your sabre. Do you still feel nothing then?'

'Don't move your head!'

She pouted but adjusted her position.

'Answer my question, then.'

'You're right, of course. Taking life is terrible. Anyone who can do it and be completely unmoved is a monster not a man. That's one reason why I wasn't happy in the army. I wanted to enhance people's lives not destroy them.'

'Dear Aristide. You are so gentle. I can't imagine you deliberately hurting anyone.'

He frowned. 'I've told you before, you mustn't say such things. I'm just an ordinary man, not a god.'

'You are a god to me.' Once more Yvette turned to look at him. 'A beautiful, kind, gentle god.'

'Don't look at me—especially like that!' The words came in an angry shout. 'I'm not the person you think I am.' He lowered his brush and his voice. 'Oh, Yvette, if you only knew...'

'Knew what?'

'Very well, I will tell you. This "gentle god" you admire so much killed his own brother.'

'How?' No shocked reaction; just a flat question.

'We had a fight.'

'Then you didn't kill him on purpose.'

'No, but what does that matter? I killed him and ran away.'

'What was the fight about?'

Aristide sat on a tussock of dried marsh

grass and put his palette down beside him. 'Oh, I don't know. Lots of things, going right back into childhood. Finally, I suppose it was over a woman. Edouard was in love with the girl I was going to marry.'

Yvette shrugged. 'So you both wanted the same woman and you fought for her to the death. What is strange about that? It is the way we do things here, also.'

'Well, it isn't the way they do things in Paris. Anyway, it wasn't like that. Edouard was in love with Eloise but I wasn't. Yet it was I who was going to marry her. Poor Ed. It must have been intolerable for him.'

Yvette walked through the stream and sat beside Aristide. 'It's like us, isn't it?'

'What on earth do you mean?'

She lay back, gazing up at him with wide eyes. 'François doesn't love me but he is going to marry me. You do love me but you're not going to marry me.'

Emma spent most of Thursday clad in ancient, baggy overalls painting the *auberge's* sun-bleached woodwork. She was released from her room by a grumbling Jeanne. Men never seemed to realise how much work was involved in keeping a place clean and tidy, she complained. She had been on at Edgar for weeks to

307

freshen up the establishment's appearance and he had kept on promising to do the redecorating. But, of course, it was she who had had to go out and buy the paint and even then, when the tins were stacked prominently on the terrace, her husband had refused to take the hint. She blamed Denis Lebec. Oh, he was strange, that one, always hanging around as though neither he nor anyone else had work to do. Now today—an excellent day for painting; not a suggestion of wind or rain—Edgar had gone off, God knew where. Well, she could wait no longer. She was going to make a start on the doors and windows. Perhaps Edgar would be shamed into taking over when he deigned to return.

Emma's offer of help was motivated partly to stave off boredom and partly in the vague hope of making her escape. If she could engineer events so that she was out of Jeanne's sight for long enough she might be able to slip away. It was a slim chance: the only exit route from the hotel lay along the straight, hedgeless track which stretched a couple of kilometres to the main road. Jeanne proved more than equal to such naive schemes. She set her guest to work on the front of the building and wielded her own brush a few metres away. Together they laboured through the morning, Emma never out of her guardian's sight. Together they partook of a leisurely lunch. Together they resumed their labours in mid-afternoon.

Emma's attempts to extract information from the diminutive Frenchwoman were no more successful. Did she know anything about this Brotherhood her husband belonged to? Jeanne shook her head. She knew nothing and cared less. If it amused the menfolk to huddle together in gangs like little boys and have solemn oaths and shared secrets, what was that to her? She had a business to run and little help Edgar was in running it. Oh, he was very good at drinking with guests into the small hours and at leading riding parties across the *marais*, but when it came to routine jobs he was nowhere to be seen.

Emma very quickly discovered that every conversational door led into the same room, and resigned herself to concentrating on her own thoughts. Even they refused to wander far from her own fear and frustration: she was isolated here in the middle of a flat, menacing terrain, able to do nothing to help herself and knowing nothing about what her friends were doing to help her.

She might not have found very reassuring an account of the frenzied activity the Lacys and George Martin were involved in.

# CHAPTER 15

The details Tim had been given at Tarascon led him to an address in Paris's Ile de la Cité. The discreet offices behind ancient façades in the lee of Notre Dame are part of the capital's most expensive real estate. The businesses that pay handsomely to operate behind those façades are buying respectability and the probity conveyed by their hallowed and historic surroundings. *Etienne Bellecourt—Expert Comptable* was the discreet inscription on a discreet brass plate beside a door painted in discreet black. At a little after ten o'clock Tim checked the accountant's name, spoke into an intercom and ascended a narrow staircase to a first-floor office.

The reception area fell—discreetly—short of opulence. M. Bellecourt presumably did not want to give his clients the impression that the not-inconsiderable fees they paid were lavished on extravagant display. The receptionist referred Tim to M. Bellecourt's secretary whose stern demeanour proclaimed, *Ils ne passeront pas,* but who softened noticeably at the name Labardie. She withdrew into an inner office and reappeared moments later followed by a tall, moustached man who was already pulling on a topcoat.

He nodded to Tim. 'Mr Lacy.' Statement not question. 'Let's take a walk.' He strode towards the outer door ignoring his secretary who stood in the middle of the room protesting and brandishing an engagement diary.

Outside, the accountant opened an umbrella against the light drizzle and initiated a brisk pace in the direction of the gardens to the east of the cathedral. Reaching the lawn layered with wet leaves, he slowed down. There were few other people in the Square de l'Ile de France. Bellecourt obviously decided that the place was discreet enough to talk.

'So, M. Lacy, how may I help you?'

'I take it that M. Labardie Junior has notified you of our mutual interest in the circumstances of Auguste Jollibone's death?'

'He has indicated that I am free to discuss with you any matters that are strictly relevant to the possible location of a collection of paintings.'

'You handle the official accounts for M. Labardie and his father?'

'No. My clients have numerous business interests. I simply advise on certain aspects of them.'

'Principally financial investments.'

'That is correct.'

'Purely legitimate investments?'

'Of course.'

'In other words, you don't concern yourself with where the Labardies' money comes from. You simply tell them how to redistribute it. The technical term is "laundering", I believe.'

'I beg your pardon?'

'*Blanchissage*—it's one of the few words of French that I do know.'

Bellecourt halted abruptly. 'M. Lacy, if you are accusing me of unprofessional conduct this interview is over.'

'Relax, Bellecourt. All I'm interested in is the circumstances of Jollibone's death and what connection it may have with the group of paintings by Aristide Bertrand. I assume you know all about the pictures?'

The rain had eased. The Frenchman lowered his umbrella, shook the drops of water from it and furled it meticulously. 'Yes, young M. Charles consulted me.' He resumed his leisurely promenade.

'And you advised?'

'I told him that the Bertrands would be a very good investment if the price was right—and, of course, if they were properly authenticated.'

'Which is where Jollibone came in—and Josephine Tarantin.' Tim watched carefully for the accountant's reaction.

'Précisément.' The muscles tightened around Bellecourt's mouth.

'Young M. Charles has a lot of confidence in Mme Tarantin, hasn't he?'

'I believe so.'

'Oh, come off it, Bellecourt! Labardie has invested heavily in fine art, largely under Mme Tarantin's guidance. You must have approved many of his purchases. So you know her well and you're a party to their business relationship.'

'I have met the lady a few times.'

'Does young M. Charles trust her?'

Bellecourt gazed up at the flying buttresses arching against the church's bulging eastern apse. He gave a long-suffering sigh. 'Has this anything remotely to do with your efforts to locate the Bertrands?'

'It could have everything to do with it.'

'How exactly?'

Tim hesitated but realised he would have to reveal more of his hand if the tight-lipped accountant was to be drawn into continuing the game. 'The elegant Josephine is ripping your boss off.'

Bellecourt's eyes narrowed. 'You have proof?' There was inadequately suppressed excitement behind the question.

'I know she lied about the Bertrands and their whereabouts.'

'Ah, so you *have* located them?'

'No, but I know where they're not and, if you tell me everything you can about Madame T's relationship with the Labardies, I'm pretty sure I can track them down.'

They had reached the row of dripping trees along the river wall. They turned and began to retrace their steps while Bellecourt carefully calculated his response.

'You appreciate that I have to be extremely careful,' he said.

'I appreciate that if you upset your Marseille clients they won't content themselves with simply taking their custom elsewhere.'

Bellecourt ignored the barb. 'Balancing my clients' confidentiality with their best interests calls for the drawing of some very fine lines.' He paused. 'As for Mme Tarantin, I have never trusted her.'

'But young M. Charles won't listen to your reservations?'

'He prefers to form his own judgements.'

'Were you content to leave it at that?'

The Frenchman hesitated. 'I may have occasionally expressed my concerns to M. Labardie Senior.'

'I gather from young M. Charles that there is considerable friction between him and his father on the subject of fine art investment.'

'That's an overstatement. If anything,

M. Labardie is too indulgent concerning his son's tastes. What does worry him is the family's reputation.'

'Which would suffer badly if it became known that young M. Charles had been swindled by someone he trusted?'

'It would certainly affect business confidence.'

'That's why Papa decided to keep a close personal watch on Tarantin and Jollibone in London last week, I suppose?'

'Last week?' Bellecourt looked puzzled. 'M. Labardie was in New York. In fact, he has only just returned after a fairly extensive stay.'

'Are you sure about that?'

'Certainly. I exchanged phone calls or faxes with him most days. How did you get hold of the idea that he was in London?'

Tim thought hard. Was the accountant protesting too much? If old man Labardie had been staying at the Wellington and had been involved in the killing he would certainly want to cover his tracks. Being three thousand miles away was a pretty good alibi. But why ruin it by booking into the hotel in his own name—something that could very easily be checked? Tim pulled a piece of paper from an inside pocket. He read off the names of the two men booked into suite 2A with C.

Labardie. Do those mean anything to you?'

'They're members of young M. Charles's entourage.'

'Do you know where he has been these last few days?'

'He travels around a good deal.'

'He has his own plane, I presume?'

'Two. What's all this about?'

Tim ignored the question. 'Are you sure Labardie Junior has no idea Josephine Tarantin is cheating him?'

'She's made a very good job of ingratiating herself. And he believes that he is an excellent judge of character.'

The remainder of the short walk back to Bellecourt's office passed in silence. Tim was occupied in trying to assimilate the new information. The accountant was relieved that the interrogation was over. They parted with few words just as it came on to rain again.

Tim tried to phone George Martin from the Gare du Nord but there was no reply from his number. Not till late afternoon, when he was back in London, was he able to make contact with his colleague.

'George, how are things at your end?' Tim prowled the sitting room of the flat as he talked into the handset.

'Bloody boring, Major. I'm not being much use here.'

'On the contrary, mate; you're the lynchpin. How's Emma?'

'Frightened and trying hard not to show it. I spoke to her last night and I'll give her another call this evening.'

'You can tell her she's well out of it. At least the murderer doesn't know where she is.'

'Got your tabs on the killer then, Major?' George's voice brightened.

'I think we're getting close. We now know that the Tarantin woman's the key to everything. It's time for another chat. I'm coming over first thing in the morning. We'll either wring a confession out of her or get her to finger the assassin. Then we can hand her over to the gendarmerie and persuade the Lebecs to let Emma go. Are you managing to keep track of Charles?'

'No need, Major. He's round here about twice a day wanting to know what we've discovered. He's dead worried that his old man will panic and do something to Emma.'

'He's not the only one. Look, George, try to impress on him that we're within an ace of unmasking the murderer—*but don't tell him anything.* We don't want him or his stupid Brotherhood chums doing anything on their own initiative.'

'Right you are, Major.'

'Priority number one is stick to Josephine Tarantin like glue. What's she up to at this moment?'

'Carrying on as if nothing had happened. She leaves her apartment—it's about ten minutes' walk away—and opens up the gallery on the dot of ten, takes a couple of hours for lunch and shopping, then goes back to work till seven.'

'She hasn't got wise to you?'

'I don't think so. I keep out of the way as much as possible. Once she's ensconced in her office I don't hang around. If she saw me lounging in shop doorways she might get the wind up.'

'Well, I'm afraid you're going to have to step up the surveillance for the next few hours. If she does a bunk now we'll be right up the creek. Sorry about this, George, but as I say, I'll be with you first thing tomorrow. Then we'll see if we can't get some truth out of our elegant, accomplished liar.'

Tim detected a resigned sigh at the other end of the line. 'A bientôt, mate, as they say in France.'

'Do they now, Major?' George put down the receiver.

A few minutes later Catherine walked into the flat. After a quick kiss and hug she dropped onto the sofa. She eased her feet out of high-heeled shoes. 'Ooh, that's

318

better.' She looked up at her husband. 'Have you eaten?'

'Yes, lunch on the train. How about you?'

'Liquid lunch in a pub opposite Victoria Station. Tim, where does Jock put it all? The guy must have hollow legs. I feel distinctly light-headed and I was on straight orange juice after the first couple of rounds.'

'You got him definitely involved, then? Good girl! Tell me about it while I fix you some coffee and sandwiches.'

'Thanks, I could sure do with a bit of cosseting. I've spent most of the morning being ballgirl in a very unfriendly tennis match.'

'Armstrong versus Edgerson?' Tim moved into the little kitchen.

'Yeah. Hang in there while I try to organise my thoughts.' She went to the bedroom, peered into a mirror and brushed some stray strands of honey-coloured hair back into place. Returning to the sofa, she said, 'OK, let's take it from the top. I called Jock around half nine. I said if he wanted evidence of Labardie's involvement in Jollibone's murder we had it. He said, "OK, come round." So I went to his office and showed him the Wellington Tower's guest list. He wanted to know which Labardie we were talking about.

I said I wasn't sure and that you were working on it.'

'It was the young one,' Tim called out as he sliced ham from a small joint.

'Really? What do you suppose he was doing at the Wellington Tower?'

'I've been working that out all the way back from Paris. Young Charles has implicit trust in Tarantin but his old man and his accountant both seem to have taken her measure. They've warned him about her but he refuses to listen.' Tim assembled the sandwiches and brought a plateful through to the sitting room. He returned for the *cafetière* and two mugs. 'But, of course, the Bertrand deal was very big. Either he wanted to keep tabs on it himself or the warnings about the fair Josephine had begun to penetrate.' He poured coffee and added milk to Catherine's.

'So, you reckon it was one of Labardie's thugs who knifed Jollibone?' Catherine spoke through a mouthful of sandwich.

'That's how I see it. That solution certainly fits all the known facts together. If Labardie turned up unexpectedly La Tarantin would have had a nasty shock. Here was her boss, sniffing around and not liking what he was smelling. What could she do?'

'Divert suspicion to Jollibone?'

'That's right. Labardie's not going to stand for being double-crossed so he gets one of his thugs to terminate the dealer.'

Catherine sipped her coffee thoughtfully. 'But Mme Tarantin could just as easily have got rid of Jollibone to prevent him blabbing to Labardie. If Jollibone confirmed what Charles Junior's father and accountant were both saying; if she was unmasked she was dead. She'd go to any lengths to prevent her partner talking.'

'That's possible but it doesn't explain why Labardie was in such a hurry to contact us. As soon as he realised we had taken an interest he had to find out what we knew. He couldn't run the risk of anyone being able to connect him with Jollibone's death.'

'So it's not the pictures he's interested in?'

'I think they've taken second place. Survival's the name of the game, now. That's why he pointed me in the direction of his father and why he wanted me to waste time talking to Bellecourt. The accountant knows nothing.'

'So you had a wasted trip to Paris?'

'On the contrary. Bellecourt inadvertently put Labardie Junior at the scene of the crime. What Labardie couldn't possibly predict was that we'd get to see the Wellington Tower's guest list and, by a process of elimination, prove that he and his bodyguards were in the right place at the right time.'

'But he'll know as soon as Bellecourt reports back on your conversation.' Catherine looked at him with alarm.

'Very possibly, if the accountant gives him a blow-by-blow description. That was a risk I had to take. Time's running out fast. We've got to get together every scrap of proof. As soon as we can work out what really did happen at the hotel we can give La Tarantin the third degree—and the fourth and fifth. So, what did you manage to glean at Scotland Yard?'

'Well, as I said, Jock was very interested in the hotel printout. He grilled me pretty thoroughly and I told him everything I could think of about Jollibone, Tarantin and Labardie. I said I reckoned Edgerson would never make the connection with syndicated crime unless his nose was rubbed in the evidence. Jock said, "And dar'st thou then To beard the lion in his den, The Douglas in his hall?" And I said "Walter Scott". And he was no end impressed.'

Tim scowled. 'He would be. Was he suggesting that you both confronted Edgerson there and then?'

'He was and we did.'

'That must have been fun.'

'As I said, it was like a particularly bad-tempered tennis match, with me scurrying around the court trying to collect the balls. Edgerson wanted to know why I hadn't gone to him. Armstrong said that didn't matter; what was important was catching criminals. Edgerson said that was fine because he was close to making an arrest. Jock asked "Who?" and Edgerson wouldn't tell him. Then Edgerson asked if the pictures were stolen and Jock said not as far as he knew and Edgerson came straight back with, "Then why the hell is the Fine Art Squad sticking its nose in?" They went at it, back and forth, for ages. At last, Armstrong said that refusing help from colleagues was bad police procedure and that he was prepared to go to the chief superintendent and say so. My God, you should have seen Edgerson. I thought he was going to burst into flames on the spot. What he did do was fling the file at Jock, tell him to take whatever copies he wanted and have it back on his desk in half an hour.'

'Do you reckon Edgerson was bluffing about making an arrest?'

'He didn't give that impression. When Jock looked quickly through the file he commented that Edgy Edgerson seemed to be taking a particular interest in someone called Conrad Lebec. Of course, I played the innocent but my stomach fell through the floor.'

'Damn! Damn! Damn! Things are happening too fast.' Tim prowled the room. 'After that fracas what's the betting our bad-tempered young inspector jumps the gun and brings Conrad in—simply to prove a point. Is Jock going to move quickly? He's our only hope, now.'

'He said he was going to go through all the statements and the forensic report during the afternoon, then visit the hotel. He reckoned he'd be there about six. If you just happened to turn up there about the same time, he wouldn't say no to an offer to buy him a drink.'

Tim looked at his watch. 'Half an hour. I think perhaps I'll give Emma a quick call—to keep her spirits up.'

Catherine rose and carried her plate and mug through to the kitchen. 'I hope you have better luck than me. I called a couple of hours ago and got some woman who made out she couldn't understand what I was saying.'

'You're sure you had the right number?'

'I rang it twice, just to make sure. I got the same woman both times.'

'What the hell are they playing at? The arrangement was we could talk to Emma any time. Where's the number?'

Catherine called from the kitchen. 'On

the pad by the window.'

Tim picked up the phone. Carefully he punched in the appropriate digits.

'Allo!' A woman's voice, cautious.

'Bonjour, madame. C'est M. Lacy à l'appareil. Je veux parler avec Mlle Kerr.'

'Non, monsieur! Ce n'est pas possible!' The line went dead.

Yvette's marriage to François was a joyful but also a muted event. The couple were brought back from the church at Gageron on a cart decorated with flowers and bunting. There was feasting and dancing till long beyond nightfall. The couple were escorted to their chamber with traditional ribaldry. Yet, as he watched the celebrations—an observer keeping deliberately in the shadows on the edge of the crowd—Aristide saw a bride and groom who seldom looked at each other and who seemed to derive little pleasure from being the centre of everyone's attention. Their reticence conveyed itself to the whole company. The merrymaking had about it a feeling of routine, of convention.

After the wedding day life at the *mas* continued as normal. Yvette moved to the house across the yard occupied by François and his widowed mother. Madeleine found plenty of work for her to do and often deliberately created it, but Yvette refused to submit to her mother-in-law's authority. As a result Madeleine, who had urged her son into the marriage, found no contentment in the changed domestic situation. Quite the reverse. She and her daughter-in-law were constantly at loggerheads. Madeleine told her son to put his foot down but the rangy François took no sides. He kept aloof from kitchen squabbles, preferring the company of the other men.

What most outraged Madeleine was Yvette's frequent absence from the *mas*. She would wander off at will in search of Aristide, and make no secret of the fact. The more her mother-in-law taxed her with the impropriety of such excursions, the more determined the young bride became to continue them. Eventually the embittered old woman reached a decision. Her indolent son could not see what was going on under his very nose. Very well, she would find proof of what was afoot. Then François would have to take action. She began to follow Yvette on her sorties.

Aristide spent less time at the *mas*. The Brotherhood made a chimney at one end of the sheepshed and installed some primitive cooking arrangements. Aristide fell into the habit of fetching kettles of Aunt Lou's soup or boiled fish or meat which could be reheated day after day. Sometimes he was too absorbed in his painting to concern himself with domestic trivia. On these occasions he made do with bread and a flask of wine and wrapped himself in a blanket beside the fire instead of returning to the farmstead to sleep.

It was on one of his rare evenings in the Bardol kitchen that Aunt Lou confronted him across the table. They were alone. Jean-Marc and his friends were in the near meadow practising the *course à cocarde,* which involved trying to snatch a rosette tied between the horns of a young steer. Like all Camargue boys, they yearned to be *razetteurs,* participants in the real games held in the town arenas. On many summer evenings they played their dangerous game until darkness or injury brought them to a halt. As Aristide and the old woman sat in lamplit silence they could faintly hear the shouts and whoops of the boys in the nearby field.

'When will you go, young man?' Aunt Lou did not look up from the patch she was sewing on her nephew's trousers.

'Soon.'

' "Soon" is a restless word—always on the move. You, by contrast, seem very settled.'

'This is a difficult place to leave,' Aristide observed lamely.

'You mean, Yvette is difficult to leave.'

'I think she will be very sad when I go.'

'There will be great sorrow whether you go or stay.' The reflected lamplight in her deep-set eyes was like the flicker of light in the depths of a well.

'Why should that be so?'

'Don't pretend to be an idiot!' Aunt Lou snapped the twine with tough fingers. 'She has made her choice—the right choice, fortunately. There is nothing but misery for you both if you remain. And there's another thing; you may bring bad luck on Mas Maraques.'

Aristide looked at her in alarm. He asked the question apprehensively. 'Why should I bring bad luck?'

'The police are not welcome here. Oh, don't look so surprised. Yvette has few secrets from me. I know about the fiancée who saw you in Les Saintes Maries and about the brother who loved her. Yvette told me your story when she came to ask me if she should marry you.'

*'Marry me!'*

'Your astonishment proves that my advice to her was doubly right. Ours is a very different world to yours. You could not become a part of us.'

Aristide sighed deeply. What is my world, Aunt Lou? Where is it? Can you tell me that?'

The old woman reached into the basket beside her for another garment to mend. She squinted at it shortsightedly. 'There was a priest at Albaron some years ago. Quite a scholar he was and had very many books. He might have become a bishop, people said, but there was some scandal and he was sent to the *marais*—"premature burial" he called it. Anyway, he used to lend me books. One was called *The Wandering Jew*. It was about a wretched man who mocked Our Lord as he stumbled under the weight of his cross. "Can you go no faster?" the Jew taunted. "I shall die soon enough," Christ replied, "but you must await your death till I return." Thus, the poor man wandered the earth for centuries and lived many lives seeking what he could not find. The old priest told me that the story was about man's quest for redemption. Do you know what he meant by that?'

'Yes, I think so.'

'You will not find it here.'

'No. I had hoped... Saving Jean-Marc, helping to drive out the shepherds, painting God's creation... How much does it take to atone for a life?'

They sat in silence for some time. Then Aristide rose. 'I'll sleep now and leave in the morning. It will be best if no one knows.'

Aunt Lou nodded.

He stood looking down at the old woman thoughtfully. 'My paintings...what...?'

'You can trust the children to look after them till you come back for them. They will make sure they remain well hidden and that no harm comes to them.'

Aristide smiled lightly. 'Do you know what they call themselves?'

'Yes, the Brotherhood. They have been good brothers to you.'

'Indeed they have. I hate leaving without saying goodbye to them...and to Yvette.'

'I will say your goodbyes. They will understand.'

Across the yard a very different conversation was taking place. Madeleine had followed her son when he went to shut up the sheds for the night. She cornered him in the hay barn and for fifteen minutes she poured out her revelations in sentences that became more shrill and breathless as their content grew more scandalous.

'Naked! Yes, utterly naked! Not a stitch! I told you they were not to be trusted. They're making a fool of you. Dishonouring your name! My name! Now perhaps you'll do something! Go to her now, boy. Beat the truth out of her!'

François made no answer. He glowered at his mother, then pushed past her and strode back to the house.

But later, as she sat by the kitchen stove, Madeleine had the satisfaction of hearing, from the room above, the swish of François's belt and the agonised screams of his wife.

It was soon after dawn the next morning that Aristide left the Bardol house. He stood in the still air and looked around the familiar homestead. He had come to love every bit of Mas Maraques. Even the long shadows were familiar and lovely. With a sigh, he turned, shouldered his knapsack, and walked away towards the *étang*.

Moments later a figure detached itself from the darkness beside one of the other buildings and followed.

In the middle of the morning Yvette was winding water up from the well when Aunt Lou came across to her. She had chosen her moment deliberately when no one else was within earshot. She noticed how the girl winced with pain as she moved her arm and guessed the reason.

'My child, there is something I must—'

But before she could say any more, Yvette demanded, 'Where's Aristide? I must see him.'

'You cannot. He's gone!'

'Gone!' With a wail, Yvette let go the handle which spun back as the full bucket plunged down the shaft. 'Gone where?'

'Gone away, as you know he must.'

'No! No! Oh, Aunt Lou, you don't understand! When did he go?'

'At first light. He will be far away by now.'

'Oh, pray God you are right!'

Without another word Yvette ran across the yard to the shed where the horse tack was stored. She grabbed a bridle, went to the meadow, whistled up her favourite mare and moments later was seen cantering away from the *mas*, her hair streaming out behind her.

Shortly before nightfall the horse came back alone.

Tim spotted Jock Armstrong sitting alone at a corner table of the Salamanca Bar with papers spread before him. He collected two scotches from the bartender, diluted his own heavily with water and walked across the room whose walls were hung with framed newspaper reports, cartoons and other memorabilia of Wellington's Peninsular campaign.

'There you go, Jock. What progress?'

The policeman accepted the whisky without a word and gulped it down. He gazed at the military mementos on the wall beside him. 'I think I know how the Iron Duke felt at Waterloo when the battle seemed lost and there was still no sign of Blücher.'

Tim sat down. 'That bad?'

'We've got one eyewitness who probably saw the murderers but, by his own admission, he was so much under the influence of John Barleycorn that he doubts if he would recognise them again.'

'We can't all hold our drink like cynical old cops with cast-iron livers, Jock. Have you been able to get a picture of the sequence of events surrounding Jollibone's death?'

'Aye, for the most part. But without reliable eyewitnesses it doesn't help us. The fact that one of the Labardies and the Tarantin woman were staying in the hotel doesn't by itself get us anywhere.'

'For what it's worth, I now know that it was the younger Labardie who was booked into suite 2A with a couple of his strong-armed cronies.'

Armstrong shrugged. 'They'll all alibi each other—and probably the woman as well.'

Tim looked at the photocopies strewn over the table. 'So what exactly have we got?'

'Forensic are being cagey about the time of death. When a body is soaked in Thames water for several hours it tends to play havoc with vital signs. All they'll say is that Jollibone was dead by midnight.'

'And we know he was alive shortly before eleven, when he left the grill room.'

'We can do a bit better than that; we can see him right back to his own door. He took the lift to the fifth floor—and stepped out into a lecherous mini-drama.' He picked up a single typed sheet. 'A Ms Susan Myllar was lodged in room 533. She was part of a large corporate conference that was being held here. They'd just finished a big formal dinner. It seems she was being pestered by some office Lothario who was far from gay. This Desmond Pocock apparently believed that natural charm fortified by copious ambrosial draughts rendered him irresistible. His attentions throughout the meal became less and less discreet and, as soon as she could, Ms Myllar left the party to seek the sanctuary of room 533. But she was not sufficiently fleet of foot. Beauty was pursued by the lumbering beast. He caught up with her at her door and there ensued a long argument. Pocock wanted to get into her room, and not only into her room. The virtuous maid was determined not to sell the pass. They actually began to struggle for the key. Then, enter the gallant Don Quixote.'

'Jollibone?'

'The very same. He emerged from the lift and lurched along the corridor. Susan reckoned he was hardly more sober than Pocock. Anyway, he took in the situation at a glance and went for the libidinous Desmond brandishing a bottle of wine. Perhaps he had visions of Jean Margueritte's futile charge at Sedan. Anyway the sortie ended scarcely less disastrously. Jollibone fell over, picked himself up, abandoned his crusade and retreated to his own room. Meanwhile Ms Myllar had taken advantage of the distraction. She disengaged herself, got inside her room and shut the door—very firmly. Exit one witness. The frustrated satyr, of course, lumbered off to his own lonely bed.'

'Going back past Jollibone's room?'

'Yes.'

'Did anyone get a statement out of Pocock?'

'Yes, someone from his local cop shop in Leicestershire persuaded him that he ought to talk—so that he could be eliminated from our inquiries. Here's his version.' Armstrong found another, shorter piece of typed text. 'You'll not be surprised that his account reads somewhat differently.'

I left the function room with Ms Myllar about 10.50 and escorted her to her room because we had some matters of company business to discuss. It was a friendly conversation—on a

335

purely professional level. I was just saying goodnight when a man came staggering along the corridor from the lift brandishing a bottle. I advised Ms Myllar to go into her room and shut the door while I faced this man who was obviously drunk. When he saw me standing my ground he decided not to risk a fight. He turned back and I saw him let himself into a room along the corridor. When I had satisfied myself that he was not coming out I went to the lift in order to return to my own room. When the lift came two men got out. I could tell from their conversation that they were French. I did not see where they went to. I cannot describe them accurately. I only saw them for a few seconds. I had had a very convivial evening and I was probably not as observant as I might normally have been.

'So he didn't notice whether Jollibone's door was still open when he passed it?'

'Presumably he was a "chaos of thought and passion all confused".' Armstrong smiled at the aptness of the quotation, then added for his companion's benefit, 'Alexander Pope.'

Tim clenched his eyes and tried to think. Pocock's account dovetailed exactly with Conrad's. The two Frenchmen coming

336

out of the lift must have been the Lebecs. But that could not have been more than a minute after Jollibone had been seeing going into his room. Yet, according to Conrad, the dealer was already dead when they found him, seconds later. Tim's stomach suddenly felt full of lead. The Lebecs had been lying all along. There could be no other explanation.

Armstrong was still talking, unaware of Tim's preoccupation. 'It's a pound to a penny that Pocock actually saw the murderers—Labardie's bully boys. By the way, we know that Jollibone was expecting visitors. He told Alfred, the head waiter, as much.'

'So, you reckon these thugs had a quiet drink with the dealer, then, sometime in the following hour, they knifed him?'

'That's the way Edgerson figures it, but I've been looking very closely at the forensic evidence and it appears a bit different to me. Come on, we'll go to the room and you can tell me which theory you prefer.'

They took the lift to the fifth floor, turned to the right and went through a fire door. They were confronted with a corridor some hundred metres long.

Jock walked almost to the end of the corridor and stopped outside number 533 on the left. 'Here's where the Myllar-Pocock sparring match occurred. They saw Jollibone go to his room. Then, after the fair Susan had made good her escape her hamfisted would-be seducer walked past 518, towards the lift. Now, Tim, would you mind strolling back to the lift with a nautical, rolling gait? Press the button and when the lift comes up, walk back as far as 518.'

Tim made the short journey while Armstrong pulled out his half-hunter and timed him. When he reappeared through the fire door Armstrong looked at his watch, snapped it shut and slipped it into a waistcoat pocket.

He came up to Tim. 'Just trying to account for as much time as possible from the last moment Jollibone was seen alive. So far I've got fifty-three seconds but, of course, that depends on how long Pocock had to wait for the lift. So, our assassins stand here and knock.' He took out a key-card and opened the door. 'Jollibone comes to greet them.' He pushed the door open wide. 'Would you mind being Jollibone, Tim? Stand just there, facing me. OK, now turn and lead the way into the room.'

Tim did so but before he had taken a step he felt a thump between the shoulder-blades. He staggered forward and had to grab at the wardrobe handle on his left to stop himself falling. 'What the—'

Armstrong's commentary smoothly continued. 'Of course you're younger and more agile than poor Jollibone and you don't now have nine inches of steel buried in your back. Would you mind just letting yourself fall?'

Tim crumpled to the beige carpet and lay face downwards.

Jock stepped over him and stood looking down with satisfaction. 'Aye, that's about right.'

Tim grunted. 'Can I get up now?'

'Yes, but on your way look at that stain by your left side.'

Tim peered at a small, brownish, linear mark about two inches long. 'Blood?'

'Aye, and that's all the blood there was. According to forensic that's entirely consistent with a stab wound in the back and a body lying on its front. There's a lot of blood but most of it gets absorbed by the clothing. Just some trickles round the side and onto the floor.'

'But that doesn't prove that Jollibone was stabbed facing *into* the room.' Tim dusted his suit down. 'He could have been attacked from inside the room later on.'

'That's what Edgerson prefers to believe. But he's ignoring the bottle.'

'Bottle?'

'Oh, come on, man! Use your head! The

bottle of Burgundy Jollibone brought back here to share with his guests!' Armstrong sat heavily on the end of the bed. 'Before the murderers left with the body (and we know how that was done; we've found a housemaid's trolley with smears of blood inside it) they went over the place meticulously. There wasn't a fingerprint to be found. But they didn't notice the bottle. "Why not?" I hear you cry. Because it was under the bed where forensic found it. And why was it under the bed?'

Tim thought hard. 'Because Jollibone dropped it when he was attacked and it rolled out of sight?'

'Weel done, Cutty-sark! Now, I can only see one way that can happen. When Jollibone comes to the door, he's still holding the bottle. Why? Either he hasn't got round to putting it down or he wants to show it to his guests—"Come on in, lads, and we'll have a bit of a party." He turns round—and wallop! There's no other way it can have been. If they'd all sat down and had a drink, or if they'd talked a while and left the bottle unopened, either it would still be here, wiped clinically clean like everything else, or it would have disappeared.'

Tim sat in an armchair and pondered the inescapable logic. He looked at the narrow entrance passageway into the room—bathroom on one side, wardrobe on the other. He imagined Jollibone arriving, clutching the Aloxe-Corton. He saw him go to the door after scarcely a minute. There stood Charles Lebec with his brother behind him. Jollibone turned and Charles—or was it Conrad—raised a hand in which something glinted.

Armstrong stood abruptly. 'The devil is, we can't prove a thing. Labardie's been too clever for us—clever and lucky. Even if we could get his assassins extradited to take part in an identity parade we couldn't rely on Pocock pointing them out. And if he did, you can imagine what an expensive defence counsel would do with his evidence.'

Lacy sat looking gloomily into space. 'And there's no other evidence at all? What about the body?'

'There was no diary or wallet, no letters—he was identified from his passport; nothing to indicate whom he might have been meeting.'

'And the wound?'

'Made with a long, thickish blade, driven in exceedingly hard.'

'Right or left-hand attacker?'

'Forensic won't commit themselves. They only say the wound was straight and deep. Let's go. There's nothing more to see here.'

As they walked back down the corridor Tim asked, 'What's Edgerson doing now? Catherine said he was muttering about an imminent arrest.'

'The silly wee man!' Armstrong snorted his contempt. 'He wants to bring in some poor bugger called, what is it...Leclerc, Lebec, something like that...for two stunningly brilliant reasons—this chap is French and Jollibone spoke to him on the phone.'

'When's he going to pick this chap up?' Tim asked anxiously.

'The super has warned him off for twenty-four hours to give me time to come up with something on Labardie. If I don't I shall be floating paddleless up excrement creek. So, what have you got for me?'

Tim gave a version of his talk with Bellecourt as they made their way back to the bar.

'So Labardie doesn't want anyone to know he was here when Jollibone was killed. So he's keeping tabs on you to find out what you know. That's not enough to put him in the dock.' Armstrong settled himself gloomily onto a bench seat by the window.

Tim picked up the file from the table. 'Could I possibly borrow this overnight? I just might be able to see something from a different angle.'

Jock shrugged. 'Why not? I'm in up to my neck. Releasing classified information can hardly make matters worse.'

'Thanks. I'll see that Catherine gets it back to you first thing in the morning.'

'And where will you be, the while?'

'Following up the one lead we've got left. And doing something the police can't do: putting Josephine Tarantin on the rack.'

Jock looked at his watch and rose to leave. 'Well, needless to say, I've just been smitten by sudden deafness.' He rested his hands on the table and leaned forward. 'Do you know, there's something you haven't told me, young Lacy. I'm not altogether sure I want to know, but I must ask. Why are you so obsessed by this case? You weren't a friend of Jollibone. You've no professional interest in these paintings that appear to have gone missing. So, where's the method in your madness?'

Tim got wearily to his feet. 'Believe me, Jock, I wish I could tell you. And I hope desperately that I'll be in a position to tell you very soon.'

Back at the flat Catherine jumped from the sofa as soon as Tim came in. She rushed to throw her arms round him. 'Oh, darling. George has just been on the phone. Terrible news.'

# CHAPTER 16

After his telephone conversation with his
boss George Martin finished the plateful
of pastries and the coffee he had ordered
from room service. He reflected that this
business Emma had involved them in was
costing Lacy Enterprises a pretty packet.
He hoped there would be some profit
in it somewhere. Neither the Major nor
Catherine mentioned finances to him
directly but everyone at Farrans knew that
things were very tight. The last thing the
firm needed was unnecessary foreign hotel
bills. So—he stood up, brushing crumbs
from his lap—best get this business over
quickly. George was glad the Major was
coming over for another crack at Mme
Tarantin. If it had been up to him, he
would have given her a thorough grilling as
soon as he realised she had been lying. She
was obviously stringing along the Labardies
and the Lebecs. That meant she was tough
as well as devious. It would not be easy to
get the truth out of her. He checked his
watch: 6.35. If madame kept to her usual
schedule she would leave on the dot of
seven. He wrapped a scarf round his neck,

pulled on a heavy topcoat and thrust his hands into woollen gloves. A glance out of the window told him it had come on to rain again. He shivered, picked up his stub umbrella and left the room. He was resigned to a long, uncomfortable night.

Few shoppers were left on the rue Gramont. A couple of storekeepers were putting up the shutters early. George picked his way between the puddles scattered among the glistening cobbles. He stared absently into a jeweller's window where an assistant was dismantling a velvet-draped display of diamond and emerald adornments unsullied by the vulgar indiscretion of price tags. As he approached number 24 he saw that the soft lights were still on inside the gallery. He walked past. The tiny 'Open' sign was showing in the corner of the glazed door. He strolled on, rain drumming on the black canopy of his umbrella.

At a pace that was leisurely without being suspicious it took about six minutes to walk the length of the short street. George timed his perambulations. It gave him something to think about apart from his miserable surroundings and the depressing prospect of the night ahead. However, by seven fifteen he was beginning to grow alarmed. The suspicion increased to a certainty that Mme Tarantin had given him the slip. She must have realised that she was under surveillance and let herself out by the back door, leaving the gallery lights on to fool him.

As he approached number 24 for the fourth time and peered into its empty, well-lit interior George cursed his over-confidence. He went to the door and tried the handle.

The door opened. The electric buzz was loud and made him jump. Quickly he pulled the door and withdrew. Well, that was a relief. The bird had not flown. Just working late. From across the street George kept watch, expecting to see the elegant gallery proprietor emerge from the rear office. She did not.

George gave her a minute, then retraced his steps. This time he held the door open for several seconds, allowing its urgent signal to sound loud and long. There was no response. All George's anxieties returned. Surely the Tarantin woman would not do a bunk and leave the premises wide open? He stepped inside and closed the door behind him.

The sudden silence remained unbroken. He collapsed his dripping umbrella. He walked quickly to the far end of the picture-hung room. He entered the inner sanctum.

'Good God!' George stood transfixed by

the sight which confronted him.

The office was undisturbed. The red chairs stood in a neat semi-circle before the wide desk upon which two piles of correspondence were neatly arranged. Slumped forward across its surface was Josephine Tarantin. She was wearing a suit of lemon yellow linen. In the centre of the back there was a wide red stain.

George stood very still. He took several deep breaths. As a measure of calm returned he looked around the room more carefully. Nothing seemed to have been touched. A hideous, but doubtless valuable, painting stood on the easel in the corner. A small safe set in the wall to the left looked to be securely locked.

He advanced around the desk. None of the drawers was open. George drew off one of his gloves. Cautiously he touched the back of the dead woman's right hand which lay palm-down on the desk. Cooling. Whoever had done this was long gone. George decided to follow the assassin's example.

He put his glove back on, opened the office's outer door, which was unlocked, and slipped through into the courtyard. It was unlit, dark. It took George a couple of minutes to locate the exit which led to a side alley. Having found it, he peered out cautiously. Satisfied that there was no one about, he emerged into the world of the living and made his way, at a brisk pace, back to the hotel.

In the Cour des Loges there were two things he had to do urgently. First he went to the bar, ordered a cognac and gulped it down. Then he went to his room and phoned through his report.

Tim Lacy also needed a brandy to help him cope with the news. After Catherine had relayed George's story he poured himself a generous measure of his best armagnac. He crouched over it in front of the gas fire.

'God! I've been so stupid!'

Catherine came and sat beside him on the hearth rug. She stroked his hair. 'It's not your fault. If anyone had it coming to her it was Josephine Tarantin. Playing both sides against the middle is a dangerous game.'

'Of course it's my fault. I blabbed our suspicions to Bellecourt. I'll bet he couldn't wait to report back to Labardie. And that cultivated young thug wasted no time in paying off Josephine and also ensuring her silence.'

'Well, at least no one can pin this murder on the Lebecs.'

Tim groaned. 'Damn! I hadn't thought of that. Of course they can. And, knowing

Edgerson, he will.'

'What do you mean?'

'Sometime tomorrow he's going to take Conrad in and try to bully a confession out of him. By then the French police will probably have told him of Mme Tarantin's demise.'

'So?'

'So, can't you see him putting two and two together and making five hundred? Auguste Jollibone is killed in London. Conrad Lebec lives in London. Josephine Tarantin is killed in Lyon. And where does Conrad's little brother, Charles, live?'

'Yeah, I see. But he won't be able to make it stick.'

'It doesn't matter, does it? Not for Emma. As soon as Denis Lebec hears that his sons have been taken onto custody on suspicion of murder...'

'Don't!' Catherine sank her head onto his shoulder. 'Oh, Tim, what are we going to do?'

He turned and put his arms round her. 'Don't worry, darling. I'll get her out somehow.' He kissed her on the forehead, then stood up. 'We can forget all about finding out who killed whom. The time for bargains and deals is over. We'll have to go in like the seventh cavalry—and fast.'

He crossed to the Charles II dresser and refilled his brandy glass from a Bristol green decanter. 'We've got to act before anyone else has a chance to do anything. That means, first of all, getting the Lebecs out of police clutches.' He rubbed a finger up and down the bridge of his nose, concentrating hard. 'We'll take them with us.'

'Where to?'

'What's the nearest international airport to the Camargue?'

Catherine thought for a moment. 'Marseille, I suppose.'

'Right.' He reached for the phone.

Seconds later he was talking to George Martin. 'OK, George, here's what we're going to do. Get hold of Charles Lebec p.d.q. Find out from him exactly where they're keeping Emma. Beat the information out of him if you have to. Make sure he doesn't talk with any of his cronies. Then I want the two of you to go to Marseille.'

'How am I supposed to persuade him to come, Major?'

'I don't care how you do it, just do it.'

'Thanks a bundle.'

'Sorry, George, but it's desperation measures. I'm scraping the barrel so hard I've got splinters. If you like, you can tell Lebec that I'm coming with proof of his innocence. I'll be on the first flight in from Heathrow.'

'And have you got proof that clears the Lebecs?'

' 'Fraid not. I know damn well that Jollibone's death was the result of a deal involving Labardie and Tarantin that went wrong. And I'm sure that Labardie has now got rid of the woman to cover his own tracks, but I don't have a shred of evidence. But don't let Charles know that.'

'Right you are, Major. We'll be there, somehow. Oh, Major, have you been in touch with Emma? I called earlier but that moron, Edgar, wouldn't let me speak to her.'

'No, we haven't been able to raise her, either. As you say, Edgar's a moron. He probably hasn't the wit to accept responsibility for letting us talk to her. At least, I hope to heaven that is the explanation. If old man Lebec has laid a finger on her I shan't be answerable for my actions. Anyway, see you tomorrow, George—and good luck with Lebec.'

Catherine had moved to the sofa. She frowned up at him. 'Would you mind telling me exactly what you have in mind?'

He sighed. 'Sheer, bloody brute force. We've tried the subtle options. Now it's a case of in through the front door with guns blazing. I'm going to go with the Lebec boys to wherever it is they've got

Emma and try to bounce them into letting her go.'

'That's just putting your lives at risk as well as Emma's.'

'I'll make it clear that if the three of us don't walk away, everything we know will be with the police and the leading Marseille crime syndicate within hours—and that'll be the truth. Labardie and Edgerson can fight over their carcasses for all I care.' He saw the alarm on Catherine's face. 'But it won't come to that. The Lebecs must know by now that holding Emma can only make matters worse for them.'

Tim sat beside Catherine and gave her a quick hug. 'I'm going to see Conrad now. Can you book two seats on the first Marseille flight tomorrow?'

'How are you going to persuade him to go?'

'The honest answer is, I don't know. I'll just have to play it by ear.'

After Tim had gone Catherine called the Air France office and made the necessary arrangements. She took a shower. She made some coffee. She settled by the fire with her mug and the *Evening Standard*. When she had read the same paragraph three times and still did not know what it was about she threw the paper aside. She looked at her watch: 8.33. By this time tomorrow either they would all be here in this room—Tim, herself, George...and Emma—or...

'Catherine Lacy, this brooding will not do!' She shouted her frustration out loud. 'Get on with something useful.'

She walked through into the tiny spare bedroom which she and Tim used as an office. The PC stood on a small table. She switched it on and selected the file entitled 'The Secret Years'. It was the name she had given to the story of Aristide Bertrand and his paintings. In odd moments over the last couple of days she had been typing up Emma's fragmentary notes and turning them into a readable narrative. Sometimes she told herself that the exercise might bring to light some useful clue. At others she regarded her text as a draft for the catalogue which would be necessary when the Bertrands went on display. When she was honest she admitted that what she was doing was keeping her mind occupied.

Catherine found the scrawled page in the old diary where she had left off and adjusted her eyes to the cramped writing. She moved her fingers over the keyboard.

Aristide Bertrand, thus, left the little community at Mas Maraques as suddenly as he had joined it. Aunt Lou explained to the members of the

Brotherhood that the artist had charged them with the responsibility of looking after his paintings until he returned for them. But weeks passed, then months and years and Aristide Bertrand did not come back.

Thanks largely to the determination of Yvette Bardol—or Yvette Robert, as she now was—the little group of the painter's friends took their task seriously. They made sure that his works were safely wrapped and stored and they guarded the secret of their location. Not that anyone else was interested. The other inhabitants of Mas Maraques had never understood the genius in their midst and they sustained no warm memories of him. If any of them ever saw the boys going out to the old sheepshed, which rapidly disappeared behind a steadily thickening wall of trees and creepers, they displayed no curiosity. Neither they nor the other *gardians* had any use for the rotting building.

Yvette Robert lived until 1935 and to her, above all, must go the credit for the preservation of this remarkable collection. It was she who held together the original members of the Brotherhood and ensured that its sacred trust was passed on to later generations. She had only one child of her own, a son,

Georges, to whom the secret could be conveyed. [Margin note: check this with Conrad's story about other children dying in infancy.] She lost her brother during the First World War, a conflict which also claimed the life of Philippe Simier. However, her descendants and those of Paul Lebec and Gaston Simier cared for and guarded these magnificent works and it is thanks to them that we can now see all these paintings together.

For a hundred years Aristide Bertrand has been one of the enigmas of Postimpressionist art. The exciting discovery of his Camargue paintings and the account of his life there in 1888–9 have given us a vivid picture of this 'lost' genius. But what became of him after his departure from Mas Maraques remains a mystery. He appears in no police records either under the name of Aristide Bertrand or Albert de Bracieux. Did he escape from France and, like Gauguin, end his days in some distant haven? Will a careful study of the recently discovered paintings enable us to attribute other works to his brush? The Camargue paintings of Aristide Bertrand may be the prelude to fresh discoveries or they may provide us with no more than a tantalizing fragment of the *oeuvre* of an artist we can now recognise as one of the Postimpressionist greats.

Traffic along the Embankment was unusually busy for the time of night. 'Bomb scare on the tube,' was the driver's only attempt at explanation as the taxi crawled its way eastwards. Tim was not bothered by the enforced leisure. It enabled him to give more thought to the problem of how he was going to talk Conrad Lebec into a sudden trip back home. If the Frenchman pressed him he would have to admit that he had failed to produce any evidence which would extradite the Lebecs from a homicide prosecution. All the circumstances of Jollibone's death pointed clearly and vividly to Charles and Conrad as the only possible perpetrators. One had to face the fact that their incredible story about finding the body and disposing of it in a fit of panic was exactly that—an incredible story. He would have to explain to Conrad that DI Edgerson—perhaps more by luck than judgement—had stumbled on the truth and that Josephine Tarantin's murder in similar circumstances only confirmed his convictions. Nothing could save the brothers from arrest. So continuing to hold Emma could gain them no advantage and would provide the prosecution lawyers with more ammunition.

And yet! And yet! Tim's gut feeling told him that both Edgerson and Armstrong were wrong. The Lebec's explanation of events was so implausible that it had to be true. And the double assassination had all the marks of gangland score-settling. The murders of Auguste Jollibone and Josephine Tarantin were vicious revenge killings as well as callous means of silencing the victims. They were not the acts of disgruntled clients who suspected that the dealers were swindling them. The Lebecs had got their pictures back, for heaven's sake: what could they possibly gain by murder? What bothered Tim most of all—perhaps, if he was honest with himself, even more than Emma's plight—was being proved wrong.

How *had* Jollibone been killed? Tim closed his eyes and went over the re-construction of the crime that Jock had staged for him. He was standing in the open doorway. He turned. Immediately he felt Armstrong's 'dagger' between his shoulder-blades. He fell—probably not as suddenly as the stricken Jollibone would have fallen. Jock stepped over him and started talking about bloodstains. Tim got up. No! Wait a bit! There was something else. Go back to lying on the floor. Recall every sensation. The smell of dust in the carpet. The sound of a dripping tap in the bathroom. Something touching his left ankle. The door! The door did not close until he stood up. So, if Jollibone died on the same spot, and was left lying there—as the bloodstain suggested—his killers must have moved his legs in order to shut the door.

Tim knew this was important. But why? According to the Lebecs they had found the door of 518 closed with the card on the floor. What did that suggest? Haste. Perhaps panic. That would tie in with the murder being committed as soon as Jollibone reached his room. Tim tried to imagine the scene. The dealer reaches his door. Transfers the bottle of wine from right hand to left. Takes out the key-card. Opens the door. He pushes the spring-loaded portal. The assassin comes up behind. Stabs the victim. Jollibone falls. The key drops to the floor. The bottle rolls away under the bed. The murderer pulls the door. Jollibone's feet in the way. Murderer steps into the room. Shifts the legs to one side. The door begins to close. Hears someone coming. Hides. But hides where? Cupboard? Emergency stairs? Tim could not recall seeing any such close to 518. Another room, then? But most of them were taken up by the conference. Those allocated to Labardie and Mme

Tarantin were on different floors. Damn! There was no way round the problem of timing. If he presumed the Lebecs' story was true he came up against the same objection, again and again. It was the old chestnut beloved of thirties whodunit writers—the problem of the murder in the locked room.

Tim had brought Armstrong's file with him with the intention of reading it during the evening's cab rides. He opened his briefcase and took it out. He found the hotel printout and ran his eyes down the list of names.

And there it was.

For several seconds he stared at it in mingled excitement, disbelief and horror.

Then he tapped on the glass partition. 'Driver, take me back to Great Smith Street, as quick as you can!'

# III

## HEURES PERILLEUSES

Painting is a way to forget life. It is a cry in the night. A strangled laugh.

—Georges Rouault

# CHAPTER 17

Tim rushed into the flat and immediately grabbed up the phone. Most of the next hour was spent on frenzied calls.

The first was brief.

'Allo?' A man's voice.

'Bonsoir. M. Lacy ici. Puis-je parler avec Mlle Kerr?'

'Non!'

'Pourquoi? Je—' Tim stopped as the line went dead.

Catherine entered the room. 'Hey, where did you spring from? I thought you'd gone to see Conrad Lebec.'

'I'll call him in a minute. Can you find the Wellington Tower number?'

'It'll be in the book.' She picked up the directory from the windowsill. 'So what's with this change of plan?'

'Tell you in a minute.' He dialled the Lyon hotel and left a message for George Martin to ring him as soon as he came in.

Catherine put the telephone book on the table in front of him, her finger marking the Wellington Tower entry. Tim got through to the switchboard and asked for the manager's office.

'Good evening. Detective Inspector Edgerson, Metropolitan CID.' Tim adopted the policeman's abrupt manner. 'That's right, the murder of Auguste Jollibone... Yes, I'm sure you are, sir. Well, you'll be pleased to hear we're very close to an arrest... No, I'm afraid I can't, sir. Not yet. When we do you'll be the first to know. Right now, I need some urgent information.' Tim asked a series of questions and tapped his fingers impatiently as the man at the other end of the line went away to consult the hotel records. At last the voice returned with the answers. 'Excellent! Excellent! You've been most helpful. Thank you... Yes, sir, of course. Just as soon as we have anything definite. Goodbye and thank you again.'

Tim turned to his wife and punched the air. 'Yes!' he shouted triumphantly.

'So, now do you want to tell me what's going on?'

'Not just yet, darling. I ought to talk to Conrad Lebec. Did you book the Marseille flight?'

'Yes. Nine thirty.'

'Good. Do you think you could knock up some supper? We're in for a long night.'

Catherine grimaced but walked through to the kitchen.

When the banker's voice came on the line it was to a background of loud, very brash music. Tim thought that another party must be in progress but once Lebec realised who was speaking he called out to someone and the noise subsided to a monotonous thumping.

'Have you found out anything?' The voice was anxious, tremulous. Not the over-confident young financier Catherine had described. Perhaps her home truths had got through to him.

Tim decided to tighten the rack a bit more. 'Have the police been in touch with you today?'

'Er, no.'

'Well, they will be tomorrow.'

'What do you mean!'

'Detective Inspector Edgerson believes he has a cast-iron case against you and your brother.'

Lebec groaned. 'I said we should have called the police as soon as we found the body. It was Charles who insisted—'

'The way I heard it, the entire brilliant scheme was yours.'

There was a strangled screech at the other end of the line. 'No! No! It was Charles. He—he gets these crazy ideas sometimes and then there's no way of stopping him!'

Tim thought, So much for brotherly

love. Suddenly it's a case of *sauve qui peut*. He said, 'My only concern is for Miss Kerr's safety.'

'I had absolutely nothing to do with that, Mr Lacy.' The man was gabbling now. 'I was quite appalled when I heard about it.'

'Then you'll be only too pleased to help us secure her freedom?'

'That's going to be rather difficult from a prison cell.'

'Listen, Conrad. Listen carefully. I have evidence that will clear you and your brother.'

'You have?' The relief was almost tangible.

'The deal is this: you come with me tomorrow to wherever it is my friend is being held. As soon as she is safe I will hand over my evidence to the police. If anything goes wrong I won't lift a finger to help you.'

There was silence at the other end of the line as Conrad's shrewd brain struggled to dispel the mists of panic. 'Hold on...I can't just drop everything. Anyway, what proof...?'

'In this country, life imprisonment means at least fifteen years, Mr Lebec. Be at Heathrow in time for the nine-thirty Marseille flight. Your ticket will be at the Air France desk. Goodnight, Mr Lebec.'

366

Tim put the phone down and went into the kitchen. Catherine was spooning scrambled egg onto two plates that already held thick slices of ham. 'Great. I could murder that.'

She gave him a wry smile. 'Not a happy choice of expression. Here, carry the plates through. If you're still hungry there are some cans of soup.' She followed him into the living room carrying an already opened bottle of Petit Chablis and a couple of glasses. 'Now sit down and tell me exactly what's going on.'

Just as they sat at the small dining table the telephone rang. Tim grabbed up the receiver and heard George Martin's weary voice.

'You wanted me to call, Major?'

'Yes, George, thanks. How did you get on with Charlie-boy?'

'Fine. He's here with me now.' George lowered his voice. 'He got the message—one way or another. We're catching the last shuttle to Marseille tonight. We'll book in at one of the airport hotels and be on hand to meet you.'

'Good. Our flight doesn't leave till nine thirty, so we're not going to be there till gone twelve your time. Now look, George, I want you to do something else before you leave.'

'We're already tight on schedule, Major.'

367

'This is important, George. I'm getting worried that we can't make contact with Emma. Has Lebec told you where she is?'

'Yes. His father's crony, Edgar, runs a small hotel. They've got her there.'

'That's what I was afraid of. Get Lebec to call his accomplice and tell him to let you speak to Emma. Impress on Charles that this is important.'

'Would you prefer us to go straight to the hotel and wait for you there?'

'No!' Tim's voice was sharp, insistent. 'We've got to play it calmly. I don't want anyone to be panicked into doing something stupid. I just need to be sure Emma's OK. Call back as soon as you've made contact. Then you can be on your way.'

As Tim sat down at the table again Catherine stared at him, fighting back a rising tide of foreboding. 'You're really worried about Emma. Why, Tim? What's happened? Is she in more danger?'

'I hope not. Dear God, I hope not. But I must confess it's not looking good.' He attacked the food hungrily but distractedly. 'I've got it half worked out but not well enough to be able to convince the police. I need to work it through with you—from the beginning.'

'I'm listening.'

'Well, it was you who made the real breakthrough. You purloined the hotel's guest list.'

Tim fetched the file from his briefcase and extracted the computer print-out. 'Now are there any names there that ring a bell?'

'Yes, of course, Tarantin and Labardie.'

'Right, we saw those immediately. We were looking for the woman's name and when Labardie's cropped up as well we were excited because we thought we'd hit the jackpot. But have a look at the others.'

'What, all of them?'

'No, you can forget all the conference delegates.'

Catherine ran her eye down the non-asterisked names. 'Philipson, Jonquil, Roberts, Andries, Hamid...' She looked up puzzled. 'They don't mean anything to me.'

Tim pointed to one name. 'How about that one?'

'E. Roberts?' Catherine shrugged.

'Sounds very English, doesn't it? But supposing it was French: E. Robert...Edgar Robert?'

'What, Denis Lebec's gormless sidekick? Oh, come on, Tim. That's a bit farfetched. According to George he's a typical peasant who's probably never ventured far from his

369

beloved quagmire.'

Tim shook his head. 'We've never met this bloke and George only saw him briefly. We shouldn't draw any hard and fast conclusions. Now, look again. What room was he in?'

Catherine referred to the sheet. '519.' She looked up. 'Is that—?'

'Slap opposite 518. They were the only two rooms on that corridor not allocated to conference delegates. Now when Jock and I visited the scene of the crime earlier on I was convinced that the Lebecs must have done it. They were condemned out of their own mouths. There simply wasn't time for anyone else to have stabbed Jollibone. Other people saw him go to his room. Then, within a minute, the Lebecs arrived. They claim that the dealer was already dead. If that was true, where was the murderer? Answer: he could only be in a nearby room. By far the best for the job was 519. The assassin could have waited there with his door open, seen Jollibone arrive, then, as soon as the coast was clear, stepped across the corridor, knocked on the door, stabbed his victim, and shut the door. He ran into a slight problem there because the dead man's legs were in the way. He spent valuable seconds moving the obstacle. Perhaps by the time he'd done that he could already hear the

Lebecs' voices. He just had time to retrace his steps.'

Catherine shook her head. 'Neat theory but I don't buy it. The timing is too tight. And what about the key? The Lebecs say they found it on the floor. Anyway it's easy to check out Roberts's identity with the hotel. You'll probably find that he's a mild-mannered travelling salesman from Smethwick.'

'That's precisely what I did check as soon as I came in. The hotel don't have an address for this particular guest because the room was booked in his name and paid for by someone else. Would you care to guess who?'

'You're the one with all the answers.'

'Mme Josephine Tarantin!'

Catherine stared, wide-eyed.

'It begins to add up, doesn't it?'

'Yes, I suppose... But no, it sets a whole hen-coop of new questions fluttering. How was Edgar involved with Tarantin? Why did he kill Jollibone? Did he kill Tarantin, too? And if Edgar and Tarantin were partners in a murder plot why did they use Edgar's real name—or something very similar?'

'I don't think the last one presents much of a problem. Josephine would want to keep Edgar out of sight. He was the ace up her sleeve. No one—especially

Labardie—must know of his existence. That means he would have had most meals in his room.'

'And he would have to sign for them.'

'Precisely. Josephine would reckon that she couldn't trust him to use an alias. Much easier to let him sign his own name, especially as anyone looking at it quickly would assume that it was "E. Roberts", a nondescript English name.'

Catherine pushed her plate away and sank her head in her hands. 'Tim, if you're right, Emma is cooped up with a psychopath who's already killed twice.'

'I know—and there's not a thing we can do about it.'

'Why don't we tip off the French police?'

'And have them raid the place in the middle of the night brandishing handguns and rifles? That could tip Edgar over the edge. Siege situations are not very healthy for hostages. No, I'd rather go in there, tomorrow, with the Lebecs and rely on them to talk him into letting Emma go.'

That was when George phoned again.

'Major? Good news and bad news. Lebec has spoken to Edgar's wife. She says that Emma's OK but that she can't come to the phone. She claims her husband's shut her in her room and gone off with the key.'

'Gone off? Where?'

'She doesn't know. Apparently he was

372

out all day, came in for his supper, locked Emma up, then went somewhere with Denis Lebec.'

'Do you reckon we can believe her?'

'Charles thinks so. He said she's dead worried. Edgar occasionally has bouts of violence but he's been much worse recently. She thinks he and Denis are up to something.'

'Ask Lebec if Edgar is dangerous.'

Tim heard a brief, muttered conversation. Then George was back on the line. 'Good question, Major. He says Edgar's lift doesn't go all the way to the top floor. He's given to sudden fits of temper. That's why old man Lebec keeps an eye on him. He's had a few brushes with the police but Denis has always managed to keep him out of serious trouble.'

'OK, thanks, George. I won't hold you up any longer. See you tomorrow.'

Emma sensed the change of atmosphere before she reached the kitchen. She had showered and washed her hair to get rid of paint smears and the smell of white spirit. She had pulled on a sweater and a pair of slacks produced by her hostess. They were clean and a reasonable fit. Emma felt fresh and as relaxed as her strained circumstances would allow. Her mood changed as she descended the staircase and heard raised voices. She hesitated on the threshold of the kitchen. But the door was open and Jeanne saw her before she could turn round. Mme Robert was standing with her back to the stove, holding a large wooden spoon before her almost as though warding off a blow. She muttered something to her husband. Edgar was by the outer door, eyes glowering, shoulders hunched, stance bull-like and menacing. He waved Emma into the room and pointed her to a wooden chair.

She took a couple of paces into the kitchen and stood defiantly in front of the heavy *armoire*.

'Assieds-toi!' Edgar half-shouted, half-hissed the command.

Emma stood her ground. Edgar roared an incomprehensible oath. He grabbed a plate from the shelf beside him. Skimmed it through the air. It missed Emma's right cheek by a few centimetres, struck the door jamb and shattered. Keeping her gaze fixed unflinchingly on Edgar, Emma moved slowly to the table and sat down, determined not to show her bewilderment and fear. What had come over the man? She watched him as he shouted a peremptory order at his wife, tweaked a chair away from the table and sank heavily onto it. This was more than sudden anger, she decided. A profound change had come over Edgar Robert. His whole frame radiated a quivering intensity. He was no longer the dull, uncommunicative, biddable ox, easily manipulated by others because he did not understand the potential of his own strength. Now there was about him something determined, fanatical—and very frightening. Here was a man who could and would do anything. A man who had turned his back on whatever capacity for rational thought he possessed. A madman.

Judging from Jeanne's reaction, she was used to these outbursts. She watched her husband warily as she ladled food onto a dish and set it before him, careful, Emma thought, to make no sudden movement. With a grunt, Edgar hunched over his meal and began to eat greedily. Mme Robert filled another dish with *coq au vin* and brought it across to Emma. She served herself and took her plate opposite her husband. For a couple of minutes the only sound was Edgar's noisy slurping of chicken broth and his gulping of wine from a large tumbler.

Then the door opened and Denis Lebec came in. Emma saw the anxious glances which passed between Jeanne and the newcomer. The older man grimaced in Emma's direction with the disapproving sneer he usually reserved for the reluctant and unwanted guest. Then he clapped his friend on the shoulder in forced bonhomie and sat beside him. The two men fell into a *sotto voce* conversation of which Emma could distinguish only the occasional, unhelpful word. But the mood of their discourse was quite clear. They were arguing. And it was no longer Denis who was taking the initiative. The once-taciturn Edgar was urging a course of action that his companion did not like. Gently but firmly the older man tried to deflect his friend. Over and again, Emma distinguished the words 'Impossible!', 'Non!', 'Mais pense-tu!' What was alarming was that Denis's efforts to moderate the big man's designs were obviously ineffective. What was even more alarming was the frequency with which both men glanced in her direction.

Emma's brain whirled. She fought to control it, to prevent it spinning in useless panic. The situation had suddenly become very, very dangerous. Something had gone wrong.

The telephone rang. Mme Robert half rose from her seat. Edgar motioned to her angrily and she subsided. He crossed to the machine.

'Allo!' he snapped. He listened briefly and stared hard at Emma. 'Non!' He slammed down the receiver.

Emma knew that her only contact with her friends had now been cut off. She had been surprised and worried that neither the Lacys nor George Martin had called during the day. Now she realised that they probably had done so and had been refused access to her. If her abductors had broken their word over that, if they were frightened and angry at something that had obviously gone wrong, and if she was now an embarrassment to them... Well, there was no telling what they might do. One thing was clear to Emma: she was not going to hang around to find out. She began to put together the rudiments of an escape plan.

She affected lack of interest in the muttered conversation at the other end of the long table and applied herself to the food. That was not difficult; Mme Robert's version of a traditional chicken stew was delicious. Emma finished her plateful and asked Jeanne if she might help herself to some more. Receiving a nod and a wan smile Emma went over to the stove. She set down her dish, removed the cover from the large pot and began to ladle out chunks of meat, *cèpes, petits oignons* and wine-rich sauce. With her free hand she picked up a cloth hanging in front of the stove. Then, shielding the action with her body, she put two large pieces of chicken into it, rolled it up and tucked the bundle inside her sweater. She returned to the table.

The *coq au vin* was followed by a lemon tart which was as delectable as it was simple. After this Mme Robert produced thick, black coffee which the men took with cognac. Emma declined the spirit. For what she had in mind she would need a very clear head.

Search parties with lamps were out all night from Mas Maraques looking for Yvette. They covered a wide area, some on horseback, some on foot. They explored copses and derelict sheds. They combed the marshland calling her name. They called at neighbouring farmsteads. But when they returned at about four in the morning for a couple of hours' sleep they had found no sign of her.

As soon as it was light enough they set off again. This time their numbers were augmented by men from other settlements and they were able to cover a wide area more scientifically.

Even so, they almost missed her. It was the Simier twins, riding together along the shore of the lagoon, who stumbled upon her. They had been methodically searching the reed beds, and had come at last to the jetty where fishing boats were sometimes tied and from which they often swam. They were about to ride past when Gaston called out and pointed. Something that might be a bundle of cloth was lying on the boards at the end of the little pier. The boys jumped down and ran to investigate.

Yvette was sprawled on the very edge of the ramshackle structure, one arm and leg dangling in the water. The boys pulled her clear and laid her down on the boards.

'Is she dead?' Philippe whispered, kneeling beside her. He bent his head close to Yvette's face and answered his own question. 'No, she is breathing.'

They stared down at their friend, not knowing what to do. Yvette looked dreadful. Her dress was torn and covered in mud. Earth and blood streaked her face. Her hands and arms looked as though they had been deliberately plastered with thick, black clay.

Philippe said, 'You go and get help. I'll stay with her.'

After his brother had ridden off, he pulled a kerchief from his pocket, dipped it in the lake and gently washed Yvette's face. After a couple of minutes the girl's eyes opened.

Philippe smiled down at her. 'Yvette, are you all right? Everyone's been very worried about you.'

She gazed up into his face with a wistful expression—half smile, half frown. Slowly the frown took over. 'Who are you?' she asked.

379

Tim reported to his wife the gist of his conversation with George.

'That ties in, doesn't it? If Edgar's been away from home all day he's had plenty of time to get to Lyon and back to kill Josephine Tarantin. But why? Why? What *is* it all about?' Catherine's mind was a fog of fear and bewilderment.

Tim finished his meal. He collected the plates and carried them into the kitchen. 'Let's see if we can work it out, shall we?' He spread the contents of Armstrong's file over the table. 'It's pretty pointless going to bed. We're both too strung up. So, we've got all night. We ought to be able to come up with something.'

Half an hour of virtual silence passed as they each read the statements and reports relating to the first murder.

At last Catherine looked up in exasperation. 'We know La Tarantin brought Edgar Robert to London but we don't know anything about their connection with each other before that.'

'OK. Let's work on it. The Lebec brothers fell out with their father—and therefore with Edgar—over the sale of the Bertrands. But they went ahead anyway, and set up a deal with Jollibone and Tarantin. Supposing the others got wind of what was going on?'

'I guess that would hit Edgar pretty hard. All that stuff about "betrayal of the Brotherhood"—Conrad and Charles might scoff but to Edgar it would be deadly serious.'

'He's potentially a violent man with faulty mental circuits. All he can think about is protecting the paintings and stopping the deal going through.'

'So how come he's in league with Tarantin? I mean, I can picture him going berserk in the Lyon gallery and killing both dealers. But entering a conspiracy with one to wipe out the other...?'

'We mustn't assume that Edgar's stupid. If we're right about him, he's carried out two perfect murders—no witnesses, no scene-of-crime evidence, no direct connection with the victims.'

'Well, he's sure been too clever for us.' Catherine sat back with an exasperated sigh. 'We're not getting anywhere, Tim. All we're doing is guessing—probably guessing wrong.' She stood up. 'I'm going to make some coffee.'

Tim stretched wearily. 'Good idea. While you're doing that I'll read Emma's notes. Did you finish typing them?'

'Yes. They're beside the PC.'

Tim found the five neatly typed pages and settled in an armchair to read them. 'It's an incredible story,' he observed a few minutes later, when his wife handed him a steaming mug and seated herself in the chair opposite. He sipped the coffee and went on reading.

Catherine was busy with her own thoughts. She spoke them aloud. 'Poor Emma. I wonder what sort of a state's she's in. I'll bet she's feeling guilty as well as scared.'

'Guilty?' Tim was only half listening.

'Of course. She'll be worried about all the trouble she's caused us. And worried about her mother, naturally. Since her father walked out and subsequently died they've only had each other. If—when—we get Emma out of this, we'll have to help her to think seriously about whether she stays with us. I'd hate her to have a clash of loyalties, and family's more important than job, in the last analysis. I feel horribly guilty just being away from the boys for a few days.'

Tim lowered the typescript and stared at his wife. 'Yes, me too. Family is crucial, isn't it...I wonder...'

'What is it, Tim?'

'This note, here, towards the end of your story. You say you've got to check about Yvette Robert's children.'

'Oh, it's just a detail. Emma's account says that she only had one child. Conrad reckoned there were others but that they died in infancy—diphtheria, he thought.'

Tim turned to the family tree. 'According to this, Yvette and François Robert produced one son, Georges, in 1890, the year after their marriage. At that time she was—what—eighteen or nineteen. The marriage lasted another forty-one years, till François's death. Yet there were no more children.'

Catherine shrugged. 'These things happen. They happened a lot more often a century ago before the marvels of modern medicine.'

'Sure.' Tim interrupted impatiently. 'There could be a dozen good medical reasons why this couple only had one surviving child. But supposing François was incapable.'

'Then there wouldn't be any children at all.'

'Or supposing Yvette refused him his conjugal rights. It seems pretty clear that she didn't love him.'

'I doubt whether that would have stopped him. But what's all this got to do with Edgar being a psychopathic killer?'

'What if he is Aristide Bertrand's grandson?'

'What!'

'Look at this genealogical tree of the Brotherhood.' He handed her the papers.

'Is there anything there that proves that François Robert was the father of Yvette's only child?'

'No, but...'

'Yvette was besotted with Aristide, wasn't she? This glamorous, sophisticated, sensitive man from another world came into her life when she was at a highly impressionable age. She fell for him hook, line and sinker. That's obvious from the narrative. And she continued to worship his memory. She lived in hope that he would come back. It was she who created the Brotherhood. It was she who was determined to preserve his paintings. She turned that isolated barn into a shrine and made sure that there would be others who went on caring for it. It was her obsession and it was so strong she made the Brotherhood share it.'

'Yeah, I guess that's true, but...'

'And what did Aristide make of her? Think of all those balmy afternoons. The two of them alone in the marshes under a Mediterranean sun. Aristide gazing hour after hour at that lovely young body. Don't try to tell me that he looked at her with artistic detachment—that nothing ever happened between them.'

Catherine closed her eyes and saw again the paintings of Yvette propped against the wall of a shabby office, bringing to life their drab surroundings. She recaptured the sensual thrill of vital colours, sinuous shapes, the overwhelming sense of exuberance and joy. 'No,' she said. 'I wouldn't try to tell you that. But where does this theory get us?'

'It gets us just about all the way.' Tim jumped up excitedly. He walked around the room making point after point. 'Yvette keeps to herself the secret of Georges's true parentage—until he's grown up. Then she tells him all about his father, the great artist. Georges passes on that knowledge, in turn, to his own son, Edgar. So Edgar grows up knowing that he is the grandson of Aristide Bertrand—*and his heir*. The paintings belong to him, and to no one else. The other members of the Brotherhood know nothing of this. They all assume a proprietorial right over a collection of pictures they've looked after for three or four generations. Now, none of this matters until Charles Lebec wakes up to the fact that the paintings are worth a fortune. Suddenly, he and Conrad are talking about selling them. This is the point at which a conflict of loyalties develops between the family and the group. Edgar doesn't want to turn against his friends but he's not about to let them steal his birthright. If anyone's going to get rich on Grandpa's pictures it's going to be him.'

'So what does he do?' Catherine was getting caught up in the narrative.

'I think that somehow he finds out the name of the expert Charles has gone to. I think he goes, quite openly, to the gallery in rue Gramont to say that there's no deal, or that if there is it must be with him alone.'

'That's how he meets Josephine Tarantin?'

'That's the only way I can see of bridging the gap.'

'But how does she get Edgar to murder Jollibone, and why?'

Tim was silent for several moments, thinking hard. 'Well, we know that Josephine was clever and totally unscrupulous. I reckon she was also getting desperate.'

'Why desperate?'

'She knows her stock with Labardie is running out. He's beginning to suspect that the rue Gramont gallery is ripping him off. She needs to put a considerable distance between herself and her former associates. But to do that she needs money—lots of money. Then up pops this fabulous cache of paintings. It's the answer to all her prayers. Securing them for Labardie will restore his confidence, and her personal rake-off will enable her to disappear into the wide blue yonder. Then, just as she's got the negotiations rolling along nicely, this rural slob, Edgar Robert, suddenly appears, saying No go.'

'That must have been a shock.'

'Understatement. She's raised Labardie's hopes. Now she's faced with having to disappoint him. And young Charlie isn't the sort of lad who can accept disappointment philosophically.'

'Wouldn't he assume that his hench-woman was trying to pull a fast one and had found another buyer?'

'I'm sure that's the way his mind would work. He was being forced into the humiliation of acknowledging that his father and Bellecourt had been right about La Tarantin all along.'

'I can see that losing face would make him very angry. Anyway, how does Josephine plan to wriggle out of this impending crisis?'

'Well, let's see... She knows she has precious little time. Jollibone has vetted the sample pictures and she's arranged to show them to Labardie in London. She daren't go back on that arrangement.'

'But how does murdering Jollibone help?'

'I don't know!' Tim pummelled his temple with a clenched fist. He went to the dresser and poured himself a brandy. 'Let's look at it from Labardie's angle.

He comes to London quite openly and books in at the same hotel as the dealers. Suddenly, Jollibone is being fished out of the Thames. Now, what would you do if you were our gangster chum?'

'Get the hell out of London, a.s.a.p.'

'That's it then!' Tim was triumphant. 'That's the motive—or part of it. Josephine couldn't deliver the goods, so she did her best to put Labardie off. He's a vicious bastard who doesn't think twice about having disloyal employees knocked off. But his assassinations are carried out by experts, whose actions can't be traced back to him—like the murder of the Russian woman in New York. If he organises a hit the first thing he makes sure of is that he's miles away.'

'So when the police make the connection between him and Jollibone...'

'They're going to be buzzing around him like flies.'

'You said putting him off was only part of Josephine's plan.'

'I can't imagine her letting the Bertrands out of her clutches. They're still her passport to long life and happiness in some South American haven. So, she works out a plan to get all the Bertrands for herself. It wouldn't take someone as shrewd and sophisticated as the fair Josephine long to get the measure of a simpleton like Edgar.

She realises that this Camargue peasant has the rough power of a steam loco. All she needs to do is stoke up his anger and point him in the right direction. She tells him what a fabulous artist his grandfather was and how right Edgar is to come to her. She can sell the paintings for what they're really worth and make him very rich indeed. How monstrous that these wicked Lebecs, and even her own partner, should try to swindle him out of millions of francs that are rightfully his. She does all this with consummate skill. If lying was an Olympic sport she'd be a medallist, for sure.'

'Do you really think she organised getting Jollibone killed in such a way that the Lebecs would be arrested for it?'

'I certainly wouldn't put such a Machiavellian scheme past her. But no, I imagine the original idea was something much simpler: Edgar knocks off Auguste and leaves the body in his room to be discovered the next day by the hotel staff. Edgar returns home straight away. Josephine stays to act the part of the victim's tearful business partner, hinting regretfully at Jollibone's involvement in shady deals—of which, naturally, she knew nothing. Labardie, meanwhile, has beaten a hasty retreat. But Josephine knows that he's not going to waste any time before he sends for her to find out what the hell's going on. She's ready for that with a story about Auguste doing his own secret deal behind her back and, presumably, falling out with either the sellers or the prospective buyers of the Bertrand collection. What she hopes is that the gangster will want nothing more to do with the affair and that she'll be free to make her own arrangement with Edgar.'

Catherine swallowed the last, now cold, mouthful of coffee. 'It *seems* to hang together.' Doubt still tinged her voice. 'But did Edgar kill Tarantin, and if so, why?'

'I still haven't acquitted Labardie of that crime. If he hadn't already decided to disembarrass himself of Josephine, Bellecourt's report of our conversation might have made up his mind. On the other hand, George's description suggests a very similar killing and we now know that Edgar's been away from home all day.'

'We also know that his wife is bothered about his odd behaviour. Oh, Tim, I'm frightened. If he's got locked into a psychopathic pattern of murder he's not going to stop. He'll lash out at anyone he thinks is in his way. There must be something we can do now. Tomorrow may be too late.'

'I wish there was.' He rubbed tired eyes. 'Perhaps...look, we need to get this down on paper in a coherent form, anyway.

Supposing we draft a report and fax it through to Jock's desk. Then, you could go along first thing in the morning and suggest that a little bit of back-up in Marseille might help.'

Catherine stood up. 'That's fine—except for one small detail. I'm coming with you.'

'Oh, no.'

'Oh yes. The seats are already booked—three of them. I should have gone in the first place. If I'd insisted, we wouldn't be in this mess. And another thing: if—when—we get Emma away from this monster, she's going to need me.'

Emma had stopped pretending to herself. She was scared—terrified. She lay fully clothed on the bed with the duvet pulled over her. And still she shivered. She looked at her watch: 1.52. The house had been silent for about half an hour. Silent after the arguments and Edgar's tirades had finally stopped. After supper Edgar had ordered her to her room and personally locked her in. She heard his little camion drive away from the *auberge* and assumed that he and Denis had departed for some nocturnal tryst. Anxiously, she had listened for Edgar's return. She could not make her escape bid until the bulky peasant was safely abed and asleep. It was well past midnight before the vehicle returned. Even if she had not heard the engine she could not have failed to be aware that the master of the house was home. The domestic quiet was shattered by loud voices, rising with each exchange to a tympanic crescendo. They were accompanied by the sounds of crashing furniture and splintering china. The row had lasted the greater part of an hour. But at last quiet returned to the White Horse Inn and soon afterwards Emma had heard the heavy clump of Edgar's footfall on the stair. With some relief, she had also distinguished Jeanne's lighter tread.

And now half an hour had passed. Half an hour during which Emma had lain motionless listening for any nuance of a sound, every change in the texture of silence. Waiting, longing for the right moment to move. Yet also fearful of the possible consequences.

She willed her body into action. She eased herself out of the bed. Quietly she pulled off the bedclothes and piled them in a heap before the door. She slid the mattress onto the floor and dragged it across to the window. She switched off the bedside light and stood for a few moments allowing her eyes to grow accustomed to the darkness. She half-felt her way back to the window and drew the curtains. The two panes of glass opened inwards without a sound. Emma unfastened the shutters and pushed them gently. One hinge squeaked. Emma stopped, heart thumping, waiting for the sharp bark which would indicate that the prowling dogs had detected the noise. But no sound was carried in on the soft, moist air. She tried again and found that, by lifting the shutter slightly, she could prevent its high-pitched protest.

Emma leaned out. She heard the breeze hissing across the marsh. She smelled the faint odour of putrefaction. She saw the black shapes of outbuildings and the line of lighter hue where the road to freedom lay straight across the menacing sepia of the *marais,* neither land nor water. She craned her neck but could detect no chink of light from any of the other windows.

Now for the tricky bit. Emma's room was on the first floor. There was a drop of some four metres from the window to the paved terrace. There was no ledge, no drainpipe, no conveniently placed lower roof. Just a sheer drop to the hard flagstones. Emma struggled the mattress onto the windowsill and pushed. The clumsy object bent in all the wrong places and the wet paint did not help. At last the mattress was hanging, more out than in, ready to fall under its own weight. Emma let it go. The soft flop seemed to echo round the walls.

This time the dogs did hear. There was a half-yelp, half-bark and she saw the two shapes come bounding round the corner of the shed. She drew back into the room and watched as the alsatians sniffed around the unusual item which had fallen from the heavens into their domain. They pawed it. They walked across it. Emma was suddenly afraid that they might decide to attack it, tearing it and worrying it noisily. Worse still, they might decide that it provided a comfortable base for their nightly vigil. At last, they contented themselves with lifting their legs and marking it. Then they ambled off into the darkness.

Emma gave them five minutes to settle down. Then she picked up the duvet and spread it over the sill. She climbed up and sat on it. Ahead, somewhere out in the starry marsh, was freedom. But between her and freedom lay two alsatians, the front yard of the *auberge*, the double gates, the long exposed trek to the main road and several kilometres of highway whose few travellers could not be automatically trusted. Not a hopeful prospect. But in the quiet house behind her was a monster who would go berserk when he discovered this attempted escape. Having come so far she was committed and there was no drawing back. Emma gazed down at the pale rectangle of the mattress and launched herself into space.

'Oof!' The jolt was harder than she expected and drew from her an involuntary grunt. Emma rolled as she landed and lay for a moment straining her ears for any sound above her own heavy breathing. Had the dogs heard? A slight yelp suggested that they had. Within seconds the two creatures were padding across the gravel of the drive. Quickly Emma pulled from her pocket the cloth containing the pieces of chicken saved from supper.

'Here, boy!' she whispered, holding out a drumstick to the leading animal. He advanced slowly, growling and suspicious. 'Nice dog.' Emma hoped that the smell of the food was stronger than the scent of her fear. The alsatian fastened his teeth on the meat and yanked it from her grasp. His companion padded up to see what he was missing. He tried to grab the chicken leg, snarling his rivalry. The last thing Emma wanted was to start a fight. 'OK, boy, here's yours.' She proffered the second piece of chicken. As the dogs settled onto the mattress, crunching bones, Emma patted them cautiously. They took no notice.

She eased quietly away. She sidled along the wall of the house. She crossed the gravel to the sheds. They were fronted by a paved path which would deaden the sound of her step. The gates were fifty metres away. Emma knew she had to reach them and close them behind her before the alsatians came after her. She also knew that it would take them very little time to demolish the chicken pieces, bones and all. She ran lightly along the line of outbuildings. She reached the corner. A twenty-metre sprint would carry her to the barrier. Now there were sounds behind her. Emma braced herself.

Something whizzed past her ear. It thudded into the woodwork. Emma turned her head. Ten centimetres before her eyes a long-bladed knife glinted in the starlight, still quivering.

## CHAPTER 18

They had to bring Yvette back to her old room in the Bardol house so that she could be nursed by Aunt Lou. At the mere sight of her husband she went into convulsions. When Madeleine Robert tried to feed her she spat the food out and screamed. Left on her own she grew thinner and weaker. Custom insisted that she remain under the marital roof. She was no longer a free agent, with a will of her own to be respected. She belonged to the man she had married. It was her lot to obey him and to defer to the wishes of his mother. It took a show of force by young Jean-Marc and an uncharacteristically strident protest from Aunt Lou to force a breach in the stout walls of tradition. Yvette's brother demanded a hearing by the leaders of the Mas Maraques community. Emboldened by anger, he told the old men that his sister was days away from death and that, if the elders would not act, he and his friends would remove her physically. Aunt Lou confirmed the sick woman's condition and announced that the house of Robert would have blood on its hands if Yvette was not released immediately. If François wanted a son and heir he must relinquish his wife into the care of those who alone could help her back to soundness of mind and body.

Yvette's subsequent recovery was little short of a miracle; but a bigger marvel was that the growth of the child maturing inside her was not damaged. Throughout her pregnancy the young bride remained bedridden, recouping her strength slowly, aided by her aunt's nostrums. Most days she lay propped on pillows and gazing silently out of her window at the level monotony of the *marais*. She seldom spoke to those who came to sit with her. Only slowly did her mind turn from her unsatisfied longing for Aristide to expectancy for the one who was coming.

It was on a day of March storms that Yvette said in a distant voice, 'It will be soon now.' She had been watching the lightning flickering somewhere out over the distant sea and she did not turn her eyes away from the window.

Aunt Lou looked up from the strips of leather she was plaiting into a fancy bridle. 'Two weeks. Perhaps more, perhaps less if it's a girl. They're always more impatient.'

Yvette frowned. 'You know it's a boy. I told you.'

The old woman shrugged. 'Perhaps.'

'Will I die?' The question seemed to be echoed by a grumbling roar from the piled clouds. The tempest was heading back inland.

'What a question, child!'

'I might, you know. I shouldn't mind.'

'Well, I have asked Our Lady to give you a safe delivery so you can forget all this nonsense about dying.'

Yvette pulled herself into a sitting position with a sudden movement which caused her aunt to look up in surprise. 'Aunt Lou, there's something, no, two things you must do. Promise.'

The old woman grunted. 'You know what happened to the rabbit who made a blank promise to the fox, before he knew what it was.'

'I want you to teach him—my son—to read and write. You will do that for me, won't you?' There was a new vigour, a new strength in Yvette's voice.

Aunt Lou was relieved to detect a fresh sense of purpose in her patient. 'Yes, I'll do that, if I'm spared. And the other promise?'

'I want you to write something down for me.'

'About Aristide?'

'Yes. Everything about him. If I die nobody will know—ever. That would be terrible.'

'It is for him to tell his story—or as much of it as he wants to tell.'

Yvette shook her head and stared again out at the marsh as a nearer flash of lightning illumined her pallid, glistening cheeks. 'We must start now.'

'Now, child, you must sleep.'

'No!' A petulant cry. 'No, Aunt Lou, please. I must tell his story.'

To humour the patient, the elderly nurse went in search of paper, pen and ink.

On the first Sunday of April 1890 Yvette's baby was born. It was a boy and his father named him Georges. According to custom, François took him, on the third day, to the priest at Gageron to be christened. Now he insisted on his wife being brought back under his roof to care for him and his heir. Yvette took up half of that responsibility with enthusiasm and joy. From the first moment she held the male child in her arms she devoted herself to his welfare. With her husband it was very different.

The morning after the christening she brought her few personal treasures to the Robert house. When she had arranged them to her satisfaction she decided to bathe. Alone in the kitchen, she heated a pan of water and poured it into a bowl on the table. She removed her dress, pulled down her chemise and began washing her upper body.

Because of the splashing of the water she did not hear François come in. She jumped when he laid his rough hands on her shoulders. His fingers closed on her flesh and clumsily he bent to kiss her neck. Yvette's body went rigid. François turned her round to face him. She jerked herself free and backed away. She grabbed up her dress and held it in front of her.

'What's this!' the man shouted angrily.

'Don't come near me!' Yvette's heart was pounding but her voice was level and calm, as though belonging to another.

'I'm your husband, woman! I'll come near you when I want—and a good deal more.' His hand flashed out to grab the dress.

With a yelp he withdrew it quickly, staring in enraged disbelief at the teeth marks and the trickle of blood at the base of his thumb. 'Mother was right,' he roared. 'You need to be tamed.' Slowly he unbuckled his belt.

Yvette turned her back on him and pulled on her clothes. But as she did so she continued speaking with a quiet authority. 'You will never lay so much as a finger on me—for any purpose.'

François wound one end of the broad leather strap round his hand. 'We'll see about—'

'Because if you do I will tell what I know.'

He swung the belt whistling through the air and brought it down with a crack on the table. 'And what's that supposed to mean?' he sneered, but did not come towards her. In its cradle in the corner the baby awoke suddenly and began to cry.

Yvette turned. 'I *do* know. And I have proof.' She walked across, picked up her son and held him close to her, making soothing noises. She carried him to the table, seated herself on a chair and presented her back to her husband.

For several seconds François glared at her with mingled fear and hatred. Then he strode from the room, crashing the door behind him.

For the first time in months, Yvette smiled.

The cupboard door opened and Emma blinked at the sudden light. Instinctively, she shrank back into the corner. But the figure outlined against the hard rays of the morning sun was not Edgar Robert.

'Venez.' Jeanne beckoned her out.

Emma struggled to her feet, letting fall the blanket in which she had wrapped herself. She emerged cautiously into the downstairs corridor of the *auberge*.

The Frenchwoman stared at her and winced. 'Barbare!' She led the way to a ground-floor bathroom, gave a little smile and a shrug expressive of both sympathy and helplessness and told her guest that there was breakfast in the kitchen.

Emma peered at her reflection in the mirror. God, what a sight! Gingerly, she fingered the red weals across her left cheek where Edgar had struck her. She looked more closely. The skin was not broken but the bruising would be there for several days. She peeled off her sweaty clothes, noticing as she did so that Jeanne had provided a pile of fresh garments. She climbed into the shower. The warm water was soothing. Emma wished that it would wash away the memory of her ordeal.

She did not need to close her eyes to see again the dark, bulky outline of her captor. His hand was raised above his head and she knew that it held another knife. Emma had cowered against the shed wall. Edgar had come up to her bellowing incomprehensibly. He had lashed out with the back of his left hand, knocking her to the ground. He had yanked her to her feet and frog-marched her back to the house. He had made her pick up the mattress and struggle with it, unaided, through the kitchen, up the stairs and back into her room. He had made her tidy up the jumble of bedclothes. Then, just when she thought he was going to leave her alone, he had pushed her back down the stairs to the deep linen cupboard and locked her in. The darkness was terrifying but it also provided comforting security. She had felt fumblingly for blankets, wrapped herself in their warmth, found space to lie down and, by degrees, managed to bring her trembling under control. After that she had obviously slept, her mind deliberately asserting healing oblivion.

Emma towelled herself and tried to batter down the fear barrier separating her from

403

rational thought. What now? In the small hours she had known stark terror; had felt herself moments away from violent death. She had been shut up in a black hole, victim of a raving psychopath. Now here she was being offered food, clothes and civilised comforts as though nothing had happened. She turned the enigma over and over as she brushed her hair deliberately slowly, finding something soothing in the motion. At last she dismissed it as insoluble. There was nothing to be done but to stay vigilantly on guard and take each moment as it came. She dressed unhurriedly, then made her way cautiously to the kitchen.

She peered into the large room and was relieved to see that Jeanne Robert was there alone. Emma sat down at the table while her hostess brought coffee, croissants and jam as well as cheese and cold ham. She was very attentive but even less communicative than usual. To the question 'Où est-il, votre mari?' she responded with no more than a shrug. Emma needed and enjoyed the food but she could not relax over it. Every sudden noise made her jump. She had almost finished her breakfast when the outer door opened and Edgar slumped heavily in.

He looked around morosely, then nodded at Emma. 'Viens!' he commanded.

Emma stared back. 'Non!' The word came out as a stifled gasp. She looked for support to Jeanne.

The woman muttered something to her husband, who replied gruffly. She turned to Emma. 'It's OK. He will not hurt you. He needs your help with something.'

'With what?'

Again the shrug which suggested that her husband's cranky behaviour was none of Jeanne's business.

'Viens! Vite!' Edgar left the room.

Slowly Emma followed him. He walked round to the front of the house to the van which was parked on the gravelled drive. He opened the passenger door and motioned Emma to get in. She hung back. To go with this madman would in itself be madness. It would probably mean a one-way trip to some never-visited, waterlogged killing place. But what was the alternative? Make him angry and he would simply attack her here. Then another thought struck her. Could it possibly be that he was letting her go? Perhaps he and the Lebecs had at last grasped the fact that keeping her a prisoner would gain them nothing.

Edgar shouted impatiently. Emma climbed into the camion. Oh well, at least she was gaining time. Perhaps on the journey the chance of escape might present itself.

Edgar let in the clutch and with a spurt of gravel the vehicle leaped forward. It reached the main road, turned left and rattled northwards at over 100 kph. But not far. Within a couple of minutes Edgar swung the camion off onto a narrow track that bounced its way between banks of tall reeds. Emma caught occasional glimpses of gleaming water. Then the vegetation on the right gave way and they were driving along the edge of the *étang*. Wavering mist still obscured its borders but a low winter sun was slowly dispersing the miasma and unrolling streamers of firegold across the surface. A heron wheeled black against the sky only to be swallowed up by the distant haze as though it had never been. Here and there clumps of rushes broke the drum-tight surface of the mere like the despairing arms of the drowning. Emma shivered. This was a haunting, treacherous place. Beautiful, yet none the less menacing for that.

Edgar also seemed to be moved by the atmosphere of the lake. Or was it just his own madness? He drove at manic speed over the pitted, twisting track. He stared straight ahead. He kept up a constant muttering, occasionally punctuated by shouts of anger. Or was it remorse? When Emma turned to look at him she saw that tears were rolling down his cheeks and through the stubble on his chin.

For twenty minutes the van bucked and skidded along, now beside the *étang,* now through groves of reed or bamboo and clumps of red-brown glasswort. It stopped when it could go no farther. Before it, two watercourses converged on their way to the lagoon. They were little more than crevices in the vegetation and the black earth but they effectively closed the track. Edgar jumped out, shouted 'Viens!' again and continued on foot. He moved easily and quickly from one clump of vegetation to another. Where the path was waterlogged he splashed through it. Where the path was non-existent he parted the reeds with his arms and flattened them with his boots. Emma slipped and slithered in his wake, sometimes up to her ankles in the oozing, sucking slime. At one point she fell to her knees. She stopped to wipe the mud from her trousers.

Looking up she saw Edgar standing a dozen metres ahead, staring out over the lagoon. Their track had led them to the edge of the water, where the reeds fell back to make a sort of inlet. Three stumps of rotting wood indicated that a structure—presumably a jetty—had once stood there. There was no sign of human activity now. Suddenly her heart was pounding, and not just with the physical effort. Emma gazed around. Was there a more desolate spot anywhere on the face of the earth? She looked back at Edgar and remained stock still. She would keep her distance. If he made a grab for her she would at least have a slight start.

But Edgar seemed to have no interest in her. Again he was talking to himself. Or was it to her? Was he trying to make her understand something? Emma could distinguish only a few words from the babble of thick dialect French: *'Elle l'a trouvé ici!'* Several times he repeated the sentence. 'She found it here!' The words made no sense.

While she was struggling to catch any other fragment of Edgar's ramblings, he turned abruptly and walked in a line directly away from the water. After about eighty metres of rising ground they came to a clump of trees. And suddenly Emma knew where they were. She followed Edgar along a well-worn path through the undergrowth and found herself facing the old sheepshed which the Brotherhood had made into a shrine to Aristide Bertrand.

But Edgar did not go into the building. He turned to the right and walked along the edge of the clearing. He stopped, pointing at a space between two feathery clumps of tamarisk. 'Grandpère,' he muttered.

He crossed himself. Again Emma saw the tears.

She peered into the short tunnel between the overarching shrubs. She could make out nothing. There was just a patch of earth strewn with grass, weed and stones. Then she realised that the stones were not strewn. They marked a rectangle—one metre by two.

Something seemed to be expected of her. 'Votre grandpère,' she said. 'C'est triste.'

He was not pacified by this attempt to humour him. 'Regardes!' he shouted. 'Regardes là.' He grabbed her arm and forced her to her knees before the grave.

Emma winced with pain and fear. What did he want from her? What was he going to do with her? So, the madman's grandfather had chosen to be buried out here. So what? It only indicated that the insanity was hereditary. She stared at the stone-bordered plot. Then she saw the other stones. In the middle. She leaned forward and brushed away some leaves. There was a pattern. With a sudden shock, she recognised it:

She sank back on her heels. She looked up into the large face with its wild fringe of hair. 'Il était votre grandpère?'

Edgar nodded.

'Et il est enterré ici?'

'Oui.'

409

Emma waited for more explanation. None came. With another abrupt instruction to 'Come!' Edgar turned and strode towards the building.

He entered, propping the door open to provide some light to the interior. He crossed the empty expanse of earthen floor and made straight for the racks where the Bertrand paintings were stored. Energetically, he began tugging the wrapped canvases out of their wooden compartments. He handed the first two to Emma. Then, with one under each arm, he marched out of the barn. Emma followed, struggling to keep a grip on her awkward bundles.

Edgar took a different path through the copse. Scarcely a path. Several times he had to stop to batten down the undergrowth or cut away overhanging branches with the sheath knife attached to his belt. Emma followed with difficulty. Reaching twigs grabbed at her precious burdens and became entangled in the protective sacking. Somehow she had to keep the pictures safe and at the same time watch where she was putting her feet. Every time she stumbled she expected to see some jagged, projecting treestump thrust itself right through one of the canvases.

The going was scarcely easier when they emerged into the open marshland. The ground was slippery and criss-crossed by tiny watercourses. The parcels were heavy and unmanageable. Emma's fingers hurt. Her arms ached. She longed to rest, or just pause for a moment to readjust her grip. But she dared not lose sight of her blundering guide.

He stopped, at last, at the edge of the *étang*. Emma saw a small boat moored to the reeds. She recognised it from pictures in the guidebooks she had been given to while away her captivity in the *cabane*. It was a traditional Camargue fishing vessel with a wide, flat stern from which a triangular net could be lowered into the lake. From this boat the tackle had been removed, leaving an empty space. Into this Edgar placed the pictures he was carrying. He took Emma's and arranged them on top. Then, without pausing, he set off back along the path.

They made another arm-wrenching journey between the sheepshed and the waterside. By then, eight wrapped paintings had been stacked and they came well above the level of the gunwale. Edgar motioned Emma to climb in. She sat gingerly on the seat in the centre of the boat. Edgar pushed the vessel out into the lake, scrambled in and settled himself heavily beside her. She noticed with alarm that the sides were only a few centimetres clear of the water. Edgar grabbed an oar and indicated that

411

Emma was to wield the other. Slowly, ponderously, the rowers eased their craft out into the wide expanse of the *étang*.

By now the early mist had evaporated and the sun stood high in the sky. Emma was glad of its warmth on her back. For all her exertions she felt a chill that went deep within her. She pulled levelly on her oar, glad of the season she had spent as a member of a ladies' college eight at Cambridge. Edgar did the steering by simply easing or increasing the pressure on his own blade. After a few minutes Emma tried some questions. Where was M. Lebec? Why wasn't he helping in this removal operation? Where were they going? How had Aristide Bertrand come to be buried in such a remote spot? All she received by way of reply was a series of impatient grunts.

She fell silent and stared glumly out over the friendless water. There was something funereal about the steady rhythm of the oars which scooped reluctant ripples from the otherwise oily-calm surface of the lake. Emma could not drag her thoughts away from death—ancient and modern. Jollibone floating along the Thames. Bertrand meeting a mysterious end close by the shores of this very lagoon. Perhaps her own killing being plotted even now by the silent, crazed man beside her. She watched the retreating shoreline and recalled Tennyson's description of the dying Arthur being ferried over the lake to misty Avalon,

...till the hull
Look'd one black dot against the verge of dawn
And on the mere the wailing died away.

'Là. A gauche!' Edgar's peremptory command broke in on her thoughts.

Half turning, Emma saw what might have been no more than a large clump of reeds but was, in fact, a tiny island. The boat swung towards a small opening among the tall stems and ran on until it struck solid ground. Edgar waded ashore with a rope and made it fast.

Following him, Emma became aware of a flimsy structure of wooden uprights, walled and roofed with plaited reed stems. It was obviously an old hide used at one time by birdwatchers or, more likely, wildfowlers but, to judge by its condition, long since abandoned. Surely this was not going to be the new depository for a collection of priceless paintings? It was. Edgar began ferrying the bundles from the boat and stacking them inside the rough shelter. As soon as the unloading was finished he ordered Emma back to the vessel for the return journey.

They made another identical trip as the sun climbed to its zenith. Identical except for one factor. Emma was becoming exhausted. The unremitting physical labour, hour after hour, was for her the final straw. It came on top of days of tense uncertainty followed by a night of terror. Now, every time she struggled through the undergrowth with awkward, heavy packages or pulled on an oar she felt her strength seeping away. Weakness brought frustration and breached from within the barricades she had erected against fear. Every wearying moment was a struggle, not just to keep her body functioning, but to hold back the tears of pain, anger and dread. Twice she asked her tormentor to let her rest. He refused with an angry shake of the head.

Once, leaving the barn, Emma stumbled. The bundle under her left arm caught on a protruding nail. The coarse, old hessian ripped. Edgar rushed up and grabbed the painting. He hunched over her, yelling a string of Provençal oaths. She cowered, sure that he was going to strike her again. But he turned and strode off towards the trees.

By the time they returned to the barn to begin the third transfer, Emma was virtually on her knees. She no longer cared what Edgar did; she had to relax her aching limbs, if only for a few moments.

She watched her captor leave the barn carrying a painting under each massive arm. As soon as he was out of sight she looked for somewhere to sit. In the shadow beside the door there was a rolled-up tarpaulin. Thankfully, she dropped down on it.

It gave beneath her weight, less rigid than she had thought. She looked down. One corner of the stiff cloth slipped away. Emma found herself gazing at the pallid, blood-drained features of Denis Lebec.

She leaped up screaming and rushed from the building. Straight into the arms of Edgar Robert.

'I suppose the only crumb of comfort in this wretched business is that Emma doesn't know she's in the hands of a murderer.' Catherine spoke half to herself as she gazed out at the spiky southern tail of the Alps, clearly visible on a brilliant cloudless morning.

Tim adjusted his seat back to the upright position. 'Yes, being locked in her room and denied phone calls won't be pleasant but at least she won't be in fear of her life. According to George, she believes in the innocence of these people. That may help her keep her sanity. I just hope to God we get there before her illusions are violently shattered.'

They had passed most of the journey from Heathrow in silence. Tim had slept for much of the last hour. Conrad Lebec, in his seat across the gangway, seemed cocooned in his own gloomy thoughts. Now there were about fifty minutes before scheduled touchdown and the stewardesses were bustling around with the 'Champagne Brunch', Air France's latest business class gimmick. The Lacys accepted the trays and made their selection from the trolley of *petits salés, hors d'oeuvres,* cheeses and small croissants.

Catherine returned to a question she had already asked three or four times. 'Do you think Robert really *would*...harm Emma? I mean, what would be the point?'

'Darling, I wish I could give you the reassurance you're looking for. But if we're halfway right about this character, there's no telling how he'll react. Perhaps our French friend can give us a better picture.' He tapped Lebec on the shoulder. 'Tell me, Conrad, how well do you know Edgar Robert?'

The Frenchman was sipping his champagne suspiciously and with little sign of approval. 'Huh! The man's a peasant!'

'OK, so he lacks Parisian refinement. But what's he like apart from that? Your brother reckons he's a bit odd.'

'Oh, sure. It runs in the family. His

father was what is politely called eccentric. He was well into his fifties before he got married and then he chose a girl of sixteen.'

'That must have caused some raised eyebrows.'

'Before my time. This onion tart isn't bad... But, yes, I believe it aroused some comment, even in our beloved Camargue.'

'Meaning?'

'Incest, in-breeding, blood feuds, mysterious disappearances, sexual deviations that would make the Marquis de Sade blush. I could tell you stories you wouldn't believe.'

'I'm sure you could but right now I'm interested in the Robert family. I take it Edgar's mother is still alive?'

Conrad drained his glass and refilled it. The champagne, he had presumably concluded, was drinkable. 'Oh, no. Died soon after Edgar's birth, apparently of some very mysterious illness. According to the stories my parents tell, there was a lot of police interest in the poor girl's demise. But the Roberts' neighbours either knew nothing or said nothing.'

'So young Edgar was brought up by his father who was, you say, eccentric.' Catherine mused. 'That doesn't sound like a very healthy situation for a young boy.'

'No, Edgar grew up to be a withdrawn

character—a bit of a recluse like his aged sire.'

Catherine probed further. 'Is it true that your parents took Edgar under their wing?'

'My father was sorry for him. He didn't have any friends. Most women were frightened of him.'

'Why was that?' Tim and Catherine asked the question simultaneously.

'He didn't know how to relate to the opposite sex. How could he? He'd never had any women in his life.'

'Would you say he's a violent man?'

'If he's been at the bottle. When I was a kid it seemed that my father was always collecting him from some bar or other where he was making a nuisance of himself. The *patrons* got in the habit of phoning Dad up. He was the only person who could handle Edgar when he was trying to drink his way out of a depression.'

'How did he get to be a hotel keeper?' Catherine asked.

'He came into quite a lot of money when his father died. The old boy had obviously been hoarding his wealth. Edgar had no idea what to do with it. Then Jeanne Picard set her cap at him. She was desperately trying to keep the White Horse going. She'd inherited it from her parents but it was very rundown. Needed thousands spending on it. And thousands was exactly what Edgar Robert had. So, Jeanne needed money. Edgar needed a home and something to keep his mind off knives. It was a *marriage de convenance* in every—'

'Knives!' Again the word came out as a Lacy duet.

'Oh yes.' Conrad's tone remained matter -of-fact. 'He's obsessed with them. That's why, when he was younger, he was such a dangerous man in a brawl. He collects the things, or perhaps "accumulates" would be a better word. He has all sorts—hunting knives, fishing knives, throwing knives, bayonets, knives for wood-carving and leather-working—you name it, he's got it.'

'Throwing knives?' Tim almost shouted the words.

'Yes. He's pretty handy with them. He has a sort of circus act. He used to scare the pants off Charles and me when we were boys. He'd stand us in front of a wooden fence—'

'That's it! That's it!' Tim closed his eyes and rested his head against the seat back. 'Oh, God, it's so beautifully simple and I've been trying to make it complicated.'

Catherine glowered. 'Explain!'

'What's been bugging me about Jolli-bone's murder is that it seemed so intricate, so cunning, so planned down to the last second. Someone had set up the perfect crime. It was the old locked-room mystery. Yet, on the other hand, the whole thing was obviously haphazard. The killer couldn't know that the corridor was going to be empty long enough for him to walk across, stab Jollibone, close the door and get back to the safety of his own room...'

Catherine protested. 'I told you that I thought the timings were too tight.'

'Yes, and you were right. But it wasn't like that at all.'

'So, what was it like?'

'Simple! Simple! Simple! It would have to be, with a man like Edgar. He gets the tip-off from Josephine that Jollibone's on his way up. All he has to do is lie in wait in 519, with the door open. The dealer comes along, unlocks his room, steps inside and Edgar lets fly with a throwing knife. That's why it went in straight and with such force.'

'But anyone in the corridor would see it.'

'Not unless they were very close—and very sharp-eyed. The couple along the corridor didn't notice anything.'

'But according to the Lebecs there was no sign of a murder weapon.'

Tim gave a little laugh. 'No. And that's what's caused all the confusion. But that bit wasn't planned. It was pure chance. Look—Edgar's standing just inside 519. He sees that Jollibone's door catches on his foot and doesn't close. Then he sees Pocock go past. He peers out. No one about. Why lose a perfectly good knife? He steps across. Recovers his weapon. Shuts the door. Retreats. Ten seconds. Fifteen maximum.'

Conrad had been following this exchange with a puzzled frown. Now he protested. 'What's all this about Edgar? You're not seriously suggesting—'

Tim nodded. 'Edgar Robert murdered Auguste Jollibone and probably Josephine Tarantin.'

'Oh, don't be ridiculous! Edgar going all the way to London to bump off a complete stranger—absurd! The man's hardly ever left the Camargue. My God!' He slipped quickly from contempt to anger. 'You raised my hopes. You persuaded me to come on this outing. You said you had proof that someone else had murdered the scumbag Jollibone. Is this it? This crackbrained theory about Edgar Robert!'

'How do you know Edgar seldom leaves the Camargue? You're hardly ever there. Just because you think of him as an uneducated clod—'

'Mr Lacy?' The stewardess smiled down at Tim. 'A telephone message.' She handed

421

him a folded slip of paper.

Tim opened it. It was short and to the point. 'Inspector Coutances of Marseille Sûreté will come aboard the aeroplane to meet you as soon as we land.' Tim passed the note to Catherine. 'Good old Jock.'

'Yeah, good old Jock, indeed. I didn't think he would exactly rush to our aid when he read our report.'

The Lacys had faxed an account of their version of the crime to Armstrong's office at Scotland Yard before leaving London. They had worded it as carefully as possible but there could be no disguising the fact that they had been withholding information from the police—particularly about Emma's abduction.

'What's going on now?' Conrad demanded angrily.

'The police are going to meet us at Marseille.'

'Police!' The word exploded from Lebec.

'Relax, they're not going to be interested in you. They'll be helping us rescue Emma—I hope.'

Lebec took refuge in his familiar attitude of contempt. 'That's what all this is about, isn't it—getting your friend out of a spot of bother she was stupid enough to walk into with her eyes wide open. And you really do believe that Edgar Robert is a homicidal maniac who goes around killing strangers.

You couldn't be more wrong. Edgar is no serious threat to anybody—certainly not as long as my father's around to keep an eye on him.'

## CHAPTER 19

Edgar thrust Emma roughly aside. He marched into the barn. Instinctively Emma ran. She forced her tired legs to carry her across the clearing. She reached the trees and plunged down the path leading back towards the van.

It was hopeless. She heard the man's heavy footfalls behind her. Within a few metres he grabbed her arm. He yanked her round, lifting her clean from the ground. He pushed her against a treetrunk. He unfastened the sheath at his waist and drew out a broad-bladed, viciously efficient-looking knife.

Emma's mind wrestled to turn her panic-swirled thoughts into simple French. Thoughts that said, 'Please don't! I won't say anything. I promise! I promise!'

The knife's point was inches from her stomach, making small circles in the air. Mesmerising. Otherwise, Edgar made no movement. Emma forced herself to look into his eyes. They were the eyes of a bewildered animal and tears were issuing from them freely.

Emma repeated, with as much calmness as she could muster, 'Please, put the knife away. I won't say anything.'

Edgar shook his head. 'That's what Denis said. But how could I believe him? I can't believe anyone. They all tell lies.'

'No, not everyone, Edgar.' She struggled to control her rapid breathing. 'I don't tell lies.'

The big man tilted his head to one side, like a dog trying to understand its owner's wishes. He gazed down at her for long seconds, saying nothing.

Quietly, and as evenly as she could, Emma said, 'Shouldn't we finish hiding grandfather's pictures, so that they can't find them?'

Edgar thought about the proposition. 'Yes, we'll do that...first.' He inclined his head.

Emma eased herself away from the treetrunk and began backing up the path, watching Edgar's knife all the time.

Inspector Coutances was a short, slim man with greying hair, bespectacled and businesslike. He came aboard the plane with two uniformed officers. After introductions that were brusque rather than brief, he announced, 'I will speak English. In my experience it saves time and misunderstanding when dealing with you people.'

Tim thought, no wonder the French invented chauvinism. He said, 'Thank you very much, Inspector. That will be most helpful.'

'Right. We've had faxes and phone calls going back and forth between Marseille and London all morning. I gather we have a hostage situation.'

Tim began to explain but Coutances interrupted. 'This is obviously complicated. We can't talk here. Come with me.'

He led the way into the terminal buildings. They travelled through various corridors and arrived, eventually, in the offices of the airport police.

As soon as they had been shown into an empty room, Tim said, 'I have a colleague meeting us here. Could someone find him?'

Catherine left with one of Coutances's men. She returned a few minutes later with George Martin and Charles Lebec. A couple more chairs were brought into the small room.

The inspector perched against a desk. He took a file from under his arm. 'Well, first things first, as I believe you English say. You are Charles Edmond Lebec and

Conrad Philippe Lebec?' He scrutinised the two brothers. 'I have a request from Scotland Yard...' He consulted his papers. 'From Inspector Edgerson, to arrest you in connection with the murder of Auguste Gaston Jollibone in London on the seventeenth of this month.'

Conrad jumped to his feet, shouting angrily, 'I knew it! I knew it! I knew this was a trap!'

The work of transporting the pictures went on. Somehow Emma found the strength to carry the bundles, two at a time, from the sheepshed to the boat and row the cargo across the lake to the new hiding place. Edgar rewrapped Denis Lebec's body but every time Emma passed the roll of tarpaulin she averted her eyes.

Yet she could not avoid the question which flashed like a neon sign in her brain. How long before she was trussed up, lifeless, in a corner of the barn, or weighted down and lying at the bottom of the Etang de Vaccarès? She deliberately took as much time as possible over each operation. Not that much exaggeration was necessary. Her feet felt like sacks of stone attached to her legs as she dragged them through the undergrowth. Her arm muscles seemed to have turned to jelly as she rowed with increasing clumsiness. Over and again

Edgar exhorted her, 'Vite! Vite!' Over and again Emma fell, or paused, or caught a crab with her oar. Eventually, she did not know whether her gaucheries were intentional or not. She had long ceased to hope for any intervention from her distant friends. They were hundreds of miles away. They knew nothing of her predicament. What could they possibly do from distant London, or even Lyon? At one time she heard a helicopter crossing the southern end of the lagoon, but its roar soon died away leaving only the liquid sounds of the *étang* and the wild cries of foraging gulls.

Edgar led her back to the barn for the fourth journey. Emma looked at the seven wrapped canvases standing in the racks and knew that this would be the last trip.

'M. Lebec, sit down!' Coutances's command came in clipped French that was as ferocious as it was softly spoken.

Conrad collapsed like a deflated balloon. He contented himself with glowering at the Lacys.

Tim spoke up. 'Inspector, may I suggest that there is something more pressing—'

The policeman held up his hand. He referred to another sheet of paper. 'I also have a request from a certain Detective Inspector Armstrong of Scotland Yard to apprehend Edgar Robert in connection with the murder of Auguste Gaston Jollibone in London on the seventeenth of this month.' His lips widened into what was probably meant to be a smile. 'Such communications do not overwhelm one with a feeling of confidence concerning the Metropolitan Police Force.'

A clock on the wall behind the inspector noisily clicked away the seconds. Tim tried again. 'Armstrong is right. Robert is dangerous and he is holding my colleague, Miss Kerr, as hostage.'

'I've checked Robert on our records. A few cases of common affray. One of assault with a lethal weapon. No custodial sentence. That's a far cry from killing and abducting people, wouldn't you say?'

Tim tried to contain his exasperation. 'It's a long and complicated story. Look, I'm very concerned for Miss Kerr's safety. Couldn't we—'

This time the interruption was a buzzing noise. Coutances took a mobile phone from his pocket. He held a rapid conversation of very short sentences. That done, he punched in a number and gave orders to some other underling. He put the phone away, turned to one of his uniformed men and had a few quiet words with him. The officer left the room.

Coutances looked at his small audience. 'When it comes to efficiency, perhaps we poor Marseille *flics* can offer the great Scotland Yard a few lessons. I have already sent some men by helicopter to the home of this Edgar Robert.'

'But, Inspector,' Tim protested, 'that could be dangerous. Supposing he panics—'

'My sergeant has just reported. Apparently neither M. Robert nor the Englishwoman is there. He made a thorough search. Mme Robert says that her husband and their "guest" have been out all morning. She doesn't know where but she thinks they are not far away. I have instructed my sergeant to do some sweep searches to see if they can find Robert's van. I am now going to join them. Perhaps you would like to come as well, Mr Lacy.'

Tim jumped up. 'Very well, Inspector. May I suggest you also take these gentlemen.' He indicated the Lebec brothers. 'They know Robert. If it comes to reasoning with him...'

Coutances shook his head. 'These men are in custody.'

Conrad shouted his protest. 'That's absurd, Inspector. Mr Lacy is quite right. Edgar Robert is a savage brute, perfectly capable of a crime like this. I have always known it was only a matter of time before he did something really terrible. He's the one you should be concentrating on.'

By way of reply Coutances turned to the uniformed officer by the door. 'Take this...gentleman...and put him somewhere his shouting won't disturb anyone.' He turned his attention to Charles, who had sat in morose silence ever since he had entered the office. 'You'd better come with us. Mrs Lacy, Mr Martin, please be good enough to remain in the airport buildings. I'm told that the restaurant is of a passable standard.'

'Can't I come, too?' Catherine pleaded.

'With the three of us, the pilot and a couple of marksmen, I'm overloading the chopper already. The airport police will inform you as soon as there's any news.'

'Marksmen?' Tim was alarmed. 'Is that really necessary?'

The inspector turned to him with a sigh. 'With your permission, Mr Lacy, we'll do this the French way.'

'I'm sorry. I wasn't implying criticism. It's just...'

Coutances relented slightly. 'I understand, sir. You're worried about your friend. So am I. Her safety is my first concern. But this isn't like an urban hostage situation. I can't put a squad of men on the ground and talk the madman into giving himself up—not in that terrain. If we find him—and frankly, it's a pretty big if—we'll have to go in quickly and hard. Give him no chance to disappear among the reeds and the bogs. So, shall we make a start?'

'Attends!' Edgar made Emma wait while he locked the sheepshed. Then he motioned to her to precede him to the boat with the last of the paintings. It was while they were among the trees that they heard the helicopter again. Edgar shouted to her to stop. The machine was somewhere behind them, over the *marais*. It was certainly nearer. But not, Emma knew with sinking heart, near enough. She longed to fling down her burden, dash for the open ground beyond the copse, and wave her arms at whoever it was who was flying over the waterlogged terrain. But she knew that such a course was hopeless, and even as her mind registered the possibility the whirring sound of the rotor blades faded away northwards. Edgar waited until the noise of the machine was no more than a distant hum, then waved her on.

They reached the boat and stacked the packages. Mechanically, Emma took her seat on the bench running athwart the vessel. Edgar pushed off and carefully climbed in beside her. Half a dozen strokes pulled them clear of the reed cover. Emma looked at her watch. The crossing to the island took twenty minutes. That meant that she had ten minutes before putting into practice her last desperate attempt to escape.

Tim peered down at the helicopter's shadow crossing the green-brown Grand Rhône close to where it finally escaped from sandbanks and marshes into the white-flecked blue of the Golfe du Lion. Beyond it and to the left he could see, as the machine flew rapidly onward, hectare upon hectare of fervid salt pans. Then they were over the Camargue proper—the dully gleaming expanse, pock-marked with islets, mudbanks and wodges of floating weed.

The chopper swung in a wide arc to the right, and ahead there appeared a much larger area of open lagoon. 'Etang de Vaccarès,' Coutances shouted above the noise of the engine. He was sitting in the front beside the pilot surveying the scene below through binoculars. Tim was sandwiched between two policemen in blue combat dress, clutching automatic rifles. Charles Lebec was tucked into the space behind them.

Tim gazed mournfully at the seemingly empty fluid world, neither land nor water; a drear waste, potentially hostile to strangers unused to its moods and machinations. Somewhere down there was a lively, courageous, fun-loving young woman scared for her very life. Perhaps already dead. Spontaneous, vivacious and affectionate, Emma was the very antithesis of that clammy, foetid domain of creeping decay. The thought of her life-affirming spirit being sucked down, smothered by the evil influences of the oozing *marais* was intolerable.

Coutances was talking into his headset mike; short urgent sentences. He turned to Tim and called out. 'My men have located Robert's vehicle on the north shore. It's near some old buildings.'

'What do we do now?'

'The other chopper has pulled away. We don't want to scare Robert. If he's under cover we'll have to go in on foot. The difficulty will be finding somewhere to land. We're going to circuit the lake at a higher altitude and join up with the others.'

Tim watched the *étang* tilt and diminish in size as the chopper banked and rose.

Emma stole another look at her watch. The ten minutes had passed. They had reached the halfway point. She estimated the distance to the shoreline. Half a mile, perhaps. She could certainly swim that far. *If.* If her limbs were not too weak. If the water was not too cold. If she could struggle out of the sweater before it became too waterlogged. Yes, she could get away. *If.* If Edgar could not swim. If he found it impossible to manoeuvre the boat fast enough by himself. If, with his detailed knowledge of the country, he did not find some way to cut her off.

No good calculating the odds. It was her only chance. No one else could do anything for her. She was alone, and alone she would either survive or die. She heard the helicopter again but it was now much higher and certainly not interested in her predicament. This was it, then.

She had already loosened the laces of her trainers. Now, as she braced her feet against the crossbeam, she eased them out of the shoes. With a sudden, jerking movement she tossed them aside. She dropped the oar. She stood up. As the boat swung, she jumped.

But Edgar was quicker. He made a grab for her arm. Emma fell into the water but the man maintained his grip. She felt his fingers biting into her flesh. She struggled to free herself. Her head went down into the opaque water. She came up spluttering. Edgar's other hand grasped her hair. Emma screamed and took in a mouthful of lagoon and slimy weed. In her panic of pain and fear she did not know whether her assailant was trying to haul her back in or push her under. She hooked her fingers over the side of the boat, which rocked violently. She felt something slither into the water beside her. It was one of the paintings.

Edgar bellowed in rage. He let go of her arm but coiled his fingers more firmly around her sodden strands of hair. Emma could not see what he was doing with his free hand until he suddenly raised it above his head, clutching the knife held dagger-like.

The helicopter followed the eastern shore of the lake. Coutances continued to scan it with his binoculars. He called a sudden instruction to the pilot and Tim became aware that the chopper was circling back and descending.

'What is it, Inspector?' he called.

'I don't know. Something odd. Look for yourself.' Coutances handed the glasses to Tim and pointed.

Tim leaned across the man on his right. With difficulty he focused them on the water below. His gaze swept an arc of empty, gleaming *étang*. 'What am I looking for?' he shouted. Then he saw it. A boat motionless. There was a figure—a man in it. He seemed to be struggling with something in the water. Something or someone? The craft disappeared from view as the chopper passed over it.

Coutances said, 'Probably nothing to do

with our problem but we shall have to take a closer look.' The pilot throttled back and put the chopper into a tighter turn.

Tim turned suddenly to Charles Lebec. 'Quick! Change places!'

In the confined space the two men struggled past each other.

'What's going on back there?' the inspector called anxiously.

Tim explained. 'I want M. Lebec to get a good view of the man in the boat—see if he recognises him.' He thrust the binoculars into Charles's hands and pointed as the little craft came into view again.

The chopper steadied twenty metres above the water and about fifty metres from the boat.

Charles adjusted the focus of the glasses. 'Yes, that's him! That's Edgar Robert! My God, what's he doing?'

Emma concentrated all her attention on the knife. She was cold. Her clothes were heavy with water. She felt as though her hair was being torn out by the roots. But she made herself watch the knife.

As it arced down towards her, she let go of the boat. She threw both hands up to clutch the descending arm. The blade struck the water close to her left shoulder. Edgar shouted something. She felt his hold on her hair relax. She tore herself free. She went down under the water. Fought up to the surface, gulping air.

There was a roaring sound in her ears. And other sounds she could not identify. They did not matter. Get away from him! Must get away from him! She rolled over and struck out in the direction of the shore. Too slow! Too slow! The weight of her sweater dragged her weakened arms down with every stroke she attempted.

Emma glanced back. The boat seemed to be no farther away. She saw Edgar standing in it. What was he doing? Brandishing an oar. He swung it towards her. She felt it strike the side of her head, then her shoulder. With something akin to relief she slipped into the darkness.

Tim watched, horrified and helpless. Coutances was screaming through a loud-hailer. The chopper was now only metres from the boat. The blast of its rotor blades whisked the surface into peaks and troughs. The tiny craft rocked. Water slopped over the side. Edgar Robert seemed oblivious to everything. Again he lifted the oar above his head. Sitting in the open doorway, one of the marksmen aligned his rifle. Coutances again yelled at Robert to stop. Again the murderer ignored him. He swung the heavy pole at the figure in the water. The gunman let off a short burst of rapid fire. The explosion was deafening. Edgar staggered, dropping the oar. The boat overturned, strewing the water with debris.

'The woman! Get the woman!' Tim shouted.

But the other member of the helicopter's crew had already donned a harness and had begun to lower himself on a rescue line.

Tim craned his head in the doorway. He saw Emma floating but inert. He watched the policeman splash into the water beside her. Momentarily the figures below were out of sight beneath the helicopter. As the rope swung into view again Tim saw the man, now linked by a second harness to Emma's slumped body, wave at the pilot.

Minutes later the two had been gently set down on the shore. Tim slid down the rope.

Coutances called over the loudhailer. 'We're going back for Robert. I've already called an air ambulance.'

Tim dropped on one knee beside Emma, who was lying very still.

She looked very different four hours later. She was sitting up in a hospital bed with a bandage round her head, but the colour had returned to her face and she gazed round at her visitors with bright eyes. Tim, Catherine and George had tried to talk cheerfully about other things but Emma insisted on hearing the details of the afternoon's events. Tim gave her a sanitised version of the rescue.

Emma sighed. 'Poor Edgar!'

'Poor Edgar, phooey!' Catherine grasped Emma's hand on top of the bedclothes. 'Don't waste your sympathy there! The guy only tried to kill you.'

'That's true, of course. The last couple of days have been absolutely ghastly. Most of that time I've been terrified out of my wits. And yet... Oh, I don't know...somehow I can't think of Edgar as a criminal, or evil...just sick.'

Tim was unconvinced. 'Some sick animals get very dangerous. Then they have to be put down.'

Catherine mused. 'Well, he's certainly been put out of his misery. And from what I can gather, it was a pretty miserable existence.'

Emma frowned at her friend. 'I still don't understand what it was all about, Tim.'

'None of us do. Not completely. Not yet. Of course, Bertrand's paintings were at the bottom of everything.'

'The paintings!' Emma clapped a hand to her mouth. 'Have they found the paintings? Edgar was moving them to a new hiding place. That's why we were on the lake.'

Tim and Catherine stared at her. Tim said, 'The police picked up a couple that were floating near the boat...'

'Well, they must go and get the rest. It would be terrible if anything happened to them now. They're on a tiny island...' Emma described the Bertrands' new resting place.

Tim made some notes. 'OK, I'll pass this on to Inspector Coutances. He said he'll be in tomorrow to talk to you and get a statement.'

'Tomorrow!' Emma stared in wide-eyed indignation. 'Hey, I can't stay here.'

Tim smiled at her. 'Oh, yes you can. You need sleep, lots of it, and good French food. You make sure you don't move until they chuck you out.'

'But I can't. It's Mummy's birthday this weekend. She'll be terribly worried if I don't turn up.'

Catherine squeezed her hand. 'Not half as worried as she'd be if she saw you like this. You wouldn't exactly make the front page of *Vogue* right now! You can phone your mother tomorrow. Meanwhile I'll give her a ring and explain that you're doing a job for us in France and it's gone on a bit longer than we expected. Which, of course, is the truth—though not, perhaps, the whole truth.'

Emma looked doubtful. 'You don't know

her. She'll be terribly disappointed.'

Tim said, 'You can phone her, too. She'll understand—as long as we all stick to the same story. Then, as soon as we've got you looking presentable again you can go and stay with her for a week or so. That should make up for it.'

Emma was suddenly crestfallen. 'Look, I know I've been a hell of a nuisance. And I hate to think what all this has cost you. If I've become too much of a liability...'

'Don't even think it.' Tim stood up. 'We're just glad you're OK. You concentrate on getting yourself back in fighting trim. Now we must go and let you have some rest. Catherine will stay on for a couple of days. We'll see you when you get back to Farrans.'

When they were outside the private ward and walking along the corridor, Catherine said, 'She's incredibly resilient. I don't know what that brute did to her but she's obviously been terribly knocked about—not to mention half-drowned.'

Tim shook his head. 'It'll hit her later. She's bound to go through delayed shock. She may need some cosseting for quite some time.'

George Martin stopped suddenly. He tapped his pockets. 'Forgotten something. Shan't be a moment.' He went back into Emma's room.

'Hello, George.' She smiled faintly.

He stood at the side of the bed, hands deep in his overcoat pockets. His face wore an embarrassed frown. 'I've got something to say to you, young lady. They'll tell you some other time.' He nodded towards the door. 'But I have to say it now. We're all...I am...very proud of you. You've got guts. You'll do.' He bent swiftly and kissed her on the cheek. Then he turned abruptly and marched from the room.

# Epilogue

## RESTORATION

Tim was right about Emma. It was not until after the Christmas break that she was able to return to Farrans Court. Her young body recuperated quickly enough, but it took weeks for the sudden shivers and the terror-haunted sleep to leave her.

Meanwhile the days following the tragic events in the Camargue were extremely busy for the Lacys. Trayloads of accumulated correspondence had to be dealt with. Neglected clients had to be soothed. Staff who had felt 'put upon' by the unexpected absence of Tim, Catherine and George had to be pacified. Nor had the Bertrand affair finished with them. Police on both sides of the Channel had plenty of questions to ask and the Lacys soon became embroiled in the arguments over the fate of the rediscovered paintings. It took quite an effort to get the business ship back on an even keel after the violent and sudden tempest that had shaken it. Tim and Catherine both devoted most of their energies to steering Lacy Enterprises into calmer waters.

However, it soon became clear that Jollibone's death and the events following it could not simply be labelled as memories 'Not Wanted On Voyage'. Emma came back with her mind full of questions. Frequently she punctuated business discussions or inconsequential conversations with urgent queries: 'Why did Edgar have to kill Denis Lebec?' 'What was Josephine Tarantin up to?' The Lacys tried to satisfy her with matter-of-fact, piecemeal answers, believing that the best thing for their friend was to forget all about her ordeal. Then one morning, Emma blurted out, in genuine anguish, 'Look, it's not fair. You've got the whole thing worked out but I was in the middle of it all and I'm still all muddled about it.' It became obvious that, together, they would all have to head once more back into the storm.

That was why they drove one evening to the Cranville Arms in Little Farrans for dinner. On a Tuesday in early January the four of them—Tim, Catherine, Emma and George—had the small panelled restaurant virtually to themselves.

As soon as they had ordered, Emma said brightly, 'OK, let's take it from the beginning.'

Tim leaned back in his chair. 'Well, I guess the beginning is over a hundred years ago. That was when the first murder occurred—the one that, indirectly, led to all the others.'

Emma shook her head. 'You're supposed to be explaining, Tim, not talking in riddles.'

'Quite right, Emma! He's being deliberately mysterious.' Catherine opened her handbag and took out some sheets of folded typescript. 'The fact is that we've only just discovered what lay at the root of all these killings. Jock Armstrong sent us this a couple of days ago.'

'What is it?'

'When Coutances's men went through all Edgar's belongings they found an old letter in a locked drawer. Coutances realised it was important so he sent a copy to Jock. Jock had it translated and made a photostat for us. It's an astonishing read—quite an important historical document. It was written by Yvette Robert. Or, I guess, it was written for her—she didn't sign it; just made her mark. She put down everything she knew about Aristide Bertrand—things he'd told her about his former life; things nobody else knew. She must have done it for her son, Georges, so that he would know as much as possible about his real father. But the most fateful part of poor Aristide's story was how he met his end.'

Emma was concentrating hard. 'Was

445

he the first murder victim Tim talked about?'

'That's right. It was one of life's little ironies—and worthy of a Hardy novel. Aristide settled happily at Mas Maraques and did his best work there. But eventually he came to see, or was made to see, that his relationship with Yvette was potentially destructive to the life of the community. So, early one morning, he set out to leave. Unfortunately that was the very morning that François, Yvette's husband, decided that enough was enough. He wasn't going to play the half-witted cuckold any longer. He went after Bertrand to have it out with him. He caught up with the artist not far from his secret workshop. They had a fight. François drew a knife. Exit one Postimpressionist genius. Now, Yvette—'

Emma gasped. 'I know what happened next. Edgar told me, or tried to tell me. Only I could make neither head nor tail of it. He kept on saying, "Elle l'a trouvé ici." What he meant was, "She found the body here." Yvette must have followed...'

'According to her account she had a terrible sense of foreboding when she realised both men were missing. She found Aristide stabbed to death near the barn.'

'Then she dragged his body through the trees, and... Oh, my God!' Emma closed her eyes imagining the scene. 'She somehow dug a grave and gave her lover as decent a burial as she could.'

'That's right. She must have been pretty tough. Even so, it took her several hours.'

Emma sighed. 'Poor girl. Do you know what she did when she'd finished? She couldn't write and she wanted to mark the grave. So she copied the monogram from one of Aristide's pictures and marked it out in stones. Oh, it's so sad.'

Catherine agreed. 'You could almost set it alongside the great romantic love stories—Antony and Cleopatra, Romeo and Juliet—except that Yvette didn't commit suicide in a fit of despair. That was because of the baby, of course. She had something of Aristide inside her. Something to preserve. Something to love. And she made sure that Aristide's son knew all there was to know about his father.'

At that point Mike Turnbull, the landlord, arrived with their food. Having few other customers to attend to, he was disposed to chat and it was some minutes before the diners could resume their own discussion.

George was looking pensive. 'So, sometime or other, Yvette gave her son the full story and that meant telling him that his real father and his stepfather were both murderers. How, in the name of all that's unholy, could he live with that?'

Tim set to work on the Cranville Arm's excellent and far-famed game pie. 'According to Conrad, Georges Robert was a recluse and an eccentric.'

'Can you wonder at it?' George muttered. 'Mind you, I reckon anyone would have to be a bit crazy to live in a place like that. It certainly gave me the creeps.'

Emma was only toying with her grilled trout. 'So all the time the Brotherhood was guarding this cache of old paintings, the Roberts were sitting on a much darker secret?'

Tim took up the story again. 'Yes, but still more important, they knew that, whatever their friends might think, the Bertrand paintings really belonged to them. That's why Edgar got so upset when the young Lebecs began to talk about selling. He protested. So did his mate, Denis. And they thought they'd warned the others off the idea. Imagine how furious Edgar was when he heard that Charles and Conrad had actually spirited some of the pictures away. He was so determined to stop the sale that he went to Lyon and accosted Josephine Tarantin.'

'And that put *la belle Josephine* in a spot because she'd already told Charles Labardie about the paintings,' Catherine explained. 'It was—literally—more than her life was worth to disappoint Mr Big. But, being a resourceful and ruthless woman, it didn't take her long to figure out a way round the problem. She strung poor Edgar along, told him that the real villain of the piece was Auguste Jollibone, and that he was about to sell the six "stolen" Bertrands in London. She made all the arrangements, booked Edgar into the Wellington Tower as E. Roberts, and gave him precise instructions. The deed was done. Labardie took off over the hills and far away as fast as his custom-built jet would carry him. E. Roberts checked out—or, more likely, Tarantin had already checked him out officially. And Josephine stayed to play the grieving and shocked partner.'

Emma listened intently. 'You've already told me how the Lebecs got involved. Was that a bit of Machiavellian plotting on Mme Tarantin's part or just bad luck?'

Tim shrugged. 'I guess we'll never know for sure. I'm inclined to think that it wasn't planned. It distracted any possible attention from Edgar but it could have led to the Bertrands coming to light and that was the last thing she wanted. The final stage of her scheme was a private deal with Edgar whereby she sold off the pictures very discreetly, a few at a time, keeping the lion's share for herself.'

'And it all went wrong because Charles Lebec posed as Jollibone and showed us the pictures. What was all that about? I can't see how or why we got involved in the first place.'

Catherine explained. 'We were just cards in a game of poker, Emma. Jollibone had played his hand badly and the Lebecs had decided not to hang around for another deal. Jollibone was desperate to get them back to the table. He knew as well as Josephine what would happen if he failed to deliver the goods to Labardie. So he decided to bring in another—*bona fide*—art dealer. The plan was that he would show us the Bertrands, get us enthusiastic about them, offer us a partnership deal and introduce us to the Lebecs, who would be convinced by our probity, even if they were dubious about his.'

'Yes, but why us?'

'He couldn't go to one of the main London dealers. That would have created much too much interest. It had to be someone with a good reputation but not so prominent. For all I know, he phoned half a dozen other dealers before he got round to me. I was the only one dumb enough to fall for his invitation to a half-empty office block.'

Emma frowned. 'And that's another thing. How come a provincial French art dealer could get hold of the key to an unfashionable London office?'

Tim put down his knife and fork. 'Ah, now that's where Edgerson's plodding routine turned up the answer. He, or rather some wretched underling, discovered that the office is rented by a company which, via a chain of subsidiaries, belongs to Calroutiers, which is the Labardie organisation's transport company. I guess Jollibone had used it before for various iffy art deals. He told the Lebecs all the arrangements for the meeting over the phone and, of course, they found the key on his body.'

'But why on earth did Charles keep the appointment, posing as Jollibone?'

'Despite their experience with Jollibone, both the Lebecs were wedded to the idea of realising money—large sums of money—on the paintings. Conrad says it was Charles's idea to go through with the meeting but I reckon he was just as keen. Their attitude was, "Since the pictures are here and since Mrs Lacy has agreed to see them, why not? At least we can get some idea of their value." '

'But that was terribly risky.'

'Not really. They made two miscalculations, but they were very understandable miscalculations. They thought Jollibone's body would not be discovered for a long time—perhaps never. And they under-estimated the sheer bloody-minded per-severance of my two favourite women.' Tim grinned across the table at Catherine and Emma. 'It was you who brought the whole house of cards crashing down.'

Emma separated the last of her cooling fish from its bones. 'My bumping into Charles in the rue Gramont obviously threw the Lebecs into a panic. That's why they kidnapped me and then didn't know what to do with me.'

George expanded on the point. 'Charles told me that seeing you in the gallery was the biggest shock of his life. He'd heard that Jollibone's body had been discovered and was terrified that the police would come looking for him. He phoned his father, who came up to Lyon. They decided to talk to Josephine Tarantin and find out what she knew. What do they see when they walk into the shop? One of the two people who know that Charles masqueraded as Auguste Jollibone. They had to get hold of you. They needed to know, beyond any doubt, exactly why you were snooping around, what you knew, what the police knew.'

'Did they intend to...silence me, if necessary?' It was the question that had recurred most frequently in Emma's mind since the end of her ordeal.

George weighed the question carefully. 'I don't think the brothers would have done anything. They're not killers. They were in a blue funk, but no, I don't reckon that would have driven them to murder. Edgar, of course, was a different kettle of fish. As we now know, he was angry enough and unhinged enough to do anything on the spur of the moment without weighing the consequences. Papa Lebec? Well, I guess he would have done whatever was necessary to protect his boys.'

Tim nodded agreement. 'And, of course, the Brotherhood weren't the only ones who were panicking. When I went to see La Tarantin she covered up very well. She produced a very credible story on the spur of the moment and when I insisted on being given a name she put me on to Labardie—anything to keep me away from the Camargue, and the truth. As soon as I left, of course, she was on the hot line to Labardie straight away. He wasted no time checking up on Lacy Enterprises. Hence my summons to the gang boss's palazzo. He intended to pump me for information and he hoped, by keeping tabs on me, to discover how the police investigation was going.'

Catherine said, 'Do you really think all that stuff about wanting you to track down the Bertrands was hogwash?'

'I'm sure he was still interested in the paintings but they'd become secondary. What really mattered was keeping a jump ahead of the police and checking up on Tarantin. He needed to know whether she really was double-crossing him and whether she was likely to come under investigation. The moment she looked like becoming a liability she was dead.'

George finished his steak with a satisfied sigh. 'Ah, so it *was* Mr Big who had Josephine bumped off. I thought it looked like a clean, professional job.'

Tim laughed. 'No, George, I'm almost certain it was Edgar. But the connection between Labardie and the gallery gave the Sûreté the chance they'd been looking for to pull him in. They gave him a real grilling and they sniffed through all his papers like pigs hunting truffles. Of course, they couldn't tie him to the murder but they've found enough to get him into court for tax evasion and various financial irregularities. Bellecourt tried to do a bunk. He was picked up in Cairo of all places. My guess is that he will crumble as soon as he's extradited and subjected to the Sûreté's third degree.'

Catherine added, 'And that's a bit of luck for us. I was expecting Jock Armstrong to be absolutely furious at the way we strung him along with half-truths. But he's delighted to have shaken Labardie up. He's working closely with his counterpart in Paris to see what other dirt they can dish on the oh-so-cultured Charles. There should be quite a few Brownie points in this business for him. So, what with one thing and another, we're still on speaking terms.'

Emma frowned. 'Tim, you say you're not absolutely sure that Edgar killed Josephine Tarantin.'

Tim drained his glass of bitter. 'I'm convinced in my own mind. It's the only explanation that fits. What I can't understand is what made him suddenly take off and drive all the way to Lyon, intent on striking down his mentor.'

George snapped his fingers. 'Do you know, I reckon I've got the answer to that one. Emma, do you remember when I phoned you at Robert's place you asked me how our investigations were going?'

'Yes.'

'Was Edgar in the same room at the time?'

'Yes, but that didn't matter. He couldn't understand a word of English.'

'No, but he recognised the name "Tarantin". You did mention it and it did ring a warning bell at the time but I didn't think any more about it.'

'Yes, of course!' Emma followed the

point up enthusiastically. 'It was after that that he refused to let me have any more phone calls. And the next morning he went out early and was gone for most of the day. By the time he came back he was absolutely crazy with anger.'

Tim nodded with satisfaction. 'That's it then. Edgar thought Josephine was under investigation and that that would lead the police straight to him. To his simple mind there was only one way of preventing that.'

'That still leaves the murder of Denis Lebec,' Emma said. 'I suppose by then Edgar had flipped completely?'

Tim shrugged. 'Well, of course, we'll never know what passed between them when they went out to the barn that evening. My guess is that Edgar was in a turmoil. He instinctively turned to the one person he always turned to to get him out of scrapes.'

'Made a clean breast of everything, you mean?' Catherine asked.

'Something like that! Good grief! Can you imagine the impact of such a confession on Denis Lebec? Not only was his old friend a double murderer but he was prepared to keep quiet while the Lebec boys went on trial for Jollibone's death. Charles and Conrad were in deep trouble and desperately worried and all the time Edgar could have cleared their names of any suspicion. I imagine he told Robert that he must go to the police and make a clean breast of everything. Perhaps he even said, "If you don't tell them, I will." Anyway, whatever was said, Edgar once again went for the simple answer: dead men tell no tales.'

Emma sighed. 'And all that business of moving the pictures, was there any point in it?'

Catherine mused. ' "Though this be madness, there is method in't." It was probably possessive obsession. No one was ever going to find his pictures. He would hide them where they would never be seen again. But he was also concealing evidence. If the police and the Lebecs turned up at the barn talking about a cache of paintings, he could say, "What paintings?" The trouble was, he couldn't shift them quickly by himself. He could get rid of Denis's body easily enough. But over thirty wrapped canvases—that was a different matter. So he had to subject Emma to one final ordeal.'

Emma shuddered. 'It would have been final, wouldn't it?'

Catherine put an arm round her. 'Yes, I'm afraid so. In Edgar's twisted logic there was no way he could let you live. You were quite right to try to escape.'

'But if it hadn't been for Tim...' She looked across at him with something akin to adoration.

He deliberately lightened the mood. 'Well, it all worked out. Now you know as much as we do. And, thank God, it's all over. So, who's for some of Mike's fabulous rum syllabub?'

Tim was wrong. The Camargue Brotherhood affair was not over. In fact, it was destined to run and run. Thanks largely to Conrad Lebec.

His fears about the bank's reaction to his involvement in such 'distasteful' proceedings were fully justified. Next time the directors decided to 'downsize staffing levels' his name was on the blacklist. His new freedom enabled him to devote all his energies to exploitation of the Bertrands and their history. He fought a long and very public battle with the French government over ownership of the paintings. He lost. That was inevitable. There was no way that the Elysée Palace was going to permit a newly discovered collection of national treasures to remain in private hands and—horror of horrors—risk being dispersed. Reorganisation and various structural changes were planned at the Louvre to make space for a permanent display of Bertrand's paintings. Meanwhile, the museum's staff spent months carefully cleaning, and where necessary restoring, the masterpieces.

Conrad Lebec was not the sort of entrepreneur to withdraw gracefully in the face of such powerful competition. The pictures might be denied him but there was still a story to be exploited. He turned himself into a marketing company. As soon as the Camargue affair broke, he sold an exclusive to *Paris Match*. But that was only the beginning. He engaged a top lady novelist to write the 'official' biography of Aristide Bertrand and had the leading publishers of five continents fighting in the aisles to secure the rights. Before the book was even half written he was negotiating a film deal for the Yvette and Aristide romance which he modestly billed as 'the greatest love story since Eloise and Abelard'.

To mark the successful signing of this contract Conrad threw an extravagant party at the Savoy. The Lacys and Emma were invited. Without much enthusiasm they went along. It proved to be the sort of affair they had expected: a crush of people pressing flesh and forgetting each other's names. Emma met one or two old friends and seemed to be enjoying herself but, after half an hour, Tim and Catherine slipped away.

It was a warm, early autumn evening and they decided to walk back to the flat. They strolled down to the Embankment, hand-in-hand. For a while they leaned against the parapet, looking out over the darkening river.

Tim was in cynical vein. 'I suppose that proves with a vengeance the old saying about an ill wind.'

'Well, this one's certainly blown lots of people no good.' She stared into the dark, slowly moving water. After a long silence she sighed wistfully. 'Poor Edgar. Despite everything he did, you can't help feeling sorry for him, can you?'

Tim grunted. 'Speaking personally, yes I can. I don't go along with this modern idea that we're all creatures of circumstance. Take away individual responsibility and you can end up in a moral quagmire.'

Catherine turned away from the wall and faced him. 'That's very hard, Tim. What chance did he really have? Or Aristide, come to that? In a sense they were both victims as much as culprits.'

Tim took hold of his wife's hand as they resumed their walk. 'Well, for my money Edgar Robert's death left the world marginally a better place.'

'And Aristide Bertrand's?'

Hand-in-hand the Lacys strolled slowly towards Westminster—arguing.

The publishers hope that this book has given you enjoyable reading. Large Print Books are especially designed to be as easy to see and hold as possible. If you wish a complete list of our books, please ask at your local library or write directly to: Magna Large Print Books, Long Preston, North Yorkshire, BD23 4ND, England.

This Large Print Book for the Partially sighted, who cannot read normal print, is published under the auspices of

**THE ULVERSCROFT FOUNDATION**

---

**THE ULVERSCROFT FOUNDATION**

. . . we hope that you have enjoyed this Large Print Book. Please think for a moment about those people who have worse eyesight problems than you . . . and are unable to even read or enjoy Large Print, without great difficulty.

You can help them by sending a donation, large or small to:

**The Ulverscroft Foundation,
1, The Green, Bradgate Road,
Anstey, Leicestershire, LE7 7FU,
England.**
or request a copy of our brochure for more details.

The Foundation will use all your help to assist those people who are handicapped by various sight problems and need special attention.

Thank you very much for your help.